M

ANN ARBOR DISTRICT LIBRA

31621012758914

WITHDRAWN

W9-ALM-244

HOT JOHNNY

(and the Women
Who Loved Him)

HOT
JOHNNY

(and the Women
Who Loved Him)

Sandra Jackson-Opoku

ONE WORLD
BALLANTINE BOOKS • NEW YORK

A One World Book
Published by The Ballantine Publishing Group

Copyright © 2001 by Sandra Jackson-Opoku

All rights reserved under International and Pan-American Copyright Conventions. Published in the United States by The Ballantine Publishing Group, a division of Random House, Inc., New York, and simultaneously in Canada by Random House of Canada Limited, Toronto.

One World and Ballantine are registered trademarks and the One World colophon is a trademark of Random House, Inc.

www.randomhouse.com/BB/

The Cataloging-in-Publication Data for this title is available from the Library of Congress.

Manufactured in the United States of America
First Edition: February 2001
10 9 8 7 6 5 4 3 2 1

In memory of my father, Roscoe Jackson, Sr. 1923–1982

To the special men in my life I have known and loved

And Richard Thelwell,
Muse and amanuensis

In those days came John the Baptist,
preaching in the wilderness of Judaea.

> *—Matthew 3:1*

Great accomplishment seems imperfect,
Yet it does not outlive its usefulness.
Great fullness seems empty,
Yet cannot be exhausted.

> *—The Tao Te Ching, chapter 45*

HOT JOHNNY

(and the Women
Who Loved Him)

Stone Soup

He knew just how to feed them

You see all our hungry faces in the photo album of his life. And you wonder. Who is he and what is he to you? You would never understand unless you know our story. So I'm going to tell you a fairy tale. Maybe you haven't heard this version.

Once upon hard times Little Grandma Gracita planned a potluck picnic. We reached into cupboards and took out what we had. Every woman thought the other might bring something better to the table. Oh, it was sad. No fried chicken, no potato salad, no watermelon. Nothing but scrap bones, carrot tops; a pitiful spread. The mushy potatoes could hardly believe their eyes. I was the last to arrive, the one who brought pearl onions.

Into this all steps a man named John, too good-looking to be good. Or so they say. If you didn't know different, you would cast him as the snake. Don Juan, con man, rogue. He said he knew just how to feed them.

He brought out a pot and made a big fire. Into it went all their offerings, along with something special: a stone from his pocket, glowing with his own warmth. Bubbling in the broth of magic, stone soup was made. It was a miracle, and it was good! Each one ate until she was full. And they all lived happily ever after?

Hardly. Real stories never end like the fairy tales do. Hot Johnny would stay so long as the soup simmered, dishing miracles into everyone's bowl. When the pot boiled over or turned cold, he would leave with his soup stone. Have you ever wondered where he went? He with all his hidden fires. We with all our hungers.

Yes, we have our hungers. Don't be tempted to cast us as the victims. We take him in, hoping to touch his magic, and we ourselves are remade.

I remember Hot Johnny like a ray of sun that touches your skin. It warms you for a moment, but you can't keep it with you. I remember him in tomorrow's dream, the bright one that dashes across your eyes right before you awaken. I remember him like John the Baptist. A chanted blessing and a splash of water, and those he touches are forever changed.

But God's gift to women is not easy to be. He has never been sure of his power, you see. He doubts our intentions, questions our devotion. Those closest to him have even seen his scars.

Cooks don't always get to enjoy what they create. What's the use of having cake unless you eat it, too? What's the sense in making stone soup unless you have a taste? Dishing up miracles for everyone else, what happens to Hot Johnny's own hungers?

The beginning of the story starts at the end.

Destiny

I could almost be what he saw in me

I didn't inherit much from my natural mother. Not a memory, not a snapshot; not even a surname. Just a sickle-cell blood trait that would blow up like a bomb one day. Just a lacy, tattered pillow with *Who art thou, my daughter? Ruth 3:16* stitched in faded thread. A question on a pillow is all she left me. That and a prediction: Destiny. My mother knew I was an accident waiting to happen, destined to wind up with a broken heart.

Mrs. Malveaux was a little coupon-clipping white lady, the last foster mother in a succession of six. What little I learned about men in my life, she's the one who taught me. When she found out I had a crush on the cutest boy at school, Mrs. Malveaux told me to lower my expectations.

"If you're going to love a man that other women want," she warned, "get ready for a broken heart. Better a butt-ugly man who is faithful than a handsome heart-stopper sharing his loving all over town."

Maybe she thought marrying that hairy gorilla of hers would guarantee her a lifetime of fidelity. But it didn't go down like that. I know for a fact that butt-ugly Franklin was not faithful to Vivian Malveaux. A fine man cheated because he could, an ugly one because he had something to prove. What possible hope did that hold out?

I knew I was doomed the moment I laid eyes on him. No, I'm lying.

I couldn't have known that, because I never thought a man like Johnny Wright would give me the time of day. Maybe I'm lucky winding up like Mrs. Malveaux predicted—my big nose wide open, my stupid heart broken. At least it was Johnny who broke my heart, which is more than dozens of more attractive women can say.

Any girl on Pope Air Force Base would have given her last dime to get with Hot Johnny. I'm the one he chose over any number with longer hair, lighter skin, slimmer hips. I may be nursing a broken heart now, but at least I had his love to myself for four whole years. At least I'm the one who got to have his baby.

I remember the first time he spoke to me. I was on KP, slinging hash in the NCO mess hall. I would chat with airmen on the chow line: the older white enlisted officers, the women, one or two of the brothers who seemed safe for conversation. But Johnny Wright was one I refused to recognize. I was frightened of him, plain and simple. Afraid he might see the panic in my eyes.

It was hard for me to look a handsome man full in the face. It would be like trying to stare at the sun. The glare of his beauty would almost blind me. My eyes would smart with tears and I'd have to turn away. So I focused on the hands pushing along a military-issue green plastic tray. Knuckles with sparse strands of sandy hair; long fingers with bitten nails. Those chewed-off nails were much easier to look at than the golden perfection of his flawless face.

I would thrust Johnny's plate toward him without looking up at him. If he tried to make small talk, I would mumble a response and turn to the next in line. One day he didn't take the plate from me so quickly. I held it out to the empty air, my face shiny with sweat and shame.

"You got a kind word for everybody but me, airman. How come? Is it because I'm black?"

I didn't answer.

"I'm going to make you look at me tonight, you luscious little chocolate drop." I couldn't see his face because I was looking down.

But I could hear the chuckle in his voice. It had to be his idea of a joke, calling attention to my color. Pretending to like my looks, when everyone within earshot could see just how plain I was.

"Look me in the eye when I address you, airman. And that's an order."

"Yes, sir," I muttered, staring down at the steaming pan of hash. I tried to hand him his plate of food once again. "No excuse for my behavior, sir."

"I'm not going to take that slop until you look at me."

"Look at the fool, for Christ's sake," someone down the line muttered. "We're getting hungry down here."

I was so humiliated. He was holding up the chow line and the others were enjoying a joke at my expense. I stole a glance at him, catching gold sparks glinting in olive green eyes.

"Take your food, Sergeant Wright," I whispered. "Please, sir."

He noticed the tears I was blinking back and grabbed the plate, brushing my hand as he did.

"Aw, baby girl." He leaned forward, murmuring in a voice meant for my ears only. "I didn't mean to make you cry."

I was nobody's baby girl, had never really been. It just made me want to cry all the more. I held it in until my duty ended, the steam table cleared and the chow pans scrubbed. I went out behind the mess hall, sat on the steps, and bawled into my hands.

I was like a hot-water bag somebody filled up, put away, and forgot about. People might have called them curves, but I knew it was years of unspilled water that swelled the contours of my skin. Six different foster homes, no family to visit on leave, empty spaces in a photo album where a father and a mother should have been. Not even a safe place to cry. Saltwater tears leaked out, punctured by the random pinprick of a man too blindingly beautiful to behold.

Then there he was. I don't know where he came from or how he got there.

"What did I say to make you cry?" he whispered, sitting down beside me. He reached over, mopping up tears and snot with his clean white handkerchief, chanting some kind of gibberish beneath his breath.

Sana, sana
colita de rana
Si no sanas hoy,
sanarás mañana.

"Huh?" My tears dissolved in sheer surprise. "What did you just say?"

"Just a little something my great grandmother used to sing when life had put a hurting on me. I don't even know what it meant, but it always made me smile. I see it still works, that grin struggling beneath all those tears. Don't you know that brown sugar should always be kept dry? You don't want nothing melting marks into that pretty face."

"I . . . am . . . not . . . pretty," I hiccuped. "You're just messing with me, sir."

He had the nerve to look surprised. He tucked a hand under my chin, tilting my head back in consideration. He seemed to reassess my broad, tearstained features.

"Girl, where were you in the seventies?"

"Not even born."

"You're probably, what? Eighteen years old?"

"Nineteen last Tuesday," I told him.

"Almost young enough to be my daughter."

I shook my head.

"You're not old enough to have any grown kids."

"Thirty-seven years old? Hell, it ain't impossible. I did get started awfully young. I cut my teeth on morsels like you. My first true love was a dark little something I called Black Pearl. Churchgoing girl, all straitlaced and buttoned down. But hot as hell and sweet as honey under those high collars and long skirts. She used to sell candy bars for the church. World's finest chocolate. Lord knows, the girl wasn't lying."

I felt a sharp stab of jealousy. My reaction shocked even me.

"Church girls usually are loose like that, sir."

He smiled at my outburst.

"Loose and juicy. Nobody had to tell me—the blacker the berry, the sweeter the juice. I wish you'd been around to hear it," he whispered into my ear. "Black is beautiful."

I kissed my teeth, suddenly irritated. Who was this golden boy to be preaching me the gospel of blackness?

"By your leave, sir. I've been in this body nineteen years and I know better. Nobody thinks girls who look like me are beautiful."

"Then they ain't got eyes," he said solemnly. "Because you are one fine figure of a woman. Your mama should have named you Midnight."

He pulled me up so quickly I hardly had time to react.

"What are you doing, sir?"

"Nobody here but us chickens, airman. You don't have to keep calling me sir."

He took my hands and danced with me, swaying to a slow song he murmured in my ear. My heartbeat underscored the off-key melody, one of those ballads that comes on the oldies station late Sunday nights. A song about a pretty little girl named Black Pearl, worthy to be rescued from the background and placed upon a pedestal.

"Don't even know how fine you are," he scolded. "Come here, girl. Let me lift you up where you belong."

With me giggling like an idiot, he lowered me down into a dip, then hoisted me up toward the moon. The kiss I was foolish enough to anticipate was a lazy salute he threw my way before disappearing through the lighted doorway. It even hurt to look at him in silhouette. I figured he and his buddies would have something new to laugh about.

But later that week on my narrow cot, tucked under the *Who art thou, my daughter?* pillow was an envelope and an unwrapped white jewelry box. In it I found a simple gold chain, a glowing black teardrop-shaped opal dangling from its end. The birthday card inside wasn't even signed; I opened it and read the eight-word saying scrawled there.

The blacker the berry, the sweeter the juice.

"I couldn't find a black pearl, although I know they exist," he admitted one night, unfastening the top two buttons of my uniform shirt. "But why do I have to look anymore? I've got my pearl."

"But Sergeant Wright," I whispered as he positioned the opal in the cleft of my cleavage, "my name is Destiny."

It was a series of mixed signals, an endless pluck of a daisy petals: *He wants me, he wants me not.*

"Whoa—down, boy." He pulled away in the middle of our first kiss, addressing himself below the belt. "Who told you to raise your ugly head? Don't mind me, baby girl. This licking stick needs a strong dose of military discipline."

I thought our relationship was a secret until people started sniggering behind my back, whispering, "Saltpeter." The hottest brother on base was dating the homeliest virgin, or so they thought. Every weekend of his leave was spent taking classes at a monastery of wandering Taoists in Chapel Hill. He was going for holy, practicing celibacy, and seeing me on the sly. A lot of people figured it for a ruse, an evasive maneuver.

Johnny used to manage the fitness center at the base but had been busted down to staff sergeant and given desk duty while under investigation for sexual harassment. The brass claimed to be conducting a confidential inquiry, but everyone had their own version of the story.

Some called it racism, a put-up job. It was an unwritten courtesy in basketball to throw the game to a senior officer. Johnny pulled rank in one-on-one, wiping the floor with his stationmaster. Now the command chief was pulling strings to get him drummed out of the force.

Others said he was guilty as sin. That at one time or another he'd slept with all three of the white women under his command. It was even rumored in some quarters that a gay man had been his accuser.

Damned liars, that's what I said. Whichever one of them blew the whistle, and all those doing the whispering. Hell has no fury like a lover scorned, be it male or female. All four of them had dropped the ball in his court at one time or another, but Johnny swears he never picked it up. Not a once.

"I've been twenty years poking around the candy box," he insisted. "Why fool around with vanilla creams and hard candies when you know what you like is dark chocolate?"

Look at me. Chocolate can't hardly get darker than this. Anyway, why would a man as fine as Johnny have to force his attention on a woman, or even a man for that matter? Everybody out there was trying to give him some.

Cashiers at the Fort Bragg PX would slip their phone numbers into his grocery bags. High school girls would follow him in town, giggling and asking to feel his muscles. Transvestite hookers would call to him from darkened doorways. Every woman from airman basic to staff officer would make their way over to his table for ladies' choice at the NCO club.

This would go on right in front of my face, with me sitting next to him or across the table. We were playing pretend, *we're just friends*. But I was really practicing invisibility. I had become so dark I almost disappeared. No one seemed to notice me there in the glare of Johnny's sunshine. If you don't say boo, people will step all over you to get what they want. If nothing else, that's one lesson I learned in the force.

His male buddies baptized him "Hot Dick Johnson." They would watch him shag some girl across the floor, a dance step I was never able to master. Slapping five in a mixture of envy and admiration. Commenting on his every move and posture. He was like the alpha male, the only one in the pack who got to mate. The other wolves got excited just yapping around him.

"Look at that," one would call out. "Watch him bend her clean over backwards. Hah! Johnny calls that 'dipping the cherry.' "

"Celibate, my balls. Hot Dick Johnson ain't fooling nobody." Lazing at the bar, guzzling beers. "That boy get so much pussy thrown at him, he got to go out with a helmet on."

An explosion of sniggling and back-slapping, beer suds flying. *Helmet* must have had more than one meaning.

"That's right," someone else would testify. "I seen that nigga on the basketball court, sure do know how to duck and dodge. Now me, I wouldn't be dodging no pussy."

"You ain't got to. Don't see none raining down on your head."

Johnny seemed bored with all the attention. Maybe that's what led him to me in the end. A woman who wasn't bold about wanting him. Who didn't chase him, never threw herself at him. Who barely spoke unless prompted. Not because I didn't want to.

I was so nervous and insecure, whenever he turned his eyes my way I would quickly look in the other direction. He could have helped himself to whatever he wanted. What was I going to do, just say no?

My quiet desperation must have looked like innocence. In fact, everyone assumed I was either a virgin or a lesbian. Johnny seemed to take my inarticulate silences for modesty and reserve. He made me out as the good girl on base. An untouched flower in a garden of sin, one he could sniff but wouldn't pick. He must have been mixing me up with that sanctified girl from his high school days. Maybe he felt guilty about taking her virginity and was trying to make it right by preserving mine.

Fat lot of good it did. We were seen out together on many a we're-just-friends occasion, and Johnny was hit with a fraternization charge. People who hadn't even been there reported that he had sexually harassed me that evening on the chow line at the NCO mess hall. Insult added to injury.

I just knew a jealous female was behind it. Probably Nelda, that weasel-faced wigger from Florida. She acted like talking black and sleeping black would make her into something she wasn't. Wanna-bes like Nelda were the worst kind of white folk. Acting like they're down with the homies, when all they want is to take something from you. It was Nelda, I'm convinced, who took those pictures of the ugliest African-looking faces from the Benetton ads and stuck them to my locker for everyone to laugh at.

"I hear you and Wright got a thing going on." She gave me the once-over in the showers one day, checking out my hair, my face, my figure.

"You know he don't want nothing but your body. You know he going to drop you the minute you give it up, just like he did that little white girl year before last. You got any sense, you'll hold out for as long as you can."

Holding out was never a strategy, at least not on my part. I would have been glad to give it up. He just never asked for it, not once during all the time we were courting. Although sometimes I could see him struggling.

I slowly came to understand that I must have had a nice body, or so some men seemed to think. Even though I saw myself two sizes too big, with flaring hips and breasts so abundant they were a constant source of embarrassment.

Those breasts had gotten me in trouble the moment they made their appearance. They bulged out as bodacious as two street-corner whores. I wasn't quite twelve, and I felt like cutting them off. Maybe it would have kept the boys and men from staring. Would have kept foster father number six from sticking his hairy hands under my sweater and squeezing them every time we were alone together in the house.

If it hadn't been for those breasts, maybe I wouldn't have been in the United States Air Force, looking for a father whose name I never knew. Maybe the Willises would have adopted me and I'd be gone off to college.

They had been the happiest two years of my life. Elegance Willis was dark like me, but his wife was cream-colored with long, pretty hair. Lorraine could have had her pick of brown-skinned children or even a biracial baby. She didn't have to settle for someone as black as dirt, way past the cute-and-cuddly stage. But she said I was just what she wanted, a girl child who looked "just like my husband's people."

Lorraine Willis could have almost passed for white if it wasn't for all that African jewelry and clothes she draped herself in.

"Oh, no, you are not drawing pictures of little pink people," she'd scold, grabbing away my crayon box. "Where's that purple? Here. I want you to make me a beautiful eggplant-colored girl, just like you."

I had never seen an eggplant before, but I looked it up in the *World*

Book encyclopedia. I learned it wasn't a plant at all, but a squash with purple-black skin. A pretty color, though I never imagined myself quite so dark and shiny.

Mrs. Willis called them my "womanly curves." She was tall and flat-chested, just like a model. When I started developing womanly curves by the age of twelve, she snapped the strap of my new brassiere.

"You're getting too big too quick. Don't let your boobies write checks that your butt can't cash. You know what I mean, Destiny darling?"

I knew but didn't worry. Nothing could hurt me now. I had my very own room, a frilly bed where I could leave my *Who art thou, my daughter?* pillow out without worrying about it being taken. I was in a good home with nice parents and an older brother who promised to "kick ass and take numbers" if anyone ever messed with me. Jamal Willis called me "sister-girl." I never thought I'd have a family, never even imagined I'd have a big brother to call me "sister-girl."

Both the Willises were high school teachers. Elegance taught gym and coached the track team most days after school. Lorraine was a painter and an art teacher, always taking evening classes—herb gardening, calligraphy, tai chi. The family owned the apartment building where we lived, reminding their tenants in writing each fall that "we keep your rent low by keeping the furnace turned down during the day."

I always got home first, walking from the middle school two blocks away. Jamal, three years older and in high school, only had an hour to wait before one parent or another arrived to turn up the thermostat. Until then, we'd just be cold. On days when we could see our breath in the air, my foster brother would crab and complain about those "penny-pinching misers" who were his parents.

I didn't mind. I'd been through much worse hardship than that. The cold apartment was kind of companionable. We wore thick sweaters, hobo gloves with the fingers cut out. We drank endless mugs of hot chocolate.

I would put on my hobo gloves and tuck my cold feet underneath me, doing my homework under a mound of blankets on the living room sofa. Jamal would let himself into the apartment, blowing to see if he could see his breath.

"Sister-girl, I'm freezing," he'd groan, diving for the sofa. "You better share those covers."

We would cuddle together, keeping warm. We'd sit up and talk, or lean back and watch TV. This was the life. Having a sibling to cuddle with and watch TV on the living room sofa.

Jamal challenged me to a tickle fight one afternoon. He won, of course, straddling me and tickling until I cried uncle. Tickle fights became a regular game. One day he didn't let up even after uncle. When tickling turned into touching, I didn't try to stop him. It was only a game.

"Ooh, sister-girl. You're soft under there." He lay on top, fully dressed at first, clutching at bulges under clothes, rubbing his body between my legs. I knew it wasn't right, but it didn't seem so very wrong. "Sister-girl got some big titties."

He would hold his upper body away, not heavy on me. Not crushing me. I would lie still as a little girl listening for Santa Claus while my body warmed, thawing like icicles. Drip, drip, drip. It's not like we were really brother and sister. Maybe this was love. Maybe someday we'd get married.

The games got more frequent, more demanding. Clothing would be shed, a little more each time. The day it came down to naked skin, where else was there to go?

I'd spent a lifetime yearning for a mother, but that was the moment when I wanted a father. I lay there quiet, not protesting. Trying hard to make my father materialize.

I could almost picture him. Tall and fine like Richard Gere in *An Officer and a Gentleman*. Only difference, he'd be brown, but not too dark. I could almost hear him at the door. He'd walk through it with purposeful strides, splendid in full-dress military whites. He'd scoop me into his arms and carry me out through the open door, pilot of his own aircraft. I'd close my eyes and we'd go flying, soaring off into the wild blue yonder. Then the fantasy popped like an overstretched water balloon.

"Ooh. You came, too." Jamal whispered panted congratulations. His movements slowed to a grind, erasing my father's face. "Sister-girl, you sure know how to do it."

"No, I didn't." I denied the fading throb, the confusing wetness between my thighs. "No, I don't."

Jamal smiled, self-assured. Like he had been the pilot, the one who had taken me into the skies.

"Oh, yes, you did." He thrust out his open palm, then squeezed it shut. "I could feel it."

It wasn't my father who stepped through the door just then. It had been Lorraine Willis's key turning in the lock, catching us both red-handed. She flew across the room, yanked Jamal from the sofa, slapped him across his face, and sent him to his room. But I was not comforted. I was not whisked away to safety. Clothing was tossed carelessly at me. Questions were too, cold and demanding.

"Who got this started? El warned me I might get a damaged child. I should have listened to him. Is this the kind of thing you learn in foster care?"

After two court-ordered family counseling sessions I left the Willises' without explanation, with no further contact. Foster father number six made Jamal's tickle fights seem like a walk in the park. I would have to leave my body to go looking for my father on a regular basis.

When I turned eighteen my birth records were unsealed. I slammed into another brick wall. I learned that my mother had been a minor: no name, no phone number, no forwarding address. The surrender of custody had been arranged by the pastor of one Pentecostal Sanctuary in Chicago. I wrote and got back a typed letter with no signature: *We are sorry to say that Bishop Peter Paul Pleasant has recently passed into the Lord's care.*

See? I couldn't win for losing. There went my one chance of finding my parents. The letter went on to inform me (while certain that I had "no connection to this church or anybody in it") that my father had left

Chicago years ago and may have joined the Air Force. The rest of it was filled with Bible quotes and hard-sell preaching: *I'm putting you on my private prayer list, child. You don't need no mother or father now. What you need is the Lord in your life.*

Maybe it was that rescue fantasy, a man in a military uniform swooping in to save me. I knew it instantly. My father must be an Air Force pilot! I enlisted on a whim, convinced that even without a name, I would know my father the moment I saw him. After all, how many black pilots could there be?

I had gone through basic training and been stationed in North Carolina when I realized what a wild-goose chase this really was. After nearly a year in the service I still hadn't found the slightest trace of my father. But I did find someone.

Johnny was an enlisted officer, not even a pilot like in the movie. What he felt for me was no kind of father love. He was attracted to my body just like Jamal and the rest. He made that very obvious. Still, he was an officer, and a gentleman in his way.

It wasn't just about body parts. I wasn't just a distraction to draw attention from his sins. Yes, he would gaze hungrily at my breasts. But he also looked into my eyes as we sat together in a parked car on steamy summer nights, watching the view from a lookout point above the airfield.

I never told him how I had grown up. Knowing that I had been an unwanted child might give him ideas I couldn't risk. I would talk to him about safer things: the books I was reading, movies I had seen, my hopes to one day learn to fly.

He talked about his new experience with God and religion. He had grown up in the Pentecostal Church, then studied Islam in Africa several years before. Now he was reading from Chinese metaphysics, the Tao Te Ching. He seemed to be testing the ideas he spoke, trying them on for size. He posed questions, philosophical riddles that neither of us could answer. Did abstinence prepare the soul for a state of grace? What was it like to be filled with grace? Would it be with you forever, or did it need to be replenished from time to time?

He spoke about his struggle with celibacy, admitting he had been a fornicator most of his life: "I abused the privilege until it lost its magic." He was now "sexually weary," but filled with the conviction it would one day be redeemed in the wedding bed. Johnny was a reformed womanizer, saving himself for marriage.

Then he would turn attention to my breasts. It may seem hypocritical, but it wasn't fornication. Johnny was no teenager; he had been around the block a time or two. For a man like that, titty squeezing wasn't real sex. Besides, what was I going to say? No? I never had before, not to other men who hadn't meant half as much.

I would take a deep breath and steel myself against the familiar intrusion of a man's hand stealing under my shirt. I would turn my body toward him but my face away, swallowing back my secret shame. It was easier if I didn't have to look.

Johnny liked to see me in bras that fastened in the front. He said unhooking them was like opening a present on Christmas morning, the contents tumbling into his waiting hands. These words were meant to reassure, but they only frightened me.

Still, it was a ritual I grew accustomed to and gradually learned to accept as the price I paid for being with him. His fondling hands, his caressing lips, his searching tongue. He could nuzzle for hours at a time, sucking and stroking like a contented baby. At first it was a sacrifice, something I did to make him happy. Then it became mildly pleasurable. I even began looking forward to it.

There came a night when something surged, a tsunami of sensation rising out of nowhere. I felt throbbing in other places. A cord connected my nipples and genitals, a chord he strummed with teeth and tongue. Teasing and tasting and tugging. I tried to push Johnny away, to quell the slippery suddenness in my groin.

To my dismay, I found myself moaning. Attempting to twist away from him, while at the same time pressing his head into the pillow of my bosom. A thing strained down there, swelling open like floodgates. It was something I had felt before, several nightmares ago. I was flooded with fluid, a disturbing déjà vu.

I burst into tears and bolted from the car, the crotch of my panties wet, naked breasts bouncing in the moonlight. I rushed into a night that smelled of pitch and pines, Johnny fast on my heels. He grabbed me and pulled me to him, laughing away my tears.

"It's all right, baby girl." Patting my back like I was a child, kissing my neck like I was a woman. "Why'd you run off like that?"

"I didn't mean for that to happen," I sobbed. "You must think I'm some kind of freak."

"If you're a freak, then you're my kind of freak. To see you get off like that, I know just how our honeymoon is going to be. Think of it as basic training. Your first climax, baby girl."

Wrong again, Johnny Wright. But how could I tell him that? Hadn't he just said "honeymoon"? That is why I didn't protest when he lowered me to the ground, laying me on a bed of pine needles that seemed placed there just for us. Touching me all over again. My hair, my eyes. Kissing all the lipstick from my mouth. Cupping my buttocks. Caressing my thighs, then finding something tender in between them. Testing that thing with one finger, fiddling it like a harpist. Pointing a breast toward his mouth again.

"This time," he made me promise, just before his lips engulfed me, "I want you to tell me when you come."

It didn't take long. The warning flare of lights, the buzz of an aircraft on night training exercises, the whine as it passed overhead—it seemed like some kind of signal.

"It's coming," I whispered, clutching at him against the approach of this *it*. It was different this time, calmer, steadier. Less like a dam bursting, more like . . . like flying. Like stretching out and gliding on a cloud of pure silk. "Johnny, it's coming again."

Only when the plane had disappeared, the endless moan had faded from my lips, the pounding of my own blood had settled in my ears— only then did the motion of his hand cease, the sucking cadence of his mouth subside. There in the stillness of stars, a night bird twittering in the pines, his face pressed against my ear, Johnny whispered six strange words.

"Baby, I need you so bad."

How could he? Why should he? What had I done but follow him down a road that had already made him weary? Something else Mrs. Malveaux taught me sprang to mind.

"Ever see a man in the supermarket, Destiny? He'll grab what he craves before buying what he needs. Beer, snacks, cigarettes. You don't want a man to need you. Need is a perishable thing. Even if the man doesn't love you, better that he should want you, desire you. Hunger has a longer shelf life."

I leaned back and closed my eyes, letting his lips follow the trail his hands traced yet another time. I pushed those words away, back into memory where they came from. Because I could hardly push Johnny away, the best thing that ever happened to me. The only thing that had happened to me. I wasn't used to having much of anything in life, and look what I wound up with. If what it came down to was needing me, then I'd take that and be happy with it.

I never saw him completely undressed until the day we married. I had neither touched his body nor knew jagged "war wounds" were carved into his thighs until the night of our honeymoon. It is not because I wanted to wait.

Sex was something that had always been forced on me. I had no experience in asking for what I wanted. He seemed quite happy with the kissing and petting we did when we slipped off the base. To undo all seven buttons, unhook my bra, suck and fondle my breasts. He seemed content to see me writhing in passion, never taking anything for himself. If he asked no more, then why should I? Johnny just assumed I was a virgin, and I never told him any different.

When he was hit with fraternization charges, Johnny was purely livid. He was a practicing Taoist, after all. Why was it assumed we were sleeping together when he had exercised such restraint?

"A simple medical exam would put that lie to rest," he'd complain. Then, looking over at my worried face, he'd give me a reassuring hug. "But I'd never put you through that, baby girl."

I never told him the truth, not even on our wedding night. My virginity had been canceled a long time ago, courtesy of Jamal Willis, foster family number five. Franklin Malveaux had left a more lasting mark. I had already had an abortion by the age of sixteen.

That is when I had enough. No more. I left the clinic with the blood still flowing from an unhealed wound, a few items of clothing and the *Who art thou, my daughter?* pillow crammed into my knapsack. I walked away from the foster care system in Memphis, Tennessee, and never looked back. I was afraid what might happen if another foster family member tried to touch me again—afraid not for me but for him.

I was practically homeless those last two years, living here and there, on the streets, with a varying assortment of well- and ill-meaning friends and acquaintances. But I managed to finish high school, number twelve in a class of a hundred and eighty. Not bad for a girl who slept on city buses and did homework on park benches.

If Johnny figured out my lie of omission, he never said a word to me about it. Anyway, I was a virgin in a way. It wasn't the first time I had sex, but it was truly the first time I'd made love of my own accord.

I had to pinch myself constantly to remind myself I wasn't dreaming. This man was mine, all six foot four of him. Every square inch of his fine brown frame, every wiry curl in that head of sandy hair. Every kiss that fell from his lips was mine, as free as the rain. The golden magnificence that still hurt my eyes, I learned to take in snatches, in furtive glances.

Get ready for a broken heart.

When the voice of Mrs. Malveaux intruded into my happiness, I put it aside. Just because Mr. Malveaux was a no-good cheat who liked to force his attentions on a fifteen-year-old foster child didn't mean my man was like that. I had me a good man.

Johnny soon had to leave the service, forced out on general discharge after a fifteen-year tour of duty. It might have been dishonorable had it not been for his Joint Service Commendation Medal. He lost most of his benefits and our lifestyle went way down. I got work in a convenience store. Johnny was hired on entry level in a furniture factory, working on the side as a fitness trainer at a gym in Asheville.

The first few years were the best, even though they were lean ones. I was happy being married, although my inadequacies sometimes caused me to suffer. Everywhere we went I felt women sizing me up, wondering what Johnny saw in me. I'd feel left out when he got into intellectual conversations that floated just above my head. I'd barge in with big words I'd read in the dictionary or seen on TV. I could tell by the amusement on people's faces that I only succeeded in making myself look dumber than I already was.

I was painfully suspicious, slow to make friends. Always afraid that women were after my man. There was this middle-aged lady who used to do my hair.

"Lucille, the original," she would introduce herself, laughing. "Honey, B. B. King named the guitar after *me*."

I never got tired of hearing it. Every time she told that joke, she seemed to be tickled to death, like she was telling it for the very first time. A big-boned, easygoing woman with a hardworking husband and a passel of kids. The kind of woman I fantasized my mother might have been.

Lucille Moseley knew we had no relatives in town, and invited us to her family reunion on the grounds of the Biltmore Mansion one Fourth of July. Black folk in the East really don't know how to barbecue right, but I never criticized her cooking. Lucille and her husband welcomed us like family. The least I could do was sit at a picnic table, chew her vinegary pulled pork, and act like it tasted good.

I learned over the years what got Johnny into trouble with the opposite sex. It was his gentleman complex. He treats a woman halfway nice, she thinks she has a hold on him. He could never bring himself to tell a girl, "Go to hell, get out of my face." Even obnoxious women like the one at the Moseley family cookout. Lucille's husband had a cousin visiting from Ohio, cussing up a storm.

"Ali," she introduced herself, looking a long way from any kind of Muslim I'd ever met. "But I'm a lover, not a fighter."

She looked more like a little teapot, short and stout. A loud-talking, bid-whist-playing, ghetto-acting woman a good twenty years older and at least one shade darker than me. Drinking whiskey and slamming down her cards like a man, her pants zipped open at the waistband and her belly sitting in her lap. When the soda water ran out, she cussed her family for their carelessness.

"Y'all hillbilly niggas don't know mixoloy for shit. Bunch of rotgut-swilling, moonshining muthafuckas!" Lucille's relatives laughed like they thought it was funny, but I was offended for them. "You can't put no tap water on top of no Old Grand Dad. Come on, Chicago. Run me over to the Food Lion."

Johnny had been her bid whist partner. He looked around for the mystery man, not realizing that he was the one she called "Chicago."

"I think I'll go too," I piped up. "I need some Mylanta."

It wasn't really a lie. That pulled pork was tearing up my stomach. Ali cut her eyes across at me like *Who is this hussy horning in on my action?* When Johnny opened the front door on the passenger side, she elbowed her way in past me.

"Girl, my ass is too fat to squeeze in that narrow little backseat. This here body is a Studebaker classic. Built for comfort, not for speed."

She said it like she was proud of it or something. The supermarket was closed for the holiday. Johnny drove to the mini-market where I worked. Ali shifted in her seat but made no move to get out of the car. She pulled a wad from her bra and peeled off a sweaty dollar bill.

"You get a discount, right? Run get some soda water and a ten-pound bag of ice." She flipped it over her shoulder, not even bothering to look back and see if I caught it. "Let me know if that ain't enough."

All that stuff for one lonely dollar? What did I look like, a magician? And since when had I become the errand girl, anyway? I leaned forward from the backseat, tapping my husband on the shoulder. *My husband.*

"You coming, Johnny?"

"No, baby girl. I'm drunk and funky." He kicked his seat back to semirecline, turning up the air-conditioning full blast. "You go ahead."

"Take your time," Ali simpered as I climbed from the backseat. "Us old heads will be in here chilling."

Didn't I tell you before? If you don't say boo, people will step all over you to get what they want. When I got back in with the ice and soda water, the air-conditioned interior was rank with whiskey fumes. They must have been passing the bottle, soda water or no. Why'd he have to go and drink with that old nothing woman? It just gave her ideas.

Johnny was stretched out, hands folded behind his head, eyes closed. Maybe he was asleep, not noticing the drunk woman leaning over him. Or maybe he had and was just ignoring her.

"Open up them pretty-ass eyes, Chicago." Reaching for his face, prying open his lids with her pudgy hands. "You got a real woman sitting here next to you."

I have never been a violent person. I was always the kid who backed down from confrontations, a favorite target for bullies. Men like Jamal Willis and Franklin Malveaux knew just where to push and I wouldn't say boo. So this wasn't like me at all.

I didn't realize I had lunged across the seat until I had cracked the windshield with the woman's forehead and Johnny was pulling me off her. Lucille never spoke to me after that and I had to find another hairdresser.

That wasn't the first time I would embarrass myself in public with jealousy over Johnny. I went from being a woman who wouldn't say boo to biting back at the drop of a hat. At a hole-in-the-wall nightclub some skanky stripper came gyrating up, jiggling her titties in Johnny's face. I stood up and lifted my top, showing which of us had the bigger treasure chest.

"You want to take my man, you need more than that to show for yourself."

"Bitch," she spat back. "Who says I want your man?"

But you better believe she backed off, went to shake her flabby tits in some other man's face.

At a church fund-raiser a girl dressed as a gypsy stepped between us. She snatched Johnny's hand from mine, offering to read his palm. I offered to show her the back of mine if she didn't leave my man alone.

I'd make five kinds of fools of myself, then weep with shame afterwards, begging Johnny to leave me. I'd point out the finer qualities of other women.

"What about Lisa, with all that long hair? She's perfect for you. Or Monica, that schoolteacher who talks so proper? That's the kind of woman you really want."

But he'd kiss away my tears, my fears. Figure out the worst aspects of those very same women and run them down.

"Lisa ain't got no chest to speak of, and you know I'm a breast man. If I wanted something like that, I would have married an ironing board. And that old talk-me-to-death Monica? She's in love with every word that falls from her own mouth. Baby girl, I'm not thinking about all those tired hos. All I want is you. Why can't you believe that?"

He'd light all kinds of candles and place them around the full-length mirror. He'd strip me naked and force me to look. Draping himself over my shoulder, stroking the curves of my body. The irony of it burned in the candlelight. He loomed over me like a long yellow flame, trying to make me love my blackness.

"Baby girl," he would whisper into my ear. "Dark wonder of my life. Just look at yourself."

If I twisted away, he'd take my head in his hands. Make me turn to face my reflection.

"Open your eyes, Destiny. Behold God's finest creation. I want you to see exactly what I see."

The flickering light would cast a pattern across my body. Shadows wandered over me, just like his hands. Just as I had calculated the charms of other women, Johnny would point out mine.

"Your hair," he'd croon, his fingers winding through it, "it's like a rain forest. Thick, dark, mysterious; a man could get lost in it."

I'd laugh his compliment aside.

"I guess it's time for my touch-up, then."

"Listen to me," he'd command, his voice husky with tenderness. "Your mouth. Baby girl, I love your lips. So full and soft and shapely. That behind. Woman, that's the kind of butter butt men write poems about. 'Ode to an African Ass.' And your breasts. Oh, my God, your breasts."

And here language would fail him. He'd sink to his knees, a priest worshiping at the shrine of some pagan goddess. He'd take one into each hand, the excess spilling over, his fingers molding me like a piece of sculpture. He'd guide a nipple to his own mouth, reverent as a Christian taking holy communion. Teasing me with his tongue. Tasting me until I melted in my own liquid, tears running from my eyes, my voice no longer my own.

"Oh, Johnny. I love you so much."

"I know you do, baby girl." He'd take his lips away just long enough to tell me. "I want you to love yourself, to know how beautiful you are."

I would swell open for him like a night-blooming flower. He would enter me like a probing honeybee. Safe in his arms, his body moving in mine. With the candles burning low, the lamps switched off so I wouldn't be blinded by his radiance. So he couldn't double-check the width of my nose or the rough texture of my hair.

It was not the pounding of the current, the arc of the waves that moved me. It was faith. No matter how rough the storm or strained the moorings, I knew I was in a safe harbor. With Johnny loving me, teaching me to love myself, I could almost be what he saw in me.

I learned to dress well, to apply makeup expertly. I never missed my weekly beauty shop appointment. I may have dark skin and nappy hair, but no one could say that Johnny Wright's wife wasn't well put together. I felt my man deserved an educated woman by his side, so I started making myself into one. Working part time, I carried a full course load at Warren Wilson, working on my sheepskin with Johnny's support, if not his approval.

"I want it if you want it," he'd assure me, staying up late to help me write my papers and study for exams. "But just make sure you're doing this for yourself, not for me. After all, I don't have a degree and I don't miss it. It ain't nothing but a piece of paper."

It was easy to say that when you had those big-city ways like Johnny did. The kind of poise where you can talk bad English just for style and not be afraid somebody would think you were ignorant.

Nobody could talk down to him, because Johnny had been so many places in life. He survived that embassy bombing in Africa and lived to tell the story. The war wounds on his thighs started throbbing, warning him to get the hell out of there. He escaped by the skin of his teeth, then went back into the rubble to help with the rescue. He'd seen tours of duty in the Philippines and Panama, Grenada and Somalia. He had shaken hands with General Colin Powell.

That's the kind of man I was married to. Self-educated, self-confident, self-made. I guess it was his growing up in Chicago, his travels in the service that gave him that polish. I rubbed a little of his polish off on myself, parlaying it into a part-time job as a clerk in the Asheville Public Library. And we were happy for a while.

I should have known it was too good to last. When I was ready for a baby it just wouldn't happen. I read all the gynecological texts and articles in the vertical file. I worried about the abortion I had had four years before. I had myself checked out numerous times and everything seemed to be in working order. I tried to get Johnny to go in, but he stubbornly refused.

"I'm not having some doctor poking around my privates. Just let nature take its course. Ain't no hurry; you're still young."

The only cooperation I got was making him change from briefs to boxers. I read that tight underwear could elevate the temperature of the testicles and cause a low sperm count. Johnny didn't want to go along with it, said he'd been wearing briefs all his life and didn't feel right dangling around loose. He said nobody but old men wore boxer shorts. Maybe he just didn't want to have a baby with a woman who looked like one of those black Africans in the Benetton ads. I cried, I begged, I finally threw away all his briefs. I was pregnant within six months.

I still don't believe I made such a pretty baby. I would sit holding her for hours, my old *Who art thou, my daughter?* pillow propped beneath her sleeping head. I was so amazed that this perfect little creature came out of me. Beauty looked more like Johnny than he did himself. She was long and golden, with a halo of sandy curls and a mouth like a little red bow, every bit her father's child. She had nothing from me but

3 1621 00929 6266

her big dark eyes. I always dreamed my babies would have green eyes like Johnny's, but the moment I saw Beauty, I knew I wouldn't change a thing about her. She was such a good baby too, so easy to take care of. She rarely even cried.

It was right after the baby came that we started having problems. My body had changed in alarming ways. I picked up fifty pounds during the pregnancy, lost half of it after giving birth, and seemed to plateau at that point. Twenty-five pounds overweight and all of it in my breasts. I started feeling self-conscious again, burdened by the weight of those basketballs bouncing in my bra. I was still wearing my maternity tops six months later for camouflage.

I couldn't bring myself to accept Johnny's heated assurances that he was aroused by all that extra flesh. I started avoiding his touches, for some reason thinking of that foster father whose hands would steal under my sweater when no one was looking.

All during the pregnancy Johnny was on me about breast-feeding. Constantly. He would be so proud to have his child nourished by her mother's own body. What could be more natural? I told him I'd think about it, but secretly began laying in a supply of baby bottles.

I couldn't stand the idea of nursing. It brought to mind those primitive women in *National Geographic* with babies on their backs and teats hanging to their waists. It made me think of a bitch nursing her litter. I couldn't bring myself to offer for nourishment that part of my body so closely connected with our lovemaking.

When the baby was delivered and the obstetrician offered a shot to dry up my milk, I ignored Johnny's protestations. After all, this was my body. I said I'd be back at the library within weeks and couldn't organize nursing a child while going back to school and work. He seemed to accept this explanation, even started getting up nights to help with bottle feeding. And backed into the corner of my lie, I rose from the birthing bed in just two weeks. I wound up taking her to a baby-sitter, when all I wanted was to stay home with my Beauty.

But when my stitches had healed and my blood dried, Johnny begged me to reconsider. If not for the baby, then for him. He had dreamed all his life of nursing from a woman's overflowing breasts. I could make his fondest fantasy come true.

"I'm just an old titty freak," he confessed, balancing a breast in the palm of each hand, the way he sometimes held a basketball. "Probably wasn't weaned right. Won't you do this for me, little mama? I need you."

Need is a perishable thing.

He'd never begged me before. And he'd never called me "little mama," either. I didn't like it. Before Beauty came, his pet name for me was "baby girl." Not that I was jealous of my own daughter. All I wanted was to have my endearment back. I wanted to be his baby girl again, not his mama.

"I already took the shot, Johnny." I found myself squirming under the pressures of his hands, the familiar searching of his lips. "It's too late now."

"No, it isn't. Your hormonal levels are still high. Prolonged, repeated stimulation will get you flowing in no time flat. Women who've never had a pregnancy manage to nurse their adoptive babies this way."

And he proceeded to demonstrate the technique. I was surprised he knew so much about the secrets of women's bodies. It wasn't much he was asking of me. And I really wanted to please my husband. But I couldn't bring myself to do it, I just couldn't. Where before I used to enjoy his attentions almost as much as he did, now his amorous squeezing and fondling, licking and suckling simply left me cold.

Why are men so fixated on breasts, anyway? They're really nothing but bags of fat. It is no coincidence that *bust* also means "failed, collapsed." The very fullness of them was a mockery, a contradiction.

I rarely examined my own body anymore. Between lullabies and diapers and midnight feedings, there was never any time for those candlelit sessions at the full-length mirror. But I would catch the occasional glimpse of myself while changing for bed or after showering. Nipples seemed to stare me down with dark accusation.

Breasts bulged from my chest, symbols of a lifetime of bad luck.

How could these sacks of shame bring forth sweet mother's milk? They were containers for my twenty years of sorrow. If anything flowed from them at all, it would be bitter tears.

Our sex life suffered, especially after Beauty started getting sick. At first it was frequent, persistent ear infections. Then she was diagnosed with FTS, failure-to-thrive syndrome. I was spending half my nights avoiding my husband's attentions, the other half walking the floors with my sickly baby. Wondering if maybe I was the cause of her suffering. If only I hadn't started back to work so soon. If only I had breast-fed her like Johnny wanted, maybe my beautiful brown-skinned angel would be thriving now.

I admit it. I was neglecting my husband. After a while he stopped making the effort. Our love life simply fizzled out, and I was relieved. I told myself I'd make it up to him. I'd have him climbing the walls again as soon as Beauty was well. Maybe I'd buy one of those electric breast pumps I'd seen on the maternity ward, the kind that made me think of cow-milking machines. Maybe I could bring myself to give this man what he needed from me. Once my baby was better.

I guess it was bound to happen. I knew it the first time Johnny was with that other woman. Not because he was tense and tight as a wind-up toy, but just the opposite. He was relaxed and easygoing, just like he'd been before the baby, when our lovemaking was going strong.

Hunger has a longer shelf life.

I'm not going to lie. I'm not going to put on a brave face and pretend my heart wasn't broken. It destroyed me. Even though it was bound to happen eventually. Even though I'd brought this on myself. Especially when I found out that the other woman was white.

When Beauty was rushed to the emergency room and I discovered him there with her, I felt like dying. If my baby hadn't needed me at that moment, I might have climbed the bridge and jumped into the French Broad River.

When I confronted him, he confessed quickly enough. He seemed almost relieved to unburden himself. He apologized, promising me it was over. It would never, ever happen again. And he thought that was enough.

He started making love to me again, and I didn't refuse him this time. But whenever he kissed me, I knew he was really kissing her. He seemed to drift away before my eyes. When he closed his eyes, as he always did during lovemaking, I knew it was her he was thinking of. Her blond hair streaming across the pillow, her rosy nipples in his mouth, her creamy thighs opening up for his golden rod.

I had been on the receiving end of Franklin Malveaux's passions too many times. Maybe this was my payback. I'd let that white woman's husband lay his hands on my body, and now another one like her had my husband's soul.

It was a torture worse than anything I'd endured at the hands of foster fathers and brothers. I was desperately afraid of losing my husband, but completely unable to respond to his touch.

I'd leave Johnny's arms while he made love to the empty shell of my body. My mind would go searching for my father. He would walk through the door with purposeful strides, scoop me up, and take me flying. I don't think Johnny was fooled at all by my pretense at passion.

Too empty to cry, I lie awake nights while my husband sleeps. I spend almost every visiting hour at the hospital, watching my daughter fight for her life. I guess I'm just a throwaway child, after all.

I was just a dark-skinned daughter named Destiny whom nobody wanted to keep. It seemed almost natural that what I wanted most in this life, I would always have to lose. I'd been loving out of my league all these years, lucky to have had a taste of happiness for as long as it lasted. It was just like Mrs. Malveaux said.

If you're going to love a man that other women want, get ready for a broken heart.

Lola Belle

It was my moment to tame the unicorn

He was in my bed when the phone rang. I take this fact and own it. I say it with neither pride nor shame. There was nothing either of us could have done to change the course of events. It was there before he met me, simmering like a volcano.

I was on top, as is my customary position. I answered the phone as I rarely do. Don't ask me why, I just did. Maybe I was trying to get a rise out of him at the moment.

"Lola Belle's Pleasure Palace," I purred, bouncing him back against the pillow when he tried to rise. "Who's on the line?"

It was his wife, speaking in that hesitant, deferential tone of voice so common to her kind. I handed him the phone and watched his face tighten. His pupils widened, like a cat's in the dark.

He didn't go soft inside me. Instead, he seemed to stiffen, maybe with the shock of the news. He hung up softly, flipped me underneath him, and quickly dispatched the deed.

I know it sounds cold. You hear unexpectedly that your one-year-old daughter is hospitalized with some dire, undiagnosed emergency. And you finish your business before you rise from your bed of adultery, pull off your sodden condom, sponge off your flaccid penis, pull on your boxer shorts, your blue jeans, your Personal Trainers Do It in the Gym sweatshirt, before you drive to the hospital to be with your wife and ailing child.

But it's not as bad as it seems. Maybe he needed to squeeze out that last drop of pleasure before facing what might be a long period without any. Maybe he needed to be on top just then, because God knows when he would be again. And Johnny Wright is not a boxer-shorts kind of man. I know this for a fact. It's that woman who has made this of him.

If there's anything I've learned from my limited experience with men, it's that you leave him with the kind of underwear he came to you wearing. If he's in briefs when you meet, don't squeeze him into bikinis. And don't envelope him in boxers, either.

No, it's not like me to provide an alibi for male insensitivity. And I'm not anyone's expert in the male underwear department. But this was a special case. And Johnny was a special man.

It's not like I was trying to steal the woman's husband. It was only the third or fourth time it had happened. If nature had taken its course, it might well have been the last. If the truth be told, I think he was getting tired of me. I was a distraction, a dalliance. My novelty was beginning to fray around the edges.

I was never really a threat to her marriage. I mean, look at me. I'm a victim of my upbringing, my own "alternative lifestyle." I don't like darkies all that much. And I like men even less.

Yes, I know. It's not a politically correct term nowadays. He's not a darkie, he's a black man. She's not a colored wench, calling up my house at all hours, contradicting herself with incoherent threats and tears and tantrums. She's a suffering black woman. At least that's what they tell me in support group.

"Where are your morals?" Bonita frowns, wrinkles her pretty pug nose, tugs her shiny black braid like that's what's worrying her. "You're buying into the same male-dominant culture that oppresses all women of color."

Get off your high horse, I feel like telling her. *You're just one step out of the teepee.*

But I don't. She's round and brown like a chestnut, a luscious full-blood from the Blue Ridge Mountains of Cherokee, North Carolina. Among those overlooked when they were herding them westward along the Trail of Tears. I could go for the likes of Bonita Bittwinter.

Don't ask me how she got that name. It doesn't sound the least bit Cherokee to me.

But she's a tad too civilized, too academic for my tastes. A Native American lesbian nerd, if you can imagine that. If only I'd gotten to her when she was rough and raw, before graduate school squeezed all the juice out of her.

"Wouldn't you call your actions a bit, er, hypocritical?" Lisa Lewiston suggests in her tentative way. "Sleeping with a man, a married man at that."

Do as I say, not as I do. Lisa is the homely, "bi-curious" middle-class housewife of the group. I've seen her herding her two and a half kids around the Ingles Supermarket. She always turns beet red when she sees me, and veers her shopping cart in the other direction.

"It sounds like Darnell Oates to me." Malaika Mugo would have to stick her two cents in. "Déjà vu all over again. Another black man made into a plaything."

I could kick myself every time I look into that black face I have to see at work nearly every day. Malaika is a colleague, a visiting scholar in the women's studies program. When she told me of her research interest in the lesbian experience, I joked about the assortment of oddballs I'd encountered in support group. Next thing I knew, there she was. Sitting across the semicircle with a smirk on her face and a notebook in her lap. I open the door to give her a peek, and she barges all the way in.

"But I want to sensitize myself to the lifestyle issues of lesbian women," she wheedles. "Surely there's no harm in that. I will respect your confidentiality."

I have suggested, to no avail, that she be banished for sneaking in under false pretenses. But everybody's so bleeding-heart liberal, so politically correct these days. They don't want to lose their token Negress, even if she is an impostor. Especially one that's a real live African. Two for the price of one. This uppity, proper-talking, Jill-come-lately jungle bunny as much as admitted she's not even gay.

I don't think it's even a case of being bi-curious like Lisa. She's just a peeping-Tom straight chick, eavesdropping on the seamy details of our deviant lives, jotting them down in that notebook of hers. Confidentiality, my cunt. If I ever see myself in any those journal articles she writes, I swear I will sue the pants off her overgrown ass.

"I don't see how you can wallow in the mud with any scummy man, black or white, married or single." That was Sonja Meyers, a hefty weight-lifting dyke with muscled forearms and a jaw line like Martina Navratilova. Her Betty Boop speaking voice is a shock, squeaking up out of all that brawn. I like her spirit; it's her butchiness that turns me off. I'm often mistaken for a fem myself, but don't let these blond lipstick-lesbian looks fool you. I'm the one who likes to be on top. Always.

Sonja only has herself to blame. If she hadn't been trying so hard to get inside my pants, insisting that I come to that musty downtown gym where she works out, I would never have met the "scummy man" I've been wallowing in the mud with.

I'm not usually a group joiner. I didn't go to therapy to get myself together or cry on anybody's shoulder, "Why am I queer? Is it nature or nurture?" I thought the Women's Alternative Lifestyles Support Group might be a good place to meet women, okay? A better class of dyke than those drug-addicted white-trash barflies I pick up at Saph Fires and places of that ilk.

I got fed up with the slim pickings and tired of driving two hours to Greensboro just to be disappointed. Because, of course, it would never do to go cruising for girls in my own hometown. My family would never live it down if word got out among the genteel society of Asheville, North Carolina. As dysfunctional and hypocritical as the Belles are, I don't relish rubbing their noses in it. Denial is a finely honed family trait.

I'm a strange breed of lesbian, I know that. A bull-dagger with breeding. Southern, overeducated, flush with family money I never had to lift a finger to earn. Teaching women's studies in a third-string state university in western North Carolina. Not because I have to, but because I rather enjoy it. In another era I'd have been one of those dowager do-gooders, wearing sensible shoes and support hose, handing out dog-eared novels in some bookmobile.

I'm a child of the fifties, coming of age in the seventies, right on the tail end of the sexual revolution. Not that the sexual revolution made it out here to the mountains, to the Reconstruction-era homestead that has been in my family over a hundred years.

Papa could probably kick himself for sending me to Massachusetts. Or rather, Mama could do it for him. Probably did many a time, once the word got back. Mama Belle had been pushing for Vanderbilt, her alma mater. A nice, stately, predominantly white college for young ladies from old southern families. Dear doddering old Daddy would hear nothing of it.

"I want her to experience the changing of the seasons," he'd quaver over an after-dinner liqueur served up neatly by Benjamin, the faithful retainer. I guess it wouldn't do to call him the family darkie. "Not a few leaves flickering in the fall, or a paltry snowflake every other December. I want her to know the true drama of autumn, the snowy beauty of a New England winter."

My paternal grandmother was French, "an effete intellectual blueblood who raised her boys like sissies and made them good for little or nothing useful," to hear my mother tell it. Sometimes I wonder if old Daddy might have had something of the true sissy in his heart, only to have it ground to a pulp by my ball-busting mother. It would have made sense. I could always point to the old gene pool.

Papa won, undoubtedly the only argument with my mother he ever did. The fallout is probably what sent him into the full-blown Alzheimer's he'd been practicing for most of his life.

Smith College was a hotbed of all the things my mother suspected: Yankee liberalism, effete intellectualism, drugs, antiwar activity, experimental education, and possibly something she never imagined. The place was chockablock with lesbians, wall-to-wall lesbians. Lesbians of all stripes and persuasions—trim preppie WASPs with diamond tennis bracelets, Jews tortured with angst, New York dykes with crew cuts, black queers in dashikis giving each other the power sign. Even the imported hothouse variety like my campus roommate.

We were walking, talking, completely opposite stereotypes, the two of us. Me with my southern accent and rose-apple cheeks and fluffy blond hair. Just the epitome of the southern belle, even if my mother hadn't been watching *Damn Yankees* when she was pregnant and given me this ridiculous name I've been trying to live down my whole life.

"Whatever Lola wants, Lola gets," Mama Belle would remind me sternly whenever I threatened to change it.

I wanted Ayesha from the moment I saw her brown eyes peering out at me from behind the veil, and it didn't take me long to get her. Ayesha was probably what shaped my taste for the exotic. She was a pure, chador-wearing Egyptian girl, saving that stitched-up virginity for a prize in some arranged marriage back home. And relieving her erotic urges with me every night. It's a venerable old Middle Eastern custom. Those neglected harem wives were bound to get into trouble with all that free time on their hands.

Now let me say something to all you radical feminists beating your breasts about the poor victims of genital mutilation from the Third World. I know it's a crime against nature and I'd never wish it on any of the daughters I'm unlikely to have. But I will tell you this. Those girls get their thrills just like us, believe you me. Well, maybe with a few minor modifications. Even a scalpel or a sharpened shell can't scrape away all the nerve endings. They do get off. If you don't believe it, ask Ayesha. Better yet, ask that oil baron husband I'd been warming her up for all those years.

Mama Belle, in pure poetic justice, blames *Damn Yankees* for spoiling my marital prospects with any number of genteel, land-owning gentlemen somewhere south of the Mason-Dixon line. We never openly discussed my sexual orientation; it was an unspoken agreement between us. Some things are better left unsaid.

I don't know how she'd take the news of Hot Johnny in my bed. Probably trigger that heart attack she's been faking for the past twenty years. Though you might think she'd be happy he was a man at least, although black as the ace of spades.

No, I exaggerate. Not all that black actually, more of a dull burnished gold with a body like a piece of sculpture. Even the scars on his thighs possess aesthetic interest. Like David's missing arms, the flaw becomes a necessary foil for his perfection. Just because I'm queer doesn't mean I can't admire a fine male specimen, now does it? Still, we don't go into the fineness of distinctions down here in Dixie. A nigger is a nigger is still a nigger.

Until quite recently there were local statutes on the books against both crimes, miscegenation being a misdemeanor, while sodomy could have me doing hard time on a felony rap. I guess the good old founding fathers had to leave a legal loophole for creeping across the color line themselves whenever they had a hankering for some dark meat. Which must have been often, considering the various gradations of coloring among our North Carolina Negroes.

There is a family of notorious wife beaters up on Black Mountain. They all have the same surname (which I won't mention here), the same freckles and glowering Irish temperaments. That goes for the white ones living on one side of the mountain and their multicolored cousins squatting on the other. Boys will be boys, after all.

Now down here in the Bible Belt, a deviant is a deviant, whether it's your garden-variety homosexual or a white woman sullying herself in animal passion with some buck Negro. You'll be happy to know that I'm doubly damned.

It's actually not that unusual for a lesbian to take a man to bed every now and then. I'm not talking about these so-called bisexuals, who as far as I'm concerned are lesbians in a state of denial. It's an interesting change of pace is all, feeling something hard and sinewy against you, rather than something smooth and soft.

And men, let me tell you all about yourselves. If you think my being queer turns men off, you've got another thought coming. Either they've got a savior complex and want to prove how a good old-fashioned fucking will straighten me out, or they want me to bring along a girlfriend to join in the romp.

So I don't know how I wound up with Johnny, who fits neatly into neither category. First of all, he's retired military, with all their little tiresome quirks and tics. Second, he never seemed interested in my body except for pounding it into proper fitness. Then he is mocha, which I'll readily admit is not my favorite of the thirty-one flavors. My limited experience with black lesbians up at Smith and the southern fried variety down here has been far from ideal—they all seem convinced that if you scratch a well-to-do southern white woman, there lurks an evil plantation mistress with a mint julep in one hand and a cat-o'-nine-tails in the other. I am tired of their anger, their knee-jerk nationalism, their guilt trips. I don't have to set myself up as a sitting duck just to get inside some woman's drawers.

So when I want to taste something exotic, I usually go for spicy East Indian curry or the fiery salsa of Latino cuisine. Nor am I opposed to hauling some visiting New England schoolmarm out of the closet or knocking moccasins with my buckskin beauty from Cherokee, whom I am determined to have.

It was just as well Sonja dragged me into the gym, because I was getting soft in my middle age. My proud Pocahontas probably wouldn't want someone who could take on an Indian name herself: Princess Thunder Thighs. I chose Johnny Wright as my personal trainer because he was the simply the best they had to offer. And I am accustomed to having the best. A former athlete, graceful, and quite good-looking with those unexpected greenish hazel eyes. But I was usually immune to such obvious charms.

Frankly, I'm relieved that the servile culture of the old South is gone with the wind. The Johnnies of today know how to deliver service in a way that is familiar without being intrusive, witty without being ribald, even sensitive and sophisticated. But always slightly aloof. Always professional, even when handling a white body by force of necessity. Placing a hand in the arch of a back, repositioning a leg, steadying a hip.

I can't imagine how "Hot" got in front of his name. I don't know any other way to describe Johnny but "cool," a quality I realize I grudgingly admire in these black Yankee men. Southerners can be such a writhing mass of contradicting emotions. I guess it comes from all that inbreeding.

Nothing ever seems to faze this man. He's all careful control. He never lets a hand "accidentally" brush a buttock, graze a breast, flick against a crotch. But he's no sexless Uncle Ben, no emasculated Uncle Tom. Underneath the cool breeze blowing off him, I detected the musky burning of a male fire. I assumed it was something he saved for women of his own kind.

Malaika was halfway right, that nosy African anthropologist. There was something about him that reminded me of Darnell Oates, the spawn of our family housekeeper and butler. I'd told the group about the games we played freely as children—hide and seek, house, doctor, nurse, naked movie star. I, of course, would be the movie star and he the butler who would do my bidding. In the beginning he never questioned my orders about what to touch, which spot to kiss.

He never failed to let me know that my plump freckled ass was not built exactly to his specifications. We'd watch TV together, munching our apples or popcorn. And he would point out the various women he found desirable.

"Ooh, I want me some of that," he'd squeal at Kim Novak's bland blondness, Jayne Mansfield's overdeveloped breasts. "I could just tear me up some of that."

As he grew older Darnell failed to acquire the servile manner that fit his parents like a glove. Maybe it was that pretentious name they gave him, a name unbefitting his station as the son of servants, the descendants of slaves. That name, and his funky attitude, is probably why they had to send him up north to live. He wouldn't have made it far into manhood in the 1950s South. I could imagine him going the way of Emmett Till. I can easily see him in O.J.'s shoes.

He began avoiding playtime, keeping to himself in the servants' quarters. I'd have to come looking for him, flaunting my little-missy authority. I'd have his mother rout him out of hiding and force him to come out and play. Even our games of sexual exploration failed to hold his attention. I'd open one eye while we were French-kissing and find he wasn't paying attention at all. His eyes would be wandering the room, sizing up the mahogany furniture, the velvet draperies, the original oil paintings on the walls. He even had the nerve to refuse me once.

"Girl, I am tired of touching your nasty pink pussy."

I was damned nice letting him be on top in the first place. He was the doctor, and I had consented to be the patient he bent over in the woods behind the stables. In the distance I could hear the scornful whinny of Danny Boy, the chestnut stallion who refused to be ridden. Papa was always threatening to send that horse to the glue factory. I flinched at the scorn in Darnell's eyes, pulled up my panties, snatched down my skirt, and sneered in my coldest Mama Belle voice, "Oh, I see. You don't like girls."

I lost that faint comfort when I stumbled upon him in the gazebo that summer he turned fourteen, pumping the bejesus out of some whimpering colored girl from the wrong side of town. She saw me watching and clutched at him for protection, peering with anxious blackbird eyes over his oblivious shoulder. How could he possibly prefer her to me?

Malaika Mugo seemed stunned when I first mentioned Hot Johnny.

"Who is this man called Johnny Wright?" she demanded arrogantly, although I'm sure I hadn't said his surname. "Tell me. I must know everything about him."

I sensed a hidden agenda and became cagey.

"Nothing you need to know."

Although really, there wasn't very much to tell.

"This must be the reason you went lesbian," Malaika pontificated in her overdone Cambridge accent, reading glasses pulled down low on her nose. She did everything but wag a finger. "You could not have him, so you decided to join him."

I was surprised to hear it from a trained anthropologist, an outdated theory that had long since lost its credence: One bad screw makes a girl go gay.

Johnny didn't look anything at all like Darnell. Yet his manner suggested the same sort of detachment. A maddening kind of don't-care-if-I-do-don't-care-if-I-don't. And I went after him for all I was worth. I'd learned a little finesse since the days of ordering Darnell around behind the stables. This one had to be handled with slow, steady, stealthy strategy.

He was relieved to find someone to talk to, someone who would listen to his run-of-the-mill marital problems. His wife had become a changed woman since the birth of their only child. Her weight gain, her fits of depression, her vague inadequacies were taking their toll in the bedroom. Their intimacy was suffering, their special moments together becoming fewer and farther between. There had even been times he had tried to make love to her and couldn't rise to the occasion.

Imagine that. All the mythology about the big black ever-ready buck, and here is one crying on my shoulder because he can't get it up anymore. I purred and petted, coddled and comforted, manipulated him gently as only a southern belle can. Then I moved in for the kill.

The first time I offered it to him, no strings attached, he looked at me with genuine astonishment. Something of the old Darnell Oates shame lit my cheeks. What did I have to prove to this uppity nigger? I was ready to pull up my pants and cry rape, when I detected something stirring in the depths of his changeable eyes. Something akin to curiosity penetrated his coolness.

"But I thought you were . . ." He stopped and looked at me in confusion. "Aren't you . . . ?"

"Yes, that's right," I admitted. "I am. You thought you were safe with me, right?"

He didn't know how to answer. I could see him puzzle it out before my eyes. Then he smiled a little-boy smile.

"And you thought you were safe with me too."

He kissed me then, leaning down to meet me at my own level, his red lips as soft and full and gentle as any woman's. Kissing my face, my arms, my shoulders. He put his whole body and soul into kissing like . . . like the way Reggie Jackson used to hit the ball. You know, the way he would pull that powerful body into itself, then release it in a controlled fury. I can't ever remember being caressed so fully, so thoroughly. I think he would have been content just to fondle me indefinitely, pausing every now and then to look at me, sizing up the situation.

The next time it happened, I had to practically commit rape to get him to move down lower. And despite his initial resistance, he had no trouble performing once I got him where I wanted him.

"You understand, of course," I told him as we eased back into our sweats (the deed had taken place on the carpeted floor of the deserted gym), "that this can never happen again."

"Of course," he answered, perhaps a little too easily. "I understand perfectly."

Which made me want him even more. Darnell Oates all over again. He resisted. He even tried to palm me off on a black lesbian he'd dug up, some gangling ex-girlfriend he'd dated in college before she realized she was gay. He went on and on about how precious his family was to him, how dedicated he was to his marriage vows—and this to some bitch he couldn't even get it up for.

I reached into my bag of tricks, my lesbian cornucopia of sexual bliss.

"Does your little wife ever do this in bed?" I'd flutter into his tight anal opening, tug at his nipples with my teeth. "Or this?"

"No, no," he'd mumble around his moans. Yet even in his fits of sexual arousal, he'd glance up at me with a sardonic glint in his eye. "But that doesn't mean I haven't tried it myself a time or two."

All right, Malaika. I'll admit it here before the whole wide world. One of the reasons I like being with women is they're so lovely to overpower, all soft and warm and sweet and pliable. But here's a delicious little secret Darnell never learned to appreciate: Men too can learn to savor sweet surrender.

Johnny never complained about me being on top. In fact, he seemed to like it that way. Oh, he could be as helpless and ravaged as a nubile young virgin. He'd lie on his back with hands behind his head and eyes closed, waiting for the *soupe du jour* to commence. Intercourse, outercourse, tantric sex, sixty-nine, nipple clamps, ben wa balls, and perhaps the most potent instrument of all, the erotic imagination. We took the cherished myths and fetishes of the antebellum South and turned them on their ear.

He would even go along when I wanted to role-play Mandingo in reverse. In this game I would be the randy buck slave slipping into the big house under the cover of darkness, sticking it to him with my oversized dick. He in turn would be the unsullied white plantation mistress, writhing beneath my crude punishment. He only demurred when I bit or scratched too hard, or wanted to try certain aids of, shall we say, the tough-love variety.

"Hey, I don't take a whipping from nobody," he would warn, staying my hand with the upraised riding crop. "And you can't be leaving any marks on me. Remember, I've got a wife to go home to."

I relieved him of the responsibility of being the sexual aggressor. He could be ravaged and plundered, a passive recipient of someone else's passions. Then he could get up and go home with a clean conscience. Why, he had been the one seduced—raped, even. He could always say, "The devil made me do it," the devil in this case being a zaftig white woman with wobbly thighs.

And what did I get out of the deal? He found a place inside me that had not been touched before. And it wasn't just about penetration. After all, I owned a complete set of latex dildos in graduated sizes.

I don't know how else to explain it, except that I got to be the prince in all my favorite fairy tales—to wield the sword, fight the dragon, and capture the heart of the fairest maiden. It was my moment to tame the unicorn, that wild, lithe, magical creature I'd never before been able to capture. I could do with him exactly as I wished—bend him to my will, let him sweep me away in his wings, if only for a time.

What if the unicorn had been been mine to keep? No, I don't kid myself. He was Darnell Oates after all, a bird of passage in the end. He was Danny Boy, the chestnut stallion who wouldn't be ridden. Even with his body erupting inside me, a part of him always seemed to be somewhere else. I told him that once.

"Funny," he mused, seeming to drift away from me even as he spoke it. "That's what my wife always tells me."

So really, we were sisters of a kind. A middle-aged blond lesbian in a heterosexual dalliance, a round-faced young black woman fighting for her husband's love.

I've never met her face-to-face. I only knew it was round from the picture I'd found while rifling through Johnny's wallet. At least the snapshot made it appear like a shiny disc. She didn't seem happy to be having her picture taken. Her head was ducked, and a tiny frown creased the spot between her eyebrows. One arm cuddled a blanket-wrapped bundle of baby. The other clutched a square pillow against her bosom like a shield. The words *Who art thou, my daughter?* could be faintly read. Frankly, I don't know what he sees in either one of us.

I swear, I wasn't trying to keep him for myself. Would that be too ridiculous, or what? He'd be somewhat out of place by my side at Saph Fires, the gay bar in Greensboro, or the Women's Alternative Lifestyles Support Group on campus, even if I had been that kind of woman, with that kind of hunger to have a man of my own. There was something elusive and untamable about that long cool drink of water. He was like a ray of sun that warms your skin for a moment. But when you reach for it, it can't be held.

And this is what I try to explain to the distraught woman who telephones me in the middle of the night, begging for the secret that will bring her man's heart back to its original resting place. I think of Bonita Bittwinter's stern admonition and try to do the right thing. I resist the urge to inform the caller that she should be grateful to me after all for sending him back with his manhood restored, his batteries fully charged. I push back irritation and try to answer the questions that increasingly become more intrusive.

"No, I am no longer sleeping with your husband. . . . I don't remember exactly how many times. Three or four. Maybe more. . . . No, I can't tell you why, it just happened. . . . Yes, I heard that your daughter hasn't been doing well. I am sorry about her illness, so very sorry. . . . I know it isn't my fault, it's just my way of showing—okay, I realize you don't need my pity. . . . No, Johnny hasn't tried to contact me lately. . . . Yes, I understand that he is all you have in this world."

I don't really blame you. I always knew something like this would happen. Do you understand what I'm trying to say? I think so.

I hate to keep bothering you like this. I just need to know, is all. It's eating me up inside. There is no reason to apologize to me. It is I who should be apologizing to you.

Can you understand how much I'm hurting? Of course I can.

I try to be patient with the questions, the prying, the memory of anxious blackbird eyes peering at me from beyond an oblivious bronze shoulder. The derisive whinny of a chestnut stallion who refused to be ridden.

Is he in love with you? No, I don't think so.

Did you feed his hunger, Miss Belle? I beg your pardon?

What did you do together in bed? Did you give him your breasts? Don't do this to yourself.

Did you love him? I need to know this. What can I say?

I always thought the blacks were such colorful cussers. I can tell Johnny's wife isn't used to flinging epithets.

You can answer me, you white honky bitch! Her voice rises, shrill and sad. *Do you love my Johnny?*

Carmen Quintana

This is the kind of man I would want for myself

I was waiting in my white uniform on the day they brought the baby home to die.

After months in the hospital, they finally gave up. It was not that the parents didn't try. They tried everything. Every clinical trial, anywhere in the South. New pain treatment, penicillin therapy, stem cell research. The parents flew like birds with Beauty in their arms. A bone marrow study at Duke University finally took her in. But bad news soon followed after good. Neither parent made a matching donor.

They came on TV, spoke on radio, told their story to the papers. They cried, not ashamed to let people see them begging bone marrow for their child. No suitable match could be found. It seems their people, they are superstitious to give blood and organs. Like the Negritoes back home in the Philippine highlands, none of them likes to see some part of the body living on after the person is gone. When the body won't bury, the soul won't rest.

How could anyone seeing his pain ever say the black man doesn't make a good father? This man, Johnny. So sad to see how deeply he loves. One of the best fathers I have known in all my days of private-duty nursing, even in my years as a physician back home.

Okay, it is not bragging, not to make myself bigger in somebody's eyes. I was a medical doctor. That part of my life stayed behind when I decided to leave home. I don't look back ever to regret.

The money I make one month in private-duty nursing is three, four times better than my salary as a medical doctor in the Philippines. When my immigration came through, the need for doctors was not there. So I lowered my qualifications, happy to come here to make my way in the United States.

I keep up with the latest research. I read the *New England Journal of Medicine*. Who knows, maybe in time I will study again, take training, become qualified to practice medicine here. Maybe I can return one day to my first profession. Right now I am happy to work hard hours. The money I save, the money I send home to family, the money I put aside to sponsor Miguelito, is all for a good reason. Maybe this year, maybe next I will be a married woman.

It is lonely here for single women; not too many other Filipino people in Asheville, North Carolina. Yes, Sanchita, the woman who runs the agency employing me, is a Filipina too, but she is only half in, half out of the culture. She must change her way of life because of the man she married.

You see, Sanchi married black, not even a Negrito like at home. With their no English, no education, you hardly ever see a Negrito traveling to the U.S. Sanchi's man is not even black like Jeremiah Lee Jackson, the military American I met as a teenager. After ten years I still think about this man. When I saw Jeremiah at first I thought he was a well-dressed Negrito.

He was out of uniform, walking in Manila like a civilian. Short and brown with wavy hair and almond eyes. Funny how some American blacks look Asian in a way. The man who sings Motown oldies on the radio, what is his name? Ah, Smokey Robinson. Looks pure Negrito to me, only except for the eyes. Just like Jeremiah Lee Jackson did that time, tipping his hat and smiling at me.

When he began speaking in English, the Negrito in him was all gone. I wondered how I could even think this man was anything but what he is.

I knew as a child I wanted to immigrate to the U.S. someday. I learned English in school on Negros Island, but mostly we spoke

Visayan every day. I didn't come to Manila until I was sixteen. Before medical school, I spent two years taking classes and working on my English. In the city, English came so easily to everyone—even the man selling *lumpia* and duck egg embryos on the street, even the Luzon hookers selling their bodies near Clark Air Force Base. So I encouraged the friendship with Jeremiah Lee Jackson as a way to practice my English.

Soon I begin liking Jeremiah for a friend, because he makes you laugh. It is not easy to do, to make a woman laugh at your jokes when she's struggling with your language. After that I begin liking him as a man. When the family back home on Negros found I was seeing an American military man, a black one even, it was serious bad news. They were some of the same bad beliefs people might say about Negritos.

"Carmen," my mother whispered in Visayan. "A woman like you can't take a man like that. He will split you open like a melon. The black man's body is . . . different."

She measured her hands in front of her, about length of newborn baby. You don't say certain things to your mother in the Philippines, all right? I was still a young girl. This was before medical school, before I had assisted births in the hospital and saw how a woman's body could stretch to deliver the biggest newborn baby. I couldn't bring myself to tell my mother that hookers who had been with military men seemed to be walking the streets of Angeles City just fine.

Still, I never knew for sure. I was seventeen years old and I didn't want to be split open by any man. One day in the park Jeremiah kissed my hand, then rested it in his lap. Maybe my superstitious mind made me imagine this. What I felt was long like a piece of wood, hard like a baton. I was afraid my mother was right. I broke off with him after then. Jeremiah went back stateside. Before long, I met my Miguelito.

Miguelito was the first man I had in life. Miguelito, *el guapo,* handsome like a movie star. His body did not split me like a melon, did not tear into me like a wooden baton. The size was not so big like a newborn baby, but he never let it stay in his trousers from the moment I left home.

How do I know? I get the news, don't worry how. Sometimes I think twice about bringing Miguelito here. Okay, when a woman goes away a man might fool around. But what happens when he meets me here? What if he shames me with girlfriends, girlfriends again, all over Asheville, North Carolina?

Look at me now. I am like the Christian missionaries coming to our islands long ago. Looking under grass skirts, studying ornaments the men wear on their organs. I always wonder about the size of Sanchi's man. I watch the bundle riding in his trousers. I look to see if she walks in pain, seems in ill health from being split like a melon every night.

I have never had a full-grown black man for patient yet, but some other Asian nurses talk about ones they have seen. Sometimes it looks like contest for who has seen the biggest size. It makes me wonder, because a man in sickbed is probably not having any normal erection. So how can one organ be so big?

"I saw one, big like donkey."

"I've seen it big as a bull."

"Other day, go to High Point. Nee-gaw man in bed with diabetes, had it big as elephant."

Rosie wasn't in the U.S. one month even. Already she is the expert, has seen the biggest black-man's penis.

"Where did you see this elephant?" I ask Rosie. "In the streets of Seoul?"

Rosie said something the other day in her broken English. Something that really bothered me.

"If it one thing I don't like, it nigger."

She doesn't even pronounce the insult the proper way. "Nee-gaw" is the word coming out of Rosie's mouth. I tell her, "You can't be a bad citizen like that. First time coming to a new country you learn to disrespect the people living here before you."

Like the colonial Spanish first coming to the Philippines, renaming our islands for their white-man spider king. Like the American military coming later. Calling us "flip" and "little monkey." If I am a little monkey, then don't come to my country. Don't eat from the fruit of my islands, shitting out seed like a *balatiti* bird.

"I know what I see," Rosie insisted. "You ask Sanchi."

I don't want to disrespect Sanchi's man, Sanchi's marriage. Sanchi is a friend, my boss too. But I am curious. And sometimes I wonder. Maybe I could have married that Negrito-looking man I met in Manila, loved him every night without being split open like my mother said. Maybe I could be living in Chicago, Mrs. Carmen Lee Jackson. Dr. Carmen Lee Jackson, American citizen with no quota of Filipina doctors to expire.

I brought it to her very carefully. "Sanchi, what is it like to marry a man from Africa?"

Sanchi was married before at home. At least she has something to compare. She laughed.

"No different way than any other man. Except he likes his meat well peppery."

I looked away, trying to think how to say my question better.

"Is true, Sanchi? Some people say a black man's body is made different?"

I found myself making the same hand size of my mother, warning me against Jeremiah Lee Jackson. Just about length of a newborn baby. Sanchi looked hard at me like she couldn't decide to be angry or not.

"It's not to disrespect," I quickly said. I could not afford to lose this job. "Only curiosity. It is just what some of our people say."

Sanchi took a long, deep breath. I think she has been asked this question before.

"My husband is a king," she said finally. "An African king. And he treats me like queen. End of discussion."

I never knew Sanchi was pregnant, she was so slim right up through the final trimester. I went to visit her in the hospital and saw her propped up in bed with her African king by her side. She was nursing the overgrown Negrito son her husband gave her. How could Sanchi's thin body hide such a big baby?

"He was born with eyes open," she said, all excited. "Eyes wide open. You were a doctor at home in the Philippines"—somehow the news had slipped out—"did you see babies born with eyes open, ever?"

"Sometimes," I admitted. "Negritoes in the mountains, their newborns are alert. If you look at a regular Filipino baby and at a Negrito baby, it's almost like the difference between a newborn hare and a newborn rabbit."

I didn't like the animal example coming to my mouth so quickly. It was too much like the nurses' talk of elephants and donkey size. I looked at Sanchi and Ade, to see if it struck them as a racist idea. Both were nodding, like they could see the point clearly.

"Negritoes?" Ade, the African king asked. "Is that some kind of Filipino African?"

I don't really know where Negritoes came from first. I think they were always there thousands of years, before any of us came to the islands.

"No, they come from Africa," Sanchi decided. "A long time ago."

She was full of facts about Negro babies that I didn't know. How quickly the milk teeth come in, how soon they start to walk, how advanced their development is compared to other kids. Breast-feeding that Negrito-looking boy was making our Sanchi into a real African queen.

I don't blame my mother anymore. She didn't understand how a man is measured not by his organ, but by the size of his heart. How he would make you feel like the queen of his village. That is a good man. Not the man who must test the thing between his legs on every whore in the city of Manila.

My mother only tried to protect her teenage daughter. It was reasonable enough to be careful of the American military. Some of them could be very rough and racist, even the black ones. But everything is not black and white.

After long talks with Johnny, I learned things I never knew in school. During the first occupation some black soldiers even deserted the American military. Maybe it was because of how bad the white people treated them. Maybe some had sympathy for our cause. Some soldiers even came to fight on our side. Some were caught and court-martialed, even hanged. True, you find racist black soldiers in the Philippines. Some of them just the same as whites. But I won't forget that black men died and were buried in our islands, fighting for Filipino freedom.

Johnny is a good man, I can see that in his eyes. Strange green eyes, just like Smokey Robinson. He is not Negrito-looking like Smokey or Jeremiah Lee Jackson or Sanchi's child. He is yellow-brown, very close to my color. He is tall, tall like Sanchi's husband. Tall like the Americans who played basketball at Clark AFB.

His dying daughter is Beauty. It is not I who say it, even though it is true. Her mother gave her this name, I think. Destiny Wright is a pretty woman, but I don't think she knows it, really. She covers her naturally dark lips with too much lipstick. She wears a certain shade of foundation too light for her skin. She reminds me of how a *durian* melon can look really sweet and ripe. But when you split it open, it is full of terrible secrets. Bitter water and a rotten smell. It is too important for her to have a bright-skinned daughter who can be the beauty for both of them. And now that daughter is dying.

I don't think Johnny cares what color Beauty is. He loves her too much. It hurts to see, I tell you. When he thinks no one is noticing, he holds her to his heart. Like holding her tight could take the pain from her small body. He cries over her. Ah, so sad. So many times he has told me, "I love my daughter more than life itself."

When I was a young physician in the Philippines, I did my practicals back home on Negros Island. I saw such men in the mountains, family men much smaller than Johnny Wright. They looked like maybe half his height. Such devoted fathers. Negrito people, how they love their children. I saw it every day: Men walked for miles over mountains, fathers with babies tied to chest. We were countrymen and country-women, but I never learned their language. It seems strange to think how hard I studied English. I ate English! But the black people of my own island, I never took the time to learn their language. One day, if I ever return . . .

But you don't need language to see the love in a father's eyes. He unties his child, holding the sick body out for you to heal it. There were too many times I had to shake my head: *No, there is nothing I can do now.* He ties the child to chest again and walks back over mountains. Taking the baby home to die.

Johnny is a good father, a good man. Very easy to talk to. He speaks to me like an equal, not like a servant. The kind of man you can talk to about anything. *Anything.* Jeremiah, Miguelito. Love, loneliness. The world and people in it, brown, black, and white. I'm sorry I didn't know him when he was stationed in the Philippines. With a friend like Johnny, who knows? Maybe my mother's warnings about Jeremiah Lee Jackson would have never even entered my ear.

Johnny loves Filipino food, he begs me to make *pancit molo* and chicken *adobo*. But when the wife finds things in the fridge she doesn't know, always she throws them away. This is from ignorance, not jealousy. Even though I can see that she is a jealous woman. She is so afraid to lose her husband. So afraid to lose her baby.

As sick as she is, Beauty is an alert child. Bright, like Negrito babies back home. Still developing, even with sickle cells piling up like branches in her bloodstream. She laughs and plays, throwing toys for her father to catch.

It surprised me so much to hear Johnny singing "Sana, sana," a little nonsense Spanish rhyme to sing to kids when they don't feel well. I don't know how he learned it, maybe in the Philippines. When I told what it meant in English, we laughed so much. "Heal, heal, little tail of a frog. If you do not heal today, you will heal tomorrow."

But to hear Johnny crooning the lullabye when Beauty cries, rubbing her small, suffering body. When she hugs so hard her security pillow, *Who art thou, my daughter?* I tell you, it hurts you hard. I try not to become involved with patients, try not to let their pain get into my heart. But I am not a statue, I am a woman.

A day came when the baby was not walking too well. She was losing her balance a little bit, and the leg was kind of weak. Her mother said it was only a little clumsiness, that is why the child kept falling over. But I knew it wasn't normal, a baby just wakes up one morning and is not walking well. I talked to Johnny about it, we took Beauty to the hospital right away. The child had a stroke just that morning.

How can you see a father crying in the emergency room and not feel his pain? Do you let tears roll away like rain on a statue, when he is begging you to help his child?

"There must be something we can do. Sometimes I wonder if it's right to keep her suffering like this, if it would be better just to let her go."

I can't let him give up his hope.

"She can recover," I tell him. "You must keep looking for a donor. The best match is a blood sibling. Your family, your wife's family. There must be someone."

The man shakes his head.

"My wife has no family. She was a foster child, she never knew her folks. And my people. God, I haven't been in touch with them in years."

"You must find them. The faster you find them, the sooner you can get your Beauty back to health. I am not speaking in ignorance here. I was a physician back home, I studied sickle cell disease in medical school. Other places have people born with this disease. Some live, some die. But I know this child can be healed."

This is honorable work for a husband to do. For a father to do. Not to sit helpless watching his daughter die. But to go find a miracle somewhere, somehow. Even if the miracle doesn't work, he can say, "I tried. I tied that baby to my chest and walked across mountains to heal her."

It was hard for Johnny to leave his child. The wife didn't want him going, even if it might mean new life for their little daughter. I see nervous fear gathering like clouds, like sickle cells piling up in her eyes. The wife is not like Johnny, not so easy to talk to. Sadness makes her stone. To her I am like equipment in the baby's sickroom. A hospital bed, a hypodermic. I want to comfort Destiny, to tell her, *Don't worry. Your man is a good man, not a ladies' man like mine.*

Women all over the world suffer this, the wondering if you will lose your man when your back is turned. Gossip comes floating to North Carolina across ocean and mountain, on long-distance telephone lines to tell me what bad things Miguelito is doing without me. And me putting away pennies, emptying bedpans and watching babies die to bring him here to be my husband.

Me, I'm not too sure about marrying Miguelito. Okay, I can't get back the lost years of Jeremiah Lee Jackson. Not every Filipino man in the world is like Miguelito. True, I don't see many single Filipinos in Asheville, North Carolina. But there are nice, hardworking Mexican men who look a little like us. They don't speak English too well, some of them. And my Spanish is *muy limitado*. But I don't care if he is a gardener and I am a private-duty nurse, if he doesn't have much education and I was a physician back home in the Philippines. If he is a good man, who cares about all that?

Who knows, I might not say no if a nice black man asked me out tomorrow. I don't think I've heard of anyone dying from being split like melon.

I want a man who will make me the queen of his own village. A man who will walk miles barefoot across mountains with a baby tied to chest. A man who weeps for his dying daughter, then dries his tears. Who gets on an airplane to Chicago to go and find a miracle. Who will come back one day, holding the gift of life in hands.

This is the kind of man I would want for myself.

Cara

Oh, how I wish I had been your first

Someone before me left it turned up too high. Maybe the chambermaid, a hard-of-hearing hotel guest. Bass tones boom like a clap of thunder. The shock of his voice reverberates, pulsing through my body like a tuning fork.

"Some Africans believe the firstborn child to be a wayfarer, one who clears a passage for the rest to follow. I say that this is too great a sacrifice."

I think my ears are playing tricks on me. I lean forward, adjusting the volume.

"Oh, my God," I murmur. "He's alive!"

I think immediately of Frankenstein's monster. A man made of scavenged parts, stirring back to life at a stroke of lightning. And then I find myself editing my thoughts. It's the invisible mother in my head, scolding me by proxy.

"Frankenstein's monster—a macabre notion indeed. What sort of African is this I have raised?"

"The kind of mongrel," I must remind her, "with an Italian name, an expatriate upbringing, a Western education, and no real mother tongue or country."

The invisible mother chooses the point she wants to argue.

"Do not blame me," she rationalizes. "You are also your father's child."

My invisible mother and Frankenstein's monster. Not such a mixed metaphor as you might imagine. The voice on the radio and barrage of attending images stir such an intense déjà vu, it is as though I am living in two times at once.

At this moment my millionaire lover has left me alone in our Manhattan hotel suite. He sits beside a dispirited woman at the lobby bar, dropping the bomb of yet another black wife. I am not altogether sure if Hector's mother will be among the group of last-minute guests. My own, as usual, will remain invisible.

In another time I find myself at a more modest beachfront inn, my first lover having left on a preparatory mission for our union the next day. As now, I am rifling through clothing. Back then, the radio also transmits a message that threatens to upset the apple cart of my hapless life.

Back again in the present. It is the witching hour and I am wide awake. Not with prewedding jitters, but the more mundane matter of what to wear for the ritual that will change us from live-in companions to legally married couple. Despite publicists' statements to the contrary, we will be wed tomorrow. And I have not yet chosen a wedding dress.

I sit in the penthouse suite of an obscenely expensive hotel. I rifle through a rack of designer gowns by famous names. I prepare myself for marriage to a man whom I admire but do not adore.

I really should be sleeping, or my dark circles will be more pronounced in the morning. My agency has recommended an eye lift on more than one occasion. I've always had smudges beneath my eyes, the kind that are deepened by fatigue but easily covered with concealer. This is a feature I cannot be bothered to correct. In fact, I rarely follow any beauty regimen, despite the invisible mother's warnings that "one day, Cara, you will balloon, like me."

I sleep irregularly, eat haphazardly, exercise infrequently. I do little to preserve the face and figure I could comfortably live on if need be. Maybe it is the security of a wealthy man's support. Maybe I have accepted Hector's oft-repeated assurance that a bush flower grows best untended. Or maybe I do not trust in beauty, because I do not trust those who define it.

"To be a clotheshorse," the invisible mother always chides, "a mannequin upon which capitalism hangs its garments, is nothing to be taken seriously."

My identity is clay, constantly reshaped to suit the whims of a world delighted to be ignorant about Africa. I have been everything from Cape Colored to Egyptian Bedouin to Falasha Jew.

The fashion world went through a phase of "Masai-itis," as my mother terms the fleeting fascination with postcard-picturesque Africans. I shaved my head and stained it ocher, donned a "tribal-inspired" sheath, let myself be draped in lengths of designer beads, and was photographed bare-breasted for the cover of *British Vogue*.

"A Masai maiden from the jungles of Kenya," read a caption on the inside cover.

"A Somali damsel" was another incarnation, "daughter of a camel-herding tribesman."

I am the biggest fake since those other two stateless Africans, Milli and Vanilli. I am a blur in the margins of African aesthetics. Those in power cast mixed-race beauty as an ethnic ideal because something in the exotic reminds them of themselves. But I am also culturally generic, forever ranked as an ethnic "other." They even call us by each other's names: Alek Wek, Iman, Waris Dirie, Cara Bondi.

"When it is Africa," my mother complains, "the West will always get it wrong."

I slip naked into a delicately embroidered dress of Eritrean cotton, softened by many washings. I study myself before the full-length mirror. Though the dress is usually worn as a nightgown, I have suddenly decided this will be my choice. For my wedding I will be a counterfeit Eritrean bride. It may well make the front page of *Women's Wear Daily*, be touted as the up-and-coming fashion trend. Some struggling dressmaker in the Horn of Africa might actually see a few dollars before designers hijack the business.

I am surprised to hear music on talk radio, a haunting rendition of an

American Civil War marching song. Perhaps Hector will cover it on his next album. African-inspired, with kora and percussion replacing the fife and drum. I will suggest it to him.

> *When Johnny comes marching home again*
> *Hurrah, hurrah*
> *When Johnny comes marching home again*
> *Hurrah, hurrah*

The music fades. A female announcer introduces "a decorated airman who served our nation during military campaigns in far-off Africa."

"I've held dying babies in my arms." His voice is reflective, restrained. He could almost be an actor, reciting scripted lines. "Victims of war and famine. Nothing could be more humbling, more heartbreaking . . . until tragedy strikes closer to home."

An image springs suddenly to memory: a tall brown man in military blues, kneeling in the dust, trying to breathe a child back to life.

"What tragedy has stricken the life of John the Baptist Wright?" the fruity voice of the female announcer intrudes. "Tune in tomorrow evening for one man's personal war: the battle for Beauty."

The music reemerges with a flourish.

> *Oh, the men will cheer, the boys will shout*
> *The ladies they will all turn out*
> *And we'll all be gay when*
> *Johnny comes marching home.*

It suddenly seems wrong to be in my wedding gown. I take off the dress, perch naked on the bed. I strain toward the radio, although his voice does not return. My mind lurches backward, a vehicle set in reverse gear. It journeys me miles down the back roads of memory.

The summer of Mogadishu, 1992. There were always three people in the relationship, although the players shifted. Me, Johnny, my mother.

Me, Johnny, Raqiya. Johnny always in the middle of it. People might find it odd that three women shared one man. But he was a different one to each of us; Mama's plaything, my playmate, Raqiya's would-be redeemer.

Before mine became a household image, Raqiya's was the face of Africa for a time. Hers was a beauty that might have been her downfall, except that she refused to fall. It may have cast her as the poster girl of famine, but that she endured.

Her image was just one of many pouring out of Somalia. My gut twisted with pity and shame, as if witnessing relatives in public nakedness. Children with distended bellies and eyes bigger than their own faces clutched empty bowls in outstretched hands. The headlines wagged an accusing finger: clan rivalry . . . scorched-earth warfare . . . famine outbreaks.

One-quarter of my blood connected me to this land of hunger. What right had I to a full plate of food? I wasn't eating well at the time and must have looked like a famine victim myself. Bone thin and gawky, a concentration-camp haircut, a face full of acne, dark-circled eyes. I have always been a worrier, probably from the diet of horror stories I was raised upon. Those smudges beneath my eyes had been there for as long as I could remember. Mogadishu must have deepened them.

I usually summered in Milan, a city where six years later I would stumble into a modeling career. My looks came from my half-Italian father, Carlo Bondi. Mama said his Somali mother's surname, Bonderii, had been shortened and Romanized when he left home at seventeen to become an Afropean.

I didn't know whether to believe her; she had been wrong about names before. She said my father's imagination had been so dull he had named me after his career. But Papa himself explained to me the meaning of *"cara mia."*

His work in Somalia must have been dangerous and depressing. Maybe this is why he partied so hard. Mama always thought the worst of him.

"This is nothing but a career move," she sneered. "Do you think

Carlo Bondi cares one whit for his starving countrymen? He snatches up a discarded identity and steps uneasily into it. The prodigal returns home in order to climb the career ladder."

Because UNOSOM was a diplomatic mission, Papa was treated like a big shot. He had a nice villa, a chauffeured Land Rover, and a generous pay packet. He was on loan from the *carabinieri*, Italian military police, to advise United Nations Operations in Somalia how best to protect their supplies and personnel. Even the good guys needed their own police force in Somalia.

My father always overdoes everything. He tried to bury months of neglect in a shower of gifts: gold jewelry too showy for a thirteen-year-old girl, elegant Somali gowns I didn't have the grace to carry off, sloppy displays of affection I found embarrassing.

For a glorified policeman, he had big tastes. He courted beautiful women, entertained in lavish parties that lasted all night. He was Nero, fiddling while Rome burned. I love my father, but being with him became an orgy of excess.

When Siad Barre left power in 1991, the country fell into chaos. All those who had the means left as quickly as possible. Mogadishu and regions nearby were now run by a cowboy dictator named Aideed. Warlords of rival clans controlled the rest of what country there was left to run.

Papa said Mogadishu was once a lovely seaside city. This was hard to imagine. It was a helpless time for decent men, struggling to protect their families in a land without law. Gangs of drugged youths roamed the streets in pickup trucks rigged with automatic weapons. The sound of gunfire and sight of corpses became almost familiar. To go outside the UNOSOM compound without an armed guard was risking your own life.

UNOSOM was not classified as a family post, so there were few other children and nothing to do. I spent hours at the villa alone, bored and restless. It wasn't long before I began to count the days. In the beginning I had been eager to escape my mother's ruthless preaching and proselytizing. Now I was thinking of creeping back to Cape Town to finish up the long holiday before returning to my girls' boarding school in the foothills of Mount Kenya.

I was the first of us to meet Hot Johnny, although he doesn't seem to remember me crouched on the staircase during one of Papa's all-night parties. I was supposed to be sleeping in my room. But I enjoyed watching adults drink and sing and flirt and misbehave. Perhaps my dark circles made me appear rather solemn. A man in military uniform lowered himself onto the step below me, teasing like he already knew me.

"Hey, pretty, why the long face?" he boomed in a broad American accent. "It's a party, you're supposed to be enjoying yourself. Come on now, show me that smile."

I gave him a snarl instead, scurried up the stairs, and plopped into bed. The nerve of these Americans! Demanding a smile like it was a debt, ordering me to enjoy myself at my father's own party. Being spotted had sucked the pleasure out of spying.

But it seems he forgot the whole incident. It wasn't until Mama arrived that he even noticed me again. My mother wasn't expected in Mogadishu. She was on assignment with Africa Watch, seeing after women's rights in the "new South Africa." She must have heard that Somalia was where the action was. She arrived in a flurry, annoyed that a case of her South African wine was being held up in customs.

News had reached her about women's plight in Somalia. Nearly everyone's plight had reached the crisis point. But there was the added danger for women and girls of being kidnapped at gunpoint and made to serve militia members from rival clans. The Mogadishu newspaper carried notices like "Waliya Jama, please come home." Seven-year-old girls were raped alongside their seventy-year-old grandmothers. My mother came to document these lives and collect their stories.

I had always yearned to have a mother and father at the same time. I was very young when my parents divorced, so I couldn't remember them living together. The very first triangle then became mother, father, and child. But it was not a happy one.

Mama tried to coax my father into her project, offering him work as translator. He said that after twenty years gone, he had nearly forgotten the language. I don't know what he whispered to the women who slipped from the villa in the morning, but it didn't sound like Italian to me.

Papa said Mama was prying into politics, a dangerous practice. Which is why Mama claims they divorced. She could not abide a man as apolitical as my father.

"I paraphrase Derek Walcott," Mama said hotly. " 'The African dies inside when he betrays, with a spy's eye, the rhythms of his race.' What did I ever see in you, a running-dog lackey for your colonial masters? I was simply loving below my means."

I am not sure Papa knew of the Nobel prize–winning poet, but he didn't let on.

"Intellectual show-off! You see, this is exactly why I do not like African women. Altogether too aggressive and disagreeable."

They hadn't lived together in ten years. It was easy to see why. Mama called him a macho sexist "who thinks he owns every woman he's ever slept with." Papa called her a shameless flirt. He became jealous of an American serviceman Mama met at one of his crowded parties.

Johnny stood there stupidly while she draped him in her *kikoi*, doing her version of the "Dance of the Seven Veils." Didn't he know that Salome demanded John the Baptist's severed head?

Papa was enraged by endearments uttered "within the walls of my own villa." When told that her first name meant "angel," Johnny learned to recite in a kind of singsong poetry:

"Malaika Mugo, my African angel."

Mama called him "soldier boy."

He wasn't really a soldier, but an airman with a rapid-deployment squad of the United States Air Force, part of Operation Restore Hope. Before they wore out their welcome, Somalis greeted them with open arms. They understood why troops had been sent to feed hungry people. If not, *shifta* bandits and militia might have looted every grain and traded it for guns.

Johnny wasn't one of those delivering food. He worked in the command center, from where helicopters and aircraft were sent to escort shipments of relief supplies.

"Not even an officer," my father sniffed. "A common military clerk."

"So says the policeman," my mother countered. "The pot calling the kettle black."

The pot and the kettle looked eerily alike. Tall, bronze, curly-haired. The two men could almost be brothers, except that Johnny was taller and bigger. Maybe he had not spent a childhood scratching for food in the streets of whatever American city he grew up in, as my father says he did in Mogadishu.

Mama's indiscretions worried me.

"You should be careful," I warned. "Papa is jealous, he might do something."

Mama discounted the threat.

"Do I tell him whom to sleep with? Carlo Bondi's jealousy does not concern me."

I do not know what power Mama held over him. Maybe like Raqiya, he believed Bantus to be sorcerers. While Papa continued to mutter beneath his breath, Mama kept seeing her American.

One day I overheard her whispering on the telephone. When the conversation ended, she grabbed me by the hand and dragged me into the bedroom we shared.

"Ready yourself, daughter." She thrust a picture at me, a crumpled photo clipped from the South African *Cape Times*. "We are off to collect this one woman's story."

On the road to Baidoa. The four of us set out: me, Mama, Johnny, and Axmed Jibril, my father's driver. Mama had borrowed him without Papa's permission, along with his Land Rover all-terrain vehicle.

We had loaded as many sacks of relief supplies as could fit in the back of the Land Rover. We would use them for their intended purpose if possible, for bribes and ransom if necessary. Food supplies were mis-used like this all the time—raided from warehouses, sold in the open market, traded for weapons. Papa always tossed a sack or two into the taxi when he kissed that morning's girlfriend goodbye.

"Sergeant John the Baptist Wright, at your service." Mama's boy-friend bent to introduce himself. "But people call me Hot Johnny."

Typical American, I thought as we drove off. Why go about with such a boastful, overbearing name? Hot for nothing! I rarely approved my mother's taste in men. We had met before, at least twice. Surely he'd been lying when he proclaimed me "a beautiful girl, graceful as a Nubian princess."

What would Johnny know about a Nubian princess? Would he rec-ognize one if she fell from the sky? I glanced out the window. Vultures wheeled overhead, swooping down on a carcass we could not see. A princess, perhaps, having her eyes plucked out.

Burned-out buildings, fallen trees, wrecked vehicles littered the land-scape. Against this backdrop an occasional man led a herd of lean camels, the odd woman or child grazed flocks of bedraggled sheep and goats.

We were stopped at the first of several roadblocks. Helmeted, brown-fatigued Americans peered in at us. They were of a singular ug-liness, with their raw and sunburned faces, their nasal voices. They frowned at the sacks of maize and rice, poking at them with the points of their weapons.

"Hey, buddy. Ya mind telling me what kind of goods you're trans-porting back there?"

"Do we look like gunmen, a woman and child?" Mama barked from the backseat. I was afraid she would ask to see his superior, his com-manding officer. "Do these men look like warlords to you?"

Axmed they ignored. Johnny they eyed suspiciously and or-dered out.

"Please step out of the vehicle. Keep your hands away from your body and don't make any sudden moves."

He was not in uniform that day, the stamp of his military identity.

But even in civilian clothes you would know he was not Somali. Why couldn't his countrymen recognize a fellow American? Did black men look that much alike?

He held one hand in the air, reaching with the other into his back pocket. He held out his identification to be scrutinized. He didn't report the weapon strapped to his calf, hidden by his trouser leg. That gun was supposed to be our protection, but it didn't seem like much firepower when people moved about with rifles and automatic weapons.

"Go easy, angel," Johnny warned, climbing back into the passenger side. He was nervous and sweating. "These trigger-happy pukes are looking for any chance to shoot. Don't get them all riled up."

Mama harangued Johnny about the undisciplined nature of American soldiers. But she didn't argue again, especially when the official roadblocks of UN troops became those of nonuniformed Somalis who could easily tell that Johnny wasn't one of them.

His height, features, and coloring compared to those of the men in the Horn of Africa. But there was a difference in the cut of his clothing, the curve of his smile, the brand of sunglasses that hid his face. I had never seen a Somali with that shade of eyes.

I could tell Mama's mind was somewhere else. She had sent it down the road ahead of us, sniffing around for a story. The crumpled photo revealed a flawless beauty, even in a land legendary for its beautiful women. A man interviewed on local television was openly nervous about so many foreign men coming into Mogadishu: "We know they will all be wanting our women."

I had already seen her on CNN. She is not well fed, but her body is more rounded than those of the others around her. She leans against a fence of thorn tree branches, not seeming to notice the cameras closing in like birds of prey.

She is frowning in concentration, her head thrown back as if puzzling out the answer to a difficult math problem. The camera angle moves down. A red stain steals over her clothing, like blood seeping into the earth. Minutes later she squats, spilling a newborn baby onto the dusty earth. Where were the doctors? What about her privacy? Why wasn't a midwife in attendance? Why didn't the newsman put down his camera to help? Mama was determined to ferret out the truth.

Although we rarely see eye to eye, I love my mother so fiercely it often frightens me. She is more than just my mother. She is Malaika Mugo, an African woman. She doesn't cling as much to her Kenyan nationality or Kikuyu ethnicity as to her African identity. For her this is the only *kikoi* large enough to wrap her spirit.

There is a tradition of the highly mobile African woman leaving children behind to be raised by a more settled relative. Yet Mama has always dragged me along with her, fighting her way from London to Milan, New York to Geneva, Nairobi to Cape Town, and countless places in between. She seemed to see me for the first time at the age of twelve and wonder why she hadn't raised an African child. Off I went to the central highlands, sent to the same Anglican mission school that she had attended.

The Kenyan boarding school had not been easy to get used to. Mogadishu was even a bigger adjustment. But nothing in my life had prepared me for Baidoa. The city was haunted by skeletal women and children, starving livestock, and a colony of flies. No hope had been restored here. The only ones with guns were tough-looking Somalis. The only foreigners you saw were the journalists with their cameras clicking.

I was suddenly boiling with anger, turning to Johnny. "I thought you were supposed to be feeding these people."

He didn't look so hot then. Confused and shaken, a little ashamed, I think.

"I heard we've had trouble setting up feeding centers in some areas . . . but this." He shook his head. "This is unreal."

To unearth one woman's story in this city of horrors seemed next to impossible. Still, Mama was stubborn. She wouldn't give up.

We had ridden around for hours asking questions before we were finally directed to a teahouse on the outskirts of town. Men sat around laughing, fondling their weapons, and drinking their tea. Some played *shax* and chewed *qaat*, a narcotic weed that stained their teeth mottled hues of black and orange. One well-dressed man didn't carry a gun. He looked to me like a gangster surrounded by bodyguards.

"Where is the girl?" Mama strode bravely into their midst. "The one who gave birth before the cameras. Do any of you know her?"

They ignored my mother, maybe because she was a woman and a Kenyan. Johnny was only the tagalong, a military clerk with a gun strapped to his leg, but he was suddenly promoted to the leader of our operation.

"Mr. American Man," shouted Axmed, our driver. "This chief wants to know what you are giving him for the girl."

They wanted all of Johnny's American guns. He denied having any. They couldn't know about the one strapped to his calf. He offered them food instead. The supplies were all unloaded. It seemed a ridiculous price, all that food in exchange for a story.

We were taken to her. She didn't seem surprised to find four strangers standing at the doorway to her room, in a circular hut with pointed grass roof. A petite young woman reclined on a woven mat, a sleeping baby at her side. My mother was suspicious, looking back and forth between the crumpled photo and the girl before us.

"I wonder if she is even the same one."

I could see the resemblance, although she had obviously lost some weight. The girl's hair was tangled, but thick and full. Her dusty skin was the color of a copper penny, cheekbones high in a drawn face. Her lips were dry and cracked but shapely. Her sunken eyes were dark and thick-lashed.

"Rather lovely, isn't she?" Johnny commented. "She could be modeling on Madison Avenue."

Mama shook her head.

"Pretty, but not tall enough. Combine Cara's body and this girl's face, you would have the next runner-up for Miss Universe."

What was wrong with *my* face? Acne only lasted so long. And why were they speaking as if the poor girl couldn't hear them? Johnny had supplies held back from the gangsters, military rations hidden in the pockets of his flak jacket. Bottled water, half-melted chocolate bars, army trail mix, oral rehydration salts. He knelt on the mat, extending a handful toward her. Mama stopped his hand.

"Only a bit," she warned. "It can be dangerous for a malnourished person to be allowed to gorge."

Mama needn't have worried. The girl took her time unwrapping a Hershey bar with almonds. She took a bite and chewed thoughtfully, nodding in approval. She might have been a taste tester in a candy kitchen instead of a famished refugee. The baby stirred, rooting and chirping like a chick. She tossed a red shawl discreetly over her left shoulder. The child nursed for a moment before drifting back to sleep.

"You speak English?" Mama inquired.

The girl nodded, seeming bored with the attention, languidly brushing away flies. Mama waved us off as she adjusted notebook and pen, recorder and tapes.

We moved beneath the sparse shade of an acacia thorn tree. Axmed reclined and fell asleep. Johnny jerked his head toward the tea-drinking men, laughing in the distance.

"I peep their cards, all right. It's a humbug, a big gang-bang."

I didn't know the meaning of his words, but I was never one to question things. For the first time he was speaking to me like an adult.

"I left Chicago hoping to never see another street gang. And here they are in Africa. Nothing but a bunch of homeboys brawling. Protecting their turf, their imaginary line in the sand."

I tried to think of an adult response.

"It's so sad, isn't it?"

Johnny sighed, shaking his head.

"It's life."

We nibbled our trail mix and nursed our silences. Mama returned, looking tired and defeated.

"She wouldn't talk to me without payment, which I reluctantly gave. Then she revealed little but her name, Raqiya Adan. I am not even sure if that is real."

I had seen Mama at work before. It was hard to imagine that tiny girl resisting her methods of persuasion. Maybe Raqiya's resolve had been fortified by the great American chocolate bar. Miles of bad roads and a ton of food had been wasted on this mission. Walking back to the Land Rover, we passed the men at the tea shop. They gestured with their guns, barking at us in Somali.

"What are they saying?" Johnny asked.

"He say you bought her, American man," Axmed translated. "Take her away, she is yours now."

Johnny's hidden gun was only one to their many. We really had no choice. There were no bags to pack, only a small pile of stiff rags to fold and tuck away—the baby's diapers or menstrual rags, we didn't ask which. Only a faded red shawl to throw over her head and shoulders. Only a short walk from a mud-and-wattle hut. Two steps up to the backseat of a Land Rover.

And that is how she came into our lives. And that is when Mama stepped out of the triangle and Raqiya took her place.

One hundred and one Somali days. She didn't come to us right away. Though claiming not to know a soul, Raqiya had us put her down in the center of Mogadishu. She said she would find and seek help from her clanspeople. Mama shook her head as she watched her trudge off, the baby tied to her back.

"Soon she will become a prostitute," she predicted.

Never one to cry over spilled milk, my mother began documenting the stories of other women refugees crowding the capital city. There were certainly plenty of them. She found them in hospitals, at the camps, and at soup kitchens run by civic-minded Somalis who hadn't fled. Except when Johnny visited, Mama would be off with her notebooks and tape recorders, all day long and deep into the evening. I would be left on my own again.

On one such day the telephone rang, a man's voice twittering animated Italian.

"*Visitatrici, visitatrici,*" he repeated.

"*Visitatrici?*" I rummaged through my memory of half-forgotten words. "A visitor? I wonder who. Never mind. *Mandamele, per favore.* Send him along, please."

"No, no, no. *Visitatrice Somale. Potete venite qua,*" he insisted. "*Venite, venite.* You come, please."

I saw her when I reached the guard post—Raqiya, wearing new clothes, arguing with the Italian sentry. She thumped her chest aggressively, pointing out the position of her heart. He eyed her suspiciously, silently. He had his rifle raised, not actually pointed toward her but not pointed away either. Raqiya grasped her bawling baby under one arm, thrusting him with her hip toward the scowling man.

"You want to shoot us, soldier man?" she taunted. "You want to kill? Here, kill me. Kill my baby."

"Stop!" I shouted. *"Aiutame!"*

"Help me" wasn't really the right thing to say, but the little Italian I knew had deserted me. I reached for the baby, cuddling him against me. Soothed, his crying stopped. I extended my free hand toward Raqiya. But as I pulled her through the gate, the sentry separated us.

"It's all right," I told him, searching for the right words. "She's a friend, *una amica.*"

He patted his body, miming his intention to conduct a body search.

"You will not touch me," Raqiya warned, "or we two will die here today. I am a Muslim woman. I will not be letting a stranger's hands touch my body."

Sighing in impatience, the sentry gestured to a uniformed woman. But as she approached us, speaking brisk Italian neither of us could understand, Raqiya took her child and turned away.

"Tell your mother," she called over her shoulder as she slid behind the guard post gates, "I am ready now to tell my story."

It all began in the courtyard garden, the barely tended, overgrown patch of dust encircled by Papa's villa. An appropriate place for a desert rose to begin to bloom again.

I would hold Mohamed Yare, "little Mohamed," who was usually sleeping. Mama would ask pointed questions, her pencil scratching and tape recorder whirring. If Johnny was there, he would hang around and listen. Sometimes he would supply chocolate bars.

Raqiya fielded questions about who she was, where she had been born, who her people were. How fate had led her to Baidoa, which was not her hometown. Her stories were long, complicated, and colorful. One would often contradict another.

Against her family's wishes she had eloped with a young man, who was soon killed by a ravenous crocodile. The beast, she insisted, had been sent by a Midgaan sorcerer who secretly loved her. She scorned the man, who couldn't bring himself to kill her, but left her alone to wander the wilderness. Another time she was a motherless child, her flight motivated by cruel treatment from her father's new wife.

"It sounds just like Cinderella," I sighed.

My mother suspected it was all a packet of lies. But whenever Raqiya came, she would bring out the tape recorder. We were caught in the gossamer of her storytelling, a web that grew wider each time, one end connected to another. When finished, she folded her hands and waited. Mama would sigh and click off her machine.

You could clearly hear her mumbling as she climbed the stairs into the villa. "Why do I entertain this tissue of lies?" But she always returned with a wad of Somali currency.

"Here." She would press it upon Raqiya. "Something for Mohamed Yare's milk."

I saw nothing wrong with storytelling. Raqiya was our own Sheherazade. The tales she spun over three months and one week were for her own survival, for Mohamed Yare's milk.

Once we sat in the garden, sleepy as bees, waiting for my mother to come. Mama had urged her to supplement feedings with bottles of powdered infant formula from Papa's store of relief supplies. But Raqiya Adan believed that if she could get her son to suckle steadily, a full supply of milk would come in. Raqiya always had Mohamed Yare at her breast, coaxing him to the nipple.

As we waited, she sang a sad Somali lullaby, which she translated into English.

Is it because hunger has stricken you?
Is it because they have gone thirsty in the desert plains?
Is it because my breasts have begun to turn dry?
Is it because your tongue has sucked only a meager drop?

"Isn't he getting any?" I asked.

No answer. Raqiya had sung them both to sleep. Mohamed Yare drooped, his head bent at an unnatural angle. I stood to straighten him. His breathing had stopped.

I shouted for help. Raqiya woke up, confused. She held the baby to her, trying to give him the breast again, patting his cheeks when he wouldn't respond.

Johnny came loping into the garden. He had dropped by to visit Mama that afternoon. As always, they had quickly retired to our shared bedroom, the better for his heart to be broken in privacy. On days he visited, I would later smell his cologne lingering in the bedclothes.

I was surprised to see him in uniform, fully dressed. He dropped to his knees in the dust beside Raqiya, taking the baby gently from her. He held Mohamed Yare's limp body in his arms, covering his nose and breathing into his mouth in quick, short puffs.

Mama stepped into the garden wrapped in a towel, her hair wet, as if she had been showering. She looked annoyed at the interruption.

"What is the problem, girls?"

We rushed him to the hospital, too late. Mohamed Yare was already cold. Raqiya never cried, not even when her son was buried. Not when Johnny took her in his arms and shed enough tears for both of them. He rubbed up and down her back, like that was where she hurt. He sang a little song that sounded faintly Italian. He told me later it was probably Spanish.

Sana, sana
colita de rana
Si no sanas hoy,
sanarás mañana.

Raqiya allowed herself one second of solace, her head slumped against his chest. Then, straightening, she pulled the ubiquitous shawl around her head and shoulders. She turned and trudged away from the grave.

"The first one always dies," she said. "He clears the passage for the others."

Mama stopped seeing Johnny soon after. Maybe because Raqiya needed him more. Mama claimed to be beyond the pettiness of romantic jealousy and possession. She often made this point while helping herself to some other woman's man.

"As an African woman, I do not buy into this Judeo-Christian construct of monogamy. I am not taking her man, only borrowing. Soon he will be returned."

Mama was a feminist, but most of her friends were men. The professional circles in which she moved tended to be male. She claimed more in common with the men than with their spouses. I suppose that is why she sometimes slept with them.

Maybe she hadn't loved Johnny enough, or even at all. She gave him up as easily as a penny that drops to the ground, too much bother to pick it up. But then, Mama's romances never lasted long. She said goodbye and left for Geneva, promising to return and collect me before the new school term began.

With Mama gone, Johnny and Raqiya still visited the garden. He joked about being a polygamous African, coming to visit "my two wives." In bits and pieces we learned the story Raqiya wouldn't share with Mama—that she had indeed been "touched by a stranger's hands." She was nineteen years old now but had only been seventeen when the troops came. From the start, it was a day of ill omen.

"Everyone knows," she explained, "that the last Wednesday of each lunar month is a day of evil."

It was the season of *abaar iyo oodo-lullul* drought, the time of the shaking of the thorn-tree fences. Why were the fences shaking? Was it by force of wind?

"The work of men," Raqiya told us. "Of desperate nomads whose animals have died. They shake the fences of strangers, people who are not their clansmen. They raid the corrals of those who still have livestock left."

But the men who raided the schoolhouse were no camel herders. They might have been bandits, or militia members from a rival clan. They struck down the men who dared to fight back. They beat and robbed the teachers, sacked the building, burned it to the ground. Some girls were raped right on the spot. Others were abducted at gunpoint. Raqiya was one of them. She never saw her family again.

She was taken away to serve the gunmen, cooking and cleaning and sleeping with them. A different day, a different man. She soon became pregnant, her baby born before the eyes of the world. She knew the men were only waiting for her forty-day ritual of isolation to end, when once again she would be forced to serve.

"It is always that the *jeer* farmers, the hard hairs, are attacked. They will raid their crops, kill their livestock, and rape their women. But anyone in an enemy clan, they also can be made to suffer."

Raqiya told her story with dry eyes. Had her tears been burned away by the drought? Was it shame that kept her dry-eyed? Or was she simply storytelling?

"If I will ever marry," she told us once, "it must be far away, where no one knows me. I have known as many men as a Mogadishu prostitute. I was deflowered by a militia man's bayonet."

Johnny jumped up, his head brushing branches of the leafless thorn tree. The chocolate bars in his lap tumbled to the dusty ground. It seemed he might set out running. He looked around quickly, then sat down again. No gunmen in this garden, no *shifta* bandits with bayonets drawn. He began to curse under his breath.

"What kind of animal is that? To rape a schoolgirl with a bayonet!"

Raqiya was impassively philosophic, stooping to scoop up the fallen chocolate.

"Men are known to do such things." She shrugged. "Even a husband on his wedding night might cut you open like a fruit."

She unwrapped a Hershey bar and bit into it with small, white teeth.

"Not every man," Johnny whispered. "Not me. Oh, how I wish I had been your first."

I don't think I was meant to overhear that remark. It just slipped out, like a sudden gasp when you see something lovely that you want. Sometimes they seemed to forget I was there. I felt I was spying on enchanted lovers, watching a fairy tale come to life.

Raqiya shook her head, lips brown with melted chocolate.

"I am glad you were not my first. It is not easy to love the man who opens you."

Raqiya was proud to be an ethnic Somali, a "soft hair." Johnny would criticize her contempt for "hard hairs," the people she called "a clan of slaves." But much can be forgiven of a beautiful woman. He scolded, but still he called her "Miss Somalia."

Johnny brought food and gifts at every visit. Nuts and fruit and flowers. Endless slabs of Hershey, the Great American Chocolate Bar. Raqiya would be singing, plaiting my hair, telling stories first in Somali, then in English translation.

But there were stories they told each other after I was in bed. There were songs. Johnny sang in a voice that was not very accomplished. I could hear it drifting through my bedroom window. Before she left for Europe, I told Mama what I thought—that Johnny had fallen under Raqiya's spell but didn't know quite what to make of her.

"Tsk, daughter. Do not be naive. A man always knows what to do with a woman, especially that man. Johnny is a safari tourist, a black version of the great white hunter. He wants to explore Africa between the legs of her women."

"I don't think he's tried anything with Raqiya."

"He cannot have her now, so soon after giving birth. He is only biding his time."

We'd given each other secret nicknames, only to be uttered in the garden. Raqiya, the beauty queen, was "Miss Somalia." She developed quite a taste for the chocolate. When Johnny arrived she would search his pockets. She wouldn't even greet him until he answered her question.

"Where is my Hershey bar?"

He would throw his arms open to her.

"Here I am, baby."

He became known as "Sergeant Hershey."

One day Raqiya took my head in her small hands, regarding me carefully.

"Cara. It is much like a strong Somali name, Araweilo. Very powerful, very deep."

"Really?" I'd been told long ago that *cara* was Italian for "darling." Maybe my father had had something else in mind. "What does Araweilo mean?"

"It is the name of a Somali queen from long ago, in the days when women were rulers of men."

"You see?" Johnny lounged under the acacia tree, peeling an orange with his fingers. "I always knew you were a queen."

"No," I reminded him. "You said Nubian princess."

"Queen Araweilo"—Raqiya preferred to peel her orange with a knife—"was a strong woman, a gifted poet. But very evil. To make the men her slaves—*shrrrr.*"

She speared her orange with the knife that had peeled it. Johnny was puzzled.

"*Shrrrr* what?"

Raqiya only smiled enigmatically.

"Use your imagination, Sergeant Hershey," I responded. "She's talking about castration."

Johnny covered his crotch with a free hand.

"Ouch. What she want to do that for?"

Raqiya shrugged lazily.

"Who knows? Only Allah."

Being my mother's daughter after all, I had a theory.

"Maybe she was angry about being cut herself. Female circumcision, that's just as bad as male castration."

Raqiya begged to differ.

"No, this is a necessary thing. That *djin* thing growing between your legs, it must be removed or you can never marry."

"If I have to be mutilated," I retorted, "then I won't get married."

Raqiya raised an elegant eyebrow and nodded, as if something she suspected all along had just been confirmed.

We argued occasionally but still enjoyed the fellowship of our triad in the courtyard garden. We could sit under the thorn tree and tell stories, eating fruit and Hershey bars. We could be innocents in Eden, each of us a child again.

Johnny could claim that, like me, he had "a little Latin in the blood." We could play fast music on his boom box, Johnny teaching us the merengue. He could dance with the two of us together, switching off partners in midstep.

Using a Coca-Cola bottle as a makeshift microphone, Sergeant Hershey could sing a silly song about a black pearl. He could promise that Miss Somalia would one day reign supreme. He could turn to me, snatching away the tea tray in my hands.

"Who are you to be serving me? It's time for me to serve my queen."

"Mind that your queen's dagger does not find some meat to slice," Miss Somalia warned.

What would happen when the triangle collapsed? When we all went our separate ways? When I returned to my Kenyan boarding school, nursing my familiar silences? When Johnny went back to America, forgetting about us both?

And what about Raqiya? Would she ever find the family left behind? Were any of them still alive? Would she come to trade her body for food and shelter, as Mama had predicted? In our idyllic intimacy, my romantic childishness, I figured out a plan.

I posed it tentatively, a smile in my voice. If they found it ridiculous, I could say it was a joke.

"Why don't we all stay here? Sergeant Hershey and Miss Somalia, why not marry? Make yourselves another Mohamed Yare and forget about the bad things going on outside. I will be the child's nanny."

Raqiya giggled at the suggestion. I couldn't tell if it was delight or derision.

"How can I marry a man with no clan? Our children would be nobodies."

Johnny did not share her laughter.

"I can never understand this business about the clans. Subclans, sub-subclans, *diya*-paying groups. What does it matter when two people love each other?"

"You do not understand. You are foreigner," she told him gently. "When you have no clan on your father's side, there is no one to lean on."

"What about the mother?" Johnny asked. "I was raised by women. I always had somebody to lean on."

"Mother is family but not clan. Clan can only come from father's blood."

"What about my mother?" I asked.

"Kikuyu from Kenya," she said contemptuously. "Infidel Africans, like *jeer* people in Somalia. Slaves, magicians, sorcerers. But you, Cara, you are lucky to be looking much more like a Somali. Your skin is light, your hair is soft. Your father's blood is strong in you."

"Y'all's royal pedigrees getting too rich for mah blood," Johnny drawled. "I should be the houseboy round here, seeing as how I'm the son of slaves."

"Slave? Oh, no," Raqiya insisted. "You are not *jeer*. You are foreigner."

Raqiya spoke clearly what others must have thought in silence. Neither of us could be counted as true Africans, of which Somalis were at the top of the heap.

"Your mother is unmarried," Raqiya told me. "Because she is uncircumcised. Have you seen the vagina of a she-camel or cow giving birth? The lips of it open, very unclean? Making love to an uncircumcised woman is like making love to an animal."

It did little good to argue, to become shocked, offended, or angry. The things Raqiya believed, she did not consider insults. She didn't even view the tragic events that altered her life as a consequence of outdated beliefs.

"These crimes," she claimed, "are committed by our clan's enemies and the *shifta* bandits who are their camp followers. All jealous men. They are using guns and violence to take what they do not deserve— women, livestock, wealth."

We constructed elaborate fantasies. Johnny would track down Raqiya's family, bring her father the bridewealth of one hundred camels, and ask him for her hand in marriage. If he refused, they would simply elope like the romantic couple in a story Raqiya once told my mother. This time no charmed crocodile would find its target.

"I got my mojo working," Johnny bragged. "Cain't no gator mess with me. I'm a main's main. I'm the son of a main. *M-a-n*. Main."

But really he was a ladies' man. Mine and Raqiya's, but mostly Raqiya's. I merely stood in the shadow of their enchantment. When Raqiya looked at him, her lips curved, her eyes sparkled. She addressed me with mock shyness, pretending that Johnny wasn't sitting there, legs stretched out before him.

"He is not too bad. Resembling of the Amarani tribe of Mogadishu. The ones who came from Persia and Arabia long ago. Some of them have such green eyes."

"See there?" Johnny thumped his chest. "Somali after all. Bring on the camels."

"Amarani are not true Somalis. They have no camels, no clan."

Johnny fell on his knees before her, kissing her chocolate-smeared hands.

"Aw, Miss Somalia. You know you want this Amara-merican man. Come live with me and be my love."

Raqiya giggled, her small hands on his shoulders, gently pushing him away.

"An uncircumcised infidel like you? Never."

Johnny sat back on his heels, squinting up at her.

"Who says I'm not circumcised? Here, I'm fixing to show you."

He jokingly reached for his belt buckle while Raqiya and I shrieked with laughter, fleeing the garden.

Raqiya refused him all the time. She wasn't a virgin anymore, but she was still a Muslim. I don't know how many times Raqiya said no before she changed her mind. Even now I can close my eyes and see it again.

I cannot sleep. Murmured voices haunt my dreams. I leave my bed. I come upon them in the moonlit garden. They are like an enchanted couple from one of Raqiya's stories, more beautiful and noble than or-dinary people.

Her eyes are closed. He is kissing her. Her back against the thorn tree and her robe open. The moon lights her face like a mask etched with bliss. His hands reach into her bodice. His head dipping to taste her breasts before she pushes him away.

I don't think it is true what Mama says, that women who are circum-cised can never enjoy sex. I saw the look on her face, and I don't think she was pretending.

I went to my own room, cooled by the breeze of a ceiling fan. I imagined myself immersed in the gaze of sea-green eyes. His mouth on my neck, his hands on my bosom. A frieze of pleasure carved on my face. Scarcely knowing what I was doing, I found my hands winding into the tangles of my own bedclothes.

The ultimate cruelty of fate was that within weeks of her baby's death, Raqiya's milk came in. So much flowed from her that she was bothered by the fullness. I brought her hot towels and compresses, beg-ging Papa to find a doctor. But when the wizened old Italian physician came to the villa, Raqiya refused to be touched by the hands of strange men. Papa regretted having gone to such trouble.

"From here on, that urchin is on her own."

Behind her doe eyes and soft manners lurked a woman every bit as fierce and passionate as my mother. A well-raised Muslim girl who could not bring herself to marry an infidel eventually found herself lov-ing one. She was not being touched by "a stranger's hands," but having a man of her own choosing.

"It was determined by the order of my birth," Raqiya admitted, fan-ning her sweaty forehead one morning when Johnny was not there. "I am *listan*, which means 'ready to be milked.' *Listan* people like love too much."

It became part of her storytelling. How he would kiss her and where. The zigzag marks on his thighs that he called "tribal scars." The heft and weight of his organ. How he had lied about being circumcised, which meant that he could not enter, only "paint" her between the thighs. Her embarrassment when her milk began to spurt. How he had begged a taste of it.

"Did you let him?"

Raqiya was a contradiction of innocence and experience, daring and shame. She pressed both hands to her breasts in horror.

"To give a man milk for a dead baby? No, Cara. This would not be right."

But she began to bring him other kinds of milk to quench his thirst. Cow's milk. Camel's milk. Goat's milk. Sheep's milk. Papa's cook went missing; he left one day and did not return the next. Raqiya took his place in the kitchen. She seemed happy and content, although she said she was used to cooking outside. She would take her fruit and vegetables, her seasonings and meat, and prepare them in the garden.

Mama didn't return in time. I would have to fly to Nairobi on my own. The day before I left Mogadishu, Johnny came to visit. I was alone in the garden; Raqiya was in the kitchen. He had brought along a goodbye present, a book of traditional Somali verse. The book fell open on "A Woman's Love Song." I read from it aloud.

> *You are poured from Nairobi gold,*
> *The first light of dawn, the blazing sun.*
> *Will I ever meet a man like you,*
> *You whom I have seen just once?*

"Cara mia," he teased. "Queen Caraweilo. I didn't know you cared."

I flushed with embarrassment but remembered to thank him, minding my manners. I found myself nervous alone with Johnny. There were usually three of us there.

"Would you like some tea?" I offered the standard Somali refreshment.

"With milk and sugar, please."

I walked toward the kitchen, calling down the corridor ahead of myself.

"Johnny's here."

"I know," Raqiya answered. "I have heard your voices, no need to be shouting."

Sometimes I think I imagined this. Maybe it was a trick of sun and shadow—Raqiya leaning over the table, her bodice open, her lovely breasts exposed, a contented smile upon her face, a ripe breast cupped in one hand as she pressed down with the other, sending a fine spray of milk into his steaming teacup.

Raqiya was unbearably complicated, like an African swan. Beneath the surface of water, webbed feet paddled furiously. Beneath the elegance of her impassive beauty, untold stories stirred.

Mombasa, 1998. I never imagined I was in love with Johnny. I loved him with Raqiya, the fantasy I vicariously shared. I was a spy in the garden of their enchantment. My own blossoming, voyeuristic sexuality. I never thought I wanted the man she had. I wanted her qualities, her elegant beauty, her *listan* nature.

I have dreams even to this day. I look in the mirror and my face is gone, her features superimposed upon it. In my dreams I am becoming Raqiya.

I was not a woman yet, but I was no longer a child. I was nineteen years old, the same age Raqiya was that summer in Mogadishu.

The holiday that followed my first year in college. For the first time in five years, I was summering in East Africa. I was dragged to Nairobi by my mother against my will. We left behind a breezy Mombasa beach house for a hotel room in the noisy, crowded capital. Mama was "networking," a concept I have never understood.

But the American embassy was beautiful that evening, hidden away behind walls in a quiet downtown neighborhood. The gleaming white buildings were surrounded by flower gardens and flagstone paths and flowing fountains. I rested on a stone bench beneath the shifting shadows of an acacia tree, reminded of another garden.

When someone sat beside me, I was annoyed.

"Do you mind?" I turned to the unwelcome visitor. "I came out here to be alone."

To my surprise he folded me in his arms. I could barely make out his face in the shadows. A tall brown American in military dress.

"*Cara mia.*" He grinned, pinching my cheeks like a little child. "Queen Caraweilo, my Nubian princess. Look at you, all grown up."

It was fitting to meet him again in a garden. We leaned toward each other and embraced, incomplete without our third angle.

"Where is Raqiya?" The question emerged as I smoothed my clothes and caught my breath. The reunion did not seem real without her.

He sighed, shaking his head. Sadness flickered in his eyes, which now seemed gray in the filtered darkness. He stared down at his bitten nails.

"Do you know I got circumcised for her? At the ripe age of thirty-plus, I put myself through all that pain. I was ready to marry her, to convert to Islam, to even consider living in her country, but she disappeared. Things had gotten very bad in Somalia."

I had read the news stories of good intentions gone wrong. A mission to feed people turning into open warfare. The unbelievable charges. Belgian troops roasting a child over an open fire. Canada's elite airborne regiment disbanding after members were found guilty of murder and torture. An American marine shooting a Somali street kid who had stolen his sunglasses. A meeting of alleged warlords, some of them elders and holy men, bombed in the quest to "get Aideed."

There were atrocities stacked on both sides. Weapons fired from crowds of civilians at a Mogadishu market. An Italian female news reporter gunned down in cold blood. An American soldier captured and killed, his body dragged through the streets.

Johnny shook his head.

"It was much worse than you can imagine. After your father went back to Italy, I put Raqiya up in a little place down the coast in Merka, away from all the violence in the capital. I thought she would be safe. I got there one day and the house had been ransacked. The village was deserted and Raqiya was gone. Soon afterward our unit pulled out. I was stationed in the Philippines for a minute, then managed to get sent out here to Nairobi. I'm now at the tail end of a two-year detail. I've returned to Somalia several times but have never found a trace of Raqiya."

I moved into his arms again, holding him in a gesture of comfort. He wrapped his arms around me, hugging me in commiseration. Between us, the memory of Raqiya lingered, fragrant as a desert rose. The third point missing from the triangle.

But another woman stepped in. Mama again, now visiting professor at a Boston college, having decided in middle age to experiment from the cover of the closet. Perhaps it is connected with her research. She is in Kenya documenting the lesbian experience, the missing chapter of African sexuality. With a generous grant from an American women's-studies operation, the two of us had been living well in Mombasa.

Her voice was accusing. Others in the garden turned to watch. She advanced upon us, silken garments swishing angrily.

"Daughter, daughter! Who is that man you're hugging there?"

I rose, pulling Johnny into the spotlight of an overhead lantern.

"Look, Mama. See who's here."

I presented him to her like a surprise package. She frowned, regarding him suspiciously. Was all her life a practice up to this point? First giving up on Kikuyu men, then Kenyans? Africans, black men, and perhaps one day men altogether?

She nodded, extending her hand for Johnny to shake. He kissed it instead.

"Malaika Mugo, my African angel. What a sight for sore eyes."

Mama snatched her hand away, shaking it as if his lips burned.

"Don't try it," she warned. "I am somewhere else now, somewhere you are not welcome."

Johnny frowned, puzzled. Maybe he thought Mama had moved up

the social ladder, was no longer interested in "loving below her means."

Mama steered me away. I waved to Johnny, a tall figure standing alone in the garden.

"Sorry about Raqiya," I called. "You would have made beautiful children."

Mama frowned at me in the taxi to our hotel.

"So, daughter, tell me this. Have you had your first sex?"

I laughed at the edge of panic in her voice. Mama's latter-day traditionalism had surfaced. The woman of many lovers, the free African spirit, the one who now secretly loved women, was urging me not to throw out the baby with the bathwater, but to center myself in my culture.

"Do as I say," I asked archly, "not as I do?"

"I need no cultural grounding," Mama insisted. "I grew up immersed in it."

As we shared a silent taxi ride, I thought back to my last year in Africa, the girls' boarding school in the foothills of Mount Kenya, overlooking the great Rift Valley.

When the housemistress had retired, we'd burn flashlights late into the night. Those girls with boyfriends would talk about their sexual experiments. Those who knew of abortionists would counsel the ones who thought they were pregnant. Those whose families were planning arranged marriages would plot their escape routes.

One night conversation swung to female circumcision. I would never have guessed it in modern Kenya, where, thanks to the work of warriors like Mama, the procedure was outlawed before they were born. It never occurred to me that among families of power and privilege, their daughters would have such stories to tell.

At least one girl had been infibulated the traditional way, being excised, sliced, and scored with a ceremonial knife, then sutured with acacia thorns. Some had had sunna clitoredectomies done in the hospital. A Baganda girl felt very superior because "my tribe does not cut." She did admit having been taught genital manipulation from an early age, protruding labia being prized among her people. A young Masai on scholarship, the first girl in her village to be sent to secondary school, explained a version I had never heard of: The clitoris was not excised but involuted, a practice said to intensify a woman's pleasure.

A student from South Yemen thought anything to inflame the senses of unmarried girls exceedingly unwise. A female cousin who allowed herself to be deflowered had brought such shame upon her family, her father had no choice but to kill her with his own hands. Those of us who had come through life unscathed had never seen circumcised genitals. An ethnic Somali from Kenya's Northern Frontier District lifted her nightgown and showed hers.

A lifelong deluge of such stories had the same effect upon me that mutilation had upon others. I had reached nineteen, wary about sex at worst, ambivalent at best. Although I fantasized and had been known to spy, I could not bring myself to experience the actual act.

"Not yet, Mama," I admitted, reaching out to squeeze her hand. "Still a virgin."

My mother sighed gratefully, wrapping her arm around my neck.

"Thank God for that. Do not be in a rush, daughter. You have plenty of time."

Little did she know, it was not for lack of trying. I had been so far as naked with a man but couldn't follow through. It was a secret source of shame. I was afraid of sex.

Over the next days Mama became obsessed with Hot Johnny.

"He is the kind," she warned, "you must give a wide berth. To men like this, Africa is just a sexual safari. To him, a woman is only about her body."

They say if you talk about it long enough, you may summon up the thing you fear. I don't know how he found me. Johnny turned up at our inn at Tagli Beach, just at the time I was growing bored with the lazy pace of my summer holiday. Nearing the end of a two-year tour of duty, he invited me to "do Mombasa," the island whose Afro-Asian admixture, coastal culture, and Islamic religion reminded me of Mogadishu.

And Mombasa we did. With Mama busy in her research, I could

easily slip away unnoticed. Johnny would meet me down the road in a rented car, a picnic basket packed. Together we explored the city market whose entrance was framed in elephant tusks, distant beaches, picturesque fishing villages. We discovered Mombasa at each other's side.

Maybe it was a suggestion made from Mama's paranoia, maybe it was a six-years-delayed reaction, but deep within me something began to stir. I wanted to explore things other than beaches and boat rides. I wanted to do more than Mombasa. I wanted to share my body, my lips and shoulders, my breasts and buttocks. Johnny at first refused.

"You don't want me, princess. I done got old and gray. I could be your father."

"I know what I want," I insisted. "And it is not my father."

Johnny would only laugh in response. But at some point he began to weaken, touching me back when I touched him, giving me his tongue when I kissed him. I wanted him to "paint me" as he had done Raqiya, and finally I told him so.

"*Cara mia.*" He caressed my chin, licked my collarbone. "Queen Caraweilo. Every woman has her own pleasure map. We're going to find your special landmarks."

"Then what are we waiting for?" I declared. "I'm ready."

"No, you're not."

I was in a hurry for his love. He urged me to be leisurely, as if we had all the time in the world to explore this terrain. We wandered the landscape of each other's bodies, touching pleasure points with hands and mouth. Caressed the ridges of tribal scars. Explored caverns and mountain peaks. Fulfillment always lingered just a few strokes away. Just a plunge in the warmth of a waterfall. But even when I insisted, "I know I'm ready," he always seemed to know.

"No, you're not."

One early evening, while rolling in bed completely naked, he parted my legs and positioned himself between them.

"I think you're ready now."

I felt my body grow cold, my lubrication drying. A throbbing inside me died. I rolled from underneath him.

"No, I'm not."

He sat up, taking my hand in his.

"I figured you were still a virgin. But is there something else wrong?"

I nodded. I don't know why I felt like crying. I always froze at the moment of truth. A script forever unfolding in my head, that sex could be dangerous, even deadly. *It is hard to love a man who opens you.*

"Cara mia." He suddenly seized me by the shoulders. He stared intently, as if seeing me for the very first time. *In my dreams I am becoming Raqiya.* "My sweet little Nubian princess. Marry me. I promise to always protect you. I swear that I'll be gentle, give you as much time as you need."

I remembered a wish once uttered in a garden: *Oh, how I wish I had been your first.*

"You want to marry me?" I was incredulous. "Knowing that I might be frigid?"

"You aren't frigid." He gave me an almost brotherly hug. "Just a little chilly. We've got a lifetime to warm you up."

Something went weak inside. I found myself swept up in the moment.

"Oh, Johnny. I think I love you. Yes, I will marry you. Let's do it soon, before Mama gets wind of this."

It was just as well I had chickened out on the actual act. Maybe she had heard me call her name. Mama burst in upon us with the fury of an avenging angel. She loomed in the doorway, silhouetted in the light of the setting sun. I don't know how long she had been there listening.

"You are doing this to my child, soldier boy? To my baby daughter?"

"Your baby daughter is an adult now." He sat unselfconsciously naked as I scurried for my clothing. "Old enough to experience her own sexuality."

"Old enough?" my mother squawked. "To sleep with her mother's one-time lover, a man twice her age? Get out of here, you child molester. Now!"

With Johnny gone, Mama ranted and raged.

"I beg you, daughter. Leave this man! I have had him before, I know this man is beneath you. If you love below your means, you will always be unhappy."

"Mama." I was impatient. "You threw the man away. Six years later we fell in love. How can you be so closed-minded about matters of the heart? You, of all people."

"Matters of the heart? Matters of the groin! Now I understand why Africans want to circumcise. They are just trying to protect their daughters."

Mama's threats, her dire predictions, her melodramatic scenes did not stop us. They only planed the triangle's edges to a point, pulling us closer together. We would be the romantic couple in Raqiya's story. We would elope, saving the ultimate pleasure for the honeymoon.

I waited on the morning Johnny left for Nairobi, headed to the U.S. embassy for a marriage license. I didn't mind a simple local ceremony, but he was insistent on this point. A military buddy trying to bring his war bride home had encountered a frustrating delay. The validity of his overseas marriage had even been questioned. Johnny wanted us to be married according to American law.

So very much like this night in New York. A radio was playing in a beachfront inn. I was rifling through clothing, preparing to pack, when a program of Swahili songs was interrupted. There was late-breaking news of the embassy bombing, a preliminary tally of the dead and wounded. Among them was an unnamed air force sergeant.

I hadn't even the presence of mind to pick up my wallet, a bag, my key. I flew from the beach house, as if to run the three hundred miles from Mombasa to Nairobi. I met my mother, driving up the road in her rental car. Her eyes were weary and her lips set.

"Nairobi," I panted, climbing in beside her. "We must go to Nairobi now."

She reached to hold me with her strong arms, with the power of her love.

"I have already heard the news, daughter. It's too late now. He's already gone."

The man who was vibrant in my arms the day before? Obliterated from the map of memory? How could it be?

"You don't understand, Mama. He can't be dead. We never made love. We were saving it for our wedding night."

Mama sighed, driving on toward the beach house.

"Go away, daughter. Pack your things and leave today. It is best to make a clean break in such matters. This man is lost to you now."

That same afternoon I flew to Europe. That same summer my father introduced me to a photographer who took my picture in a walled garden. Years later, I still have the photos that would redirect the path of my life. The camera transforms me. In my drawn face, in my shadowed eyes, I glimpse the same elusive fire that was Raqiya's.

Mama would live to be sorry she sent me away so suddenly. She thoroughly disapproved of my decision to leave the university after one year of study to try my hand at modeling. Even when my career has taken off and my face is on the cover of every European fashion magazine, she rarely speaks to me except inside my head.

A failed attempt at acting took me back to Mombasa later. It is not a total lie my fiancé told the press later, that he found his bush flower in an African village, a water jug balanced upon her head. The African village was a movie set; the tropical print, a costume; the water jug, a prop attached to my headdress to prevent it from toppling.

Despite being a white man, Hector Gutzman is a refugee like me. Another displaced, identityless person without a home or a mother tongue. Like him, I'm a rootless soul, a nomad. Flitting here and there, fitting in nowhere. Mixed bits of language in my mouth: English, Italian, Somali, Swahili, none of them spoken well. Bits of unrecognized memory floating in his blood: London, Argentina, Auschwitz.

Frankenstein's monster and his makeshift bride, made from scavenged bits of body parts. He has been described as a cultural bandit, looting the musical traditions of native peoples. The critics do not understand that he is a nomad, a contradiction of cultures. A blond Jew with a British accent, born in South America, raised in Europe, living in America. Like me, he is an empty vessel dipped into the world's wells.

The radio promo is repeated, a shorter one without his prerecorded voice.

Why did my mother bury Johnny alive? To save my heart, or to control my life? Was it an honest mistake or a sinister mission that sent me flying away from his arms?

I realize I am still waiting to feel him inside me, to be enfolded in the promise of his protection. I slip naked between the sheets, my hands tracing the road map of my own body. It was too late for one thing, though.

Oh, how I wish I had been your first.

That radio program won't air until tomorrow night, when I will be married to another man. This doesn't have to be. I know certain people in New York City. Even at this hour I could make phone calls and inquiries. Johnny wouldn't be that hard to find. I could leave this hotel room right now. I could pack in a flash and be at his side before the sun rose.

I hear the metallic click of my lover's keycard in the door. I close my eyes and feign sleep. Smudges beneath my eyes will soon fade away. I always know where to find him.

In a Mogadishu garden, he lounges beneath the leafless shade of an acacia thorn tree. A woman in his arms surrenders to his touch.

In my sleep I am becoming Raqiya. In my dreams I am loving Hot Johnny.

Malaika

He needed Africa to feed him too

In my student days, back in the time of de jure apartheid, I went to one chi-chi London function. All champagne and hors d'oeuvres, black tie and ball gowns. The guests were mostly white, a token blackie on a free ticket scattered amongst them. The entertainment for the evening was all African, though.

This had been an ANC benefit, I believe. Yes, I'm almost sure of it. I seem to recall Zulu warriors in sham leopard-skin loincloths waving their *pangas*. They dance the *tsoi-tsoi* with scantily clad maidens, their normally bare breasts sealed in white brassieres.

I can remember one thing clearly. The British hostess blushes in embarrassment when the guest of honor rises to deliver his address. The South African freedom fighter in exile has been drinking heavily all evening. He raises his glass in an impromptu toast to oral sex.

"To the European man's *rrrr*ubbish," he proclaims, richly rolling his *r*'s. "Because he does not know how to fock."

I am inclined to agree with my colleague, I am afraid. I have come to see that the more sexualized the West becomes, the less love is actually made. Intercourse might one day be a lost art, like letter writing. Why, the former leader of the free world said himself that he was only fooling around. Any African knows that bit of business wasn't really sex.

Why bother getting hot for nothing? I have never been much for fussy lovemaking. I have never liked a man toying too much with my body. Fondling this, licking that. A sandpaper friction that leaves my senses raw. Hot Johnny Wright was my last straw. After him I felt as touched-out as a mother with nursing twins, as feeble as a she-camel with a broken back. From then I learned to tell my lovers exactly what I wanted: *Right this way, please. Mind the gap. No ducking in the attic window nor sliding in the back entrance. Enter only through the main door.*"

An excessive amount of squeezing, pinching, poking, prodding is an unnecessary distraction. A watched pot never boils, nor does one that is incessantly stirred. What I like best is having it quick, deep, and hard.

Are you surprised to find an African woman so outspoken? Especially one who is Kikuyu, among the most conservative of Kenyans. Chalk it up to being a rebel. I am what I am, and I know what I want. An orgasm without penetration is simply not satisfying to me. It can even be uncomfortable when my empty walls clench against themselves, looking for something substantial to cling to.

My current lover had to be made to understand this. All this slurping and sucking the lesbians like is not enough. I need to have something deep inside. She makes whatever modifications she has to and does what she can to please me.

She has a kind of innocence, however butch she believes herself to be. Very earnest, very eager, very white. Blond and pink-cheeked, senior faculty at the college where I am teaching now. We actually butted heads in the beginning, that old race bugaboo flaring between us. Until I found we had a common fetish, a joint object of our desire. Until she tumbled for me, head over heels. She tries her best. If I love her at all, it is not for the sex.

She wants to be the man in the relationship. With me she is learning to know her softness.

"Oh, Malaika," she once murmured at the height of passion. "Love me, Mama Africa."

I am ashamed to say that I slapped her face.

"Never," I barked, twisting myself away from her. "Never do I want to hear you call me that again. You are not loving your mother here."

She burst into tears, the print of my hand red against her pink cheek.

"What did I do?" she whimpered, trying to crawl into my arms again, attempting to maneuver the artificial organ back inside me. "What did I say wrong?"

I did not answer her, but freed myself from the tangle of bedsheets. I did not listen to her weeping, did not respond to her pleas for me to come back to bed. And this one believes herself to be a butch. Hah! I can teach her what it is to be a man. Watch me.

Soon I was fully dressed and out the door, looking for the one with just the right instrument to scratch my itch. It did not take long to find him. He was not the one I really wanted, but he would do in a pinch.

"Stupid Stuart," I called him, right to his own face. Dull as a brick and thick as a board. Thickness measured in more ways than one, thankfully. I am openly living the truth most African women believe: Women are good for relationships, men are only for the sex.

Surely the elders conceived this terrible practice as a precautionary measure. This must be why 65 percent of all African women are circumcised. If not, we would all behave as polygamous males. Variety is a sensual delight that African men would like to save for themselves.

Anyone who loves me must take me as I am. So I did not apologize when I returned to my lover, still waiting in the sheets. I did not begrudge her Stuart's leavings. I did not object when she kissed and nuzzled a bit too long for my liking. I did not complain when the minutes ticked by before she was ready to strap her artificial manhood back on and mount me again. Now that I was satisfied, I was prepared to compromise.

This is not because I am a cruel woman. It is because I know the depths of my own desire. I have discovered that I can never be satisfied with just one person or only one gender.

Cara is the only one I will allow to call me Mama. Now that we are both women, I have even encouraged her to address me as Malaika. If you allow them to make a mother of you, you will soon be made a beast of burden. The proverb has reason, after all. I have seen camels splayed in the sand, collapsed to their knees from that last straw heaped on their back.

When they want you to be mother, it is because they have made some other woman queen. How do I know it to be true? That word was Hot Johnny's praise song for me, back when I thought I could mother a continent. Before he learned that a man is not meant to love his own mother.

"Mother Africa," he would moan into the valley between my breasts, licking the moisture collected there.

To think that I was swayed by his flattery! Back then I was more charitable. I would patiently allow him to nuzzle to his heart's content. I knew he eventually would get around to giving me what I needed. I waited for the moment when he would call, "Malaika Mugo, my African angel! Show me the oasis deep inside you."

And I would respond, "Send your snake to the cavern, let him come inside and quench the fire."

Oh, how he would plunge, deep as the Rift Valley. And how I would rise, high as the snowcaps at Kilimanjaro. Hot Johnny made me wait for my satisfaction, but it was worth the delayed gratification. My inflamed senses would be soothed, my ruffled feathers smoothed in a gush of warm water.

Despite the things they have said about me, I am a lover, not a fighter. Kikuyus are farmers and cattle keepers, not warriors. If I have had to fight since early adolescence, it was always for a reason.

I have always feared the sight of blood. I could never bear to watch the cattle being slaughtered, although I had no trouble later eating the meat. I knew one day I would have to see my own blood spilled, to spread my legs before the circumciser's knife. It was an inevitable reality I could not bring myself to face until that time drew near.

This was my culture, after all. Everyone knew and understood. If she wanted to become a wife and mother, a Kikuyu woman must be circumcised.

I had been an obedient daughter up until then. But the last straw is the last straw. I was being measured for new clothes when I heard that the women were planning a circumcision ceremony for all the nubile village girls. I made the first adult decision of my life. With a few shillings in my pocket, I fled. Somehow I made my way to Nairobi. I had a paternal cousin there, whom I had grown up calling Auntie. Everyone at home knew Makindu as a prostitute. When you resist mutilation and arranged marriage, you are lucky if that is all they say of you.

Even when they found me there and brought me home, I refused to submit. I fought and cursed, I faked suicide, I threatened to run again. The ceremonies would not be delayed by the antics of one recalcitrant rebel. The ritual knife was wielded, the blood of my agemates flowed, the dances were danced, new clothes were worn, praise songs were sung. The disgruntled circumciser wrapped her bundle and left; she could not be persuaded to tarry.

But my rebellion had a price tag. Like Auntie Makindu, I had earned a new title. Village children would follow me, pelting me with stones and chants. There is a whole repertoire of songs insulting the genitals of uncircumcised women. Unable to bear the humiliation, my parents sent me away to a mission boarding school.

So I learned to be a warrior. That early act of defiance not only preserved my body but ensured my education. When I return to my village now, I find that yet another of those stone-throwers has resisted the circumciser's knife.

I would not undo my decision for all the tea in Kenya. Yet perhaps having the clitoris excised at adolescence would not have been such a hardship after all. I have always been suspicious of women who claim that sex is all clitoral. I have never had much enjoyment from that knob of flesh. Too much attention can even be an irritant. All my pleasure comes from deep within me, the hidden wellspring some Africans have called "bearded meat." That is where I want to be touched.

Literary scholars are so fetishistic in their academic jargon. They have to create their own language no one else can understand. There is a term I've always hated but have recently come to appreciate: "phallic woman," an oxymoron. A female who is the source of her own agency, the master of her fate, who declines to be a follower of fools. My lover Lola calls me this, her voice hushed in admiration. If I am a phallic woman, what then is the corollary?

Maybe that is Hot Johnny, with his soft lips and hungry mouth. The one whom I allowed myself to love below my means. Though not the uneducated dolt my husband was, he was never my intellectual equal.

I never intended being with that type again. I had had my fill of pretty boys, the kind who believes that he honors you with his attentions. What did I ever see in Carlo Bondi? My only excuse is that I was young.

We would normally have never crossed each other's paths. The two of us lived in separate worlds. I was at Cambridge by then, stretching out a minuscule stipend on a trip to Milan. I had come for research on my doctoral dissertation, to document the stories of Dominican sex workers.

Imagine their plight. You are a good-looking, underpaid, uneducated young woman on your half island in the Caribbean, toiling in the countryside *campos*, the *barrios* of Santo Domingo. Some hustler comes along with the promise of money, international travel, a legitimate career.

"As pretty as you are, mamí? You could be a dancer, a model, a movie star. Or maybe a nanny or a domestic worker. Over in Europe they pay you good."

It was a thriving trade, this business of luring women into sexual servitude. They called it white slavery, but most of the women weren't white at all. Their dark skin and exotic look had become quite popular in Western Europe. When a Dominican-Italian captured the Miss Italy crown years later, people were up in arms because she didn't represent "the ideal of Italian beauty." I believe they had come to associate Dominican women with prostitution and couldn't accept one as their beauty queen.

I felt very important indeed, an African graduate student with her own bodyguard. A handsome black *carabinieri* officer was given over to security detail. Everyone knows that the military police in Italy are none too bright. Carlo tried to convince me that white slavery did not exist, even though he was assigned to protect me from the mafiosi who ran it. *And see, African* signorina, *we are not racists. We do have blacks in fairly high places.*

It was supposed to be a fling. A long-distance relationship somehow ensued, flitting back and forth between Milan and Cambridge. It was a two-year honeymoon. We had just enough time to enjoy each other's bodies before one of us would be flying off again. If we hadn't married, perhaps we might still be together. It was only because I had foolishly gotten pregnant and Carlo begged me not to abort the baby.

The honeymoon ended on our wedding day. What had I been thinking? I was seeing Carlo Bondi for the first time, and my eyes were wide open. I had the worst of the African and European in one man. I got out of that one as quickly as I could. The only worthwhile thing that marriage produced was my daughter.

I vowed to avoid beautiful men afterward, then broke my rule with Johnny Wright. He was certainly as beautiful as any woman. Almost too beautiful, in fact. His only redeeming grace was that he often seemed not to know it.

Not vain, but he was certainly arrogant. Hot Johnny came to Africa clothed in the cockiness of his military uniform, the missionary zeal of his Yankee savior complex. He was going to save a continent, beginning with Somalia. He was going to feed Africa's starving people, beginning with Raqiya. But he needed Africa to feed him too.

He never understood why Africa did not come flocking to him, the prodigal son in Uncle Sam's clothing. He could not believe he wasn't greeted with open arms. He turned instead to open legs, and there he found at least three willing victims. At least.

I was foolish then. I wanted to help him discover his lost self, reclaim his African soul. I allowed him to think of me as Mother Africa. I was as giving, as bountiful as the fertile earth. I let him dig for diamonds between my thighs, bathe in the oasis between my breasts, explore the gold mine between my ears.

He called Africa his spiritual homeland, though he actually appeared no more than 40 percent Negroid. I had to keep reminding myself of a thing my father always said: *There are no bad questions, Malaika, only unwise answers.*

I was patient with him, even when he posed the most ridiculous queries.

"If people are starving, then why don't they stop having so many babies?"

"What are the Somalis fighting about, anyway?"

"Why won't the government buy food, not guns?"

"Why do people seem to hate us when we're only trying to feed them?"

Cheep, cheep, cheep. This is what they mean when they want to call you Mama. To predigest their food for them, feeding it to them like a baby bird. To teach an instant lesson, ten-thousand years of history in thirty words or less.

This is what I try to explain to the white South Africans who evoke their four-hundred-year sojourn, to my own alienated daughter when she displays her body before the world like any *National Geographic* native.

Africa is not just a rite of ancestry, a ritual of possession. You cannot take the relationship for granted, the way you would a mother. It is a commitment to be made with the earnestness of wedding vows. It is an account that has fallen deeply into the red. Do not look to her to take on your debts. Don't just stand there asking questions. Do something to help her, soldier boy.

How could I know he would be so daft? How could I guess he'd become so infatuated with one silly girl he would risk his own life for her, or one day forsake me for my own offspring? I would never have given that soldier boy a second glance but for the fact that I caught him staring at her one night. It was not jealousy, if you must know. It was a deliberate sacrifice, a failed effort to protect my daughter. He watched her at a party as she pranced about innocently with her graceless father.

Cara learned to dance from African-American schoolmates that year we lived in upstate New York. Those children gyrated a bit too wildly for my tastes, tossing their buttocks about in wild abandon. Any Kenyan would look and know that there goes a prostitute. These girls were my daughter's teachers. But my scolding did no good. Cara would simply turn the music down low, close her bedroom door, and practice the booty dance in private.

Even with her body gawky and ungainly, her face pimply and her mouth full of braces, her buttocks swaying obscenely, Cara Bondi had a certain natural grace—a grace that is now unfortunately wasted, strutted like a peacock's tail for the photographer's cameras, up and down the fashion runways. The peacock is certainly the saddest of birds, with only a train of gaudy feathers and a strangled shriek to speak for itself.

I have made something of a study of the way men watch women's bodies. I will soon be assembling my data and compiling my findings. Perhaps I will publish a paper in *Psycho-Anthropology Quarterly*. I will entitle it "The Rape of the Look."

A wealth of information is apparent in a single glance, an instant of body language. The social dynamic of men gathered together in groups is different than that of a man alone. Yes, there are the anomalies, the ritualized wilding and gang rape. Group behavior is more commonly just window dressing, the wolf whistle and catcalls part of the male bonding ritual.

The individual male is quite another animal. He is furtive, sneaky, predatory. When he thinks no one is looking, he will caress his own genitals while watching the body of an attractive woman. Why do you think pornography is such a thriving business?

Once, while standing on queue for theater tickets at an off-price booth in Piccadilly Circus, I had the uncomfortable sensation of something butting against my posterior part. When I turned back, a man stood there in all innocence, reading his London *Times*. I felt the sensation once again. Whipping about, I caught a young man with dreadlocks bumping his crotch against my behind.

"Sorry, mum," he apologized. "Me cahn't help meself, you know now. Me like de bum too bad."

Such a pathetic creature. I barely had the heart to slap his face and box his ears.

There are also messages to be read in visual avoidance. A man deliberately glancing away rather than meeting the enticement of a certain woman's body immediately suggests a family relation, a symbolic plucking out of the offending eye. Undoubtedly the enticing body belongs to a daughter, a sister, a mother.

I happen to know that my ass is one of my best features. I have been told so enough times to believe it is true. I bear the phenotypic Bantu buttocks, proudly jutting and fully rounded. Once in a supermarket I noticed a man watching me intently from behind as his wife did the family shopping. When she caught him at it and complained, he gave such a tormented sigh.

"Damn!" he cursed, a child who has its favorite television program switched off. "I was only looking."

Men like to watch. I know that as well as anyone. Why should Hot Johnny Wright be any exception?

He watched my daughter with a dash of indulgence, granted. A twinkle in his eye that suggested he saw a child role-playing a woman's sexuality. But there was also a healthy dose of appreciation. His eyes roamed her figure boldly, admiringly. The applause that followed was not for the dancing couple, but for Cara alone.

"What a beautiful girl, graceful as a Nubian princess," he called out to her father, sweating with exertion. Poor Carlo could barely match his daughter's pace. "She'll be a heartbreaker one of these days."

I sidled over to where he stood leaning against the wall, drink in hand. I swayed my body hypnotically, even though the music had ended. I would tease him a bit, teach him the lure of subtle movements. I swung my hips ever so slightly, turned to allow him a look at my undulating ass. I removed the *kikoi* draped about my buttocks, wrapped it tightly around his neck, and pulled his face down to meet mine.

"Yes, we are a family of femmes fatales." I smiled up at him, ignoring Carlo's studied scowl. "Prepare, soldier boy, for your own heart to be broken."

I thought I might enjoy his body for a bit. I was ready to let him between my legs, with no intention of opening my heart. I was set to scorn his ignorance, not entertain his intellect.

I cannot tell you why I let him lavish me with sloppy affection when I never liked being touched in any way but deep, hard thrusts. Why I let him inflame my senses to the burning point before he produced water to extinguish them. Why I let my body become a game park for his safari explorations, my wit a watering hole for him to splash and frolic in.

How was I paid for my indulgence? Hot Johnny had the chance to be with a woman, and in the end he chose a child.

He used many terms of endearment, ecstasies uttered at the peak of rapture.

"Malaika Mugo, my African angel."

"Mother Africa."

"Show me the oasis deep inside you."

As though I were a natural monument, Mount Kenya or the river Nile. I was an African fetish, a cultural artifact. I was never a real woman to Hot Johnny Wright. He never once called me Miss Kenya. He never whispered to me, "What a beautiful woman, graceful as the queen of Sheba."

What happened to the warrior woman, the lioness? How had she become so weak and besotted? With all my education and intelligence, I allowed myself to become a souvenir. I was the local color, the object of an original case of jungle fever.

When his attention drifted to that insignificant twit, a girl with neither education nor ambition, I realized it was a matter of time before he would leave me. I have never allowed myself to be discarded. As always, I was the one who did the leaving. I pretended to toss him away with careless ease. I have no doubt that he floated straight into her arms.

I will say it right here for the whole world to witness. If I am lying, may God strike me blind. May the girl herself appear and sue me for slander. Johnny made her out to be some kind of paragon of African grace. But Raqiya Adan, if indeed that is her name, was nothing but a common con artist.

I found this girl in a backwater village, filthy as a beggar and loaded with lice. I brought her to the capital, gave her food and solace, obtained infant formula for her ailing child. I reached into my pocket for a coffin and cemetery plot when she spurned my wisdom and the baby died of malnutrition.

I paid that girl for her story. One of the first things you learn in the study of cultural anthropology is that a paid subject is a tainted subject. Still she insisted, and I gave in. I paid her. Raqiya Adan was no better than a prostitute, and I do not just refer to the service she claims she was forced into. Even that business, who can tell? So much of what that girl sold to me was a tissue of lies.

Her family, she claimed, had died in a raid upon their village in the lower Shabelle Valley. But suddenly they were restored to life, if not full health, when she realized Johnny could divert relief supplies their way. Did those supplies go to feed the starving? No, indeed. They were traded in for weapons to arm her clan's militia. Raqiya was a typical Somali, tangled in the chaos of clan politics.

I do not want to play the color card, but there it is. I cannot allow myself to stick my head in the sand like that mythical flightless bird. I am the actual African ostrich. When confronted with danger and controversy, it kicks up a storm with talons so sharp they can rip a hole in an elephant's hide.

My own daughter was made an enemy unto me. She was one of two slim, light-skinned, keen-featured women with soft, curly hair. I was a short, dark, broad-featured Bantu. And who does Hot Johnny desire in the end? Which would you choose? African people the world over suffer from this disease, keeping the skin bleachers and hair straighteners and plastic surgeons in perpetual wealth. He claimed to love Africa, but he turned away from the African in me. He returned to the motherland, then spurned the mother.

This is one of the reasons I have chosen to love women. I am tired of forcing men to see my beauty.

I returned to Somalia long after Cara was at school in Kenya, Carlo returned to Milan. Johnny was still there, neck-deep in the chaos and anarchy of clan politics. All his good intentions to feed Africa gone for guns.

It seemed Johnny developed in her an appetite for green-eyed foreigners. Raqiya was there too, living in Merka and making time with a Somali Arab while Johnny risked life and career keeping her clan in smuggled foodstuffs. If the U.S. hadn't pulled out of Somalia when it did, I doubt if he would have lived much longer.

I might have had some sympathy had he not turned up later in Mombasa. Cara was only nineteen then. She was innocent still, an untouched child in a woman's body. It was the ultimate disrespect, the unpardonable violation. To sleep with a woman, then come to lay with her own child. I will never forgive him for that. In old Africa, men were stoned and castrated for less.

Female genital mutilation, despite being an anachronistic act of barbarism, is also an ineffective means of guarding women's virtue. In Somalia itself, where nearly all women have undergone the most radical form of mutilation, rape has reached epidemic proportions. I interview women in the refugee camps who have been preyed upon by everyone—militia members, male refugees, the Kenyan police, border guards.

Their surgical chastity belts did not prove impregnable to bandits' knives and soldiers' bayonets. Slicing off their genitals and suturing them shut will not protect them from rape, ritual sexual slavery, child marriage, forced feeding, educational neglect, the AIDS epidemic. I urge Africans to protect their daughters, as I could not protect mine.

"Educate," I tell everyone who will listen, "not mutilate."

People think me a hypocrite for preaching abstinence and practicing promiscuity—do as I say, not as I do. My love life is immaterial. I am mature now, and long past my prime. The life I live is my own. The world's dangers are worst for the very young women, like my daughter, Cara. How close she came to destroying her future in the frying-pan promise that Hot Johnny offered.

I do not rejoice in the terrorist's bomb, the resulting deaths at the U.S. embassy in Nairobi. It was an international crime, a tragic waste of human life. But it did buy time for me to wrest my daughter from a lech's grasp, to spirit her away to her father's bungling care. She would not be protected there, but tossed into the fire. This is yet another force in the exploitation of young girls: the conspiracy to commodify their bodies. I see no great distinction between sexual slavery and hustling naked from the front cover of British *Vogue*.

It is all the fault of that soldier boy, who only recognized her superficial attributes. To him she was just a dancing body. He never appreciated my beauty, and he never nurtured Cara's intellect. I suppose that would have been too much to expect, the blind leading the blind. But he is the one who taught my daughter to see herself through the camera lens, to value her body through the gaze of men.

I wonder if Raqiya managed to escape such peril.

If you could see these Somalis running to Kenya with their noses in the air. Very haughty and xenophobic for a people starving and warring themselves to death. I met her years later while interviewing women in the Utange refugee camp outside of Mombasa. She was in the same city that same summer Hot Johnny Wright was busy seducing my daughter. If he knew how close he came to Raqiya, I doubt he would have been so devoted.

I never told him, of course. I would not give him the satisfaction of having the one who had stolen his heart. Why? So that he could abandon my daughter for Raqiya, just as he had done to me? I did not want to see Cara with him. But I also didn't want him to break her heart. Better that she should leave him than the other way round. It is always better to be the one who leaves.

Some things never change. Raqiya was as difficult as ever. Still demanding money, which this time I would not give. Ever the practiced liar, she would not recount her true story. Would not say what made her risk her life on an overcrowded dhow sailing from Kismayo. Would not explain the intervening years, from Mogadishu to Merka to Mombasa. Strangest of all, she would not reveal the father of the green-eyed child she was nursing.

I know African women take an extended period of breast-feeding, but this child had to be at least four years old. I advised her that if the child's father was the likely suspect, the two of them could easily be resettled in America. The girl was very stubborn and so naive. She'd earlier been in a border camp, where relief workers took the most desperate cases of child malnutrition away to an off-site feeding program.

Raqiya was of the obsessive belief that Somali children were so beautiful, the white people were stealing them to keep for themselves. Can you imagine that? She was just biding her time, waiting to be able to return to Somalia or resettle in the Northern Frontier District. She didn't want the Americans to come and take her child.

Johnny was my nemesis, the memory of him like the green mamba viper, a creature that proves difficult to slay. You may try to crush the creature with a heavy object. It gathers itself from a smear on the ground and begins to move again. You may slice it in two with your cutlass. The front part of its severed body may slither off, the fangs of it still capable of producing poison.

It could have been me buried in the fallout of a bomb blast. I had overheard the whispered plans. There would be no marriage if I could help it. I set out to follow him, fully intending to beard the lion in his own lair. I would go to Nairobi on a mission, prepared that day to issue an edict. An American predator was harassing my teenage daughter. I would stage a personal sit-in, do a war dance there on the embassy grounds until I was satisfied something would be done.

Somehow I lost him in heavy traffic on the long Mombasa road. If I had reached Nairobi just thirty minutes earlier, if I had not met the roadblocks that aggravated me until I knew the reasons for them, I might have been one of those unnamed Kenyans among the dead and wounded in the news reports.

I thought his memory was safely buried back in Kenya. I am not a superstitious African, no hostage to kismet or predestination. But I do believe in irony. In sheer poetic justice, I find Hot Johnny resurrected. He is living in the same American town where I have come to settle. What's more, I do not learn this by bumping into him at the local library or standing in line at the video rental shop.

The words hit me like a terrorist bomb. They fell from the lips of one pink-cheeked blonde with a southern drawl. A self-proclaimed lesbian, serving out salacious morsels of her erotic interludes at the Women's Alternative Lifestyles Group.

This is why I ultimately invited her into my bed. Asheville is a small town. We are bound to encounter him together one day. I might even take out a membership at the health club where he works. The two of us might stroll in one day, arm in arm. I would sidle over, doing my "Dance of the Seven Veils." I would smile sweetly into his face.

"You see this woman you have been loving? Well, now she is mine."

He would be astounded, perhaps even upset. But if he played his cards right, I might let him join in once or twice.

Before he even knows that I inhabit the same communal spaces, sipping from cups in the same coffeehouses, shopping for reading material at the same bookstores, he is taken away from me once again. I have to believe it is better this way.

I am loving the woman loved by Hot Johnny. I touch the face of the one he has touched. I close my eyes as she pushes into me, deep, quick, and hard. Yet the taint of him still lingers in my imagination. He is a virus in the bloodstream, waiting to infect me with fever.

Hot Johnny's face haunts my fantasy, his tongue licks my memory. Raking my senses until they are sore.

"Mother Africa, my African angel," he murmurs against my throat. "Show me the oasis deep inside you."

My heart breaks open like fallen fruit, like circumcised genitals on a bride's wedding night. The walls of the cave clench wildly against themselves, with nothing substantial to cling to. I am a mass of tingling nerves, a flare of raw need. No viper spitting venom will come to quench the fire.

I will never, ever forgive him for this.

Tree

My first taste of tenderness

I lied when I told Johnny that I no longer needed a man.

It was a little white lie I'd told before, one most men seemed willing to believe. They take one look at my scalp-hugging hair, my rawboned body, my rough skin, and seem to accept that I'm every inch the man they are.

I hadn't gone gay in my middle age. Just beaten, bony and sexless. What little meat there was on my bones was withered by the heat of passion, ravaged by the winds of spinsterhood. Formerly full cheeks are sunken now. My bones are much closer to the surfaces of my skin.

I am more treelike than ever before. A willow struck by lightning, still looming despite twisted limbers, scarred trunk. The curves of my calves have hardened into cords of wood. Few birds find shelter in my bare branches. Few men bother me with their attentions anymore. When the occasional one alights, rustling the warning that I prefer women is my way of shaking them loose.

But that's not why I lied to Hot Johnny. When he suddenly reappeared after so many years, I didn't want him to see the meagerness of my existence, the emptiness of life after him. I didn't want him to know I'd been nursing the dry tit of despair for the past eighteen years. When Hot Johnny left I didn't stop living my life; I just stopped loving it.

It's not like I ever gave up on him. I'd left so many doors and windows open for his return. Christmas and birthday cards with my return address on the envelope. A notice of our ten-year college reunion, even though neither of us had graduated from the University of Illinois. An anonymous subscription kept up over the years to the Winston-Salem newspaper where I work as a reporter. RaeAnn Rodgers, the first female, black or white, to ever grace the sports page. Just in case he cared to notice.

It was this last avenue that brought Johnny back to me. By then I'd given up any expectation of hearing from him again. I'd just been leaving doors open out of habit, like the old cat lady who sets out bowls of food even though the strays no longer come. So when Johnny wandered into the newsroom clutching a bouquet like some jilted bride, I was unprepared for his return.

I was one year his junior, but the deprivation of the years made me look more like his mother. He reached out with open arms to embrace me. I stood up quickly and pumped his hand—as always, noticing that even with flats on my feet, I nearly met Johnny at his own eye level.

He used to joke about my height back in our basketball days. When we bumped into each other in the athletic building, his freshman eyes would roam the length of my six-foot-three-inch frame. He'd back away slowly and marvel.

"Damn, you're a dangerous sister," he'd say with a whistle. "I bet you could take me to the hoop any day of the week."

"I bet I can, too, freshie. Wanna try me?"

Back then I still had the cushioning of curves, the confidence of the upperclassman, the protection of a full leaf cover. I was Tree, the childhood nickname Johnny never learned to call me. To him I was the "angel bird" with the eternal hang time. The girl who didn't just slam-dunk, but seemed to sprout wings and fly.

I was not a helpless little bird back then. My roots firmly planted in family soil, I was my father's Tree, the son he never had. Although I did have a twin brother who was four inches shorter, always more interested in shopping with Mama than one-on-one with Daddy. I suspected that somehow RaeMon's and my own genetic coding got mixed up in our mother's womb. I got the muscled body and competitive spirit that should have been his birthright; he got the plump hips and feminine nature that should have been mine.

Daddy was ever the master arborist throughout my childhood, training me strictly from seedling to sapling. Every day after school from the age of eight on, I could be found practicing with the Rock Island High School team my father coached. Every year we'd crisscross the Midwest for games and clinics and basketball camps.

I never gained the adolescent baby fat of other girls my age. I didn't get my period until I was sixteen. I didn't even play against other girls until I got to college. I was always the only girl on the boys' basketball team. After their initial resistance, they got so used to my presence that I became another one of the guys.

I was Tree, the honorary boy. Other girls envied my cachet, my easy entry into the locker rooms of men's lives. I'm sure that I saw more jock straps and hairy buttocks and dangling penises than any other girl in the state of Illinois. By the time I finished high school I had tried out a few, just to see what the big deal was. Familiarity breeds contempt.

What magic charm made girls blush and babble, simper and struggle among themselves just to be seen on some jock's arm? Nothing worth writing home about. Not until Hot Johnny came to my bed and touched me with his magic, transforming me from a sturdy tree to a fluttering bird. From basketball princess to lovesick Cinderella.

I had gone buck wild by junior year in college, trying to match my twin's scorecard. We competed regularly, comparing notes. By then we knew we both liked men. By then I'd bedded half of the Fighting Illini, my own assistant coach, and a visiting Olympic sprinter my brother had always had the hots for.

"You ain't no player," RaeMon would scoff at my latest escapade. "You're just playing a role. Your heart ain't in it."

"The first man I meet who makes me come," I promised him. "I'm gonna hold on to him like a handle."

But holding on to Hot Johnny was not so easy. First I had to scatter all those other chicks clucking around him. Then I had a job convincing him I knew another game to play with big brown balls. The minute we'd made love, our feet dangling from the end of my too-short dormitory bed, I knew what I'd been missing all along.

Those other boys had fucked me like the tomboy I was. These were guys whose idea of foreplay was bending me over behind the bleachers. They had dribbled, slam-dunked, and rebounded like we were on the basketball court. Johnny Wright was my first taste of tenderness.

I was a girl jock who lived on the court but had never been courted. He was the first man to ever kiss my hand, smack in the center of my palm. He took me out for cheap eats, on long walks across campus. He would walk me back to my room afterwards, kissing me good night three separate times before anything even happened.

And oh, when it did. When he laid me against him like a baby, my body almost as muscled and masculine as his own. When he rooted out sweet spots buried beneath layers of sweatshirts and athletic bras. The sensitive throb at the base of my throat. The straining peaks of my small breasts. The pinpoint of pleasure between my legs, almost hidden between folds of skin.

I never knew I had a clitoris. Never even knew what a clitoris was until the day he touched me and something down there fluttered, tremulous as a baby bird being coaxed from her cage.

"Where's my Cece?" Johnny crooned, singing her out of hiding.

> *Cece, my playmate*
> *Come out and play with me*
> *Bring all your dollies three*
> *Climb up my apple tree*

Once Cece eased her head out, he entertained her with raunchy rhymes, complete with sound effects. A mischievous smile lit his lips as he dipped his head between my thighs and whispered.

> *Put your foot up on a rock*
> *Sss-ah, sss-ah*
> *Let the boys see your cock*
> *Sss-ah, sss-ah*

If that don't do
Sss-ah, sss-ah
Let them stick it on through
Sss-ah, sss-ah

Between nudges and nips, excitement boiling and laughter bubbling, he'd tell her stories. The "cock" he knew from boyhood was not the turkey necks of male genitalia. "It was sweet meat like yours, angel bird." He poked and teased, joked about the trouble he had gotten into as a teenager in an all-boys institution. He'd fallen into bed, horny as hell, announcing to the entire dormitory room, "Damn, I could use me some cock right now."

The version he taught me to chant as he introduced his "lickin' stick" into the game began with the words *Put your foot up on a stick, let the girls see your dick.*

"Angel bird," he'd say, "would you care to meet this one-eyed dummy? We call him Jimmy Ray Johnson. A growing boy, but none too bright. What you have to say for yourself, Mr. Johnson?"

He would turn ventriloquist for his swelling dick, shaking its head and saying in a goofy voice, "Well, you can call me Jay, and you can call me Ray, and you can call me Jimmy, but you doesn't have to call me Johnson."

I'd often crest to a climax on a crescendo of giggles.

It was wild, delirious, crazy college sex. We'd do it anywhere: the back of the bus, against ivy-covered walls, the Illini Union in the broad daylight. We'd even go at it with my roommate in the next bed, pretending to be asleep. We couldn't care less that we were both in training, paid no heed to coaches' warnings not to have sex the night before a game. Two willowy trees wrapped around each other in a storm of passion. An extravagant game of one-on-one I couldn't seem to get enough of.

I now know my error. I was dizzy, dick-whipped. I let lust and laughter go to my head. I didn't leave well enough alone, never trusted nature to take its course. I haunted him, hunted him, followed him around like a six-foot-three-inch fool in stocking feet. I was going to hold onto this good loving like white on rice. But Hot Johnny cooked up very, very slippery.

I thought I was staking my claim, protecting my turf. Guarding my man, like I did on the court. There was nothing wrong with playing an aggressive game. Tales told for my own self-comfort. I am ashamed to say that now I know the word for it. I've since seen it described on talk shows where hapless men moan about being harassed by desperate women.

I was stalking Hot Johnny. Following him from class to meals, dormitory to basketball games. I even turned up uninvited for Thanksgiving dinner at the home of one Avis Ransom Jones, a woman Johnny had described as his godmother. I'd carefully copied her South Shore Chicago address from the corkboard above his desk. She didn't seem like any godmother to me.

But if I hadn't been such a damned fool in the first place, maybe Johnny wouldn't be here today. Maybe he would never have wandered into the newsroom with his bouquet of tuberoses. Nor been there to marry that young woman with dark lips, eyes that seem bewildered by the excess of her button-popping bosom. That child he's begging me to find help for now would never have been born.

Johnny would be underground, six feet four inches of scoured bone. I would have wept at the funeral and mourned the next few years. But somehow I'd have soldiered on.

And I'd have more to show for my thirty-eight years than some dusty trophies and a disappointed family and an atrophied heart. I'd have my college degree and an Olympic medal under my belt. Maybe women's basketball wouldn't have flopped the first time out. We'd be playing in the NBA by now. I'd have an athletic shoe named for me, be starting a second career as a color commentator, or even be coaching men's NCAA. Maybe I'd be whole again, my heart intact.

If only I'd turned back that early December evening. We'd been fighting ever since that disastrous Thanksgiving Day in Chicago, and Johnny was avoiding me. The first snow of the season had fallen. I was on the path to the Illini Union, tailing Johnny from the athletic building. I followed at a discreet distance, walking softly, careful not to let snow crunch beneath my feet and betray my looming shadow. Though I crept along fifty feet behind him, my shadow strained impatiently toward him, a crooked tree stretched out on the pavement.

There were three of them, none nearly as tall as Johnny or myself. But it was obvious their bodies had been honed by years of street fighting. One leaped from behind a low bush, a baseball bat in his upraised hand and a ski mask over his face. He was short and stocky but moved like a ballerina. I couldn't help admiring the athletic grace of his spring into the air. He came down on the balls of his feet, connecting the bat squarely with Johnny's back. I could hear a definite *thwack*, the muffled sound of a softball hitting home.

Johnny fell to the ground, instinctively shielding his head with his arms as he rolled over and sprang to a war crouch. Obviously he'd been involved in this sort of business before. At first I thought the banshee wail was his. But no, it had come screeching from my own throat.

I scrambled to his aid, yelping a war cry. Two against three, two tall athletes against three wiry gang-bangers, it barely evened the odds. I didn't feel any of it until it was over: my lip splitting, my tooth breaking, my stomach kicked so hard I suspect that's why I'm still having problems. But we gave as good as we got before they ran off.

I had the worst of it, because the only place I had ever fought was on the court—the kind of brawls that would quickly be broken up by referees. Johnny wept when he saw my face in the full light, wept the whole time we waited at McKinley Health Center. He wept as we were driven to my dormitory by campus security. And he wept in my arms that night. We held each other gingerly, mindful of our respective bandages and bruises. Loving had never been so sweet.

"RaeAnn, angel bird," he breathed into my open palm. "You saved my life tonight."

That was when I truly began to love him. Before then I had been a seething mass of hormones, a homing pigeon propelled by desire. But as we lay entwined night after day, that is when I learned his past: the years of gang-banging in the ghettos of Chicago, the drugs, the jail, and amazingly, something he called *chili pimping*.

That all-boys institution he joked about during foreplay was not some exclusive boarding school. How incredible it was to reconcile the two lives: that of the handsome brown basketball star and that of the juvenile delinquent who'd spent his entire sixteenth year in reform school.

There was no fear on Johnny's part, only a calm, quiet certainty: "They'll be back, Bosco Bear and his Dicks. No doubt about it. They're coming for my ass."

I tried to keep him safe at my side. But he couldn't hide out in my dorm room forever. He became bored and restless, increasingly testy. He began to chafe at the cloistered intimacy, the claustrophobia of living like "a rat in a hole." If only he could have stilled himself to stay put just a little longer.

We made plans for him to get away. He sat out the next basketball game, waiting in my dormitory room. His old wound throbbed, a warning that danger was near. That telepathic scar hadn't been lying.

His enemies were looking for him at Assembly Hall. I spotted three guys lurking around outside the men's locker room. I knew it had to be the same ones. That big, chunky thug had been the one with the baseball bat. Even without the ski mask, I recognized the body build. The face on him was frightening, all burned-looking and leathery. It looked like he was still wearing a mask.

But the police who were supposed to be on the scene never showed up. Just another case of black men trying to kill each other, I guess. All parties are guilty, and nobody cares. After that plan fell through, Johnny seemed to give up hope. He started drinking heavily and sat around all day in his underwear, cursing and fuming.

The very night he left to make a run for his own room, he met the bullet with his name on it. It caught him midstride, shattering his left femur, his college athletic career, his professional ballplaying dreams.

He had a new scar now, an almost mirror match to the one on his right thigh. One old and raised, healed into a keloid of thickened flesh.

One fresh and raw, tracing the arc of the bullet's entry, the surgeon's incision. An X marks the spot of buried treasure, the steel pins anchoring the bone beneath. Both seemed as artistic as tattoos, as jagged-edged as lightning bolts.

The university quickly got him patched up, then thrown out. His athletic scholarship was withdrawn not halfway through his freshman year; there was no longer a way there for him to make.

By that last night he had long since stopped shaving. His lower jaw was covered with tufts of sandy beard. He'd let his curls twine into a tangled bird's nest. I don't know if all this was a sign of despair or an attempt at disguise.

"I've got to get the hell out of here," he muttered. "Get as far from Chicago as I possibly can."

One would have thought that 185 miles was far enough, the cornfields of central Illinois at enough of a distance to keep the violence of his past at bay. Who would have figured those ghetto gang-bangers to be the traveling kind? Who would have guessed that type kept up with college sports?

"Where will you go?"

I said "you," but I meant "we." Where would we go? Preferably someplace we could keep loving each other in a cocoon of safety. The basketball career Daddy had been grooming me for all my life, my undisputed future as the first female NBA player—it was all forgotten in a heartbeat. The only thing real at that moment floated in the gold flecks of Johnny's eyes.

"I don't know. As far as my money and the Greyhound will take me."

I gave him all I had to ease his getaway. The comfort of my body, whatever money I could muster. The remains of that night's pizza wrapped in aluminum foil. A stuffed monkey in a University of Illinois jersey, holding a pennant that read I Got a Basketball Jones.

And in the morning he was gone. I assumed I'd hear from him in time. That he'd write, he'd call, he'd send for me. He never felt the need to inform me of his whereabouts. It took months, nearly a year, before I saw him again. I discovered him hiding out in Memphis. He eluded me and joined the military.

I was able to track down what branch of service he had enlisted in, where he was based. I never knew I was so resourceful, that I could come up with a packet of lies so smooth they could dupe the U.S. military complex into giving out confidential information on one of its enlisted men. Maybe I should have been a spy. Maybe I could have been working for the CIA instead of as a sports reporter for a small-town southern daily.

It was clear that he no longer wanted me. When I caught up with Johnny again, he'd changed, had become a different man with different ways. He wore a crisp military uniform now. He had become cool and uncaring. When I persisted, pestering him with pleas of unrequited passion, he was sometimes cruel.

I uprooted myself to follow him from base to base, town to town. I could have had the starring role in that decade's stalker movie, *Play Misty For Me*. I could have waited around a few years and tried out for Glenn Close's part in *Fatal Attraction*. I was a neglected child angling for attention, and negative attention was better than none at all. My name in Johnny's mouth as he proclaimed me a "crazed bitch," my reflection in his horrified eyes when I slid into the restaurant booth next to his date—this was easier to accept than the alternative, which was my name silenced, my shadow erased.

At times he would weaken, and those were the moments I lived for. Sometimes an evening of confrontation, a volley of verbal aggression, would end with him in my bed. Even his lovemaking had become different; there was no longer any tenderness in it. He had lost his sense of humor, his gift of laughter. He never took the time to kiss my hand. He had stopped calling me his "angel bird."

He made love to me like the tomboy I'd been, the obsessed stalker I'd become. He yanked me by my hair to punish my mouth with his kisses, pummeled my body with his pounding, grasped my forearms so hard there would be bruises there in the morning. Bruises I would savor until they began to fade away.

"I saved your life," I'd plead without a scrap of pride. "Don't you think you owe me something? I would do anything for you. Anything."

"Then get out of my life"—he'd turn away—"and go back to your own. You're no good to yourself or anybody else. I don't want a woman with nothing in her life but me. And you don't want a man dragging failure around behind him like a fuckin' tail."

Contention can't fuel an obsession forever. It was when he began waving to me as I'd tail him along the jogging trail, when he began introducing me to his dates, that I knew whatever fire Hot Johnny once had for me had burned itself out.

By then he'd become a noncommissioned officer, about to be transferred overseas. By then I was a beaten woman, with barely enough strength left to drag myself to the next town, let alone across the ocean. With barely enough emotional reserves to seek out the life Johnny sent me to find.

I don't want a woman with nothing in her life but me.

I clung to the comfort of my delusions. All right then. I would go out and find a place for myself. I would do so well, in fact, that Johnny would be proud. One day he would even want me again. When the creep of unrequited years made it obvious that our time had passed, I kept on going from force of habit, the momentum of a promise made.

I put down shallow roots, anchored myself in thin soil. I thought I was content, if not happy. Just one of those lies women tell themselves when they are too afraid to love.

If I didn't thrive transplanted here, I somehow managed to survive. Winters were never that cold in North Carolina. Even as the seasons changed, I was able to maintain a modest leaf cover to shield my nakedness. Celibacy was not even a decision; it was a natural response. I never trusted myself to love anyone after that because, well, what was the point? I barely had enough love to cover myself.

Johnny needs me now, needs me to help the dying daughter he says that he loves more than life itself. I have always been a loner here. It is with some amazement that coworkers and editors see me barging into their offices, calling in imaginary favors. Maneuvering what little influence I have built up over the years. Keeping my promise to publicize his cause, going far beyond that promise.

I am back on the court again, playing run-and-gun. Crashing through the defense, mowing down the opposition. Bullying my employers, colleagues, my few friends and acquaintances into supporting "the battle for Beauty" with their dollars and news stories.

Johnny lingers in my life's open doorway. I talk to him on the phone daily, meet with him several times a week. I try to keep my heart caged, a hood on the head of the fluttering bird. But it is no use. Wings beat mercilessly against bars. I am loving him as hard as I ever have, as deeply as I did when I was twenty-one. And now even my own lie is no protection.

He weeps in my arms one exhausting day when his daughter has taken a turn for the worse. He is desperate to find a compatible bone marrow donor. He has decided to go home to Chicago. Back to the place of his tumultuous past, to dig up his old forgotten family and lay his heart at their doorstep. He prays that his enemies have forgotten his name. He begs me for help.

It only takes a few phone calls. The hotel space is confirmed, the services of a search firm donated pro bono, several media and talk show appearances lined up. Airline tickets are contributed for a flight that will take him away from me one more time.

"Once again, RaeAnn," Johnny whispers into the palm of my hand, pressing his lips against it, "you have saved my life. What can I offer in return?"

"You owe me nothing, Johnny Wright." It speaks for me, that desperate stab at dignity. "Nothing at all. I've moved on now, and I don't deal with men."

I don't know if it is guilt or obligation that touches his lips to mine with a taste of their original tenderness. When I do not respond, he stops to check my eyes. I am struggling not to respond. To hold on to all I have left: my self-respect, my patched-together pride, my peace of mind. Johnny sees through the thinness of my disguise. He could always tell when I was lying.

"One more time, angel bird?" he coaxes. "Just for old times' sake? We were good together once."

I open my mouth to say no, but he presses a finger to it.

"I understand you're into women now. Maybe it's my fault you went that way in the first place. I know that even lesbians enjoy the occasional pleasure of a man." His hand leaves one mouth to seek out another. Coaxing Cece to come out and play, the forgotten pinpoint of pleasure hiding behind closed doors. "And I want you, RaeAnn Rodgers. I need you like never before."

Nineteen years of resolve dissolves. A cold, hardened candle catches alight at the first spark. His hands move across the cords of my back, his lips against my breasts. His fingers stretch me open, his body enters mine. My tightness yields to him hesitantly; it is almost like I am a virgin again. I try to pull away but can't seem to muster the resistance. I settle instead for gravity. He is not pushing into me; rather, I am collapsing around him.

It is different now, if nineteen years of abstinence hasn't dulled my memory. This is nothing like our original mating dance, that wild, delirious college sex. Nor is it the painful, brutal loving of the later years. It is something else, something potent and overpowering seeping into every pore of my being. I am sinking into love again, sweet, healing, harsh, tender, terrifying love.

The moment before I am engulfed in quicksand, I find my wings. Whoosh, I am elevating, entertaining air, the sun searing my skin. I am diving toward destruction only to be swooped up again. But the sensations are ever so fleeting. His charity proves more short-lived than his cruelty. More unsettling than those numb years of silence.

There is something frightening in our mutual climax. We are caught up in a storm of our own making. Oblivious of the power of our own passion, we are dashed onto distant shores. Something inside is coming undone, becoming remade. I think that Johnny felt it too.

"I thought I was doing this for you," he murmurs into the pulse of my wildly beating heart. Birds, they say, can sometimes die from the trauma of a human's touch. "I never imagined it could be like this, Tree. You've given me just what I needed to keep on keeping on."

Keeping on to save the one he loved more than life itself. To move miles beyond me, putting distance between us once again. This was a most reluctant sacrifice, the last thing on earth I could afford to give. How was *I* to keep on keeping on?

Because I am nobody's angel bird. I am a tree in spite of it all. Beguiled into bloom by the balm of an Indian summer, plunged into the chill of a sudden winter. My buds frozen in bloom. The ground is cracking, my roots are shifting. My precious few leaves have been shaken loose, blown into the whirling wind.

There are no exquisite pains to savor the morning after, only the wetness he leaves between my legs, the tears running in rivulets down my face. The bruise that is my heart continues to throb as he gathers his clothes, kisses my hand, and leaves me with the rest of my lie to live.

Cinnamon

He taught me how to slow-hand dance

"Lord, I know those lips."

It is with a start that I recognize that pursed mouth. I woke up promptly at the crack of noon, lazily reached to click on the remote. Those lips exploded at me full blown in a television close-up. Lush and red, like sliced fruit. He's wearing a neatly trimmed mustache now. His full mouth is moving beneath it.

Sparkling in the glare of television lights, it looks like he's gone and made a little something of himself. I admire his finesse, but I also feel like pointing a finger of accusation.

"Nigga, you ain't nothing!" I want to shout at the TV screen. "I knew you when you were scrounging around Memphis like an alley rat. You wasn't nothing but a po' pimp, a male ho. I knew you when you were a gigolo, living off the do-rag sisters."

I am so pissed off, I barely hear what he's peddling on the midday news. Goddamn that Hot Johnny! Still has those juicy lips. Still has that sex appeal after all these years. Of course, I am no slouch myself. If only he could see me from where he sat, he'd know I'm none the worse for wear. My breasts are still high, my ass still firm and rounded.

When his fifteen seconds end, I absently scratch down a hotline telephone number that flashes across the bottom of the screen. I stretch like a cat and switch off the TV. This unexpected blast from the past turns me on like a furnace. I feel like doing something nasty.

I ease back into bed, even though I just woke up. I enjoy these times when my husband is out on the road. It gives me a chance to do delicious little things for myself, to myself. To laze around in a nightgown all day long if I want to.

I sip my mimosas and nibble at whole strawberries, licking the juice that runs down my hands. I scoop up chocolate mousse and whipped cream, suck it off my fingers. I lay up in bed and watch TV movies and rented videos, read trashy romance novels. Take a pause for the cause when the spicy story gets the sap flowing. Fondle and flicker my own firm body, pleasuring myself like the heroes do those unsullied yet hot-blooded damsels in the bodice rippers.

I was always the entree on someone else's plate. I never even mastered the art of self-pleasure until I was pushing thirty, so I make up for lost time whenever I can.

The telephone invariably rings during one of my self-love sessions.

"What you doing, woman?" that jealous man of mine gruffly demands. Old habits die hard.

"Fucking myself," I answer frankly, "since you're not here to do the job."

He can't help but guffaw, barking out that husky laugh that always ends in a hacking cough. He really ought to come off those unfiltered cancer sticks he's been chain-smoking since the age of twelve. He's not even sixty yet, and I shudder to think what his lungs look like. And I'm only forty-eight; far too young to be a widow. I spent too many years singing "I can't get no satisfaction" to give it up now that I've found me some.

"Go ahead and handle your business, baby," he growls. "Just save some of that poontang for me. And don't let no other nigga have what's mine. You know how I gets."

I know all right. The right side of my jaw still aches when I chew steak. And though I may be tempted to creep every now and then, common sense holds me back. Not only do I know which side my bread is buttered on, I've settled into a kind of contentment.

Cupid ain't nothing but a sadistic imp with an itchy trigger finger. I learned the hard way not to place my heart in firing range. I don't lie to myself about being in love. I'm fond of my old man, happy with the pampering he's learned to lavish on me.

They say you wind up marrying a man just like your father, and I suspect it's true. My man is made after my daddy's own heart when it comes to the fine art of spoiling a woman. Although Pops was nowhere near as country as this slew-foot Tennessee walker I've saddled up.

I stifle the urge to call that hotline number. To look Johnny up, catch up on old times. To find out what's happened in the two decades since Memphis. I wonder what has brought both of us back to our original stomping grounds. I ought to turn up where he's at, wearing something slinky. Give him a taste of what he's been missing all these years.

If only Johnny Wright could see me now, my custom-built home in Country Club Hills, my designer clothes, my silver BMW, my blue fox. Of course, the new, improved Hot Johnny would probably look a lot better in this setting than the husband I have.

Everything I own outclasses that man by a mile, with his countrified ass. If he had his way, everything in this house would be covered in plastic.

Still, he's the one with the money, and he doesn't mind sharing it. He knows what to do when the lights go down. He treats me like a lady in public, a mistress in the living room, a whore in the bedroom, and he doesn't even require me to enter the kitchen. That's what we got Run and Tell It for, the alcoholic old witch who doubles as watchdog.

My husband pretty much takes me as I am. Johnny was always trying to remake me into something else. He said that I was "programmed to self-destruct." That my life of sin would be the ruin of me. He used to call me a tragic mulatto, a Jezebel right off the pages of a plantation novel.

Jezebel was just a fine sister with a bad rep, at the mercy of history's player haters. I seem to remember from catechism class that a painted whore got tossed on her head from a second-story window, but that's probably not right. We received our catechism in pieces. You never got the whole story in the Catholic Church. Jezebel's punishment always seemed too rough to me. A straying husband and his jealous wife must have been behind it.

You better believe that if I'd been back on the plantation, I'd pick the master's bed over cotton fields any day of the week. You got to use what the good Lord gave you. You can call me a hoochie mama if you want to. But that doesn't stop men from looking at me, liking what they see.

First of all, like I told Hot Johnny, I ain't hardly tragic. My father's death was the worst thing I've had to live through, but hey. Nobody gets out of here alive. Pops had always been in my corner, but I knew he wasn't immortal. Being out on the streets comes in a close second on the tragedy scale, but I turned that around right quick. I ain't begging for squat on the midday news. I've got a bank account full of money and a house full of things, some of them costing more than I used to make in a year. And I didn't have to sing the blues to get a bit of it. Somebody did, but it wasn't me.

Second, I am not a mulatto. Sure, there's healthy helping of cream in my coffee. I've got some honky stirred in, just like everybody else in black America. My cream is just closer to the surface, that's all. It's part of what makes me who I am.

I've been accused of worshiping that bit of white blood flowing through my veins. But what can I tell that Irish man who slept with my grandmother sixty years before I was born? *Get thee behind me, Satan?* Should I erase the whiteness from me, like Michael Jackson did the blackness, like those of you out there with your permed hair and blue contact lenses? Should I nap up my hair, flatten my nose, blacken my skin so I'll look more like the rest of you Negroes?

I'm not the one who made the beauty rules. But if the shoe fits and looks good on me, I'm damn sure going to wear it. I can't help it if I'm just a fine bill of goods. That I'm blessed with cinnamon-colored skin, some good hair on my head, a few curves in the right places, a face to launch a thousand ships, a tight snatch, and the know-how to wrap certain men around my pinkie finger several times over. Otherwise, there's not much else going for me. There, I've said it. Like Pops used to say, "It pays to know your own limitations."

I'm undereducated, an underachiever, a woman with no real talents. I admit I've got a certain kind of take-no-prisoners bluster that some folks admire. I've been too busy polishing my shine to pay too much attention to my character. I leave that to the homely girls.

I'm really not a nice person. And I'm too far down the road to turn around now. The most I could hope for was to snag me somebody who doesn't mind a hard edge on a piece of fine crystal. My best bet was to finagle my place as a trophy on some rich man's mantelpiece.

But I've got needs just like the next person. It took thirty years of my life to find the spice I've been searching for. When you find something you've been looking for so long, you can't just abandon it. You've got to stay with it, to see where the story ends.

When you find the spice of life, it's hard to go back to eating your food plain, no seasoning. Columbus and his kind sailed around the world for a taste of cinnamon on the tongue.

I didn't want to hurt Hot Johnny, to rub his nose in it. I didn't want it to end with hard feelings. But we were so much alike, we both had the same kind of hunger. How could we be each other's spice? We were like stray cats with our raggedy fur and our half-starved spirits, turning to each other for warmth in the dead of winter. We couldn't offer each other much comfort.

Still, it doesn't hurt for someone like him to swallow a dose of humility. That's just the way the cookie crumbles. No use crying over spilled milk. Take those cookie crumbs and sop up the disappointment.

Hot Johnny never had to work a day in his life cultivating women's love. It flourished like wildflowers for him, like those red petals he wears for lips. He never had to water, never bothered to fertilize, to re-pot or pinch back any withering blossoms. He just strolled out to the flower garden of life and plucked what he wanted. He always had women bobbing at his beck and call. Like Pops was known to say, what is easy is never appreciated.

Anyway, I can't be with nobody prettier than me. That's my bottom line. I ain't fighting no man for my place in front of the mirror. When I ask that looking glass "Who's the fairest of them all?" if it ain't me, it damn sure better be Miss America's face flashing back. Ain't but a few of those beauty queens who can match me in the looks department, even at my age. Cinnamon Brown can go toe to toe with Halle Berry any day of the week.

What did that crooked politician say about his baby deer of a secretary, the young girl everybody thought he was screwing? You know who I'm talking about, the one caught running guns to the contras down in Central America.

"She can't help it if God gave her the gift of beauty."

That's me all over. And Hot Johnny too, who was much too fine for his own good. He couldn't help it if God gave him a backhanded gift that backfired on him. Me and Johnny were both relieved of the responsibility of trying too hard. He was almost like a male version of me. Brown-skinned and curly-haired, with greenish hazel eyes and thick lashes I wish to hell I had. Lovely eyes are just wasted on a man. I was never as captivated with Johnny's white-boy eyes as I was entranced by his nigger-red lips.

I don't even know how we hooked up. I was living hard, running wild. Headed for a fall and I knew it. Johnny happened into my life to cushion my landing when I hit rock bottom.

I've done all kinds of freakish things with freakish men. I've been nothing if not experimental. I grabbed the reins of sexual aggression, literally and figuratively. I got some of my best ideas from X-rated films and wasn't shy about putting them into practice.

I encouraged one man to give toe sucking a try, took a whirl around the world (mine, not his). A little lightweight S&M action (I was the mistress, never the slave). A threesome with another woman (my idea). I'm a card-carrying member of the mile-high club, Chicago to L.A., business class. Was almost arrested for indecent exposure while dallying with a man in a skybox at a Bulls game. Got the shit slapped out of me for getting my freak on in the back room of my mother's bar during my father's wake.

In my twenties I dated one dude who worked days, another the graveyard shift at the same steel mill. One would get up to go to work, and thirty minutes later the next one would be slipping in between the sheets. There's a lot I've done that I'm not particularly proud of, but I wouldn't call it shame either. I chalk it up to experience. I just wanted to see what it felt like. Except for the steel mill brothers, I never tried anything more than once. Once a lark, twice a perversion.

But up until that point, I had never let two men have their way with me at once. When it happened it was my decision, even though some people may have read a rape into it. Rest assured, I went into it willingly. I was trying to soothe myself in the emptiness of pure sensation.

The only man who had ever really loved me had just left me forever. I was a pampered brat turned spiritual orphan. My soul threatened to slip into the cold grave right along with Pops. People don't realize that brittle chicks like me are actually quite fragile. Glass is easily shattered, after all.

Anyway, Pops' funeral led to a messy scene. One man naked on the bed beside me, another standing over us with speculation in his eyes and a leer on his lips. Me watching it all through a long-focus lens. Wondering to myself if this could be the time.

And here's the killing thing: All that sensation—four hands, two tongues, two dicks—and the shit didn't even move me. We could never get the rhythm right, figure out where to put all those extra limbs. How to arrange it so both of them were touching me without them having to touch each other. Neither man wanted me back after that episode.

After that I let myself slip. Johnny and the other addicts called it low self-esteem. I just figured there was nowhere to go from there but down. I pretty much let anybody have it who wanted it: the cab driver, the pizza delivery man, the newspaper boy. My boss at work, who took me home and introduced me to the missus. And she got some of it too. Maybe this would be the time.

None of the shit was any good. I'd wake up the next morning with my head on the pillow next to some man I didn't know and didn't want to know. I was thoroughly disgusted with myself. But I didn't stop, couldn't seem to stop. I was finally becoming the whore my best friend had called me the night she accused me of trying to take her man. Except I was getting paid nothing but hard knocks and a penicillin-resistant strain of the clap.

That's how I wound up in the room with him and a bunch of others like him. Now me, I wasn't like any of them. I didn't need no twelve steps to set me straight. I wasn't some degenerate exposing myself to kids on the city bus. I wasn't some molested child acting out her abuse twenty years later. I had nothing to do with household pets and barnyard animals. I didn't belong there.

"Hi there. I'm Cinnamon. And I'm a sexoholic." I breathed suggestion into my words like Marilyn Monroe, like a phone sex ho. I threw back my shoulders and pushed out my titties. Everyone else had introduced themselves as a recovering sexual addict. I was making fun of them, trying to get a reaction. They didn't even have sense enough to know they were being mocked. Everyone applauded at the end of my introduction, nodding at me encouragingly. Trying to nudge a sad story out of me.

I couldn't believe that with all my looks and style, my life had led me down to this dead-end road. Sitting in a basement with a bunch of perverts. Broke as a church mouse in Memphis, Tennessee.

I always thought my folks showed no imagination in naming me Pat Brown until I met up with a tall, whiskey-voiced baritone by the name of Willie Lee Williams. He was playing harmonica at a blues spot on the yuppie side of Chicago, singing a double entendre about some evil wench who "wanna sell my monkey." Staring straight at me with baleful eyes, one bushy brow uplifted in invitation.

Who'd have believed that a bluesman with a gold tooth in his mouth and a Jheri curl on his head had stretched my nose wide enough to run a train through? He had lured me to Memphis with a promise of the moon and left me singing the blues myself. And I don't usually do the soap operas or cry over spilled milk. Men are like buses—you miss one, another one's bound to come along.

See, it's usually me that does the dumping. I keep them around until I suck out all the flavor, then it's on to the next stick of chewing gum. But I was knocked off center, the better to fall. I had no job, had ventured out on a wing and a prayer to a strange city where I didn't know a soul.

I had fantasized about a future with a man who had him a little piece of pocket change, could keep me in a manner to which I'd happily become accustomed, who seemed to be taken with my good looks and evil ways. Who let me spend his money any way I wanted. It was a strategic decision. I wasn't getting any younger. I still had my beauty, but it was just a matter of time before it began to fade. As Pops used to say about his businesses, "I saw an opportunity and I seized it."

Then one slip-up and it was all over. One lousy mistake and I was kicked to the curb, went from princess to pauper. Long Tall Willie went off on me like a time bomb when he stumbled on that little affair. Hell, it wasn't even an affair. Just a one-night stand. He was on the road and I was lonely.

Men do it all the time. When a man fools around, he's a player, a heartbreaker, a lady's man. You think Long Tall Willie just says no when some juicy road ho wants to go back to his hotel room and jump his bones? You know the deal. When a woman does the same, you're a whore. A nymphomaniac. A loose woman. Yesterday's trash blowing in the breeze. The people's piece. Oh, yeah. I've been called it all.

See, if any of those jokers had been man enough to give me what I needed, which was a halfway decent orgasm, then I wouldn't have been jumping from man to man hoping that maybe this would be the time. And that's just what I told those people at Sexual Addicts Anonymous. I didn't give a damn what they thought. Wasn't nothing wrong with me. I only came for the free refreshments. I was overdue for a square meal. It turned out to be coffee and tea and cookies, that old tired shit.

I discovered we were both from Chicago. That's what made me notice Johnny in the first place, that and his juicy red lips. Johnny was hot all right, with his lanky yellow body and the most delicious mouth you've ever dreamed. I watched how it pursed and puckered like the promise of a kiss whenever he was thinking hard.

I didn't know the man from Adam, and all I wanted was to feel those lips on mine. I wanted to get up from where I sat, walk over to where he was, kneel before him, lean in, and suck his ripe fruit into my hungry mouth. To tease those lips apart with my tongue and taste what honey could be found within. Maybe this would be the time.

It was those lush red lips that suckered me into his life, since I don't usually go for the pale-skinned dudes. The darker brothers tend to treat you better, I've always found. They are more apt to value the unaccustomed gleam of gold dangling on their arm. Although my bluesman was as black as Mississippi mud, and he sent me to the emergency room with a cracked jaw. So much for my color complex theory.

Hot Johnny was addressing the group.

"I've always felt like a failure. Multiple relationships with women became my measure of success. The more women I bedded, the better I felt about myself. Nothing else seemed to turn out right. The only thing I could lay claim to was easing into some woman's life and slipping her heart into my hands."

They say women wear their hearts between their legs, and a man like Johnny knew just where to find them. A little con artist! I could see him coming a mile off with his sweet red lips. Trying to reach his hand in some woman's pocketbook for her last coin. Pretending to be squeezing her titty when he's really probing for her petty cash. Those long arms could snake right into the nest eggs of love-starved spinsters. Yeah, I had the boy's number.

Over dinner, when I learned about his domestic arrangement, I knew I was right. He'd been living in "a polygamous relationship." Two do-rag-wearing sisters sharing him, African style. He wasn't doing a lick of work at the time. But then neither were they, though pooling their welfare checks kept the wolf from the door and Hot Johnny in pocket change.

I always wondered why he never knocked either of them up. Probably iron-poor tired spunk, pooped from all that screwing. They were mad at him now because he was in recovery, had stopped giving up the dick. All they wanted was a caramel-colored baby apiece—was that too much to ask? And there he was, holding out on them. The do-rag sisters had been threatening to put him on the street.

"You're wasting your time with me," I warned over our hamburgers and Cokes. A cheap date; that clinched it. A gigolo through and through. The only reason I went out with him at all was that I was broke and hungry, in no position to turn down any free meals. "I ain't got a nickel to my name, not even a welfare check. I'm in no position to take care of no man, don't care how hot his johnson is."

I glanced down at his hands, fondling a sweaty glass of cola. Long, slender fingers with hairy knuckles. Nails bitten down to the quick. The thing about the hands and feet is really not a reliable measure, incidentally. The biggest prick I'd seen was on a half-pint preacher with hands almost as small as his mind.

"I don't believe in buying no nigga. If I got to pay for it, then I don't want it. Hell, I'm looking for some man to take care of me, not the other way around."

This man had the nerve to lean in toward me with a look of concern on his face. Not boredom and distraction, like I'd expect from a gigolo who hadn't struck pay dirt. Not like a lech who'd accept any opportunity for some free pussy. He looked at me all concerned and earnest, like the rest of those losers at the twelve-step group.

I guess it was the zeal of the newly converted. At the meeting we'd just left, Johnny had boasted three weeks of abstinence, and everyone applauded politely. A regular goddamn monk. He put down his drink and captured my hands between his.

"You're better off learning to take care of yourself, sister love," he lectured. "If I didn't know better, I'd swear you were my long-lost sister. You remind me so much of myself."

I looked back into his eyes, hazel with green sparks floating in them. I cleared my throat, tossed back my ponytail, and smiled, wishing I'd worn better clothes to present myself in. I'd show him his "sister."

I reached across the table for the bottle of Tabasco sauce. I coated one of his long fingers, raised it to my mouth, and sucked. It was pure poetic justice. The Sexual Addicts Anonymous meeting would be the ideal place to feed my need. I'd go through them one by one, whip through there like the Chicago hawk. They'd never knew what hit them.

"Now this could be something other than a finger." I swirled my tongue around his fingertip and watched his red mouth pucker in consideration. "Just use your imagination."

Maybe this would be the time.

Do you know what he did? Winced like he had been bitten, though I'd been careful not to use my teeth. Snatched away his hand, licked the offending finger with his own tongue. Dipped it in his water glass and wiped it with his napkin. Frowning faintly, a missionary without a convert.

"Damn, that shit stings. I must have had an open cut. And Cinnamon," he said to me, "bedding you down in your weakened condition would be like taking indecent liberties with a minor."

Furious, I jumped to my feet. I didn't care who in that Denny's heard me.

"A minor? Why, you sanctimonious, self-righteous hypocrite! Don't you know a woman when you see one? Any man in here would give his eyeteeth to be with me. What makes you think I want your sorry yella ass, anyway?"

He tilted his head to the side, considering. Like mine had been a serious question, not a rhetorical one.

"I don't know. Arrogance, maybe. I've been accused of it."

"Damn right. As arrogant a bastard as I've ever met." Though it really wasn't true. I sat down again to my plate of half-finished food.

"Of course, you could never be charged with that crime yourself. By the way, the hot sauce trick? That's a new one on me." He smiled ruefully, raising his glass in a toast. "And I've tried them all. Kudos to you, Cinnamon. You know your stuff."

I couldn't decide whether to be suspicious, appeased, or insulted. I caught the humor brimming in his eyes and opted for laughter.

"Yeah, that Tabasco business was pretty funky. It should have been chocolate mousse with whipped cream. Best I can do in a Denny's."

Before I knew it we were comparing trade secrets like fellow fishermen sharing tips on how to bait the hook, cast the line, reel in the catch. The lure you never thought the fish would be fool enough to bite. But they always swallowed hook, line, and sinker.

We wondered why men kept on coming back to where they'd been treated the worst. Like the one who'd confronted me after he saw me kissing another man in the front seat of his Audi. And I'd managed to convince him that his eyes were playing tricks on him, that some strange slant of sunlight or passing cloud had changed another woman into my dead ringer.

We marveled at how Johnny unerringly knew just the right balance of macho and sensitivity to make the most wary woman want to drop her drawers. How you didn't even need to touch a woman to capture her, to have her heart flipping like a fish out of water.

Although one couldn't avoid the aftermath of these expeditions, the scent of rotten fish that lingered long after the catch. The emptiness, the acrimony, the messy entanglements. One catfish had grown feelers like a swamp skipper and followed Johnny down to Memphis from Champaign-Urbana. I'd seen her myself, sitting two rows behind us in movie theaters. Tailing us through the park with long-legged strides. We concocted elaborate ruses to throw Johnny's sick ballplayer off the track.

That brother-sister business seemed to fit the bill after all. People even mistook us for siblings. Every now and then I'd test the limits of our platonic relationship by sticking a tongue in his ear or plunging a hand down his pants. He'd shake his head and push me off gently.

"We got a good thing going, Cinnamon Brown. Why complicate a true friendship with something like a roll in the hay? We're trying to get ourselves straight, sister love. We don't have to be at the mercy of our addiction."

I was stumped. Sex was the only way I knew to be with a man. But none of my bedroom tricks worked on Johnny. I gave up trying to seduce him and grudgingly accepted the rare gift of male friendship, something I realized I had never experienced.

We became more than just friends. We were fellow sufferers testing celibacy as our sobriety, falling back on each other for support. Picking up the phone when one of us was weakening, in danger of drifting into old habits. Joking about our various withdrawal symptoms, the after-effects of unrelieved urges: the blue balls and throbbing pussies.

We'd both given nicknames to our nether regions, as if they were somewhere outside of ourselves. I used the term "pot likker," not in reference to the organ itself. It was both the endless fluid that it produced when at full boil as well as the person who sampled it. Johnny proclaimed "Johnson" his "lickin' stick" for the blows it delivered, and the oral attentions he expected it to receive. I noticed we called them *the* pot likker, *the* lickin' stick, *the* breasts, *the* balls, not *my* pot likker, *my* lickin' stick, *my* breasts, *my* balls. As if our passions were something neither of us dared to own.

Like a couple of ex-drunks watching social drinkers at a cocktail party, we were getting hard-ons and wet panties at the most innocuous acts: seeing a baby breast-feed, watching love scenes in movies, happening upon couples kissing in the park. Sharing antiaphrodisiac remedies, we wondered where one could find saltpeter when the cold showers failed.

We were like recovering drug addicts reliving the sensations of their chemicals, or cancer survivors comparing symptoms. We weren't having sex, but we were always talking it.

I remember us splashing in a swimming pool among the half-naked bodies, and Johnny pointing out which kind of breasts he liked best. I looked down at his long bronzed legs. Touched the raised surface of jagged scars, running like lightning bolts along each thigh.

"What happened here?" I asked.

"Dragon bites," he explained, pushing my hand away. "Some of these broads can get awfully aggressive."

I remember sitting at a blues club on Beale Street, likening lovemaking to a pressure cooker that somebody took the lid off of too soon. Recalling the moment I would sense the built-up steam begin to dissipate, the coveted climax begin to escape.

Johnny also had a catalog of handy hints designed to turn on the faucet of sexual response in women. Only to be used with caution, only after I'd gotten myself straight, he said. He even hinted broadly that one day he might be up for a hands-on demonstration. He detailed the virtues of various sex toys and masturbation techniques; he listed the hot spots and erogenous zones men frequently overlooked. It was a decidedly mixed message when we were supposed to be practicing abstinence.

Ironically, it was those long, sometimes all-night support sessions on the telephone that taught me how to please myself. I'd recline in bed, sip red wine, and talk dirty with Hot Johnny.

"You ever made it with a bald-headed lover?" he'd ask.

"Fool," I'd murmur, waiting for the heated punch line I knew was coming. "What the hell I want with a bald-headed man?"

"Cinnamon Brown, you haven't lived," he promised, "until you've had a smooth, shaved head rubbing against your coochie. One of these days you'll have to try it."

"Johnny Wright, you are one nasty boy."

We'd whisper and tease and titillate each other for hours on end. I would close my eyes and imagine a smooth head between my legs. A pair of red lips moving all over me. Like a lit charcoal growing gradually hotter. By the time we'd hang up the sun would be rising, and I'd be nearly dizzy with untapped desire. I'd fall upon my pillow and hump it until I was sailing and it was soaking.

I finally understood the meaning of that old song Long Tall Willie loved to sing: "I Got My Mojo Working."

It was almost like a cat-and-mouse game, Johnny pushing me away with one hand, luring me toward him with the other. Two steps toward him, one step back. A long, hesitant, drawn-out dance that might have gone somewhere had not the battering ram of Long Tall Willie come barging back into my life.

It started with phone calls all hours of the day or night, designed to harass and harangue me into submission. Even after I changed numbers he hunted me down like a hound dog, tailing me home from the little poot-butt waitressing job I finally found, ironically at the same Denny's restaurant where Johnny and I had our first date. Confronting me in the street with a tangled web of aggressive accusations and guilty apologies.

"Leave me alone, fool." I'd shake myself loose from his grasp. "I never go back where I've already been."

He wouldn't take no for an answer. He became more aggressive, more desperate. He stole into Denny's once, snatched me off my rubber-soled feet, and drove me around town for hours, ranting and raging. He repeatedly called up my manager, first trying to get me fired, then begging her to intercede on his behalf.

I knew that Long Tall Willie sometimes carried a gun. He'd shown it to me several times. Had even threatened to use it to shoot the dick off that young Jehovah's Witness who knocked at the door to leave a tract and wound up leaving with some trim. It happened one day he was on the road.

There's a thin line between religious ecstasy and sexual rapture. There's no place this side of the whorehouse where more screwing goes on than in the church. I've known some smooth preachers with extravagant voices, counting out the wages of sin on both hands. When the fingers and toes failed, I'd helped certain ones of them count sins on various other extremities.

I knew some of those church sisters, too. Double-breasted true believers who shunned the evils of worldly pleasures but could eat their weight in barbecued ribs. Eager to offer up the weekly tithe, the country fried chicken, the sweet potato pie, and a hot heaping helping of poontang if the reverend so willed.

Although I was raised in the suburbs as a straitlaced Catholic, my mother often took us to her cousin's church in West Side Chicago. Sweetwater Missionary, the "shouting Baptists." I've seen how those church mothers quiver when the spirit fell down on them. I've seen them toss back their heads, lift skirts thigh high, fan the sweat that bloomed between breasts, and moan out the name "Sweet *Jee*-sus!" I used to seriously wonder what part of the body the Holy Ghost entered through.

That Bible thumper peddling salvation at the doorstep had such a fire, such a religious fervor in him. It clung to him like musk. If we were really "living in the last days" like he said, I needed some of his holiness to rub off on me. I too needed to be saved. Maybe this would be the time.

We had this nosy old biddy hanging around the house. Yes, the same one who blew in last winter on the Greyhound, so rank you'd think she'd been riding an actual dog. I didn't have the heart to turn her away, although she's the reason the right side of my jaw aches. Back then she'd do a little cooking and cleaning when she wasn't busy nipping Willie's Napoleon brandy, replacing with water what she'd tip out into her open mouth.

I saw her at it all the time and took pity on her alcoholic ass. I never once blew the whistle on Mama Roanie, always quick to remind me she wasn't just some cleaning woman, but a girlhood friend of Long Tall Willie's long-dead mother. Even when she got in my face with "I been here before all of Willie Lee's whores, I'll be here when your red-bone ass is out the door," the most I did was slip and call the witch "Macaroni." I still have a soft spot for the feisty old heifer, despite the dirt she did me.

She was a woman of many names. Her real one was Rona Tallet, though I later rechristened her "Run and Tell It." She peeped the action through the half-open bedroom door where we'd retreated to "read our Bibles." She spilled the beans, Willie went ballistic, the rest is history. My jaw still locks when I yawn, still aches when I try to chew Macaroni's pan-fried Porterhouse.

I remembered that gun, a gleaming bronze pistol decorated with ridges and curlicues. It looked like something out of the Wild West, almost too fancy to be a deadly weapon. But Hot Johnny bleeding to death in a doorway with Long Tall Willie languishing on death row wasn't something I wanted on my head.

I was determined that each man would know nothing of the other's existence. I was able to keep it that way until the night one kicked in my front door, the day the other discovered me spread-eagled in my own bed. I wouldn't even have confessed then if I could have gotten away with it.

We had been up until the wee hours with one of our phone sex sessions. The next afternoon was the Fourth of July, and we were supposed to have already left for a barbecue. It was a hot Memphis day with the windows closed, the sun slanting in through open curtains. An occasional firecracker went off in the distance. I was celebrating Independence Day in the most dependent way: T-shirt pulled up and panties pulled down, feet and hands bound to my bedposts with four of my own multicolored silk scarves.

"Son of a bitch," Johnny whispered, standing over me. "Who did this to you, Cinnamon? Tell me."

I shook my head stubbornly. I knew I wouldn't call the police, wouldn't go to the hospital. I would never report this crime. I was totally drowning in shame, self-loathing, and something slippery and confusing at the bottom of the well. Despite that it had happened eight hours before, something deep and disturbing prickled every pore of my being. Johnny's hands moved, reaching to undo the ties that bound me.

"No," I whispered. "Please don't. Not yet."

"Cinnamon." He sat beside me on the bed, focusing upon me a penetrating stare. "What the hell is going on here?"

I had to swallow hard before I answered. Swallow down the bitterness of a newly discovered secret. It was Snow White turned upside down. I hadn't been kissed and no Prince Charming had roused me.

A lanky executioner had led me to the wilderness. He'd crashed into my resting place, lashed me to my bedposts. He'd yanked me from the arms of sleep and into his own. I had fought hard against the acts he forced upon me. It was a futile battle against his violence.

Long Tall Willie had not been gentle. My lips were reddened with bite marks, my forearms and shoulders purple with bruises. The muscles in my legs ached from trying to hold my legs together against a stronger pressure that forced them apart.

And here's the killing thing. Somewhere mixed up in that utterly insane shit was a secret seam of glory. Somewhere in the struggle my body had responded despite itself. I'd been swept over the edge of the waterfall.

Was this what I'd always been looking for and never knew I wanted? To have my pressure cooker finally explode, flinging its contents against the wall? To have a man so overtaken by harsh passions that he'd let loose all his self-control and force me to lose mine?

I'd always gone after men with a certain degree of cool determination. I'd met men halfway, often leading them to me through the bedroom door. Had I really wanted to be somebody's prehistoric bitch? Caught by the hair and dragged off to a cave, to be brutalized and damn near destroyed?

"It's not that bad, Johnny. It looks a lot worse than it is."

"Not that bad? Cinnamon, you were raped, for God's sake . . . weren't you?"

I licked my dry lips, then nodded.

"Yes . . . but for some reason I liked it. I don't know why."

Johnny frowned down at me, lifting the frayed edges of my fetters.

"What have you been playing here? Some kind of sick sado-masochistic game?"

I shook my head. It wasn't as simple as that. It wasn't just the pain, the punishment. It was something else, something I could barely recognize. Something about paddling upstream against a relentless current, only to be hurled downstream into the cascade.

It was the ultimate guilty bliss. I was not responsible for the berry bursting between my legs and bleeding into every cell. I hadn't plunged to my downfall, I'd been dragged there. I had finally hit bottom. Who would have known the pit would be filled with such rapture? Who would have expected to find Heaven sizzling on the spit of Hades?

"What do we do now?" Johnny wanted to know. He had started again to untie the scarves at my ankles.

I couldn't look at him, couldn't stand the accusation flashing like sparklers in the depths of his eyes. I couldn't face his contempt. I had to turn my face away to tell him.

"I want some more."

"This is pitiful, Cinnamon. You deserve better than this."

"Look who's talking," I hissed, pushing back the velvet glove of vulnerability to show I still had steel underneath. "Don't give me that holier-than-thou shit when you've been the same kind of whore I am. I don't give a damn about deserve, Hot Johnny. I want what I want . . . *now*."

What started out as a demand had ended as a plea. He narrowed his eyes, pursed his lips, hesitated for a second. Then he dropped the edges of the silk scarf he'd been unknotting and zipped down his pants in one rapid motion. He never even bothered to take them off. He presented himself nearly flaccid, stimulated an erection with a few efficient hand strokes. Stopped, sighed, straddled me.

He never said a word during the entire act. No kisses, no sweet nothings whispered, no exquisite ecstasies lavished, none of the Kama Sutra secrets he boasted of knowing were luxuriated upon me that afternoon.

I'd had so many men by then, I could hardly count them all. Yet each had left his calling card, his specific imprint on my skin. Each had brought something slightly different to the lovemaking experience.

Up until the night before Long Tall Willie had always been a meat-and-potatoes kind of lover. He didn't believe much in foreplay, no stirring up the pot of passion. He wanted to heat it up quickly, gobble it down in big bites. To get down to the nitty-gritty in the shortest amount of time. No appetizers, no desserts.

But hell hath no fury like a man scorned. His dull imagination had been sharpened on the anvil of rejection. The fires of desperation had forged his indolence into a sword. He'd whipped it from the sheath and plunged it to the hilt. He'd been insane, insatiable as a wolf that night. Almost crazed with pent-up passion. He'd been like one confined for years in solitary, and woe be unto the one bent to fetch the fallen soap.

Long Tall Willie had seemed almost as helpless as I was. The dragon between his legs repeatedly spat liquid fire but kept rising to rear its swollen head. He'd mounted me savagely. Again and again and again throughout the night. Who would have thought that skinny man had so much semen in him?

You could tell much about the psyche of a man by the way he handled his business in bed. Because every single one of them had a point to prove.

Some men wielded their organs like a club, others like a paintbrush. Some were hunters, looking for another trophy to mount on the wall. Some were obsessed with variation, always looking for a new position. Others never strayed far from the tried and true; if it ain't broke, don't fix it.

Some were selfish, interested only in their own satisfaction. Others were scorekeepers, obsessed with the number of orgasms they thought they were producing in me. Those kind of players always held something back, watching me and measuring my response.

Some loved me more as a status symbol, worshiping my pale skin. One man was so wrapped up in the slick texture of my hair, he fucked it instead of me.

Johnny was destined to be among many firsts in my life. The first man who had ever made love to me on the telephone. And the only man who'd ever screwed me with such doleful detachment. Like a condemned prisoner stepping up to his sentence.

There was no pleasure in the grim set of his face. There were no sighs and moans, just an occasional *ummph* like a man working on the chain gang. Was that a weary tear lodged in the corner of one green-flecked eye as he pumped away? Or was it just a drop of sweat dripping from his brow?

When he finally rolled off me, I wasn't even sure that he'd come. I know that I hadn't. I didn't even have the heart to fake it. If you can't take the heat, stay out of the kitchen. The only rockets bursting were the ones being fired off outside my bedroom window. Nothing had combusted in that sweltering bedroom. Not even the smoldering sparks of the depravity Long Tall Willie had inflicted upon me the night before.

Hot Johnny's head plopped next to mine on the pillow, curly and sandy like my own. He puckered his lips in contemplation, then propelled himself out of bed. I realized then that I only knew his lips from observation, from watching them across the room at the Sexual Addicts Anonymous meetings. I had never felt them pressed against mine.

I had seen that mouth pursed in seriousness, lecturing me about the presence of some deadly strain of virus they were just finding out about. I'd linger in the lusciousness of his lips and barely hear his warning. So now he had finally fucked me. Taken me up on my standing offer of a free lunch when there was nothing but leftovers on the plate. But in the year I'd known him, Johnny had never even kissed me.

Go figure. He was way too complicated to understand. Even for me, with my advanced degree in fuckology. Maybe Hot Johnny wasn't so hot after all; maybe he talked a better game than he delivered. Maybe it was an ego thing. The arrogance, the conceit he freely admitted as a character flaw.

It could have been competition too, a kind of Betty Crocker fuck-off. Maybe he wanted to see if he could come behind another man and make the earth move on the same mattress. Or maybe it was the gigolo I'd sensed in him all along, delivering the deal to the letter of the law.

Maybe it was his way of taking me down a peg or two. If I was going to bring it to him like a whore, he was going to take it like a john. Or maybe he was just offering a mercy fuck by a recovering sex addict. Maybe he'd given up the idea of rescuing me, realizing there was nothing worthwhile left to salvage. Maybe he really believed himself to be my brother.

I looked down with faint interest as he stood, stuffing his johnson back into his drawers. Even in its limp condition it was long and yellow like him, the pigment at the tip matching his petal-red lips. I would have remarked upon the resemblance but hesitated to break the hush.

"The Star-Spangled Banner" was playing faintly somewhere, probably another apartment. There was no other sound in the room but the zipping of his pants, the silken swish of scarves untying, the padding of his footsteps to the door, the firm sound of it closing behind him as he walked out of my life.

I sat up in bed. Stretched my stiff muscles. Rubbed my raw ankles and wrists. Went to the washroom to empty my bladder. Didn't even bother to shower. I wanted it fresh and funky for him. Pulled down my shirt. Pulled up my pants. Put on my shoes. And went out in the streets to look for Long Tall Willie.

Yes, Johnny had befriended me, the only man on earth who could claim that dubious distinction. He cared about me, had tried in his own bumbling way to save me from my addiction. But that and a quarter will get you a cup of coffee. It wouldn't put no meals on my table, no BMWs in my garage.

Maybe if Hot Johnny had gotten to me before Willie did. If he had come to me the morning after he'd made me come on the phone. If he had touched me with the fullness of his sweet red lips, a brown-skinned Prince Charming. If he had kissed me, only once, he might have been the man to awaken me. And maybe that would have been the time.

If Long Tall Willie's touch triggered the exquisite wiring that brought pleasure and pain, then Johnny's was a more deliberate laying on of hands. He created a hothouse where my nature bloomed, slow and languid like an orchid. With him it wasn't about the act so much as the suggestion.

Johnny was my teacher. He taught me how to slow-hand dance. I had been snatching at sex like a greedy child. With Johnny I learned to savor the slow buildup of desire. With him I was titillated, tantalized. He taught me how to make my pleasure last. With him I learned to fantasize. And sometimes fantasy is more intense than reality.

Until Hot Johnny I had had sex everywhere but in my own head, and with everyone except myself. He had given me one long year of extended foreplay, and neither of us knew it. He was the one who primed the pump, who slow-roasted my pepper until it was so hot that it finally burst open. Long Tall Willie just happened upon the right place at the right time. But you know what they say. First come, first served.

I'd been waiting all my life for the man with the Roman candle to shoot me to the moon. I'd finally found it at the punishing prick of one crazed, crude, harmonica-playing bluesman. His gold tooth and Jheri curl be damned—I wasn't ready to give up the cookie when I'd only taken one bite. Would you? And if the cookie crumbled, you'd better believe I'd be down on my knees licking up every crumb.

When somebody gives you a gemstone smeared in shit, you don't throw it in the toilet. Hell, no. You clean it off, you polish it until it sparkles. You take that sucker and strut it like crown jewels if you can pull it off.

As Pops said, "You've got to go with the feeling." Or like Long Tall Willie sings:

You never miss your water till your well runs dry
Said you never miss that water till the well runs dry
Turn your back on this good loving, babe
Better hang down your head and cry.

My jaw still aches when I chew steak. When Long Tall Willie is out on the road he'll sometimes call me twenty times a day. If a man studies the sway of my hips too long, I catch Willie's suspicious eye. I note the warning lift of a shaggy brow. I know for a fact that Willie hasn't gotten rid of that gun; he still periodically polishes the curlicues.

I close my eyes and imagine the magic of Johnny's lips moving over me. A tantalizing fantasy, a nut on the sundae of that day's slow-hand dance. I sigh, roll over in bed, and find myself picking up the telephone.

I don't call the TV news hotline where Johnny aims to charm people out of I don't know what—their blood, their bone marrow, their hard-earned bucks. Something about a sick baby needs an operation. There had to be a con in it somewhere. I wasn't looking for a phone sex fix, nor thinking of a face-to-face. No, buddy. I wasn't about to give up my satisfaction nor mess with my meal ticket. Not for all the tea in China, nor the uncertain charms of another man's lickin' stick. But I knew someone who might.

When you get an unexpected blessing, pass it on. Still throbbing agreeably between my legs, it is with wicked glee that I dial up a girl in the Jackson Park Highlands. I use the term loosely, because Avis Jones is no spring chicken. Hell, that hussy's a good ten years older than I am, and not nearly as well preserved. But then, I haven't had any babies to stretch my body out of shape and crease my face with worry marks.

I met Avis nearly a decade ago when she shot the cover photo for Long Tall Willie's *Treat 'Em Rough and Make 'Em Like It*. I don't know what those two were smoking. Willie needs to be kicked in the dick for such an atrocity. Avis ought to be stripped naked and whipped as an accessory to the fact. Willie's just an oaf who stumbled into the big time, but Miss Sophisticated should have known better. Had my man decked out in the most ridiculous Halloween getup, I'm ashamed to show the shit to people.

Get this: a full-length shot of a rangy old fool in a metallic red pimp suit, long pointed tail dragging the ground, horns jutting out of a Jheri-curled head, grin stretched to show a shiny gold tooth enhanced by a cartoon gleam somebody airbrushed on, brandishing a phallic-shaped pitchfork like he's threatening to jab somebody with it.

Had the nerve to dedicate this mess to me, his "sticky-sweet Cinnamon bun." Putting our bedroom business on Front Street for all the world to see. I told you the man had no class. Willie's in Memphis right now recording *Long Arm of the Law*. Heaven help us.

But I was telling you about that photographer who showed my husband's ass in public. I'd never forgiven her for that. Maybe there was a way I could return the favor at last.

When I was visiting her studio one day with Willie, I stumbled on an old snapshot turned over in a frame on her rolltop desk. I never said anything at the time, but I looked around and put two and two together. I knew one day that opportunity would knock.

Guard your door and pour out your pot likker, Avis Ransom Jones. Hot Johnny's back in town with a sad story, a new mustache, the same blood-red lips and foot-long lickin' stick.

Miz Jones

We did it to and for each other

I'd been wanting a baby so long I'd almost gotten used to the morning ritual of taking my baseline temperature, the monthly futility of trying to pray my period away. Or, when it came a day late, rushing to the neighborhood drugstore for a home pregnancy test.

I had nearly convinced myself how lucky I was to reach thirty-six without a stretch mark to my frame, my hourglass figure still intact. I feigned irritation at the antics of small children, passed up invitations to coochie-coo somebody's mewling newborn.

"What biological clock?" I said brazenly to my girlfriends, some of whom were already grandmothers at my age. "I don't hear nothing ticking."

I was so busy mastering the fine art of denial, I hardly recognized the baby when it arrived, six feet tall and nearly grown. If I noticed him at all, it was in the offhand fashion an adult regards a lanky kid with a perpetual basketball underarm. You know that ungainly stage some boys grow through, with body parts developing out of sync? That was Johnny when I met him. A man's height, but a smooth, hairless face. Hands and feet flopping two sizes too big for his body, like paws on a German shepherd puppy.

We'd been waiting at the elevator the day they moved in. The door slid open and there they stood, surrounded by a sparse collection of battered belongings: mismatched kitchen chairs, a mattress and box spring, half a sectional sofa, several worn-out suitcases. Johnny stood calm in the midst of the chaos, twirling not one but two basketballs in his open palms. Even then he stood a head taller than his father. *That boy handles those balls like he's got the sun and the moon in his hands,* I remember thinking.

"Welcome to the building," Beau called out heartily. No sooner had we stepped into the next car and the doors closed than his cheery tone turned sour: "Section Eight. These welfare niggas 'bout to overrun the building."

Still, Beau was the one who initiated contact. He found out soon enough that Johnny was a high school basketball star. In the magnanimous manner he reserved for those he considered beneath him, he'd slap him five after a good game, play armchair coach to his skyhook technique, or invite him in to watch sports on a Sunday afternoon when he had nothing better to do.

He'd bulldoze any comment or comeback Johnny might make. "Beau knows, young blood. Former ballplayer my own self, college athletic coach. I ain't trying to rule you, just trying to school you."

If Beau was cast as big buddy, I soon realized I was the secret schoolboy crush. When my husband was around, Johnny studiously ignored me. When Beau left the room, he would flash a sidelong grin in my direction.

"Li'l Miz Jones. Foxy to the bone."

An artless adolescent playing dirty old man. I flirted right back.

"Hey, good-looking. What you got cooking?"

With his sweetness and boyish charm, Johnny was the goodwill ambassador of the family. His daddy always struck me as a shadowy figure lurking in the background of his life. I still have trouble remembering his name, something with a *J*. Was it Joe? James? Or maybe John senior?

They were a strange pair, those two. You'd never have guessed they were even related. Johnny was tall, brown, and straight with a grade of sandy brown hair just a shade too nappy to be what some of us still refer to as "good." And those curious chameleon eyes some black folks have, the kind that seem to take on the coloring of their surroundings; golden in the sunlight, green in the shadows. And, I would eventually discover, gunmetal gray in the light of the moon.

I'll never know where Johnny got his charm. Maybe from the mother who was missing in action. That daddy of his had a decidedly absent quality. Oh, he was there, all right. But even in his presence it was easy to forget he was around.

I always ran into him in the elevator, where he'd be crunched back into the farthest corner, like he wanted to disappear into it. He was so slouchy and stoop-shouldered, you had to bite your tongue to keep from shouting, "Straighten up, man!" Sometimes I'd catch him glancing up at his son with mild bewilderment.

How come this boy towers above me so? his dazed expression seemed to wonder.

I nicknamed him "The Little Man Who Wasn't There." What little there was of him was swallowed right up by the threadbare blue security guard's uniform he usually wore. A matching visored cap just a shade too big would be pulled down over his eyes. He looked like a kid wearing his father's clothes. The Little Man Who Wasn't There never appeared to be either stone sober or sloppy drunk, just somewhere in between.

I can remember him looking me in the eye on only one occasion. We'd generally avert our glances, mumble the obligatory "good morning" or "good evening" when we ran into each other on the elevator. But that particular afternoon we had our one and only sustained conversation.

I had gotten dressed up that afternoon. Well, for me it was dressed up: my blue-suited, ascotted, plain-pumped interview outfit. A row of gold buttons on the double-breasted jacket made it look the feminine version of the security guard's uniform Little Man wore.

This was shortly before I got an agent to do the dirty work—one fast-talking little black woman with twin pigtails and a headband who calls herself Apache. Having to sell myself was the thing I hated most about being a freelance photographer. I was lugging work around town, trying to peddle my wares to textbook publishers, ad agencies, and anyone else who'd give me the time of day.

This particular afternoon I was off to show my portfolio to a prospective client, I forget whom. As it was, I hadn't been sure what kind of work to present. So I'd brought along practically every print I'd ever shot in a huge portfolio. I'd also tucked two carousels of slides under my arm and slung a big leather bag across my shoulder. I was going to bowl them over with abundance, I suppose.

I was fumbling, trying to lock the door with all that stuff in my arms. Johnny's daddy shuffled down the hall and asked if I needed any help.

"As a matter of fact," I sighed, "could you hold these for a minute?"

I gave him the two carousel boxes to hold while I locked the door. He stood there waiting patiently, weaving slightly. You see, on this occasion the man was stone drunk. It was the first and last time I would ever see him in such a condition.

I made a move to take back the boxes when I'd finished, but he held on tight.

"Naw, thanks," he slurred. "I'm a gennilmun. A gennilmun always holds a lady's packages. Thas what I teaches my son. I say, 'Johnny. Always hold a lady's packages.' "

I must have appeared disbelieving, because he shook his head vehemently.

"I ain't lying."

It took forever for the elevator to come. When it finally did, we were the only passengers on it. The man didn't take his customary position in the farthest corner. Instead, alcohol-emboldened, he appointed himself elevator operator.

"What floor you want?" His unsteady hand wavered across the panel of self-service buttons.

"Oh. First floor."

"Hey, me too! How 'bout that? Now, lemme see here." He stood there, boxes clutched to his chest and peered blearily at the numbers on the buttons. After what seemed an eternity, he finally found the one that spelled *Lobby* in big white letters. "First floor, coming up. All-1-1 the way down!"

As we descended I stared straight ahead. He stared straight at me.

"What," he hiccuped, "what you got in all these here boxes?"

"It's my work," I answered shortly, thinking irritably, *And what's it to you, you nosy drunk man?*

He continued to stare.

"Hey, guess what?" He perked up suddenly.

I didn't answer.

"I bet I know what you is."

"Do you?" I was silently bemoaning slow elevators in high-rise buildings.

"I bet you a schoolteacher."

"No," I said shortly, refusing to elaborate.

"You looks just like a schoolteacher to me," he stubbornly insisted.

I suspect that in the profoundly drunken state, misinformation entering the brain gets fixed there. I don't know that for a fact, but I suspect it to be true. Because the next time it happened again, an aggravating déjà vu.

Again I was loaded down with packages, this time groceries. I was waiting for the up elevator rather than the down. It was the end of a very long day. I was tired and testy when father and son walked up. Johnny's loose stride seem to measure one step for each of his father's stumbling two. He was growing into the lankiness of his body by then, though he still had a bit of that adolescent coltishness about him.

"Can I help you with those packages, Miz Jones?"

"No thanks, Johnny. I can manage."

He took them from me anyway. I guess Little Man hadn't been lying. He had certainly taught his son the chivalry of package toting. The elevator arrived and we stepped on, a silent trio on the way to the thirteenth floor. Johnny's daddy broke the stillness from his position in the far corner.

"Miz Jones a schoolteacher. Did you know that, Johnny?"

"I am not a schoolteacher," I hissed between clenched teeth.

Although I rather felt like one at that moment. An exhausted school-teacher. I had done an afternoon photo shoot with a bunch of unruly preschoolers. "Miz Jones . . . Miz Jones . . . Miz Jones" still echoed in my ears, like the chirping of baby birds.

Then I had to swing by the supermarket for the weekend shopping. It seemed that each aisle held some taunting reminder of my mother-lessness. Disposable diapers. Baby formula. Teething rings. And the real thing on more than one occasion.

My attention had been caught by one cute toddler with a thousand braids, a different-colored barrette bobbing at the end of each one. A girl in tight jeans, young enough to be my daughter, must have had enough time to plait each braid on that tiny head. Maybe that task de-pleted her reserves of patience. Maybe the child's appearance counted more than her contentment. At that moment the young mother simply couldn't be bothered with the baby who toddled behind her with out-stretched arms, whimpering to be held.

"Girl, I ain't thinking about carrying your heavy ass," the girl warned with an upraised palm. "Don't make me have to whup you up in this store."

I had to quell a sudden impulse to scoop the crying child into my arms and run off with her.

Some people don't deserve the children they have, I thought peevishly.

Yet another stone to be dumped upon the heap of frustration I car-ried that day. My body was a field that refused to bear fruit, no matter how much seed was planted. The world was conspiring to flaunt that fact in my face. I was mad at myself for succumbing to self-pity. I was mad at the girl in the supermarket for not cherishing the precious baby she'd been blessed with. Now here was the last straw: Little Man and his incomprehension that a sister in a suit could be something other than a schoolteacher.

"I am a photographer. A professional photographer."

A pause.

"Well. You sure looks like a schoolteacher."

So he was going to make me be one. It seemed that everyone these days was trying to make me be something I wasn't.

My best friend called me a codependent, said I needed psychotherapy like nobody's business. My agent wanted me to concentrate on commercial work, because the arty stuff I did was fine in my spare time "but it ain't going to pay no bills." Beau didn't even want me doing that. He was pressuring me to quit work altogether and become a full-time wife and mother, like his own sainted "Muh Dear" down in Mobile. Yet he was too busy brooding over the faded glory of his ballplaying days to handle the balls that would make a mother out of me, if you know what I mean. And now Little Man was trying to make me be a schoolteacher on top of it? That did it.

I unconsciously assumed my fighting stance—head tossed back, legs akimbo, a hand on each hip. Like a time bomb going off, I was set to release the tension I'd squashed down all day. But Johnny jumped in, a deft referee.

"She sure don't look like none of my teachers, Daddy Joe."

"She don't, huh?"

"Li'l Miz Jones, foxy to the bone? Shoot, I wish my teachers did look that good. I'd be getting A's in every class."

His clumsy compliment fell on deaf ears. I hadn't the heart to come up with my customary comeback. Silence followed us out of the elevator and down the hallway. I stopped at my door and held out my hands for the bags. Johnny shook his head stubbornly.

"I'll bring them in. They kind of heavy for a little something like you."

His daddy shuffled down the hallway to their apartment. Johnny followed me into mine. He held the door open for me, effortlessly hefting onto one arm the grocery bags that had my upper arms aching all the way home. I absently noticed lean muscles rippling along his arms as he wielded the weight. Physical strength was one of the traits I most admired in a man. Don't ask me why. Maybe it was because I had always been so puny myself.

"You'll have to excuse him," he said confidentially, like a parent apologizing for the antics of a wayward child. "He just says the first thing that pops into his head."

"Mmm-hmm," I murmured, feeling around for the entryway lights. The apartment was uncharacteristically dark.

"Y'all sure do have a nice place here." His eyes glinted gray in the darkness, squinting at the huddled shapes of plants, bookcases, and the heavy Mediterranean furniture Beau had insisted on buying the moment he'd gotten back on his feet. I always thought its massiveness was more suited to a medieval palace than a one-bedroom apartment.

"Mmm-hmm," I repeated absently. Johnny always said that whenever he came into our apartment. I used to think he was just being polite.

"You can drop those bags anywhere," I told him, fishing around for my change purse.

"Don't worry, I'll take them on into the kitchen." A regular Sir Walter Raleigh of the supermarket. He must have been a delivery boy as a kid.

"All right. You know where it is."

I kicked off my shoes, padded into the living room, and switched on the lamp, about to plop down on the couch. When the light came on I saw that Beau was sitting right in the spot I was about to collapse into.

"Oh, hi. What you doing sitting there in the dark?"

I could tell from his expression that he was spoiling for a fight.

"Sitting up here hungry." He glowered. "A man works hard all day, can't even come home to a hot meal. Wife out running the streets doing God knows what with the devil knows who."

"I was not running the streets," I insisted, trying to think if there was something in those grocery bags I could throw in the microwave for a quick meal. "I was working just as hard as you. The shoot ran overtime, okay?"

Beau was the possessive type. Always had been. I used to think it was because he was so crazy about me. Now I know he was just plain crazy.

"If you can't take care of your house and your husband, then you don't need to be out there working." Beau started singing his old familiar song. "As nasty as this house is and as little time as you spend in it, I might as well not have no wife."

"Beau." God, I hated to hear myself saying his name that way, somewhere between a whine and a plea. I was usually able to tune out his nagging. But I was so bone weary, so soul sick. "Let's not get into this right now."

"Don't get into it?" he growled. "We already into it, woman. You stay out in the streets, running backwards and forwards to these goddamn doctors. Maybe if you'd slow your little ass down and act like a woman's supposed to, you wouldn't be needing to run to the doctor."

"Beau." My head was pounding, swelling. *Miz Jones. Miz Jones. Miz Jones.* It seemed ready to explode. The blue-and-gray Mexican pottery ashtray we'd bought on our honeymoon was crouched invitingly on the coffee table. Beckoning to me. I was in a dangerous mood. "Leave me alone."

"Leave you alone. I'll leave your ass alone, all right." He rose from the couch, clenching his fists. Didn't I tell you he was spoiling for a fight? "Just like you need to leave these niggas in the streets alone. Just like you need to leave these know-nothing doctors alone. You act like a woman instead of a goddamn man, maybe you'd be able to make a goddamn baby."

My hand was stretching for that ashtray some peasant woman in the village of Zihuatanejo had painstakingly crafted. And I don't even smoke. Beau should be eternally grateful to Johnny Wright. The boy probably saved his life that evening.

"Miz Jones," his voice called out, a deeper version of the infantile chirping I still heard in my head. I turned to see him standing just behind me. He was calling me, but staring at Beau. His eyes were glinting like green glass. He too was clenching his fists.

"Oh, I'm sorry, baby." All the aggression rushed right out of me. I was my mother now, backing out of a confrontation with a handy excuse. *Leave me be, Malcolm. I got these babies to see about.* Retreating from the battleground to the kitchen. The sight of this frightened teenager looking ready to deck my 250-pound husband brought out the misplaced mother in me.

"I forgot all about you. Here, let me get my purse."

I headed back to the entryway, where I'd dropped it. After a moment's hesitation, Johnny followed.

"Here you go, Johnny. And thanks." I grabbed the first thing I saw and handed it to him, a five-dollar bill. He ignored it.

His changeable eyes looked down at me, now as soft and gray as a kitten's. His brow was creased with worry.

"You gonna be all right, Miz Jones?"

"Of course I am."

"Are you sure?" Somebody caring. That was the balm I'd been needing all day. Just a dab of concern to rub into the aching places, to soothe the hurt and pent-up frustration. That was all.

Touched, I leaned up and kissed his cheek.

"I said I was going to be all right. Now go on home before your daddy starts wondering what happened to you." I crammed the five into his hand and pushed him gently toward the door.

He shoved it absently into his jeans pocket, flashed a worried glance back at me.

"If you need me, you know where to find me."

And then he was gone.

"What was that little yella nigga doing in my house?" Beau shouted from the living room.

"Carrying in the groceries," I said tiredly, going into the kitchen to unpack them.

Beau stomped back into the bedroom, still shouting. "Don't be letting these ghetto niggas in my house, hear?"

"Don't be ridiculous, Beau. You've had Johnny in here a dozen times yourself. He's just a kid."

"A little hoodlum," Beau barked. He came into the kitchen smelling like English Leather and wearing what I later learned to call his whore-hopping outfit: dark shades, pointy-toed shoes, brown leather bomber jacket.

"While you out there running the streets night and day, these ghetto niggas casing out the joint, getting ready to rob us blind."

My hand closed spasmodically around a plastic-wrapped package of meat.

"*Beau,*" I sighed into the freezer. My breath steamed back at me. "Don't be bringing that boy into this. You're just trying to pick a fight and you're grasping at straws."

"Straws? I don't need no straws, woman. What I'm supposed to think when my wife is out in the streets all day long?"

"*Beau.*" I repeated his name for the umpteenth time. Settled the packages of meat into tidy little rows in the freezer. The action seemed to calm my nerves. "When you met me, I was working. When you married me, I was working. What makes you think I'm supposed to stop working now?"

"That's right, rub it in," Beau shouted, slamming the freezer door, barely missing my knuckles. "Just because you had to support the two of us when we first hooked up, you ain't gonna never let me forget it. Is you?"

When Beau got mad his grammar slipped.

"Is I is, or is I ain't your baby?" I teased.

Levity did not help the situation. He brought his enraged face within snarling inches of mine. I felt around for the package of frozen spinach still sitting on the counter. Not much of a weapon, but I'd use it if I had to. I wasn't about to be anybody's battered wife. Yes, he had pushed before. He had shoved. He had shaken. But he had never hit. And that was where I'd drawn the line. I was my mother's daughter, but not that much. I wasn't going to sit still for a beating.

"Hell naw, you ain't my baby," Beau barked back at me. "You ain't shit."

He stomped to the front door in his whore-hopping uniform and didn't come back until Sunday morning.

That was what? Two years ago? My memories of that period are so similar that they all tend to blur. You'd hardly believe how happy we once were.

Did you know I had won Beau away from that TV weather woman? You know, the one who wears those false eyelashes a foot long. Beau was playing pro ball back then and he was a hot property. Beauregard Demetrius Jones. Big and tall and husky, finest man on the team.

"That man's too good-looking to let somebody pound him into a pulp," I told Serene. Little did I know that the very pulp pounding that put his handsome face on the sports page—with my photo credit attached—would soon come to a screeching halt.

I was taking pictures for a little suburban rag, shooting everything from PTA meetings to professional sports. That was how we met. He was soft-spoken and polite; didn't even try anything until our fourth date.

It wasn't just his money and his fame and his looks. He had this smile, a smile to just melt your heart. He was fresh from Alabama, very sweet and just a little shy. The kind of man to snatch you up easy as a child and cradle you in those big, strong, steady arms. Like I said before, physical strength was something I admired in a man.

I wanted him from the moment I saw him, but didn't let him in on it. Men like that, with women from eight to eighty hanging on them, you've got to strategize. I won him away from Wanda Weathergirl with a carefully fostered I-don't-care attitude. Played hard to get for all I was worth. Made him jealous of a boyfriend who didn't even exist. Maybe that's what set the stage for his possessive entitlement.

Beau was injured in his third season, right before his contract came up for negotiation. His money and fame were gone in a minute. But I still loved him. I married him, didn't I? I'd spent the past ten years trying to have his baby, hadn't I?

You know, I even used to find his jealousy flattering. Until I found out why it's called insane jealousy.

Beau finally found a job coaching community college sports. I stayed home that first day and did the domestic routine. Cooked a gourmet dinner and shampooed the carpets. Mopped the kitchen and bathroom with Beau's favorite concentrated pine cleaner that had such an antiseptic stink, anybody within miles had to know the floors were clean. I lifted the lid, dumped the dirty water in the toilet, and was just putting the bucket away when I heard his key in the lock.

I ran to meet him, standing on tiptoe to plant a welcome-home kiss on the lips, like somebody's Stepford wife. Except that he turned his face away and my kiss slid across his stubble-roughened cheek. My puckered lips could feel his jaw working—with anger or fatigue, I couldn't tell which.

"Hey, baby. You have a good day?"

"Yeah. Why shouldn't I?" He threw his briefcase on the couch and went into the bathroom.

I know what it is now, the psychological term for it. Serene calls it vertical hostility. I call it pecking-order oppression. Somebody out there kicks your ass. You come home and kick the ass of the person underneath you. The boss kicks the husband. The husband kicks the wife. The wife kicks the kids. The kids kick the dog. The dog kicks the cat. And the cheese stands alone. But see, I didn't recognize it back then. I just knew he was in a bad mood and somehow I felt responsible. Maybe the house wasn't clean enough.

"Avis, come in here!" Beau hollered from the bathroom.

He was in his classic pissing pose: leaning back slightly so he could watch himself, hefting big boy between thumb and trigger finger like a Wild West gunslinger. I still made a point of oohing and ahhing over his black Derringer, even though by then I'd began to suspect it was shooting blanks. Beau stood frowning at the toilet he pissed in.

"Who you had in here today?"

"What do you mean?" I was confused and dizzy, the pine fumes still smarting in my eyes. "There hasn't been anybody here but me."

"You're lying, woman. You had a man in here."

"And you're crazy," I scoffed. "What makes you think a man was here?"

He pointed to the raised toilet seat.

"That's how I met the muthafucka when I walked in. Since when did you learn to pee standing up?"

See, that's why they call it insane jealousy. Beau had a textbook case of it. I should have known right then that a quarrel over a raised toilet seat, escalating as the man shakes excess drops from his dick, does not bode well for the future. But I refused to recognize the warning signs.

Anyway, he's gone now. The night Johnny carried the groceries in wasn't the end of our marriage. It unraveled steadily over the next year and only came to the end of the line a month before that fateful day. I shouldn't have been surprised. I guess I wasn't.

You know my friend Serene the hoodoo head doctor? I'm not a patient of hers, but she's determined to make me one. She was the one who warned me away from Beau in the first place. If I don't know Dr. Weaver, nobody does; she had to practically bite her tongue to keep from telling me "I told you so."

"You're grieving," she said to me across the shiny surface of her big mahogany desk. Serene was even shorter than me. She'd bought that desk to give herself an air of authority, but sitting behind it made her look as tiny as a child.

"Your marriage is over and you're grieving. Accept it."

"Accept what?" I had taken my I-don't-care attitude out of mothballs and put it back on. I paced the room, fidgeting with the light meter. The angle of the corner cast shadows across Serene's face, the dark wood sucking up light like a sponge. Yet she insisted on being photographed behind that massive desk. "What, do I look like grieving? I'm glad to see the end of that man. The way I've been suffering all these years? I'd sooner grieve getting over the Hong Kong flu."

Serene smiled broadly, showing her braces. If the woman was so determined to look authoritative, why'd she let them put those braces in her mouth? They made her look about thirteen.

"Well, the operation was a success." Her braces glinted at me. "But the patient died."

"Don't start with me. I'm not in the mood for no psychiatric humor. Just come on out with it. And don't grin unless you want all that metal to show."

"But it's true. Divorce is like amputation."

"Lord, here you go," I muttered, snapping her with her finger pointed at the lens, the image like an Uncle Sam Wants You poster.

"You've got to learn to live with phantom pain. It hurts where the limb used to be, even though gangrene has set in and cutting it off saves your life. It hurts where the limb used to be."

"All right, then. I'm grieving. I'm grieving. Now shut up so I can take this shot."

Serene was right, though. I missed the bastard. Not his suspicions, his arguments, his accusations. But his presence. His smell. His bad habits. The space in my life he occupied for ten years.

I sat around the house in a blue funk. On days I didn't have to work, I wore pajamas 24/7. Didn't brush my teeth or comb my hair. Didn't cook. Didn't eat. Sipped away at endless mugs of Tia Maria, the last of a case we'd brought back from a miserable vacation in Jamaica two years ago. I drank it mixed with coffee. The coffee kept me awake. The booze kept me buzzed.

I did that scene for a solid month. Finished the case of Tia Maria and thought about getting another one. Got up one morning and took a good look at myself in the bathroom mirror. I looked like death sucking on a neckbone.

I ran a bath and got out my cosmetics case. Somewhere in this big city there was a nice somebody who might want me. I didn't know how to find him, didn't even know where to look. But at least I could be looking presentable when he arrived.

And that is where Johnny stepped in.

All right, now. Don't look so shocked and disgusted. I know it sounds appalling. A thirty-eight-year-old woman and a teenage boy. I know you're sitting there shaking your head. "Damn. Avis Ransom Jones must have got real hard up when Beau walked out on her."

But it's not like that. Not like that at all.

First of all, let's get one thing straight. Beau didn't leave me, I put him out. I got fed up with all the fights and womanizing. I should have listened to Serene in the first place.

She told me I should never have married him. Said I wasn't looking for a mate, but using Beau "to work out abandonment issues with your wife-battering, womanizing father." I should never have told Serene so much about my childhood. She was in medical school back then, using all her friends as guinea pigs for her textbook theories. Besides, I was in love.

"In love with your father," Serene said smugly.

Well, so far Serene hasn't found out about Johnny. I know she'd really Freud out on this one. She'd swear I was looking for the son I never had. That I was trying to replace the baby I aborted back in college, the cast-off life I believe I am now paying through the womb for. God, has it been that long? I was nineteen, the same age as Johnny was then. My unborn baby would have been nineteen too, probably a freshman in college. Just like I was when I got pregnant the first time I dropped my drawers.

What is that huge bird that just went fluttering by the window? Did you see it? It's probably an overfed seagull. They're venturing farther and farther in from the lake these days. I saw one the other day screeching from a lamppost on Stony Island. But I swear to you, this one looked almost like a chicken flapping by the thirteenth-story window. Chickens coming home to roost. Lost and whirling in the windy heights.

Okay, I've stalled long enough. Here's the story.

That day about a month after Beau had gone, the day I came back from the living dead, was the day the whole thing started. I thought work would be both healing and distracting. I went across to the lakefront to finish a roll of film, spent half the day in the darkroom developing and printing, then went back out to the supermarket to restock my empty refrigerator.

I put a little Cornish hen in the microwave and watched the baby bird rotate for a few minutes. It looked pathetically lonely in there, wings lifted slightly as though ready to take off. It was going to be hard getting back in the habit of cooking for one. I felt myself getting depressed again, so I drew another long, hot bubble bath. I was sitting there soaking when I heard the knock.

I swear, I started not to answer it. I told myself it must be some of those Jehovah's Witnesses selling *Watchtower*. Otherwise why hadn't the unknown knocker buzzed from the lobby? But something weak and irrational in me suggested it might be Beau crawling back to beg my forgiveness. I had already changed the locks.

I ran to the door toweling myself down, afraid he'd leave before I got there.

"Who is it?" I called out.

"Me," a muffled, indistinguishable male voice answered back.

Peering through the peephole, I saw a miniature image in fishbowl effect. Johnny, hands in pocket, leaning against the opposite wall, looking down at his large gym-shoed feet. It would have made an interesting shot.

But I was suddenly pissed, peevish with disappointment. I slipped on the burglar chain and cracked the door an inch, thinking he'd come to watch Sunday sports with Beau. I snapped at him that moment; I'm almost sure of it.

"What is it, Johnny? Beau's not in, and I'm in the tub."

His head came up. Eyes tired and apologetic.

"Sorry, Miz Jones. I got kinda locked out. Was wondering if I could use your phone."

I hesitated, then took off the chain.

"Come on in. But give me a second. I'm not dressed."

I dashed to my room and slipped on a bathrobe. When I came back he was standing at the living room window.

"Hey, good-looking." I owed him this one. "What you got cooking?"

The sunset streaming in lit his chameleon eyes a molten gold. There were smudges as dark as bruises beneath them. All my thwarted maternal instincts came rushing out.

"Johnny, what's the matter?" I went over and touched his arm. "You look awful."

He pulled away.

"I'm all right. Where's your phone?"

I stepped back, hands on hips.

"You know good and well where the phone is. Go on in the kitchen. You can pull the door shut if you need a little privacy."

I watched his lean figure slouch into the kitchen, a gym bag slung over his shoulder. No boy as young as Johnny should be walking as wearily as he was.

He pulled the door shut and stayed in a good twenty minutes, talking on the telephone. The timer on my Cornish hen went off, but I didn't want to go in and disturb him. I could hear a steady buzz of anxious murmurs behind the closed door.

He came out looking more weary and defeated than when he went in. I eased in past him.

"Don't go anywhere yet. I'm just checking on my dinner. I'll be along in a minute."

I put the hen on a plate. I microwaved some frozen vegetables and buttered some bread. Not much of a dinner. But I brought it out to him.

"Get it while it's . . ." The rest of the words just died in my mouth.

I wish I could describe it to you. I wish I could put into words what I saw in him. Not in his face, which was turned away from me. It was in the way he held his body. He stood at the window, shoulders hunched. Desolation is the only way to name it. He wore it like a cloak.

"Now, Johnny." I set the plate on the coffee table. "You can't tell me that nothing's wrong."

He didn't move. I walked to the window, to him. Placed a hand gently at the small of his back.

"Johnny, what is it? You didn't have any luck on the phone?"

"No." He shook his head. "Called a couple of my partners. Most of them wasn't in. The others didn't have nowhere for me to stay."

"For you to stay? I don't get it. If you're locked out, why not call your father and get the key from him?"

My eyes followed the line of his vision. Outside on the sidewalk thirteen stories below, a motley collection of belongings was strewn. Mismatched kitchen chairs. A mattress and box spring. Half a sectional sofa. Several worn suitcases. The street scavengers were thickly gathered, pawing through the meager pickings.

"Lord," I sighed. "Looks like somebody got themselves evicted."

"Yeah," Johnny mumbled. "Tell me about it."

I look at his face in the twilight. His young, brown face. Sorrowful, sixty-year-old eyes with blue bruises beneath them. Sunset and sadness leaking out like lost gold.

"Oh, my God." I touched his arm again. "I am so sorry."

He shrugged away and stalked to the couch. He collapsed onto it, long legs sticking out, long arms folded across his chest.

"That old fool." His voice broke with bitterness. "He ain't paid rent in six months and he's been throwing away the eviction notices. How was I supposed to know?"

I went and sat beside him. Took his hand.

"Poor you," I whispered. "Poor us. Just a couple of outcast souls."

"You?" Away from the light, his eyes were hazel again. They wandered the room, measuring its contents. "Y'all ain't about to lose none of this stuff."

He jerked his head in the general direction of the dining room furniture, the outsized buffet, table, and six chairs I'd always hated.

"I wish somebody would come and evict this mess. Besides, there ain't no more 'y'all.' " I don't know what suddenly made me bare my soul to this lean teenager. My predicament now seemed trivial compared to his.

His cough-drop-colored eyes were fixed on me. Anguish turned to anger.

"You mean he left you?"

I shrugged.

"Let's not worry about me right now. Let's worry about you. There's some food on the table."

"He's a fool," Johnny said shortly, pushing the plate away.

We were sitting close, too close. The moment of sympathy that had drawn me there was past, and I really should have moved away. His thigh pressed against mine, lean, hard, and muscular. I was no longer holding his hand. He was gripping mine.

"Johnny, if you need somewhere to stay until . . ." He looked straight at me, his eyes like arrows. Something lurched inside me. I really should have moved away.

Then he was weeping. Not sobbing, not crying. But weeping, as if the pain was stuck somewhere deep inside him, struggling to get out. He made no noise, but his chest quaked. His eyes streamed. Before I knew it I had taken him in my arms. Pulled his not-quite-nappy, not-quite-curly head to my bosom.

"Miz Jones." His voice was breaking through the tears.

"What, baby?" I whispered, stroking his hair. "What is it?"

He didn't answer. His tears pooled against my collarbone, trickled down the cleft between my breasts.

A moment later he was kissing me. Weeping and kissing me. His tears slick against my bosom. His lips tasting the wetness of his own tears. Nuzzling apart the opening of my terry-cloth robe. Latching onto a swollen nipple. Suckling like a hungry child. A ravenous baby bird.

"Johnny." I struggled away, lifting his head from there. "No."

His eyes met mine. Reddened, still wet with tears. His mouth sought mine. Before I realized it he was hungrily sucking kisses from my lips, his blue-jeaned knee nudging my bare ones apart with gentle desperation.

What could I do? What would you have done? Deny him? With his arms wrapped around me like I was his life preserver, how could I?

So it happened. I will not tell you how, though I know you're curious for the details. It's seamy and unseemly. A thirty-eight-year-old female locked in carnal bliss with a boy half her age. Mrs. Robinson in blackface, on the living room couch, no less.

"Poor thing," you're probably telling your friends. "A woman scorned, on the rebound with the first thing walking."

What can I say but that we were a salve for each other's wounded parts?

Johnny spent the night. Johnny spent many nights, but that was the first.

Somewhere in the interim we'd moved to the bedroom Beau and I had shared not one month before. The bedroom was full of oversized

Mediterranean furniture that was a match to the dining room set. I woke up out of sorts, head throbbing with a residual hangover that lingered even though I hadn't drunk a drop the day before. I glanced over at Johnny's sleeping figure and winced.

"Cradle snatcher," I greeted my reflection in the mirror. "Dirty old woman."

Then I thought of Beau and the poetic justice of it all. He had started going with a younger woman, you know. Not quite a teenager, granted. He wouldn't have gone to jail behind it or anything. But much younger than I. Twenty-two, twenty-three perhaps. I'd met the girl. She'd been a visitor to our house before I knew they had a thing going on.

She was tall and wasp-waisted, with a lot of hair. It cascaded around her face and down her back. I couldn't tell whether it was real or not. I know her name wasn't. She'd given herself a ridiculous one. Sparkle. She introduced herself with a decided lisp: "My name is Thparkle."

She couldn't seem to get Beau's name right to save her life. Called him what sounded to me like "Boy."

Boy had lectured me on the night he left. Lectured me as he packed his shorts and socks and whore-hopping clothes.

"A young woman," he proclaimed, "will respect you. A young woman knows how to make a man feel like a man. She ain't grown hard and fixed in her ways. She looks up to you."

"So does a twelve-year-old child," I said nastily, watching him pack. I was delighted to see he was making such a mess of it. He'd always depended upon me to do his packing for him whenever he traveled. I glared at his big, inept hands tossing things helter-skelter into the suitcase.

"If you want unconditional hero worship, then maybe Sparkle's too old for you. Maybe what you need is a teenage virgin."

Little did I know those words would come back to haunt me.

Although technically still a teenager, Johnny obviously hadn't been a virgin in quite some time. Still, he looked young and vulnerable in his sleep, curled into a narrow corner of the king-sized bed. His lean frame took up much less space than Beau's muscle-bound bulk. He slept with a long arm flung over his head, slumber erasing all signs of age from his face. He could have been a very tall twelve-year-old snoring there.

I felt disgusted and ashamed of myself. I stumbled into the kitchen and put on some coffee. My hand was reaching toward the liquor cabinet before I remembered that I'd given up my morning habit of Tia Maria and coffee.

When I got back to the bedroom Johnny was awake. The sleeping cherub was gone. In its place sat a yawning, red-eyed, evil-looking young man with a five o'clock shadow. At least he was old enough to shave, I remember thinking with some relief.

I sat down on the bed with my coffee.

"Want some?" I offered. "You look like you need it."

He shrank away from the steaming mug.

"Yuck. How can you stand that stuff?"

He stalked into the bathroom. I sat sipping my coffee, watching him through the half-open door. He stuck out his tongue and glared at it, then rubbed his whiskered face.

"There's an electric shaver in the cabinet," I suggested.

He slitted his cat eyes at me. I could see them glitter in the semidarkness.

"I am not using his razor."

He slammed the door shut.

"Suit yourself," I said cheerfully. I was somehow comforted that I had a surly young man to look at over the breakfast table rather than an innocent, ravaged angel. I was used to dealing with a cantankerous man.

I was lingering over my second cup of coffee and a slice of dry toast when he came into the kitchen.

The stubble was gone from his chin, so he must have broken down and used Beau's razor after all. He was bare-chested, a light fuzz of sandy hair covering his lean chest. I noticed for the first time a jagged mark running along his right thigh.

He wore the previous night's discarded briefs and looked in a slightly better mood. Those briefs put me in a better mood too, somehow. They made him seem more manly and mature than his nineteen years. Despite the fact that we'd been trying to make a baby, Beau had persisted in his juvenile habit of bikini underwear, worn skintight to cut off the flow of blood to his brain. I slipped a couple of slices of bread into the toaster.

"I guess you're not a coffee drinker. What can I get you to go with your toast?"

He looked around hopefully.

"You got some milk?"

From the mouths of babes! Milk, no less. The childlike request brought back my ill humor.

"There isn't a drop of milk in this house, Johnny Wright. And no Cap'n Crunch to go with it." I slung this over my shoulder as I padded to the counter to freshen my coffee. "Sorry. I know you're a growing boy."

Okay, that was uncalled-for. I was simmering in self-disgust and took it out on him. I quickly got my just desserts.

The next thing I heard was the slide of bare feet across the kitchen floor, a quick, athletic gait. Then long, wiry arms grabbed me from behind. They wrapped my body fiercely, hugging me back against a long, wiry frame.

"You better find me some milk somewhere, Mama," he murmured against my ear. His hands reached under my T-shirt, squeezing the fullness of my breasts in both hands, as if searching out a source of sustenance denied elsewhere. "I'm a growing boy, all right. I'm growing by the minute."

"Yes, I know," I murmured. His mouth moving toward my neck exhaled the scent of baby's breath. "I feel it."

Before I could protest, I found myself being lifted off my feet and maneuvered backward onto the kitchen counter. If he didn't get his milk that morning, it was not for lack of trying.

Long moments later back in the king-sized bed, the name he moaned at the moment of truth was not the one I'm used to hearing. After a decent interval I tackled him on the subject.

"Was it good for you, son?" I breathed in a Marilyn Monroe whisper.

His cat-green gaze slid over to me, a sandy eyebrow lifted.

"Son? That ain't no mother-son action we just did, Miz Jones."

"Then you've got to quit this 'Miz Jones' business. It makes me feel like an old lady. Or one of those schoolteachers your daddy's always accusing me of being."

He sat up abruptly in the bed, his eyes darkening dangerously.

"Don't mention that nigga's name, please."

I watched curiously as he fumbled around in the nightstand drawers.

"What are you looking for?"

"A cigarette."

I was amazed that someone so young had developed the unfortunate habit of smoking after sex.

"I don't think you'll find any, baby. I don't smoke and Beau took all of his with him."

He shrugged.

"That's all right. I need to quit anyway."

He was an entire contradiction, that boy. That man. If he wasn't appearing too young and vulnerable for his stretched-out body, then he was seeming too old and hardened for his years.

It was a good ten years since I'd last had the experience, but I hadn't changed. After spending a night with someone for the first time, I'm always distressed by how little I know about him. It puts me in a panic. Maybe I need to reassure myself that I haven't just slept with the Ripper. I feel seized by the insatiable desire to know every detail of his life, from when he lost his virginity to how many brothers and sisters he had and how he had gotten that scar on his thigh.

Johnny didn't take kindly to my inquisition. When I asked him what he was still doing in high school at the age of nineteen, he answered shortly, "Playing ball." He grew sullen when I asked him about his father. He said "I don't know" a lot. When questioned about his absent mother, he answered, "None of your business." He got mad and tried to leave.

He slipped back into his briefs. He marched into the living room and found his discarded jeans, his shoes and shirt. He slung the unopened gym bag over his shoulder and headed for the front door. I rushed around and blocked it with my full five feet three inches.

"I'm not letting two men walk out on me in less than a month. That's just ridiculous. If you're determined to go, you're going to have to move me."

Beau would have done so without hesitation. Johnny easily could have. But didn't. He looked down at me, bemused and confused. Then he went and sat down on the couch.

"Well, I guess I don't really have nowhere to go."

"Thanks, John," I said acidly. "I'll always cherish those words."

He laughed.

"I really don't want to go anywhere else, Miz Jones . . . Avis. But you need to quit it with this third degree. I got things on my mind."

There was no future in it. How could there be? The relationship was too tipped over, too imbalanced. It wasn't just the number of years that separated us, it was the configuration. It might have been different five years later, if I'd been forty-three and Johnny twenty-four and responsible for himself.

I was well on the road to middle age, while he was just tasting his adulthood. Cramming six wasted years of high school into one last chance and hedging his bets with hopes of a basketball scholarship, Johnny had to give up the big bucks he'd been making flipping burgers at McDonald's. I had to put him on a weekly allowance, for Christ's sake.

He had barely finished high school when he tried to pull an aimless act.

"I've been going to school all my life," he protested whenever I pulled out the college catalogs. Athletic recruiters were crowding my machine with messages he rarely got around to answering. "Let me relax for a minute."

"There will be no relaxing in here," I warned him. "Not so long as I have to bust my butt. It's either school or work for you, young man. Take your pick."

"Damn," he grumbled. "You sound like somebody's bossy old mama."

"I ain't trying to rule you." I found myself repeating Beau's patronizing platitude. "Just trying to school you."

"Former ballplayer my own self," Johnny drawled. "College atha-letic coach, don't you know."

We had a lot of fun mocking bumbling Beau. But I will admit, sometimes there were tears. Sometimes I felt discarded, useless. Tossed aside like Johnny's evicted belongings. Sometimes I felt guilty too.

"I'm sucking up your youth, just like that man sucked up mine." I'd count my gray hairs, frown in the mirror at my laugh lines. "I always thought I'd be married forever. I was supposed to be somebody's wife, somebody's mother. It's too late now. I'm all used up."

"Come here, baby." Johnny pulled me into his young, strong arms. "Li'l Miz Jones, foxy to the bone. Any man would be happy to have you."

"Then why did Beau leave me for somebody else?"

"Because he's a big old country 'bama, ain't got no good sense. As smart a woman as you are, how'd you end up with somebody like that? If you had met me first, you never would have married that doofus."

"Ten years ago," I'd have to remind him, "you were, what? Barely pushing puberty? I'd be up on charges of statutory rape. You'd be one screwed-up little boy."

"Ain't no way a little screwing would have screwed me up. Age ain't nothing but a number, baby. We just would have had more time to make each other happy."

Yes, we made each other happy, even though there was no future in it. But there was joy and happiness and passion and tenderness. Oh, it was sweet as baby's breath while it lasted. And you know what else? It's absolutely true what they say about young men at their sexual prime. Lord, that was a loving man. I won't say what, but Johnny did things to me in bed that no man has ever done before or since. I don't know where he learned it at his young age, but he certainly taught me a trick or two.

We did it to and for each other. I wanted to be his bridge between a desperate past and a promising future. I wasn't trying to rule him, only to school him. I taught him everything from table manners to English grammar, what to wear besides T-shirts and gym shoes on an evening out. He was a willing student.

Johnny tried so hard to be the man he thought I needed. I could slip on my rose-colored glasses and look at him that way. Tall and strong, committed and caring. Growing more charming and handsome with every passing day. But every so often I'd force myself to see him through unfiltered lenses: sitting in the driver's seat of my sedan, holding open the front door of my apartment, paying for dinner on the town with money I'd slipped him at the beginning of the evening.

"Wake up and smell the roses," I'd have to admit. "Your Prince Charming is a boy playing dress-up."

I wasn't trying to buy his love. I was giving him a base of experience to build upon. I knew he wouldn't be with me forever, and I didn't want to see him drifting back into the arms of the streets. God bless the child who's got his own, not to mention the man. Johnny was given more than his share of obstacles in life, and less than his share of opportunities. I was a mature woman who could provide him with some of them.

Do you know he had never been outside of Chicago? Not even so far as Gary, Indiana. For his twenty-first birthday I gave him a surprise, ten days together in the Bahamas. I intended this trip to open a window on the world for him, but I never imagined it would change my life too.

Neither of us got much sun, sand, or sightseeing. Something in the air added an extra dose of passion to an already torrid love affair. Maybe it was the full moon over Nassau. Or maybe we both sensed the end of the line looming. Most of our time together was spent in the hotel room.

If you've been to the Caribbean lately, you may have noticed that some of the more enterprising beach boys come right down to the airport to stake their claim on arriving single women. They check out the clothing, the carriage, the jewelry, calculating the relative risks and benefits. I was approached only once during that vacation. When the brother saw who I was with, he backed away with hands in the air.

"No problem, sistah." He shrugged. "Me see you already get a young one."

I will always remember that last night in Nassau. We shared an opulent seafood dinner, then strolled along the beach hand in hand. Moonlight made the waves shimmer like liquid silver. I slipped off my high heels, testing it up to my ankles.

"Come on in." I scooped up a handful, splashing him. "The water's fine."

"You go ahead." Johnny eased into a semirecline, lounging in the sand. "It looks pretty fine from where I'm sitting."

I pulled the sundress over my head and tossed it to him. Waded in in my underwear. I swam a few strokes, then turned over and floated on my back, watching the moon and remembering how at the end of dinner that evening the waiter had approached with the check, clearly confused. I could see him sizing us up, trying to decide which one had the money to pay.

Who are they to each other? was the question buried in the gaze of nearly everyone we encountered. *Mother and son? Brother and sister? Lover and beloved?*

It was a riddle even I found myself puzzling over. I pulled myself from the suck of the tide, silver drops rolling from my body. I walked to where Hot Johnny lay propped on his elbow, lazing in the sand with my bundled belongings. Looking up at me, he held out a high-heeled sandal.

"Your slipper, m'lady?"

"Why, thank you, my Prince Charming."

I stretched out a foot for him to fit it on. Watched him cradle the ankle, stroke the instep, bring it to his mouth for a lingering caress.

"John the Baptist Wright," I murmured. "I had no idea you were a foot man."

"There's a whole lot, baby," he replied, lightly licking the curve of my big toe, "you don't know about me. Lucky you got a lifetime to learn it."

I sighed. Knowing better, saying nothing. I pulled my foot away, sank onto the sand beside him, and couldn't help thinking of Cinderella.

In the final analysis, that fairy godmother hadn't done much but polish a diamond in the rough. A dose of encouragement, a dash of confidence. The carriage and coachman, the ball gown and glass slippers were really just wardrobe for the outside world. She would ultimately have to sink or swim on her own.

"I am the fairy godmother," I whispered, fiddling with the buckle on his belt.

"What?" Johnny cupped my face in his hand. His eyes glinted gunmetal gray in the light of the full moon. "What did I just hear you say?"

"Ever notice how people look at us?" The waistband fell open; I tugged at his zipper. " 'Who is she and what is she to you?' Well, I'm your fairy godmother."

I reached in and captured the magic wand, watching it transform under my touch.

"You're the fairy godmother, all right," he murmured, a catch in his voice. "The godmother of love."

I know that sex on the beach is a cliché by now, a cocktail ordered with a naughty wink of the eye. But to really make love on Caribbean sands under the unblinking light of the full moon? I can't begin to describe the magic that was made that night. I *was* Johnny's fairy godmother, after all. His teacher and lover, his sister and mentor. And yes, his mother too, those two tender years.

You know Serene went to town on a garbage truck when she found out. Freudian slips and panties to go with it, Oedipus complexes and every neurosis in the book. She has a son, you know. I hope the good hoodoo head doctor with all her theories about "black manhood training" doesn't send that boy to the psychiatrist's couch himself one day:

"I'm raising my Shaka to be a serious, sensitive man. This is going to be one black male who won't come up dogging out our women."

Yet I felt something of that same mother love for Johnny as I watched him come to life. To lap up life, in fact. Eagerly. He was a man becoming. Sensitive and serious and terrible and tender. I knew I wouldn't be around to enjoy it when he harvested the fullness of his manhood. Still, I counted myself lucky to be in on its cultivation. Some young woman was going to get herself a hell of a man.

In the end I had to push my fledgling out of the nest. His wings were ready, and how else would he know he could fly?

I keep a picture from his graduation day. I set up the tripod myself, put the shutter on automatic. He's wearing a cap and gown and we're both smiling, looking not toward the camera, but into each other's eyes. We hold each other by our outstretched hands, a princess and her Prince Charming. It looks just like we're dancing together. Depending on how the light hits that photo, Johnny's eyes seem to gleam green, gold, or gunmetal gray.

Oh, by the way, if you ever run into Beauregard Demetrius Jones, you can tell him something for me. In the two years I was with Johnny I learned something that a decade of marriage, thousands of dollars, and a dozen doctors never discovered.

It wasn't me who couldn't make a baby. It was him.

Jonavis

He's the only one I know with eyes like mine

They had so much trouble finding a vein. It seemed like my blood vessels were shrinking beneath the surface of my skin. Now it throbs in the crease of my right elbow, where they finally drew blood. I can almost feel my corpuscles rushing to the site of injury, coagulating into a scab beneath a flesh-colored bandage meant for someone with flesh considerably lighter than mine.

I never cried over shots or needle sticks as a child, not when she was there to help me be brave. It is times like this, more than anything or anyone else on this earth, that I want my Jama. More than Mom, more than Gunther, more than Gertie. Even more than José, the love of my life. I am almost reaching for the telephone, the Mississippi exchange burned eleven years deep in memory. And then I remember the letters.

I've been saving them for over a year now. I reach beneath my bed and bring out the cigar box. Jama always kept important documents in a collection of colorful cigar boxes. I don't know where she got them from. She never puffed so much as a Kool, as far as I knew. Did she have a secret addiction? Or maybe Jama had a cigar-smoking, gray-haired gentleman, a secret boyfriend we never knew about.

Even in a bundle fastened with rubber bands, I can make out some of the contents. The curled edges of old letters, photographs, greeting cards. On the very top, the printed program of my graduation ceremony from Whitney Young High School, class of 1999.

Jama had been there, inching toward the auditorium with Mom and Gunther on either side, her three-legged cane picking out a path before her. She seemed so frail, so wobbly. She trudged along so wearily.

Oh, please don't let my grandmother collapse, I can remember praying as I watched her progress. *Please let her make it to her seat.*

I didn't want to break her concentration, so I hesitated to call out and let her know I was there. Yet somehow she sensed it. Jama was like that; she had a certain kind of radar. She turned toward where I stood, surrounded by classmates in identical caps and gowns. We waited to file in, for the pianist to strike up "Pomp and Circumstance," for the class to march.

Jama squinted, searching me out among the crowd. She pointed her bony finger at me, just as she'd done when I was a child when by some instinct or intuition she knew I'd been the one who tracked mud over her clean kitchen floor, sneaked tastes of Mom's piña colada, or had a report card pitted with D's hiding in my book bag.

This time it wasn't the finger of accusation that pinpointed my whereabouts. It was one of recognition, of congratulations, wrestled from the protection of Gunther's grip. She raised it to her mouth and kissed it. She didn't blow the kisses toward me either, but sprinkled them at me, like starch water onto wrinkled shirts. Like an aged, brown Tinkerbell scattering fairy dust. Then she continued on her weary way.

"That's Jama," I whispered to Gertie, standing next to me. We had become best friends only after Jama moved down south, so she had never known her. "My old girl."

"Grandma's baby," Gertie teased. "Sho is proud of you. First one in the family to graduate high school."

Jama momentarily forgotten, I turned and eyeballed Gertie, hand on my hip.

"Hussy, please," I hissed. When we wanted the insult to sting, we cussed each other out in Ebonics. "My mother has a master's from Columbia College, all right?"

One of Gertie's hands went to her own hip, and the other snapped a circle above her head.

"Well, excuse me, Miss Green-Eyed Wench."

I snapped back, "Your man sho' was loving these green eyes when I had him last night."

Jama went back to Leland and died two weeks later. Mom said she'd been holding on just to see me graduate. We went down for the funeral, closed Great-Granddaddy's house and put it on the market, and brought back the cigar box marked *Jonavis*. I'd shoved it under my bed, unable to bring myself to look at it until now.

There was something so final in the snap of overstretched rubber bands, breaking under the tension. Dust shaken from the pages was like clods of dirt falling onto a casket. I unfolded the first page and met the shock of my own childish, carefully printed hand.

Mrs. Jamesetta Ransom
12 Honeysuckle Crescent
Leland, Mississippi 38756

Dear Jama:

You remembered I like butterflies! Thanks for the birthday present. I like this writing paper with orange and yellow butterflies on it. It is so pretty. Now I can write you a letter every week.

I miss you a lot. I miss Sunday breakfast and the way you cook eggs and grits and Samuel Crocketts. I wish you didn't have to move down south. I wish Great-Granddaddy James would get better so you can come back home and live with us again. I wish you would be there after I come home from school.

Now I'm in the Southside YMCA after-school program. We swim sometimes, play badminton and checkers. The after-school teacher helps us with our homework, but she doesn't know decimals too good. It's fun at the Y, but sometimes those kids be making fun of me.

When you get done with your homework you can have a snack and look at videos. Yesterday we were watching old-time toons. Bugs Bunny looks funny on those old cartoons and he talks funny too. Betty Boop came on in black and white singing "Jeepers, creepers, where'd you get those peepers?" and everybody turned around and looked at me. Then they went to pointing and sniggering.

Why do I have to have green eyes, Jama? Nobody in the family has eyes like mine. Every time I ask Mommy, she always says we'll talk about it later.

I have to stop writing now. It's time for me to go to bed. Thank you very much for the writing paper, and for the socks and panties too.

Your granddaughter,
Jonavis Lynn Ransom

. . .

Dear Jama:

Sorry it took so long for me to write you back. Thank you for telling me. I didn't know my father had green eyes. I never seen him in my whole life. I want to find him. Mommy says she doesn't know where he is. Do you?

I can't wait to see you this summer. Mommy says I can come down south and spend a whole month with you and Great-Granddaddy James. I hope he's feeling better now. I'm sending you my new school picture. You can't see it on the picture, but I have braces now.

Kids at the Southside Y call me the "green-eyed, silver-toothed troll." But I don't be paying them no attention. They're very ignorant. Mommy says she's going to try to get me in the after-school program at Trinity. The children there are much more civilized.

Also I don't go by Jonavis anymore. From now on I want everybody to call me Johnni Lynn. Mommy doesn't like it, she says it sounds like a country singer's name. And then she corrected me about saying Samuel Crocketts for salmon croquettes. If I was saying it wrong, how come she didn't tell me before? And how come she gave me such a messed-up name, anyway? There's a girl in fifth grade named Johnetta, and a lady at church named Johnesther. I don't know anybody else with the name Jonavis, but it's a little bit like your name, Jamesetta. Were you the one who named me?

Bye, I love you.
Your granddaughter,
Johnni Lynn Ransom

. . .

Dear Jama:

Nobody tells me anything. I didn't know until I got your letter that I was named after both my parents. It seems like you tell me a whole lot more in your letters than you did when you were living here with us. Do you think Mommy doesn't like the name Johnni because that's what they called my father? I'm going back to my old name because I don't want Mommy to think I like the John but I don't like the Avis. So you can call me Jonavis again.

I'm glad that you gave Mommy a free, unhindered woman's name. I'm not sure what that really means. But I don't think my mommy named me so I can be dragging along my missing father everywhere I go, like you said she did. I'm named after both my parents, just like you were named after both of yours.

I know you didn't know my father well, but can you think of somebody who does? I really want to find him.

I can't wait until I see you this summer. Bye!
Your granddaughter,
Jonavis Lynn Ransom

. . .

Dear Jama:

I'm glad we got to spend some time together. I'm sorry it couldn't be longer. It was very sad when Great-Granddaddy died. Don't worry, Jama. Everything's going to be all right. His soul is with the Lord and he's an angel now.

It was very nice down south, except it's too hot for me. Every-body says I came home a whole lot darker. Are you sure you want to stay living down south? I hope you won't be too lonely in your father's house all by yourself. You can always come back to Chicago anytime you want. Mommy moved her darkroom from the basement up into your old bedroom, but we still have the guest room right next door to mine. I know your arthritis hurts your knees, but I can help you up and down the stairs.

Me and Mommy developed my film from the summer. We made these prints for you to have. There's a nice one of you and Great-Granddaddy James sitting at the table at Sunday breakfast. Look at how happy he is. Great-Granddaddy liked salmon croquettes too.

Now that I'm almost ten, me and Mommy are making an experiment. We're going to see if I can be responsible to watch myself when I get home from school. It's only two and a half hours alone. Mrs. Royster's always home next door, in case of an emergency. Mommy's a little worried, but I think I'll be fine. They charge too much at that after-school program for what little they do.

Guess what, Jama? We're getting a dog to keep me company and protect me. Mommy's taking me to the Anti-Cruelty Society this weekend. I want a golden retriever or a border collie puppy, but Mommy says it's the luck of the draw when you adopt a pet.

Mommy showed me a picture of my father. It was from when he was graduating from high school. I can't see what color his eyes are on the picture, but they don't look green to me. They must have known each other a long time to be way back in high school together. If you can remember anything else about my father, please write and tell me, okay? I love you.

Your granddaughter,
Jonavis Lynn Ransom

. . .

Dear Jama:

Mommy tells me I'm a love child. Does that mean I'm illegitimate?

Last month on Father's Day I was watching this cable TV gossip special called Hidden Shame, about famous fathers and their illegitimate children. Those rich athletes have all kinds of kids out of wedlock. There was this guy who said he was John F. Kennedy's love child, but I think he was lying. Some geezer named Johnny Carson has an illegitimate grandkid who's black. The mom of that kid thinks that they're trying to kill her because she sued for child support.

There was a rumor that Muhammad Ali was Queen Latifah's father. But then Queen Latifah came on herself and said it wasn't true, she just looks a little like Muhammad Ali. They showed a picture of Queen Latifah's real father and Muhammad Ali's real daughters, he has a lot of them. You can see where they look way more like Muhammad Ali than Queen Latifah does.

And you know Bertice Berry, who has that talk show? She came on and said she never really knew her father all the time she was growing up. But then her mother all of a sudden told her that her father is Otis Redding, who used to be a famous singer. And Otis Redding's wife and kids said no, Otis Redding is not Bertice Berry's father. They can't really prove it unless they take a paternity test, but Bertice Berry said that's okay, just leave it alone. She's grown now and doesn't need a father anymore, plus Otis Redding is dead anyway.

Are you sure my father is John the Baptist Wright? I think I look a little like Smokey Robinson, the singer. Don't you, Jama? Mommy used to go around taking pictures of famous people like Aretha Franklin, Mayor Harold Washington, Bozo the Clown on Channel 9. She was the photographer of the stars. Maybe she had an affair with Smokey Robinson and he swore her to secrecy.

These famous guys never want to claim their illegitimate kids because they think you want their money. Look at Bill Cosby and Autumn Jackson. Look at Michael Jackson and Billie Jean. He said "the kid is not my son," but later in the song he admitted that "his eyes are like mine." Do you think Smokey Robinson could be my real father? He's the only one I know with eyes like mine.

Your loving granddaughter,
Jonavis Lynn Ransom

. . .

Mama:

I'm writing you this letter because I don't trust myself on the telephone. I won't have you hushing me up, guilt-tripping me out, or shouting me down. This time you are going to hear me out.

It is not right what you're doing to Jonavis. The age of twelve is a very delicate time in a young girl's life. She's coming to you, desperate for answers, and you're filling her head with poison. I saw the letter you wrote to her. I can't believe you would tell a child so many vicious lies about her father.

I know there was a big difference in our ages, but I'll thank you to not refer to my child's father as "that boy." He was only nineteen when we got together, but he was a grown man of twenty-one when Jonavis was born. And no, he didn't abandon us. As a matter of fact, he didn't know anything about the pregnancy, although I don't want this repeated to Jonavis. I was ready to be a mother, but he was in no way ready to be a father.

Maybe I was wrong, but it seemed the best decision at the time. All of us make mistakes, Mama. Motherhood doesn't come with a manual. I just didn't want to burden this man with the knowledge of a child he had no way of parenting.

I know I should have told Jonavis more about her father. I knew the time would come when she needed answers, but I thought I could protect her a little while longer. And it's not because of any "hidden shame" that I've kept Johnny's identity a secret. He treated me with honor and respect the two years we were together. You, on the other hand, lived over thirty years with a man who abused and cheated on you. Which one of us has something to be ashamed of?

I don't want to fight with you about this anymore. But I don't want my child to inherit your bitterness. The women in our family are not doomed to suffer "man trouble," and I don't want you saying that to my Jonavis. In fact, the less said to her about her father, the better. Please let me handle this in my own way.

Your daughter,

Avis

. . .

My dear Jama:

How did we get out of the habit of writing to each other? It's been something like two years, and we haven't exchanged a single letter. I know we talk to each other on the phone, and we get to visit on the holidays. But our letters used to be so special.

Anyway, the walls have ears around here, so I'd rather write than call right now. Mom tried to help me find my father, but she obviously didn't try hard enough. We tracked down some of his family, but it's like he dropped off the face of the earth around 1982, the same year I was born. Convenient, isn't it? Mom says we can't invest any more energy into looking for him, because obviously he doesn't want to be found. She says, "I tried my best. What else can I do?"

Mom won't let me date boys or anything, even though I'm a very mature fourteen. I have to wait another whole year. No boyfriends, no dates, even though every other freshman at Whitney Young High School is going out. And you'll never guess what Mom is up to now. Jama, you will be shocked. I can't think of anything worse to report. The world is coming to an end. I am helpless to prevent it.

Mom wants to bring a Nazi into our lives. A Nazi, complete with his own little pencil mustache. Can you believe it? My mother is dating Hitler.

How did she get it in her head to hook up with a white man? I don't want a white man. I know I used to beg for a father. "Where's my daddy? I want my daddy. Give me my daddy!" Okay, maybe I was a brat about it. But that was then. This is now. I am fourteen years old, nearly grown. I don't need a father like I did then. Especially not a white, German, bald-headed Nazi.

I will put an end to this relationship, or my name ain't Jonavis Lynn Ransom. You watch me.

Your loving grandchild,
Jonavis

· · ·

Jama:
It wasn't even necessary. It wasn't even that serious. He didn't have to go giving me The Diary of Anne Frank. *I already read it in the eighth grade. Then I have to hear his lecture about the Jewish Holocaust and the African Holocaust, and the many millions gone, and the solidarity of suffering people.*

I'm not a child. He didn't need to talk to me like I was a baby, patiently explaining how he can't be a Nazi because he's a socialist and a Jew. He's not even German, he's Austrian. So what? I don't care what he is, I don't want Gunther.

But Mama is determined to go through with this marriage. So there's only one thing left for me to do. I'm going on the Internet right this very evening. I will finally find my father, my natural father, John the Baptist Wright. I don't know much about him. That picture Mama thinks she has safely hidden, I've been sneaking looks at it ever since I was a child.

It's embarrassing when I look at it now and realize how much older Mama must have been than him. She was a cradle robber from the looks of it, grinning at him in her tight shirtwaist dress. Holding his hands like a proud mother. Not the mother of me, I was barely invented yet. Or maybe I was there, hidden in the picture. I might have been that little bulge beneath her waistband.

But no, I'm talking about the other baby. The one wearing a graduation gown, the cap sitting a little lopsided on top of that bushy Afro. His big, blushing grin. The boy looks like a teenager, not that much older than I am now. The man who is my father.

Remember I used to think my father was Smokey Robinson? It's Mama's fault, she's always listening to the oldie-but-moldy radio station. Well, there used to be an old song called "Get Ready, 'Cause Here I Come."

You hear me, Jama? John the Baptist Wright better get ready to be found. The wedding's in one month, and I refuse to live in a house with Mom and Gunther Abrams at the dinner table together, sleeping in the same bed every night. It's just impossible, that's all.

That boy in the cap and gown, who must be a man by now, has never been a father to me. Well, now he owes me. I'm raising up out of this place, going to find my real father. That's where I'll have to live until I'm grown. Either that or I'm coming down to the Delta and live with you.

Fee fi fo fum . . . look out, John, 'cause here I come!

Later on,
Jonavis

. . .

Dear Grandmother:

It was so nice seeing you last month. Where do you find down in Mississippi to buy kente cloth? I had to fight, I mean literally fight, with Mom to let me cut my hair this year. I was so glad to see you strutting up in the wedding with your African garb and your TWA (teeny-weeny Afro). I'm probably going to start dreading soon, but Mom says wait until we get the college interviews behind us. She's completely given up having any control over my head. Lord knows, she's got enough to control with her bald-headed husband of hers.

Get this, Jama. Before they got married, Mom would introduce the boy by his real name, Gunther Abrams. A pretty ugly name, if you ask me. But it will never be my name, so hey. Anyway, now Mom tells everybody, "Meet my huuuuusband." She says it just like that. "My huuuuusband." Like she doesn't want to let the word out of her mouth. It's disgusting.

Anyway, things are going great. I did well on my SATs. I'm getting my braces off soon. We're going to interview at Spelman, Dartmouth, and Brown. I got in all of them, hey-hey! Brains, baby. They run in the family.

I'll miss seeing you this Christmas. Mom and Gunther insist on spending the holiday in Austria, and they're dragging me along. Old bald-headed Gunther didn't turn out to be such a bad boy after all. But hey, I'm grown. Don't nobody need to be sitting under their mom and stepfather's roof when they're grown. That's why I'm getting as far away from Chicago as I possibly can.

Sad news. You remember Snoopy, my schnoodle pooch? He died last week. We'd been having this conversation about what was going to happen to Snoopy when I went away to college, because I wanted to take him with me. We've been together since I was nine years old. He used to comfort me when I was at home by myself and afraid of Dracula and Freddy Krueger. Mom said, "No way you're dragging that half-blind, incontinent old dog off to college with you." It was almost like Snoopy heard all the drama and decided to make things easier on us. I cried for a whole week.

Missing Snoopy makes me miss you. Even though we won't be together for Christmas, I promise you I'll fly down for a weekend sometime in the new year. How's your arthritis treating you? Don't let it get you down.

Oh, don't forget, Jama. Put this date on your calendar— June 11, 1999. Graduation day! Be there or be square.

Love,

Jonavis

Jamesetta Louise Ransom
1914–1999

God's own angel
Laid to rest
Loved by all
But God loved her best.

Jamesetta Louise Ransom was the eldest of six children born to James Louis and Etta Worthy Matthews in Greenwood, Mississippi. She was raised in Leland and attended the Andrew Jackson Elementary School and Quincy Colored High School in Greenville.

Mrs. Ransom moved to Chicago in 1935, where she worked as one of the first African-American telephone operators in that city's history. She met and married Oscar Ransom in 1936. Three daughters were born to that union, which lasted until Oscar's death in 1970: her daughters Avis Abrams of Chicago, Beatrice Ransom of Washington, D.C., and Gloria Jean Braxton, M.D., of Santa Barbara, California. Mrs. Ransom retired from Illinois Bell Telephone in 1978 after thirty-seven years of service.

She returned to Leland in 1989 to care for her elderly father, who passed into the Lord's care in 1990. She was on the ushers' board of Second Baptist Church of Leland since 1992, and was a forty-year member of the Society of Eastern Stars.

In addition to her daughters, she is survived by sisters Berta Rae Bullocks and Evalina Crawford; a brother, James Junior; grandchildren Jamal, Elizabeth, and Jonavis; great-granddaughter Khadija; and many cousins, nieces, and nephews, great-nieces and great-nephews, friends and loved ones.

She will be sorely missed.

The obituary had been my addition to the cigar box of memories, folded in half unread and crammed in with the rest. It didn't surprise me that Jama saved my letters. She saved everything: grocery lists, coupons, soup can labels, receipts. But then, I was also her special grandchild, the only one who had grown up with her.

I had always been Jama's girl, all my life. Sitting in her lap to eat until I was nearly four. Snuggling in her cushiony arms while watching TV. Hanging around her kitchen, the room she ruled. It was Mom's house, but Jama's kitchen. Her death had hit me hard. I had been avoiding opening that cigar box for a year and a half now, afraid I'd break down in a thunderstorm of grief and sadness.

I folded the letters back up and retied the broken rubber bands, surprised at the gentle rain of my tears. Not tears of sadness for Jama, or even myself, but for the child I used to be. I wanted to reach back and comfort her, to tell her it's going to be all right.

I weep for that child. Not a poor child, or a deprived child, or an unloved child. A child, in fact, who was pampered. A child with a mother and a grandmother and two out-of-town aunts who doted on her. A child with a great-grandfather who called her on the phone and remembered her birthdays. A child who had ballet lessons and soccer club, a beautiful home and expensive clothes and delicious home-cooked meals. But a child starving to death from daddy hunger.

What I did seemed natural, as right as rain. I pulled down the shelf of my drop-leaf desk, then found my favorite lavender pen and the last few sheets of writing paper with orange and yellow butterflies flitting across the top.

. . .

My own dear Jama:

I know you've been gone a while now. I've missed you in too many ways to count. Being on my own for the first time, living in another part of the country, I especially miss your letters. I often find myself leafing through my mail, looking for your familiar handwriting. Are you looking over my shoulder right now, reading every word that spills out in lavender-colored ink?

I'm sorry about that business with Mom when I was twelve. I really didn't know the two of you had been arguing. I always wondered why you stopped writing for a while, and why things got so strained. I didn't realize she'd read the letter you wrote about my father. It wasn't your fault. You did the best you could by me and my mother. And Jamesetta Ransom's best was pretty damned good!

Excuse my cursing, Jama. It's developed into a habit lately, and I really need to quit. It is the middle of my sophomore year at Brown University, but I am home in Chicago. I have been called back home for something I simply cannot believe.

I got here and found out that the father I'd been fretting about and searching for and pining over all these years—the one who had been so impossible to locate, the one I thought I needed so badly, the man whose eyes are green like mine, John the Baptist Wright, who used to be called Hot Johnny when he was my age (oh, I bet you didn't know that, did you? That was his nickname, Hot Johnny)—has turned up after all these years. After I hunted for him feverishly the year I turned fourteen, tried to wish him into being all those years of childhood, and finally forgot about him, here he comes.

I will never be the same again, Jama. I will never be able to look in the mirror again without seeing his eyes looking back at me.

My father is charming and handsome, smooth and manipulative. Hugging me and crying, claiming he never knew he had a daughter. And what does he want? Not to make up for old times, not to replace all those birthday cards and Christmas presents he never gave, not to make up for the father-daughter dances he never attended. None of that.

The bastard wants my bone marrow. My bone marrow! Making himself at home in my house, sitting in the den and drinking microbrewed beer with the only man who's ever been a reasonable facsimile of a father. Joking and laughing with my mother just like he hadn't abandoned her, alone and pregnant, nineteen years ago.

Trying to get in good with the family so he can ask me for my bone marrow! He wants it for his daughter—"your little sister," he says with tears welling in his eyes. A child he obviously loves more than he ever loved me, even if he knew that I existed. Wants me to drop everything in the middle of the semester, fly off to North Carolina, check myself into a hospital. This stranger hadn't known me one day, and he had the nerve to ask the impossible.

I was tested today. I've been crossing my fingers, crossing my toes, crossing my heart, and hoping, Please don't let it be me. Please, please, please. *We're all waiting for the test results to see if I'm a compatible transplant donor for my half-sister, Beauty Lynn Wright. Can you believe that? We even have the same middle name, although I've stopped using mine.*

I'm not sure what I'm going to do if it comes back positive. Everyone thinks I'm selfish for having any doubts. Johnny Wright, I believe all he cares about is his Beauty. The media has somehow gotten hold of the story: "Coed undecided while a young child's life hangs in the balance." It's probably Hot Johnny's doing, guilt-tripping the people around me to pressure me into a decision. Mama and Gunther. Even my boyfriend, this fine, fine Cape Verdean dude from New Bedford.

Well, it's his parents who come from Cape Verde, and they're really backwards. They won't claim Africa, he complains. They call themselves Portuguese. But José, he's not like that. He's really cool, Afrocentric and the whole nine yards. He said his parents almost had a fit when he came back for Thanksgiving break with a headful of baby dreadlocks. I'd twisted them myself, locking them with olive oil and beeswax. We'd only been dating a few months when I got called home. And this is after I'd gone nearly a whole year without dating anybody!

José with a hard J ("not soft like the Spanish," he explains) quietly hears me out when I cry on his shoulder during late-night phone calls. He listens, but then says at the end of the conversation, "Maybe you should reconsider. You could be saving a life here."

"Would you do it?" I asked him. "Give up your bone marrow for a sister you never knew you had?"

He answered without hesitation.

"I would do it for a stranger."

That's easy for him to say. You can be all brave and altruistic when it's not your life on the line. What about the risks I'd have to go through? It's not like donating blood, you know. What about the recovery period after the surgery, a period that could mess up my life? What about infections and stuff? What about the operation I might never wake up from? What about my boyfriend, whom at least three other chicks I know have been checking out?

What about my studies, which I had to leave in the middle of the semester? I'm a biochemistry major, and maybe one day I'll help discover the cure for sickle cell disease and save thousands of lives. Why should I sacrifice my life now to save just one?

I guess I sound pretty selfish. It's not just myself I'm worried about. It's a risk for the baby too. I've been reading up on it. They give the patient these powerful drugs to kill off her bone marrow, then you do a transplant to replace it. But Johnny told us Beauty already had one stroke. Those drugs can really be dangerous for someone who has had a stroke.

I count out the number of people I could do this for, people who love me and whom I love back. José, without a doubt. Mama, definitely. Gunther, probably. Gertina Lewis, my best friend from high school, maybe.

I'm just not sure about saving Gertie's life when she seems so determined to throw it all away. To think I used to lie to her mother when she'd sneak out to be with Teran all night. I wish she'd get rid of that do-nothing, know-nothing, drug-dealing thug and get a life. Gertie actually got into UCLA, but she stayed in Chicago just so she could be near that man.

These are people I have a history with. Memories of childhood and sleepovers and birthday parties and Thanksgiving dinners. Those other people, a father I never knew and a sister I've never met, they're my blood, all right. Blood strangers.

All those years we looked for him, checking birth certificates and college records, all those hours logged onto the Internet— and look how easy it was for him to locate us. He was a moving target, but we've been sitting still all these years. Even when Mom left her apartment to buy a house in the Highlands, she only moved four blocks away.

He didn't know about me, but why hadn't he thought to contact my mother, just for old times' sake? A woman, he said himself, to whom "I owe more than I can ever possibly repay." Something tells me he's said that about lots of women.

"Li'l Miz Jones," he teases, calling Mom by her old married name. "Still foxy to the bone."

She grins at him like a schoolgirl.

"You should know, good-looking. You still got it cooking."

"Gunther," I warn my stepfather, *"you'd better keep an eye on these two."*

Everybody cracked up like it was a joke, but I was serious. Do you think Mom could still be sweet on him after all these years?

What's so hot about Johnny, anyway? Yes, he's good-looking and all, but I never did trust those pretty-boy types. Well, except for José, but he's a different kind of man. I thought Mom was so level-headed. Besides good looks, what could this man, this boy, possibly have had to offer her at the age of nineteen? Nineteen, Jama! That's the age I am now, and I can't imagine being anyone's parent. I guess Johnny couldn't either. At least that's what Mom decided for him.

John the Baptist Wright wants the privileges of fatherhood without the responsibility. Not only does he want my bone marrow, he actually thinks he can try to raise me, old as I am.

We were getting ready for a family dinner at Leona's last night, me, Mom, and Gunther. Hot Johnny was tagging along. I had borrowed Gertie's black suede Fubu suit. I know you're still into clothes, probably the best-dressed angel in heaven. You should see it, Jama, it's really cute. You know I'm tall, so it does fit me kind of short in the legs. About midthigh length. But hey, that's the way they're wearing them these days.

So Gunther, you know he never comes right out and says something.

"Are you certain that dress is the right decision?"

Mom had no trouble at all.

"Girl, where are the rest of your clothes? I know you aren't going out in that thing."

Excuse my French, Jama. But ain't nobody asked Hot Johnny a damned thing. Here he comes putting his two cents in, trying to play both sides against the middle.

"I don't know, Avis. Our daughter is looking rather sharp tonight. But maybe, just maybe, Johnni girl, you should listen to your mother, hmm?"

Johnni girl? It was like he had been reading my letters to you when I was nine.

"The name is Jonavis. And I don't recall asking for your wardrobe advice, Mr. Hot Johnny."

"Jonavis, respect!" There goes Gunther, all red-faced with embarrassment. It doesn't take much to make him blush. "It's your father, after all."

"Don't sweat it." Johnny grins at me like it's a private joke between us. "I've been a teenager too. It's only because of the weather, Jonavis. The hawk is howling like crazy tonight. I wouldn't want you catching cold out there."

Yeah, right. Like he really cares. Or if he does, it's because he wants to preserve my health for obvious reasons. Oh, he tries to pretend it doesn't matter.

"Please don't think my only interest in you is as a bone marrow donor. No matter what decision you make, in the end you will always be my daughter. It took almost twenty years for us to find each other. The door will always be open for you, Jonavis Ransom. All you've got to do is walk through it."

See, I know when somebody's trying to work reverse psychology. That's like when you tell street people you don't believe in giving money to beggars, especially able-bodied black men. They look at you all puppy-dog sad and say, "That's all right. God bless you anyway."

I mean, it's all a bit late for me and my father. Right, Jama? I'm sure you peeped his cards a long time ago. Didn't you try to warn me about him once?

I've figured out why I used to be so desperate to find him. When you don't have a father to say "I love you," no matter how many people are saying it, you still feel unloved. It's like, if my father doesn't love me, then no man really can.

"I've been here four days," I told Gunther. "Four whole days, and my father has not once said he loves me."

He kissed me on the cheek.

"Your father does love you, liebling. *He's loved you from the time you were a rebellious adolescent, hating the ground he walks on."*

"Oh, Gunther." I kissed him back, I had to. He had his arm around my shoulders, his stubbly cheek stuck out waiting for it. "I'm not talking about you. And I'm still a rebellious adolescent who hates the ground you walk on."

Gunther only laughed. I guess he's figured out by now that my bark is worse than my bite. My white stepfather loves me and my black father doesn't, even though I look just like him. I have his long body and sandy hair and caramel-colored skin. I have his green eyes.

I have always wondered where I got these green eyes. Jeepers, creepers, where'd you get those peepers? *"Jonavis White" was one of those childhood insults, which sounds a little like what my name would have been if my father had actually given me his. But I was never Jonavis Wright. In fact, I was never John's Avis. I was my mom's Avis, and my grandmother's Avis, Great-Granddaddy James' Avis, and even Gunther's Avis (a lot of people think he is my real father now).*

I don't look at all biracial, you know that—even though this father of mine tries to lay claim to some kind of mulatto pedigree. Can you believe he actually gloats over something foreign in his blood? Talks about a grandmother who is sometimes Louisiana Creole, sometimes Mexican, sometimes Indian, depending on the story he tells. Lord, save us from backward Negroes and their Indian grandmamas! We want to be everything except what we are. I swear, Johnny Wright is nearly as bad as José's people.

I'm proud to have an African grandmama, one who loved and lived in loud colors. I've got your and Mom's bold African features, your kink in my sandy hair. I've got Great-Granddaddy James' bushy eyebrows and full lips. But these green eyes looking out of a brown face come as a shock to most people. Sometimes I catch my face in the mirror and I shock myself. No wonder kids used to think that my missing father must be a white man.

Now I know it's true. That other man, the one who has in his wallet a tearstained picture of his real daughter clutching a teddy bear and a pillow that says Who art thou, my daughter?—*he's nothing more than a sperm donor.*

The child is innocent, I know that. She's just a baby, not to be faulted for a father who has turned up too late in his first daughter's life. Too late to teach her left from right, to tie her shoe, to ride a bike. Too late for soccer games and high school graduation. Too late even to pay the bills of fatherhood: room and board, braces, a four-year-old Chevy Celebrity, a college education. Too late to say "I love you"?

But not too late for me to save a life. So I've got a decision to make, the hardest decision of my life. I need you right now, more than ever before. Is loving a father something you can learn to do? Is it too late in life to walk through that open door? Tell me, Jama, what should I do? What would you do?

Love always,
Your Jonavis

Sister Baby

I beat the boy to make him strong

Johnny claimed he lived a hard life, but you would never know it by his hands.

You know that TV commercial for dish soap? Mother and daughter, young and fresh like sisters. Even by their hands, you can't hardly tell which is which. After a lifetime of scrubbing pots and pans, the older woman's hands are twins to her daughter's, smooth and soft as a baby's behind.

Who they think they fooling? You and me know it's all a damned lie. Ain't no way a woman gonna work that hard and the hands don't show it. Look at mine and you can read my life story. You don't even need to be a palm reader when you turn them over on the black-handed side. These hands are a road map of tribulation, testimony to hard times. Tough and knobby, covered with nicks and scars. And the truth is as plain as the broken veins. I'm a workaholic. I'm a diabetic. I'm a junkie. Ain't none of it no contradiction.

I ain't never wanted no little bit of nothing. Whatever I got, I had to have a whole lot. Not just a slice, but the whole damned pie. Not just a snort or a pop, but the full mainline. Yet and still, I've always had to work hard for what I wanted. Always.

The bed I sleep in is one I make myself. If I eat the whole pie, it's one I bake myself. I don't look for no one else to feed me. Ain't no free lunch, 'less you count school leftovers would have been thrown out anyway. I never been a woman they let ride free because she looked good. Neither have I robbed, conned, or whored to feed my need. I take my smack like a man, cash on the barrelhead.

You got to work for what you want. It's a lesson I learned from my mother. Not that she followed it. I guess her way of thinking was either you did your duty, or you had the daughters to do it for you.

If we held up our hands, hers would have looked like the young girl's, mine the old lady's. She had a whole church to take care of, not just me and my three sisters. She had to portion out her mother love.

She loved us best when we were doing housework. Cooking, dusting, wiping down kitchen walls. She didn't believe in mops. The only way to get floors clean was on your hands and knees, scrubbing with a stiff-bristled brush. Polishing the bathtub so bright you could see yourself in it, that's how I got my blessings.

"Sister Baby, you so smart," Momma Niece would gush, proud like I discovered a cure for cancer. "I don't know how you get that tub so clean."

While Momma Niece shouted every night at the Pentecostal Sanctuary Church of God in Christ, we raised each other up. Each older sister took her turn mothering the rest, until it was time for the next one in line.

Mary went to college in another city, then off into another world. She ain't never looked back yet. Martha left the nest to mother her own. She was pregnant with the first of five kids by the age of seventeen. Martha got everything she could out of that public aid check, including her own place in a housing project down a ways from where we lived. That girl always could stretch a dime until it hollered.

When it got down to sister number three, Samaritan had two jobs to do: mothering me and working a church secretary job that paid little or nothing. It was how our family gave to the church, having nothing to tithe but hard work and obedient daughters.

I didn't miss having a mother much, because I had three mothers when I was growing up. I was the youngest of Deniece Wright's brood of daughters. Daddy Joe chose good Bible names for the rest. He was gone by Momma Niece's fourth pregnancy, so she just grabbed one from a TV commercial. At least that was how my sister Samaritan told it.

"The Baby Ruth bar," I had to hear all the time. "All you can eat for a nickel."

Samaritan wasn't nothing but jealous that hers was such a worldly name. See, I know my Bible. Ain't nothing wrong with the name Ruth. She was a virtuous woman, the faithful daughter. She followed her mother-in-law into the land of Judah: *Whither thou goest, I will go. Your people will be my people, and your gods my gods.* Book of Ruth, chapter 1, verse 16.

For all Ruth's loyalty God blessed her with a son, one that would be the ancestor of Jesus. You got to study your Bible. The Pentecostal Sanctuary ain't about no shucking and jiving. Just because you get saved don't mean you're going to stay saved. You got to put in your time. The devil and his demons lurk at every corner and stop sign, toting buckets full of dirty sin. They ain't happy 'less they're staining the clean robes of some saint.

That's what happened to Samaritan. She did her work, but not willingly. Lazy as a slug, that girl. Always trying to shirk her chores and put them on me, then go off somewhere and bury her nose in a book. And it don't be the Good Book neither.

"Worldly," Momma Niece sighed, and prayed for her. "Them worldly ways gonna bring down a heap of trouble on Samaritan head some day."

I loved her because she was my third sister, and because she was a child of God. But that Samaritan had a little of the devil in her. Everybody makes Samaritans out to be do-gooders, but you read your Bible. You'll see they wasn't nothing but some no-account lowlifes. That's the point of the parable. Nobody expected a Samaritan to do a good deed.

Sister Samaritan played like she was saved. Come Sunday morning she be shouting the roof down with the best of them. She get the

Holy Ghost and go to shaking, crying, talking in tongues. It take three ushers just to hold her still and keep her from showing her drawers. That wasn't nothing but false holiness. Samaritan was a Sunday saint, sinning up a storm all the rest of the week. She claim to know God, but by her actions she denied him.

Long as I been going to church, good a daughter as I tried to be, I hadn't never been blessed with the Holy Ghost. I asked Samaritan what it felt like to have the spirit of the Lord moving in you. She closed her eyes and thought about it.

"Like tongues of fire licking you all over you. Feel just like a man making you come."

See there? Just studied evil.

"You ain't been fornicating, has you? He that committeth fornication sinneth against his own body. Lawd, Sister Samaritan. I'm gone have to pray for you."

Samaritan only laughed in my face.

"Save your prayers for somebody who needs them, like Deacon Thomas. Ask the Lord to deliver him from them cock eyes. You ever try looking that man in the face? His eyes be roaming every which-a-way but straight."

She go to crossing her eyes at the needle, making mockery of the poor man.

"Sister Samaritan, you quit it." I couldn't help but laughing. "God going to punish your sinning ways, fix your eyes to stay like that."

It was when we were home by ourselves, making things to sell for the church, that Sister Samaritan's demons came down. We were always selling something for the church. Chicken dinners, chocolate candy, handmade samplers and pillow slips. We needlepointed them with little Bible sayings. *Jesus wept. Honor thy mother and father. Vengeance is mine saith the Lord.*

Samaritan be writing from the Good Book with needle and thread, yet running up sin with her evil mouth. Wasn't nothing or nobody safe from her gossip and name-calling: Sister Adamina's false teeth, Mother Monica's big butt, and poor tone-deaf Elder Willie singing in choir.

It's me, it's me, it's me
Oh, Lord
Standing in the need of prayer.

"Hmpf. Standing in the need of some singing lessons. Elder Willie need to sit his rusty butt right on down."

That girl would make un-Christian fun of everybody. 'Course, I was sinning too, sitting up there listening and laughing along. But when she wagged her wicked tongue the pastor's way, my laughing stopped right there.

"No, Sister Samaritan. You going too far. That's God's own prophet, got the gift of second sight."

"A big old stank-breath, pork-chop-eating, pot-bellied, twist-dickded—"

"You going straight to hell," I whispered, then started wondering. "Besides, how you get it in your filthy head that Bishop Pleasant got a twisted . . . you know, private part?"

Samaritan laughed like a fallen women, raising a thread to her lips and biting it.

"It match his mind."

Evil as Samaritan was, I still hated to see her go. She just run off one day, ain't even say goodbye.

"Worldly ways." Momma Niece shook her head, going off to church to pray for her third daughter's mortal soul. "Trouble on her head, just like I prophesied."

I ain't sure trouble ever fell down on Samaritan like Momma Niece said. I soon started wondering if she ain't just slipped free of her cross and left it behind for me to bear. Hadn't a year passed when trouble came in through the same door that Sister Samaritan walked out of. Trouble soon told me it was my turn to be the mother.

But that was Johnny, the second trouble. He came right on the heels of the first trouble. And trouble, they say, always comes in threes.

"If you can't bear no crosses," Bishop Pleasant taught us, "you can't wear no crown."

You can't hardly be sanctified in the Lord's sight lessen you ready to do some hard work. Hell must be full of folks with smooth, soft, unworked hands. Ain't the Lord called onto him "all ye who labor and are heavy laden, I shall give thee rest"? Ain't the gospel song promised that "if I work, the Lord's going to buy me a crown"?

My blessing had been promised to me when I was twelve years old. I was going to raise me up a prophet. You see, women weren't allowed to minister in our church.

"It wasn't me who made it that way," Bishop Pleasant preached from the pulpit. "Oh, no. God himself said it. He told me through my namesake, the Apostle Paul. 'Let your women keep silence in the churches: for it is not permitted unto them to speak; but to be under obedience, as also saith the law.' "

A woman couldn't preach, but as man is born of woman, she could raise up a preacher. That's the deepest blessing God could bestow upon a woman. *Notwithstanding she shall be saved in childbearing, if they continue in faith and charity and holiness with sobriety.* It wasn't long after Samaritan left when Bishop Pleasant told me I could be so blessed.

"I been watching you, Sister Baby. The Lord got something special in store for you. He promised that as long as you practice obedience, he will allow you to raise up a prophet. I seen it in my second sight."

I took over Samaritan's job at the church, coming in every day after school, all day Saturday. I worked so late some nights I didn't have time to crack a book or write a lesson. I never had been taught to type, so I had to pick out my letters. Nobody ever showed me filing or bookkeeping either, so I had to teach myself. But I didn't mind. I was dwelling in the Lord's house, doing the Lord's work.

Some nights we worked so late that Bishop Pleasant would send everybody home in his car. He was the Lord's servant, our own shepherd. He couldn't ride around in just any old junk. We bought our pastor a brand-new Cadillac every other year.

"You church mothers done gave a lifetime of labor, it's time you rested your weary heads. Go ahead home, Sister Lulu, Momma Niece. Mother Pleasant, please give these ladies a ride. You know it ain't safe out in them streets."

I would stay behind, typing up the bulletin, sweeping out the sanctuary, counting the collection and keeping the record. But on some evenings I would do my duty faceup on the office couch. Bishop Pleasant sweated on top of me, moving in and out like a plunger in a toilet. I was blessed, being rebaptized.

" 'Come, let us make our father drink wine.' " He would grunt and push, quoting from Genesis. " 'And we will lie with him, that we may preserve the seed of our father.' "

I would lay on the creaking couch, praying it wouldn't fall under the weight of two people. I was figuring out what made Samaritan so evil.

When I started getting big, Momma Niece asked me directly.

"Has any mens been fooling with you, Sister Baby?"

"Oh, no, ma'am," I answered back. "Nobody but Bishop Pleasant."

She drew back and slapped me hard.

"Lawd to deliver me! Go wash out your mouth, Sister Baby. Trying to soil that good man's name."

Momma Niece decided it was something unnatural in me, a spirit possession. A demon haunted me for months, growing big as a watermelon. The night it had me screaming in pain, she carried me to church for a prayer healing. Sister Lulu took one look at me, laid me on the office couch, and called Mother Bethany.

The Pentecostal Sanctuary didn't accept the worldly power of doctors and medicines. We believed in natural healing. Midwives to deliver babies, herbs and home remedies for aches and pains, prayer to heal deep afflictions of body and spirit.

"Jesus is my doctor. He writes all my prescriptions. He is the source of all healing."

I repeated this prayer over and over as I panted and pushed, laboring on the same rickety couch where Bishop Pleasant had lain with me. Something stretched out and slipped into the waiting hands of Mother Bethany. I thought I had been delivered of my demon.

Therefore are my loins filled with pain; pangs have taken hold upon me, as the pangs of a woman that travaileth; I was bowed down at the hearing of it; I was dismayed at the seeing of it.

"Praise be to God, Sister Baby. The Lawd done blessed you with a girl."

"A girl?" I hollered. "No, that can't be no girl. I been obedient. I was supposed to have a son, just like Ruth. Bishop Pleasant said I'd raise me up a preacher."

They tried to give her to me, tried to put in my arms that bloody squealing thing I hadn't been promised. I wouldn't hold her. That's the cross I'll be bearing the rest of my days. I wouldn't hold my own daughter.

The church mothers wiped her off, cut the cord, wrapped and bundled her up. They took to the corner whispering, while I tossed and wept on the rickety couch. Mother Bethany kneaded my stomach like bread dough until something like a bloody liver fell out of me. Maybe that was the demon had been plaguing me all those months.

"You got to feed your baby now."

"That girl ain't mine," I hollered. "I been good. Bishop Pleasant promised me a son."

The women held my arms while Mother Bethany raised my blouse, taking my two titties in hand. I fought and wiggled while she pressed and pumped, squeezing my first milk into the silver chalice Bishop Pleasant used for monthly communion service.

That was her first meal. Mother's milk from the communion chalice, soaked up with a clean white handkerchief and dripped into her greedy lips. When I was strong enough to stand, Momma Niece walked me home. Home without my demon. Home without my daughter.

I went back to school the next week, running to the bathroom every period to change my rag. I prayed to stop the bleeding. *Jesus is my doctor.* The milk that kept swelling in my titties, I squeezed into the toilet and flushed it down. *He writes all my prescriptions.* I prayed to stop it running. *He is the source of all my healing.* I prayed I would never go back to being church secretary.

Still I did my work. I stayed at home alone, making things for the church to sell. Fried chicken, sweet potato pie, needlepointed pillow slips with Bible sayings. Even babies need a place to rest their heads, to fix their faith. I made up a little one, *Who art thou, my daughter? Ruth 3:16* stitched in red. I stuffed it with rags, sewed white lace around the seams.

I sent it with Momma Niece, who was spending more time at church than ever before. I tried to put out of my mind that bloody, squealing thing another woman was mothering now. I ain't had no right to her, after all. I hadn't held her when she was born, didn't feed her when she was hungry. But I still couldn't stop thinking about her.

And that's when the second trouble walked through the door.

I already knew I had a half-brother, even though none of us had met him. He was born about a year before Samaritan ran off. The news had sent Momma Niece—she who had tried four times and always came up short—into a shivering fit, shouting and praying and talking in tongues.

"Lawd, to deliver me." She'd look up at the picture above our heads, the one that used to scare me: Jesus, with his running wounds and bloody heart. "Seems like I can't make nothing but girls. But I'm blessed, praise his name. Let that harlot hussy have her son. Boys ain't bring nothing but a lifetime of trouble on your head."

She'd sigh away her sour grapes, making us all sink to our knees. We had no way of knowing that the harlot son who had us kneeling and praying until our knees were raw and our voices hoarse would soon be among us.

I'd been scrubbing pots and floors practically since I was born. I'd been typing and filing and sweeping at the Sanctuary for nearly a year. But my hands didn't start chapping until the day my daddy dumped the second trouble on our doorstep.

It was my thirteenth birthday. Now, what made me think Daddy Joe came to bring a gift or take me out to eat or one of those regular father-daughter things he always promised? Here he come knocking at the door, a child laid up against his shoulder, a bulging laundry bag at his side.

"Sister Baby Ruth," he announced. "Get to know your brother John. We calls him Monkey."

The monkey was not much of a birthday present, but it was better than nothing. I went around to see him. Matted curls, bone-thin face, nose packed with boogers, eyes squeezed shut. I sang to him in a baby voice, like my sisters used to do me. Like I never done for my daughter.

> *Are you sleeping, are you sleeping*
> *Brother John, Brother John?*

His eyes flew open so fast, he couldn't have been asleep. He must have figured something serious was going down and had shut his eyes against where life was leaving him.

"Daddy Joe, what's wrong with his eyes?"

He had them fixed on me like flashlights, grayish green eyes with specks of gold floating in them. They were so big they seemed to take up half his face. I ain't never seen those kind of eyes before, and they scared me. He kept staring, like he was burning a picture of me in his brain.

"Quiero, quiero," he quavered, pointing at the front door. "Quiero Lita Gracita."

"What is he, retarded?" I couldn't get the sense of what he was saying.

Daddy Joe just shook his head. "Ain't nothing wrong with him but hard-headed. I done told his old granny Gracita not to teach him that foreigner talk. Don't you worry, Sister Baby. He soon grow out of it."

We called him Monkey, but he came to our lives like a new-hatched duckling. He fastened himself to the first thing he saw, a big sister he would learn to call Mimi.

Daddy Joe left. Never said when he would be back for his boy. After watching for hours at the window, Johnny curled up on the couch and went to sleep. He wet his self there, piss running into the cushions I would have to soak in bleach water later.

I was sure Momma Niece would hit the ceiling when she came

home from church. But I was in for a surprise. She had a sudden soft spot for the baby monkey put out in the cold. The same harlot's son who had her praying before a bloody Jesus, she decided to keep.

"Not long," she promised. "Just until your Daddy Joe get back up on his feet. Cute little old monkey, but he look so pea-ked. We got to get some food in you, little John the Baptist Wright. Ooh, ain't you got some pretty hair?"

She patted those knots on top of his head, cooing in the same tone that praised my clean bathtubs. Johnny drew back from Momma Niece, shaking his head. Even he had enough sense to know that head of hair wasn't hardly pretty. Those matted curls looked like they hadn't seen a comb since the day he was born. Next day when I stayed home from school to look after him ("just until we find a baby-sitter, Sister Baby"), I took the clippers to that mess and cut it clean down to his scalp.

That would be the first of many school days I missed watching after Johnny Wright. It's amazing how that monkey ran through baby-sitters. The first one was sick three days out of five. The second wasn't paid on time and stopped answering the door when I came to drop him off. One old lady died on us after six months. Another had a old stank dog; Johnny just loved that mangy bitch, but Tuffy one day decide to rip Johnny right through the thigh, it took six stitches to close the cut. Left a big old ugly scar he gone carry all his life. The dog had to be put down and the lady was mad at Johnny for the loss of her precious Tuffy. Didn't want no more parts of him after that.

By the time I was sixteen, Johnny had been with us three years. I'd spent more time out of school than in it. I dropped out in my junior year, same year Johnny would be spending a whole day away from home in the Kinny garden. By then I had missed so many lessons, I had no hope of catching up.

I can date my second trouble to the day that snotty-nosed, pissy-pants little monkey brother came through the door with his needs and his nightmares. Two and a half years old and wasn't no way weaned, not even potty-trained. My hands started chapping, withering up like any old woman's. I had diapers to wash every day, plunging my hands in scalding bleach water.

He wouldn't feed himself or go to the toilet. But Johnny came to us walking, talking, even preaching like somebody way older than his years. Grieving for the mother who left him, begging for the titty. Looking at me like I might have some to give him. Johnny had to learn some hard lessons right then. Like how to drink his milk from a cup, like a natural man.

He wasn't the only one with hard lessons. I would go to church and see a little girl dolled up in lace and ribbons, sitting in Mother Pleasant's lap. I was glad to see they had gave it to her. *Who art thou, my daughter?* She held on to that little lacy pillow like it was her own Bible, wouldn't put it down for nothing. Yet when I tried to speak to the child after service, reach out and play with her, little Pearlene clung up against Bishop Pleasant's stubby leg. The next thing you know some usher got me by the hand, leading me away.

"Esta bonita," a little voice come calling behind me. I turned to see my half-brother sucking on some sweet the church mother gave him whether he deserved it or not. Peppermint candy, lemon drops, sugar rocks. Following me, looking back at Pearlene. "She pretty. Who that little girl is?"

"Ain't none of your business, monkey brother. And speak plain." It took the longest to get that boy to stop talking like that. Sometimes I caught him playing at it, sitting up speaking foreign to somebody nobody else could see. I sho' didn't want him calling up his demons inside the Lord's house. I have to grab his hand and drag him from the church. "It's time for us to go home. We got our work waiting."

No matter how hard I worked to raise him up straight, Johnny learned to use his pretty-boy looks, his cat eyes, his con-man charms early on. He cut his teeth on his own stepmother. When she wasn't busy shouting, she was spoiling Johnny rotten. He never did a lick of work to earn it, unless you can call play preaching work.

Momma Niece and the other church mothers were always muching him up. They prophesied that he'd be a preacher like his daddy before him, even like the great Bishop Pleasant himself. They played like his demon babbling was talking in tongues, probably why it took so long for him to grow out of it. Johnny would break into a sermon at the drop of a hat, walking the floors and pumping the air.

"*¡Alabado sea el Señor!* (Praise the Lord!) For the wages of sin are eternal damnation. The Lawd. (Hah!) Don't like ornery. Oh, the Lawd. (Well!) He don't like evil. And my Lawd. (Y'all don't hear me, now.) Don't like ugly."

He would turn and look straight in my face, cheesing. Maybe he was waiting to hear what a cute little monkey he was. But it sounded to me like mockery, a reminder of what my Momma Niece had said all along: "You ain't got no pretty face, Sister Baby. But you sure do have a good heart."

Pretty-boy Johnny knew he had a butt-ugly Sister Baby, and had the nerve to pray it out loud. That was his first beating. Not too many days passed before he had to be chastised again. It got to be almost a daily affair.

After he had misbehaved he'd go tearing around the place, making me chase him down with the belt. Didn't he know his running just made me madder? And he be praying to beat the band.

"Lawd, Mimi 'bout to kill me. *¡Ayuda me, el Señor!* Sweet Jesus in heaven, don't let her put no more welts on my behind!"

Despite his prayers, he didn't miss too many beatings. He'd pee in the bed almost every night, leave his wet drawers in the middle of the bathroom floor, and crawl up in the bed with me, half naked. Then he'd try to charm his way out of his chastisement, hugging up on me, smiling in my face. Lying.

"Mimi, you so pretty."

That didn't keep him from getting his ass whipped on a regular basis. Wasn't "Thou shalt not bear false witness against thy neighbor" one of God's commandments? *Let no one deceive you with empty words, for because of such things God's wrath comes on those who are disobedient.* He couldn't fool me. I knew what I looked like. Short, stout, black, and heavy-busted, just like all of the Wright women.

On account of all that, Johnny ain't miss too many butt whippings. He was still getting it ten years later, after he had shot up past me.

"Monkey brother, you ain't never too big to get your ass whupped,"

I'd warn him, the ironing cord wrapped around my hand. "Long as you misbehave, that's how long you'll be punished for it."

Then the winter when he was twelve and I was twenty-one, he reached up and stopped my whipping hand.

"Mimi, I ain't taking no more beatings from you."

"What?" John the Baptist Wright, talking back to me? "You got the nerve to fix your mouth and say that to the woman who raised you? You ain't read your Bible? Ain't a creature more cursed than a stubborn and rebellious son."

"You ain't none of my mother." He snatched the broom from my hand and held it above my head. "I ain't taking no beatings from you or nobody else. And quit calling me Monkey."

Had the little monkey lost his mind? I watched, half afraid he would bring that broom down on my head. But I didn't show it.

"You too grown to take a whipping, you too grown to be living here," I told him. "Get your stuff and get out."

To my surprise, he did just that. Broke the broom over his thigh and tossed it away. When had the monkey got so strong? He didn't beg my pardon. Didn't say "you so pretty." Snatched up his coat, walked out in the snow, and never looked back, just like Mary, Martha, and Samaritan before him. And that was the beginning of the third trouble, the one I'm still living.

Momma Niece, who had taken to calling this other woman's son "my boy Johnny," never got over it. She stopped checking the garbage can and praising floors so clean you could eat off them.

"Where my boy Johnny at?"

She would come home from church every night until the day she died, looking around the apartment for her sour grapes.

Why is Lazarus the one they remember, like he made his own miracle? Yes, they do praise Jesus for bringing him back to life. But what about Mary and Martha, the ones who nursed him through a long illness? Who went running to Jesus, weeping and a-wailing? "If you had been here, Lord, our brother wouldn't have died."

Without a sister praying for him, he would have stayed there on the other side. Would have slept forever in a cold tomb, his eyes squeezed shut against where life had left him. Sisters saved that boy's life.

So yes, I beat that monkey's ass. What's wrong with that? *Thou shalt beat him with the rod, and shalt deliver his soul from hell.* I beat him so the devil wouldn't have to do it later on. I beat the boy to make him strong.

"Don't let people fool you, monkey brother. I don't care how light you are, how many curls you got on your head, nor how they much you up over the color of your eyes. Pretty is as pretty does. You got to work hard for what you want."

It was a wasted lesson.

I hadn't seen Johnny in eight years, he shows up all of a sudden looking like death eating a soda cracker. Limping into the grade-school lunchroom where I work my day job, scaring the kids and teachers half to death. Hair all wild about the head, beard on his face.

He handed me a peace offering, a cheap stuffed monkey in a basketball jersey that said I Got a Basketball Jones. What kind of worldly mess was that? Just like I didn't already have a monkey of my own by then. That monkey was looking a whole lot better than Johnny did. At first I wondered if one of the family addictions hadn't fallen down on him, like his father or sister before him.

Life had put a hurting on him, but it ain't marked his hands like it did mine. They were still long and golden, smooth as a baby's ass. Hurting like he was, he must have still had a woman somewhere doing the dirty work for him. The only roughness about them were the chewed-off fingernails. When had he started biting his nails?

He used to be a thumb sucker, I remember that. I saw the mess get started, the very day his whore of a mama dumped him, his drunk of a daddy picked him up and brought him to us. He was fiending, desperate as any junkie looking for a fix.

"*¿De leche?*" he begged, looking all up in my chest with hungry green eyes. "Mi' milk?"

That's how he got started to calling me Mimi. It was like he could look at me, see straight through me. Like he smelled me out and knew my secret.

I felt sorry for him in my heart. I guess I did in my titties too. I felt a little twinge in each one, the dammed-up milk letting loose. It dripped from me like tears, soaking through the toilet tissue wadded in my bra. But this milk was made for my lost daughter, not my baby brother. Especially not one as big as he was.

"Ain't got no titty for you here, monkey brother." I went and poured him a jelly jar of cold milk from the refrigerator. He took it, tasted it, it dribbled from his mouth. The glass fell from his hands and hit the floor. He began to cry.

He grabbed my leg and buried his face in it, looking for something warm against it. I pulled away. He looked at his thumb like he ain't never seen it before, brought it to his mouth, and went to sit by the window. He sat there sucking, watching Sixteenth Street, waiting for the mother who would never come for him. Finally he curled up on the living room couch and fell asleep in his own piss.

If it hadn't been for me, that sickly baby might have died. I knew right off that the boy needed him some food. He was hungry and didn't know even how to feed his self right. He picked at things instead of eating, pinching the middle out of bread slices, sucking up runny rice pudding. The only thing he had a good appetite for was sweet milk. He guzzled it down like it was going out of style. I figured he'd been living all his life on titty milk. That was all he knew.

Titty milk ain't no kind of food to grow a boy into a man. I gave that boy good, solid food to make him strong. Food to sink his teeth into, put some meat on his bones. Collard greens with ham hocks, grits and gravy, smothered chicken over rice, spoon bread and sweet potato pie.

He ain't did nothing but pick over the best parts. Leaving half the meat on the bone, drinking up the pot likker, looking under slabs of hot-water corn bread like his demon was hiding beneath. And me, eating my plate of food and his leftovers too. Momma Niece always said it was sinful to let good food go to waste. She was known to check through the garbage cans.

My monkey brother had grown to be a man and I believe he was still jonesing for his missing mama. Why? I worked away my girlhood for that boy. Then he up and left over a little ass whupping, walking out the door and never looking back. His leaving like that pinched the center out of my life, like the middle out of a bread slice. That's how I was blessed for my good deeds. Me, the youngest of Momma Niece's four daughters. The one been promised to raise up a prophet.

I spent ten years caring for a monkey brat that wasn't even mine. It wasn't long before another one slipped in to fill the need. Perching on my shoulder like an imp, an organ grinder's pet. Staring at me with hungry eyes. Biting the hand that feeds it. But this one won't never hold a broom over my head. I already been two kinds of fools. I ain't about to be the same fool thrice.

So what if I'm a smackhead? Even with my habit, I'm stronger than these weak-minded women so turned around behind some light skin and curly hair they let a man piss on their head and call it rain. Sister Baby Ruth don't take no mess behind no man, no more.

Fact is, the only man I'm loving these days is the Lawd. I'm a God-fearing Christian woman, don't care if I've taken up cussing and been read out of the church. Can't an addict still praise the name of Jesus? Just like the devil loves a sanctified soul, God holds sinners closest to his heart. Just like he drove seven demons out of Mary Magdalene, he will one day cure me of my affliction.

Whensoever he willest, I'll stop shooting heroin into the veins of my hands. In fact, I'm not even getting a high no more. After so many years, I'm using these days just to stay straight.

I don't do no hustling. I ain't spending more than I can make in a day dishing out school lunches, or in a night making change at a ghetto gas station. I still manage to pay my rent, even put away a penny for a rainy day. Sho'ly there are cheaper highs, but I ain't buying it. I'm loyal like a lover, like a faithful daughter. White horse is the only one I'll fool with till the day I stop riding.

Whither thou goest, I will go.

I figured my brother as a lazy-ass pretty boy who never learned to stop sucking the titty and be a man. Well, ain't no titty here. If it was one thing Johnny knew, I had pulled up the welcome mat. I wasn't 'bout to clean up his shit for him. I had done my time washing diapers and piss-stank bedsheets. So when he showed up looking like death warmed over, I knew it had to be a desperate thing.

"Johnny, I ain't going to lie. I never thought I'd see you looking this bad. 'Course, life got me right raggedy around the edges too. But I never was much to look at."

He'd been sitting across my kitchen table, staring down at his hands. He looked up and fixed his green eyes on me like flashlights, just like he did when I first met him.

I halfway expected him to run off a mouthful of demon babbling. If nothing else I did for that boy, I sho' got that devilishness beat out of him.

"I never understood why she always said that. 'You ain't got no good looks, but you sho' do have a good heart.' Momma Niece really did a job on you, didn't she?"

"On me? You the one always had to have some woman saying how pretty you was. 'But thou didst trust in thine own beauty, and playedst the harlot because of thy renown, and pouredst out thy fornications on every one that passed by.' "

He looked away, shaking his head.

"You never really knew how beautiful you were."

"Don't start with me," I warned. "You still ain't too big to get your ass whupped."

"I thought you were the prettiest woman in the world."

" 'Favor is deceitful,' " I reminded him, " 'and beauty is vain: but a woman that feareth the Lord, she shall be praised.' "

He rested his chin in his unworked hands, remembering.

"You and all the women in the Pentecostal Sanctuary, I thought you were angels. Drifting around in those long skirts and high-collared dresses."

"If you had read your Bible," I reminded him, "then you would remember. God commanded women to adorn themselves 'in modest apparel, with shamefacedness and sobriety; not with braided hair, or gold, or pearls, or costly array.' "

"Well, I do remember Job. 'Deck thyself now with majesty and excellency; and array thyself with glory and beauty.' You were gloriously beautiful. You and all those high-butt, heavy-breasted, midnight-dark church mothers who comforted me when I cried, gave me sweet things to suck on when I was hungry. 'My son, eat thou honey, because it is good; and the honeycomb, which is sweet to thy taste.' "

" 'His bones are full of the sin of his youth,' " I quoted. " 'Wickedness be sweet in his mouth, though he hide it under his tongue.' "

Johnny's bloodshot green eyes went to darting around my kitchenette, looking just like his old drunk daddy.

"Anything in here to drink?"

" 'Wine is the poison of dragons, and the cruel venom of asps.' Deuteronomy thirty-two. 'Wine is a mocker, strong drink is raging: and whosoever is deceived thereby is not wise.' Proverbs twenty."

Johnny had the nerve to raise one eyebrow.

" 'Give strong drink unto him that is ready to perish, and wine unto those that be of heavy hearts.' Proverbs thirty-one."

Couldn't no backslid sinner match up with me in Bible wisdom. I may be on dope, but I ain't never tasted liquor.

" 'He asked water, and she gave him milk.' "

I reached into the refrigerator and found five small cartons, smuggled away from the school lunchroom. I gave him four, saved one for myself. Watched him guzzle them down, one right after the other. Then he raised up slow from the kitchen table and limped into the bathroom, bladder busting with all that milk. I suddenly felt sad for the young man I had mothered but never had time to sister.

"Why you walking like that?" I called after him. "What happened to your leg?"

I had seen a lot in my thirty-something years, a whole lot of hurt and pain and misery. Been through some of it myself. But when Johnny came back in the room and told me about the bullet in his thigh, I'm here to tell you, I couldn't see nothing but a bone-thin face with hungry green eyes, a nose packed with boogers. It made me want to cry. Not for the man Johnny was now, but the baby he used to be.

Pity left my mind when he limped over and laid down in my bed.

"Remember Pearlene, the Pleasants' daughter? Something about that girl reminded me of you. Whatever happened to her?"

"What, you ain't happy to see her ruint? You leave that girl alone. She ain't been right in the head ever since she went down to Memphis and—"

I stopped and shook my head. I done said too much already.

"To what? To do what, Mimi?" He sat straight up in bed. "Tell me what happened to Pearlene. Where is she now?"

I almost broke down. Almost told him the truth about my daughter, the girl he never knew was his half-niece. But just then my monkey woke up. Scaled my back like a lamppost, reached over my shoulder to whisper in my ear.

Feed me.

"Pearlene Pleasant," I sighed, lied. I ain't held her when she was born, didn't feed her when she was hungry. Least I could do was try to protect her now. "That is a whole 'nother story. I don't know where she is now. Maybe down in Memphis still."

"Then Memphis," he decided on the spot, "is where I'm headed."

"Memphis?" I repeated. "What for?"

"To find her, to tell her I'm sorry. To put some distance between me and my demons. To try to start life over again."

Feed me!

Don't mistake kindness for weakness. In fact, don't even look on it as an act of kindness. That voice whispering in my ear must have been God telling me I was still my brother's keeper. Well, this would be my last Lazarus act. I dished up all the food I had in the house, school lunch leftovers meant to be my dinner. A big plate of chili-mac, creamed corn, the last carton of milk, a slice of buttered bread. Just like when he was a kid, Johnny pinched the middle out of his white bread, guzzled his sweet milk, and picked at the rest of his food.

Feed me!

I left him sleeping in the bed I made, rode the Douglas Park elevated to the bank. Bet you never saw a smackhead with a Christmas club account. I cleaned it out. I went to Jewtown, bought a cheap set of clothes, a washcloth, some deodorant, a disposable razor. He wasn't going nowhere without washing his funky behind and shaving that mangly beard.

We rode to the station in silence. Him sitting stiff in them out-of-style dungarees. Me on the edge of my seat with the demon monkey clawing at my back. Clicking his teeth to the rhythm of the El train riding along the tracks.

Feed me!

"Mimi, you been so good to me." Johnny grabbed my hand. "I know it was you who had me placed with the Pleasants after I got arrested. You tried to do right by your baby brother, even when it didn't always work out. Thank you for everything. I'm paying this money back as soon as I can. I promise you that."

Just like the pitiful lies he told to avoid chastisement. "Mimi, you so pretty." I snatched my hand away.

"Don't lie to me, John the Baptist Wright. You got what you wanted out of me. You ain't going to be in touch, you ain't never going to pay me back. This ain't a loan, it's a gift. Go get yourself a life. And don't come back looking for nothing else. I ain't like the rest of your weak-minded womens. That's your last favor from me, understand?"

I bought a bus ticket with money meant for that night's fix. I turned my back when Johnny climbed on that Greyhound, didn't even bother to wave as the midnight coach pulled out for Tennessee. The monkey danced on top of the moving bus, waving a lacy white pillow. *Who art thou, my daughter? Ruth 3:16.* He swung from lamppost to telephone line, following me all the way home.

Feed me, Mimi. Sister Baby Wright.

I made my way back to my flophouse digs, monkey grown to gorilla size. I cut on the lights and TV set, ate up Johnny's plate of picked-over food, laid my track-scarred hands in my lap, and steadied myself for the jones coming down like a broomstick over my head.

Miriam

He could one day be a credit to his race

Chicago Board of Education
Official Student Record

Student: John T. B. Wright
Date of birth: May 9, 1961
School: Alexander Dumas High School

. . .

October 20, 1975

Miriam Cohen
School Counselor
Alexander Dumas High School
1500 S. Independence Boulevard
Chicago, Illinois 60623

Dear Miss Cohen:
   Congratulations! You will be delighted to learn that John T. B. Wright, one of your own scholars, achieved honorable mention in the National High School Classics Competition. His project "Musketeer Mission to Mars" was the inspired adaptation as a science fiction comic-book saga of the Dumas classic The Three Musketeers.
   Our judges were extremely impressed with this young man's creativity and originality. Although the honorable mention cate-

gory carries no cash prize, all winning contestants receive their own Junior Classics Library Collection, valued at $150.

If able to attend, Master Wright and his family are cordially invited to accept this award in person. The awards ceremony will take place on January 12, 1976, at the New York Public Library.

You may be interested to know that John T. B. Wright was the only freshman to receive an award of any kind. Our three prize winners and ten honorable mentions were selected from eight thousand high school contestants from across the country. Alexander Dumas High School is lucky indeed to have a person of such promise among your student body. We predict he will go far.
Very truly yours,
Conrad Panagakis
Acting Director
National Classics Foundation

. . .

January 18, 1976

Joseph Wright
1234 N. Kildeer
Chicago, Illinois 60644

Dear Mr. Wright:
Your child, John T. B. Wright, is a freshman at Alexander Dumas High School. I want to call to your attention his attendance record. Although he is generally a good student with average-to-excellent grades, he has accumulated seventeen absences and eleven tardies in this term alone.

Perhaps you are not aware that John has missed so many school days lately. This puts his academic performance and final grade for freshman year in serious jeopardy. I am sure you will want to do all that you can to remedy this situation.

Let's try to work together to see that your child's attendance improves. If there are extenuating circumstances, such as an illness or family emergency, please do not hesitate to let me know.
Sincerely,
Miriam Cohen
Counselor
Alexander Dumas High School

. . .

Request for Transcript

To: Miriam Cohen, School Counselor
From: Humberto Rodriguez, Educational Coordinator
Date: March 23, 1976

As a result of a recent conviction for armed robbery and resisting arrest, the minor student John T. B. Wright has been sentenced to serve juvenile probation in detention. Effective immediately he will be held in custody at the Audy Home for Boys for a period of no less than one and no more than three years. Please submit an official copy of his academic transcript, so that we may begin to plan the continuation of his high school study.

. . .

February 6, 1977

Miss Mary Corn
Dumas School
Chicago

Dear Miss Mary:
I want you to see after my little brother. His name is Johnny Wright. I raised up that boy from two to twelve. He mostly a good boy. He used to go to church and know the Lord. But Satan's demons been keeping him busy. I know he done wrong, but he been off in that reformatory school for near about a year. I hasn't been in touch with him myself. But Mr. Shackleforth, his probation officer think he seen the eror of his way and is ready to come out. I done messed up my life already. I don't want Johnny to lose his chances. Our pastor say he can help get Johnny somewhere to stay, where he won't be around no more bad company. Please help him get back in school, Miss Mary. I sure do appreciate it.
Very truly yours,
Ruth Wright

. . .

April 30, 1977

Andrew Felton
Circuit Judge
Cook County Juvenile Court
Chicago, Illinois 60622

Dear Judge Felton:

I understand that John T. B. Wright's case soon comes up for review. I would humbly and earnestly implore you to suspend his detention in the Audy Home and return this young man to his school, family, and community.

John Wright was one of the first students I met when I started here as school counselor in 1975. We were both brand-new. I still remember him out of a freshman class of seven hundred students. He immediately struck me as an intelligent and sensible young man, a student with the potential to excel. He had only been at Dumas for a few months when he won honorable mention in a major literary classics competition. I have seen much in my two years here, but students like John make my job worthwhile.

A series of unfortunate family and environmental circum-stances led to Johnny's criminal involvement. He comes from a very poor family and is a member of an oppressed minority, strug-gling to survive in the urban wasteland of inner-city America. It is a constant battle against hopelessness and degradation.

I work daily in an institution referred to by the community, the students, even some of the faculty and staff as "Dummies High." Our students are no dummies, Judge Felton. They are victims of a society that has forsaken them.

Although I realize Johnny's infraction was quite serious, it was his first offense. I feel strongly there will not be a second one. I believe he has atoned for his mistakes and repaid his debt to society.

With a father in crisis and no longer able to care for him, and a mother who seems unwilling to, I realize that his home situation is of serious concern. Please be advised that the pastor of the Pentecostal Sanctuary has pledged his support in finding a wholesome foster care situation and will do all that he can to facilitate this. Attached is a letter from Reverend Peter Pleasant to this effect.

If your decision is indeed favorable, I promise to put forth my best efforts in seeing that John T. B. Wright reaches the potential that was hinted at during his freshman year. I believe he can be thoroughly rehabilitated, complete his high school education, go on to college, and become a fully functioning member of society. He could one day be a credit to his race.

Respectfully,
Miriam Cohen
Counselor
Alexander Dumas High School

. . .

Memorandum

To: Andre Thomas, Principal
From: Miriam Cohen, Academic Support
Date: December 18, 1978
Re: Fighting Musketeers, academic suspensions

The following students have been referred for suspension from school athletics due to poor academic performance: Andrew Bailey, Florestine Connors, Henry Hillman, LaSagnia Jackson, Albert Jones, Roberto Ramos, and John Wright. I realize that John has not failed any classes this term, but he is a borderline student. Although he should be in his junior year by now, he missed roughly a year and a half of studies, and his academic record still shows him as a freshman. It is my wish, and John's as well, to eventually schedule extra coursework and summer-school credit so that he might be able to graduate with the class of 1979. This will not be possible with the current demands on his time made by the Fighting Musketeers and Coach Crockett.

cc: Harrison Crockett

. . .

Miriam:

I spoke to Principal Thomas and he agrees with me 100 percent. He passed all his classes. Johnny Wright is doing just great this season and there's no way he's dropping off the team. He's got three more years to catch up on coursework. Are you trying to tell me this kid's college material? Because if you do, I'm just not buying it. I don't think you could get him into college with a crowbar, but I bet dollars to doughnuts that I can. If he plays his cards right and commits to his game, Johnny has excellent prospects for an athletic scholarship. Get off his back, Cohen. Give the kid a break.

Harry Crockett

. . .

Memorandum

To: Harrison Crockett, Physical Education
From: Miriam Cohen, Academic Support
Date: January 20, 1978
Re: John T. B. Wright

Last month's communication was not addressed to you, Coach Crockett. It was sent to the principal's office. The proper procedure would have been to reply to Andre Thomas in the form of a memo and send a carbon copy to me. However, since you did contact me directly, I must let you know how strongly I disagree with everything you said.

With a little preparation and a lot more attention to his studies, John Wright would be a perfectly viable candidate for college placement. I find it incredible that you, an Afro-American man yourself, would deliberately try to limit this boy's options for bettering himself. There is no reason why he should spend six years in high school just to play basketball. I feel that you are exploiting this student in the worst kind of way.

Basketball is not every black boy's dream, nor is it the answer to every problem.

cc: Andre Thomas

. . .

Memorandum

To: Andre Thomas, Principal
From: Harry Crockett, Phys Ed
Date: February 1, 1978
Re: Cohen's memo of January 20

Miriam Cohen doesn't know what she's talking about. If you ask me, she's some bleeding-heart do-gooder coming into the community to preen and posture, then going back to the North Shore while the rest of us have to live with the results of her experiments.

She wants Johnny to go to college. That's all fine and dandy, but who's going to pay for it? Is Cohen? I grew up in the ghetto, just like you, Andre. Came off the streets playing high school sports and college athletics, got my sheepskin out of it. I know the real deal. The Fighting Musketeers will give this young brother half a chance to do something with his life, not some pie-in-the-sky college dream she's planting in his head.

For the first time in twelve years our school has the chance to make the all-city playoffs. Think about that, Andre. Do you know what kind of attention we'll be getting? Athletic recruiters from every NCAA school in the Midwest will be watching. So why is Cohen trying to block a brother's opportunities?

Board regulations say "no student under academic probation will take part in any athletic event or extracurricular activity." John T. B. Wright is not under academic probation, but he will be if Cohen gets her way and loads him up with all those extra classes. She says that I'm exploiting Johnny. Well, she's just trying to make a guinea pig out of him.

cc: Miriam Cohen

. . .

Memorandum

To: Andre Thomas, Principal
From: Miriam Cohen, Academic Support
Date: February 6, 1978
Re: Crockett's memo of February 1

I'm blocking Johnny's opportunities? I have done nothing but support this kid since he's been back at Dumas. If it hadn't been for me, he'd still be languishing in the Audy Home. I went to bat for him in court, picked him up in my own car when he was released, bought a set of clothes for him with my own money, and saw him safely settled into his new foster home. Where was Coach Crockett then?

Crockett's representation of me as a "bleeding-heart do-gooder" is both unfair and slanderous. I marched with Martin Luther King's Chicago campaign in 1967. I spent two years as a Peace Corps volunteer in a remote village in Sierra Leone, living and working among the people. I have been here at Dumas for the past three years. I am no stranger to this community, and no carpetbagger either. I don't know why my motives are always suspect, when I have these students' best interests at heart. It's people like Crockett who make me wonder if Afro-Americans really want us to help them move forward in their struggle.

I still believe Wright's academic advancement is more important than his athletic achievement. What does Coach Crockett want, for Johnny to be a Fighting Musketeer until he's twenty? I'm working with the board to see if any of the work Johnny did at the Audy Home is transferable. If he is able to attend two summer sessions and pick up three extra credits in the next academic year, he can conceivably graduate on time. I suggest we plan a team meeting with the student in question, his family, and custodial guardian so that we can discuss this matter reasonably.

cc: Harrison Crockett

. . .

Memorandum

To: Miriam Cohen, Academic Support
    Harrison Crockett, Physical Education
From: Andre Thomas, Principal
Date: February 15, 1978
Re: Enough already!

I'm tired of all this "he said, she said" over Johnny Wright. To hear the two of you go at it, the boy is either an Einstein in training or the new Julius Erving. What do you want, for me to cut him in half and you each take a piece? You two need to stop this bickering and try to come together on it. I've met with Johnny privately and he expresses his desire to continue playing basketball. He promises that his studies will not get short shrift, but has decided not to take on any additional classes at this time. I consider the matter to be closed. Johnny Wright is not the only student at Alexander Dumas High. We've got 2,376 others here. Let's give them some attention for a change.

. . .

May 19, 1979

Miriam Cohen
Alexander Dumas High
1500 S. Independence Boulevard
Chicago, Illinois 60623

Dear Miriam:

   Got your phone calls. Sorry it's taken so long to get back to you, but I've got several other clients in crisis. Johnny's is not the only case that needs my attention. I have looked into his situation and will see what I can do. You're right, he was only seventeen when he was arrested. I don't know why he's being held at the Cook County Jail, but he did turn eighteen there. Given that, I'm not sure I can still make an argument for his status as a minor.

   You actually want to go down there and make bail? Bad idea, Miriam. I think it would look very fishy for a kid's high school counselor to come and bail him out on a rape charge. Especially a female. This is a messy situation. I think you should keep your distance and just let me handle it.

   I don't need to tell you this is a very damaging charge. If convicted of this second felony offense, he could be tried as an adult and wind up doing some serious time. I'm not as sure as you are about his innocence, but I do have my doubts. I'm reserving judgment right now on whether this violates the terms of his probation.

   They were both minors living together in the same house. It seems to have taken place over a period of time, so more than likely it was consensual sex. The girl's father is the one who brought up charges. He also tried to hit him with battery, but it seems to me that Johnny has a better case against him. He's a big boy, but he took the brunt of the beating. I just don't see him as the perpetrator. Considering that he had injuries and the preacher didn't, John must not have put up much resistance. Hell hath no fury like a reverend wronged, I guess.

I know how crucial Johnny's athletics are now. Lucky thing the season is over. Maybe we'll be able to keep this out of the media. I've got a meeting with the public defender and the prosecuting attorney on Friday. We'll try to get the charges dropped, of course. But Johnny might have to consider some type of plea bargain arrangement.

In the event that he gets off, we need to figure out whom he's going home with. Obviously he can't go back to the Pleasants. And don't even think of taking him in yourself. What about his biological parents? Is either of them ready to step forward? See if you can check it out.

I can't make any promises to you, Miriam. I'll do my best, which is all I can do. We'll just have to trust the rest to God, fate, and the criminal justice system.

Take care,
Eugene Shackleforth
Probation Officer
Cook County Juvenile Court

. . .

April 11, 1981

Benjamin Fowler
Athletics Department
University of Illinois at Urbana-Champaign
Champaign-Urbana, Illinois 61820

Dear Ben:

It was great seeing you down in Chicago last month. Some playoffs, right? We were pushing for first, but ranking up second is nothing to sneeze at. Still, it would have been great for Hot Johnny to go out of Dumas in a blaze of glory.

I know you have your eye on my star player. Yes, he's a pretty

amazing athlete. Sure, he'd consider coming out to Chambana if the price is right. I must tell you, we're still looking at some other possibilities. What kind of package can you offer? Give me a call, let's talk turkey.
Yours,
Harry Crockett
Physical Education
Alexander Dumas High School

. . .

May 15, 1982
Undergraduate Admissions
University of Illinois at Urbana Champaign
Champaign-Urbana, Illinois 61820

Dear Admissions Officer:

It is with great enthusiasm and pride that I tender this recommendation for admission on behalf of John the Baptist Wright.

I have known Hot Johnny, as we affectionately call him here at Dumas High, for nearly six years now. He is an excellent student and a brilliant young man, intuitive, charming, and very intelligent. He's always done well on standardized tests, and I think you'll find his SAT scores to be quite satisfactory.

Although his academic potential has not always been reflected in his grades, you will notice from his transcript that they have improved considerably over the past two years. You will appreciate this even more when you realize what sort of challenges this young man has had to face.

He has had to fight for academic merit in a climate that has often been less than supportive. I will not go into particulars, but Johnny has also had much to overcome on the personal and family levels. This is primarily why it took a bright student six years to complete high school. For the past two years he has been in a more stable home environment and has worked diligently on improving his grades.

Although a great deal of attention has been given to his athletic accomplishments, Johnny Wright is also a talented writer and self-taught artist. He has excelled in his U.S., ancient, and world history courses. He is also a voracious reader and a skilled chess player. I taught him chess myself, and we have played many games together over the years. In recent times Johnny always trounces me miserably.

The University of Illinois would certainly benefit by Johnny's contribution, and he in turn would benefit by study there. I am sure he will thrive in an environment that will, for the first time in his life, encourage his intellectual development. Although he is at present uncertain what course of study to major in, I believe he will excel at whatever he chooses.

Faithfully yours,
Miriam Cohen-McMann
Assistant Principal
Alexander Dumas High School

Pearlene

He made that gal forget her religion

Th Pntcostal Sanctuary Church of God in Christ calls you to Sunday srvic.

Now, that don't look right. Lord save us, this e *is jamming up again. Why it always got to be the letter you type the most that messes up? Ain't no shame this Saturday night. All that sin walking the streets has done slipped beneath the church doors and into my typing machine. Demons down among the keys, fooling with my letter* e *and making me waste my ditto masters. Ain't that devil got a nerve? Studying his evil here right in the Lord's house.*

Get thee behind me, Satan! This ain't none of your typewriter, this is the Lord's machine. Mallinalli salla meena.

Eeeeeeeee. *Oh, truly God is able! It's working now, thank you, Jesus. Lord, I'm so tired of fooling with this old manual. If it's your will, please bless us with that computer we been praying for so long, amen.*

Ri-i-i-ing!

What in the names of Jesus? Sorry, Lord. Forgive my blaspheming tongue. Who could be calling here this time of night?

Pentecostal Sanctuary, praise the Lord. Pearlene Pleasant speaking . . . Yes, Mother Dear . . . Well, just me, but the door is locked up tight. . . . Sho' you right, we're living in the last days. . . . Yes, I know it ain't noways safe out there. But we trust in God to look after babies and fools. . . . Yes, I promise I'll be careful. . . . I do remember, Mother Dear. . . . Dixie Peach Hair Pomade, a pair of white pantyhose and a pint of butter pecan . . . Well, just as soon as I finish typing this ditto and run off tomorrow's bulletin. Shouldn't be no later than nine. . . . Praise Jesus' holy name. Bye now.

Celebrate being celibate! "Saying no to the sin of fornication" is the theme of the Celibatarian Saints annual ice cream social.

Join them for this inspiring message and meet other single saints spreading the word of the gospel, next Saturday afternoon at 3 P.M.

Oh, Lord, is that somebody at the door? I ain't answering, don't care how loud and long they knock. Ain't Mother Dear just said it? Women getting raped every night of the week. Look, he's still out there. I can see his shadow in the doorway window, looks like he's trying to peep in here at me. He must can see the light burning. Oh, where does Reverend Sandifer keep that Mace?

Lord knows, I got no business being down here this late at night. But Mother Betty kept me so long at the senior citizens'. Like to talk my ear off. Bless her heart, she ain't got nobody else to talk to. Somebody got to visit the sick and old, the lonely and shut-in. Yet and still, the church has got to have its bulletin on a Sunday morning. It's always a sacrifice when you're working for the Lord. You do what you must and let God take care of the rest.

Jesus, is that man coming in here or what? I thought for sure I locked that door. Don't let me fool around and get raped in the Lord's house. Don't let that sinful man have his way with me tonight!

You got to leave here, brother. Church is closed right now, but we'll be open for Sunday service tomorrow morning. Visitors is always welcome, ain't no strangers in the house of prayer. . . . You come back tomorrow at ten. . . . Well, I do work here. But like I said, the church is closed. . . . No, I don't believe I know you. . . . Don't come no closer, please. . . . Oh, Jesus, don't touch me! Don't be trying to kiss on me. . . . Lord God help me!

> *Father, I stretch my hand to thee,*
> *No other help I know.*
> *If thou remove thyself from me,*
> *Whither shall I go?*

Well, I'll stop singing when you stop touching. Don't be trying to hug and kiss, you don't know me like that. Watch where you put them hands. I'm a Celibatarian Saint, keeping myself pure for marriage. . . . No, I have never seen you before in my life, I'm positive of that. . . . You're who? I already told you, I've never met a Johnny Wright in all my born days. You got to leave here now, don't I'll call the police.

No, you must be mixing me up with somebody else. You knew somebody who was a member of this church? Well, it ain't none of me. You must mean that other child Bishop Pleasant and them used to have around here. Lord knows she was a sinner. What-all she done, I don't even like to think about. *For it is shameful even to mention what the disobedient do in secret.* Me, I'm president of the Celibatarians, ain't never done that type of thing. I ain't married yet, and fornication is a sin before God.

What do I remember about that gal? Well, she got messed up behind some boy, I know that much. Tall and light-skinded with green eyes, kind of like yours, come to mention it. Yes, that was the downfall of her. She loved her some pretty eyes and good hair more than she loved her Lord.

Looking at him in his clothes, you wouldn't know the devil's bite was branded on his thigh. Looking at his face, you wouldn't think such a comely young man had mixed in that kind of worldly corruption. When she asked him if he was still pure, the boy just laughed and shook his head.

"Girl, you don't even know me. I used to run ho's down on West

Madison Avenue." Then he took her hands in his, leaning in and looking into her eyes. "I want you to pray for me, sister."

With that kind of past, people must have thought he done seduced that gal. Lured her from the Lord into the ways of the flesh. But it wasn't like that at all. She fretted about holding on to him, worried that he never tried to touch her. Every time he was away, she would think of him in the arms of those worldly women. Of him slipping back into his old ways, lost to her forever.

Oh, yes, she prayed on it. Then she set her cap and went after him like her life depended on it. Trying to save his soul from eternal damnation, she the one who wound up falling.

She had a good Christian upbringing, but it all went for nought the minute she opened up her heart. Seem like she was hungry all the time and couldn't get full. She was starving for that boy, and he was her food, her milk and honey. Yes, indeed. She near 'bout scared that boy to death, and he wasn't somebody who was that easy scared. He tried to hold his self above sin, he who had lain in a den of whores.

"Girl, your need is bigger than the ocean." He be trying to push her away from him. "You liable to drown us both."

See, that's the kind of trick the devil uses. He'll hold out something you want more than your own salvation, then act like he's fixing to snatch it away. It makes you lust after it that much more. Oh, Satan is a liar and a conjurer too. A psychologizing son of sin, a master of temptation.

I'm here to tell you now, that boy was fine. Pretty as an angel in heaven. He may not have been saved, but he sho' was something to see. All the gals round here was after that boy, the ones was saved and the ones was sinners. She the gal he picked out of the whole group, can you imagine that? She must have had something special to catch his eye.

What did you say your name was? . . . John the Baptist Wright, sho' 'nough? Oh, that's a powerful Christian name. You must truly love the Lord.

Well, I guess I could spare a minute or two. Seeing how we both knowed that poor child, bless her heart. Black Pearl, that's what they called her. You know what we say at the Pentecostal Sanctuary Church of God in Christ? "There are no strangers in the house of prayer." You want to sit down for a minute? We got some instant coffee.

No, I don't know what became of that gal. I ain't thought about her in years. I remember her, though. She truly loved the Lord before she got turned around behind fornication and worldly pleasures.

I remember when the boy first came here, poor thing. He had lived a hard life. Put outdoors by his family in the dead of the winter, not a pot to make water in nor a window to throw it out. Had spent some time in a home for wayward boys, I do believe. The pastor took him in out of the goodness of his heart, may God rest his soul.

Yes, Bishop Pleasant is dead now. He passed more than few years back, went home to join his heavenly father. You know that we truly loved him, but God loved him best. Lucius Sandifer's our pastor now. An able and godly man, but Lord knows he can't preach like Bishop Pleasant could. That man was God's saint on earth, he could do no wrong. Why, he and Mother Pleasant took me in when I was just a baby.

That's right. My real mother was another ruint gal, the poor little church secretary that used to work for Bishop Pleasant when he was alive. They said she run off and left me laying in the birthing bed. Can you imagine that, a mother just up and leaves her newborn child? But the Lord will surely make a way. A child born of sin, and that godly couple still found it in their heart to take me in and raise me up. But then, ain't we all born in sin? Born in sin and saved by grace.

Would you like me to show you around? It ain't all built up like those grand churches with two and three thousand members. Oh, some of them have grown so worldly, claiming to be saints with painted women all up in the Lord's house, their arms bare and their heads un-covered. Got their choirs singing blues and calling it gospel, don't make the pastor no never mind. Nothing but money changers in the temple, congregations full of drinkers and gamblers. Yes, the world is in a bad way now, I do believe we're living in the last days.

But we got our own little sanctuary in the midst of sin. It's not much to look at, but we're proud of it. Just because this is a storefront church don't mean we can't praise his holy name.

We were right up there with them big South Side congregations when Bishop Pleasant was alive. Used to be a time when we had over five hundred members, had to split up into two services. Christmas and Easter some years, it was three services. Now we're lucky to get fifty people coming through here on a Sunday. . . . Oh, you've been here before? . . . Really, that long ago? Well, wonder why I ain't never met you? I sho' was around then. I grew up right here in this church, you know. Ain't been nowhere else.

You couldn't find more loving parents on heaven nor earth, but Mother Dear and Bishop Pleasant couldn't keep that gal. They wasn't blessed to bear their own, but they sho' took care of us. That other gal? She was just too bad. Repaid the Pleasants' goodness by letting a boy spoil her virtue. How do I know? She told me all about it.

She sacrificed her mortal soul trying to save his. She loved that boy like a brother, taking him to around to Bible study, getting him involved in the Celebatarian Saints. I tell you one thing. That boy could preach him a pretty sermon. Oh, he had a way with words.

Pretty words, praise Jesus! Would fall out of his mouth like pearls, go to licking you all over like a thousand tongues. Ain't that devil a scoundrel? Using the word of God himself to create confusion in the flesh.

Those two would leave straight out from Bible study and go to committing fornication. Yes, Lord. She would lead him right here to this very room. Would lay him 'cross the couch, that very one you sitting on. Yes, she had the boy bed her down in the house of God.

See, he had already bedded down a plenty young womens, but he ain't never had a virgin. This the kind of woman a man wants for a wife. "A widow, or a divorced woman, or profane, or an harlot, these shall he not take: but he shall take a virgin of his own people to wife."

She wasn't light-skinded and pretty like some. She ain't had no straightened hair and painted face like those worldly gals he been around. She wasn't out doing that butt shaking they call dancing, playing cards and drinking spirits. See, that's why he wanted her. He wanted somebody fresh and pure. Plus she had them big old breastes on her.

Now don't be looking at me like the pot calling the kettle black, because I know I got some breastes on me too. But I'm not like that other gal. These here is for my husband, whensoever the Lord blesses me with one. I ain't never let no nasty boy get my bra off and suck on me like a nursling babe. I ain't never had no man stick nothing up in me, not even the doctor. Jesus is my doctor, rastemi challa, hah!

Right there, you see it? That's the same old couch, you can feel the springs poking through when you sit down. Right there with their clothes pulled down and the lights turned off. With her legs spread and his hands all over her. Whispering in her ear and feeling for her pearl. His thing winding all up in her, sweet like the devil's fruit.

Right here in the room where Bishop Pleasant read his Bible. Right here where I type my church bulletins. Oh, God, forgive them! Making her scream out loud and call his name instead of the Lord's. He made that gal forget her religion. Made her explode, just a-wriggling and a-writhing in Holy Ghost rapture. Except it wasn't the spirit of God moving in her. It was the possession of sin, a baptism of hellfire that felt like heaven. "Stolen waters are sweet, and bread eaten in secret is pleasant. But he knoweth not that the dead are there; and that her guests are in the depths of hell."

I remember one time the lights went out. That didn't stop their sinning. He found some candles and lit them around her. He said she shimmered like marble in candlelight. Went to worshiping her body like a heathen idol. You know fire is the devil's own element, don't you? You got to be careful what you say and do in front of a burning flame. That boy said he was drawn to her like a moth to a candle. That's just how the devil will trap your soul.

When the sinning was over, he sang to her. Sang those pretty words, straight from the throat of Satan. Calling her his Black Pearl, telling her how precious she was. See, that's how the devil gets you, appealing to your pride. And pride goeth before a fall. Mmm, seem like I can close my eyes and hear him singing right now. Telling her to come out of the background and into the world.

Oh, you the one singing! Well, how you know that worldly song, Brother Wright? What you mean, you used to sing it to her? Lord save us, you was that boy? You the one who ruined that gal? Yes, ruined her. You mean to say, you didn't know she was in the family way? How could you not know? "Then when lust hath conceived, it bringeth forth sin: and sin, when it is finished, bringeth forth death."

You know, every time it happened she would tell the pastor. Every single time. She told the pastor and they would pray on it. At first it wasn't nothing but kissing, kissing and touching her bust. She didn't know if that was fornication, so she took it to the Lord's messenger here on earth, Bishop Peter Paul Pleasant. What he told her?

Well, he said touching above the waist was no sin at all, just so long as she reported to him exactly what happened, exactly when it happened. But that gal soon lost her good sense. Let that wanton lust spread over her, didn't care where the touching went. Above the waist, below it. Every time she sinned, that gal took it to the Lord. Confessed it to Bishop Pleasant, the one who could ask God to purge her sin.

Oh, many an hour was spent in prayer. "Is there no balm in Gilead; is there no physician there? Why then is not the health of the daughter of my people recovered?" I don't need to tell you that prayer changes things. She looked around one day and the boy was gone. She was hurting for a while, hungering for him. "For the hurt of the daughter of my people am I hurt; I am black; astonishment hath taken hold on me." But praise be to God, she was clean again. The boy? Child, when she wasn't there for his lust and sinning, that no-good boy just up and left.

No, sir. No, no, that's a lie before God. Our Bishop Pleasant was a good man. He was a spiritual father to us all. He wasn't the kind of man who would beat a boy near 'bout to death, call the police to take him away. Even a young man who had ruined his adopted daughter. Not Bishop Pleasant. He would sit that boy down and talk to him, make him see the error of his ways. I know this can't be no true story you telling me.

No, I don't know what became of her or the baby. But I do know this much. That gal stole my little lacy pillow I had since I was a child, it read *Who art thou, my daughter?* from Ruth, chapter three. One of the church sisters, Sister Baby Ruth, made it for me. That gal took it with her when they sent her down south.

That just goes to show you the nature of a sinner. If you fornicate, you'll steal. If you steal, you'll kill. That Pearl was the one had a baby out of wedlock. Some people say she came back to the Sanctuary, but they're a liar and the true ain't in them. I'm the one here. I'm the good girl, the Celebatarian Saint. That bad girl never came back, and she ain't never coming back. Why you looking for her now after all these years?

Do I want to see a picture? Well, yes. But who are these people you showing me? Your wife and your daughter? No, Brother John. I don't recognize neither one of them. But that sho' do look like my pillow that little baby holding. How in heaven did your daughter get ahold of my pillow?

No, I ain't got bone marrow to give to nobody now. I don't know nothing 'bout no blood disease. Wash your feet in the blood of the lamb, that's all I know. Pray to the Lord, that's all I know. Didn't Jesus heal the lepers? Didn't my Lord deliver Daniel?

I ain't the one to judge you. Vengeance is mine, saith the Lord. Yes, Brother John, I do understand and I wish I could help. But that gal, she left here a long time ago. She suffered for her worldly ways, and all I can do is pray for her. I'll pray for you too, you and that baby child of yours.

You know you need the Lord in your life. You know you need to see after your salvation. It ain't just your mortal soul you're sacrificing. If you ain't saved, your marriage ain't saved, nor is the fruit of that union. Come, let me anoint your head with oil. Come, get down on your knees. Sister Pearlene's sending up prayers to the Lord, oh semolee falla!

Lord, God Jesus, bless this man for the sin he has done and the sin he has yet to do. Bless that gal he turned down the road of no return. Suffer the little children to come unto thee. Bless and heal his sick child, for the child is father to the man and has the sins of its father flowing through its veins. Halla simma challa, hallelujah!

I done already told you, I ain't none of that gal. How did I know he called her Black Pearl? How I know about that mark on his thigh? How I know what they did in the dark? She told me all about it, that's how. My name is Pearlene. Pearlene Pleasant, not nobody's Black Pearl.

Some child wrote here a few years back, looking to find her mother and father. Child name of Desiree, Destinary, something like that. I still got her letter in the filing cabinet. Felt sorry for that child, sho' did. But no, I couldn't help her, just like I can't help you. I never had nothing to do with it. It must have been that other gal. That fornicator and sinner was her long-lost mother.

I never been sent down south in shame, never had no baby I had to leave on the birthing bed. I'm clean, Lord knows it, clean through and through. I live in grace, sanctified in the Lord's sight. Taking care of church business, looking after my old sick Mother Dear, visiting the elderly and shut-in every Saturday afternoon. President of the Celibatarian Saints Social Club. Nobody ever laid me on a lumpy couch and went diving for my pearl.

I said, "Lord make me an instrument of thy will." I ain't never smoked a cigarette nor tasted a drop of liquor in life. I ain't never worn pants, nor skirts up above my knees. I went to the Jones Commercial High, wore my hat and white gloves to school every day. I said every day, you hear me now?

I graduated with a diploma in secretarial science and made it my ministry. I ain't went out in those worldly offices, sitting amongst the liar and blasphemer, the sinner and adulterer. I type and take my Gregg shorthand, keep the books and run that mimeograph machine, all for the Lord.

Me, I don't care nothing about no good-looking man with pretty hair. I ain't nobody's Black Pearl. Yes, I may be dark-skinded, but praise the Lord! Halla minna salla, hallelu-jah! My soul is whiter than the driven snow.

Peaches

That's what a man supposed to do

Damn, it's cold out here. That hawk got his nose up my ass tonight. I thought this bus wouldn't never come. Hold on, peoples. Don't be in such a big hurry. Lady Peaches don't get around like she used to. Feets hurting me like a dick-dog. Whew, let me get a seat and catch my breath. How's everybody doing tonight?

Well, hey, Mr. Bus Driver. What you know good, daddy? I likes me a working man. Sho' do. I bet you I can drive this bus. What kind of experience I got? I got me a-plenty experience. Fifteen years with the same pimp.

Who that laughing back there? Bitch, fuck you. You ain't walked a mile in my shoes, you ain't got no business talking. What, you ain't never seen no ho catch the CTA?

I been in all kinds of rides in my day, cars you only seen passing by. Lincoln Town Cars, Cadillac Coupe de Villes, BMWs, stretch limos. Nowadays the players like them Jeeps. That's what my man got now. You want to know why I'm riding the bus? Dollar Billy is temporarily undisposed, if you must know. When he got sentenced last week, police impounded his ride. But it ain't no thang. He'll soon be rolling again and this CTA can kiss my ass.

What you mean, creating a disturbance? What you talking, disorderly conduct? How you gonna play me like that, Mr. Bus Driver? I ain't drunk, just a little toasted. I done paid my dollar fifty. I'm gonna ride this muthafucka till I get off, just like everybody else on here. Who going to put me off, you?

Oh, it's like that. You got that radio, fixing to call the cops. Don't even bother, I see my business ain't wanted here. I'm getting my ass out on the street and walking, like the ho I am. Hey, anybody on this bus want a good time? Ya'll get off at the next stop. It ain't but a short walk to the Excess Motel.

What you talking 'bout, Es*sex*? I worked every single room in that place, I ought to know the name of it. Let me get my ass off this bus 'fore I have to hurt somebody. Driver, let me off at the corner of Madison and Kedzie.

Well hey, big daddy. I see you done took me up on my offer. My name Sheila, peoples call me Lady Peaches. What your name is?

Jimmy? Hmpf, your voice sho' do sound familiar. Seem like I know you from somewhere. Never mind, don't make no difference. Daddy, what happened to your face? Naw, it don't bother me none. I don't care what you look like, I'm a equal-opportunity businesswoman. Come on over here and check this out. You like what you see? It look good, don't it? What you want, daddy? A screw, a blow?

You say you want to talk? For what? Honey, I sell cunt, not conversation. I ain't got no talk for you, 'less it's pillow talk. Now, you want somebody to talk dirty to, I'm your girl. Fill your ear with full of *muthafuckas*, if that's what greases your griddle. But you just want to conversate, you need a shrink, not a prostitute.

What, you still here? Will you quit following up behind me, whatever you say your name is. Jimmy? Well, Jimmy, I don't mean no disrespect. But you and that face like a Halloween mask, like to scare off all my little business. All right, you want to talk, go ahead and talk. But you going to have to pay me for my time. Twenty-five dollars on the hour, that's what I charge.

Come on over to the Blues Room and buy me a drink. Let me sit my tired ass down. Whew, this has been some kinda night. Every little hype and crackhead got her ass on the corner these days, old ho like me can't hardly make a honest dollar. Either the mens want you to give it away, or they want to take what little you got. You got a cigarette, daddy?

Who, me? How old you think I am? They say a lady ain't supposed to tell her age, but I know age don't make the lady. Just turned forty-seven, but I know I look seventy-four. Feel older than that sometimes. Been out on these streets so long, it's like dog years. Every year you come through alive, that's seven years of a regular life.

You say *who* is back in town? No shitting? Hell yeah, I knew Hot Johnny the Gent. That man was my regular pot of gold. Shit, I made that nigga. Gave him his walk, his talk, his natural name. Taught him everything he know; how to shoot the rock, walk the walk, and feed the kitty, if you know what I mean.

First time I seen that boy, I could tell he was a virgin right off the bat. It was all in the walk. Take a look at a priest or sissy man. Man ain't never had no trim, he be moving all stiff-legged. Can't hardly walk for them blues balls. How you gonna call yourself a man, you ain't never had none? Me, I love to break a man in. Virgins, sissies, priests. You know what everybody used to say? "Poontang Peaches make a dead man come."

Sometimes at the end of stormy weather, a rainbow turns up. You ever seen one in a puddle on the sidewalk? I remember looking down one day, saying, "Well, damn if that ain't a rainbow!" Along come a foot, stepped right in the middle of it. I didn't know it at the time, but that was my pot of gold.

Johnny Wright was out walking, trying to look cool. You know that pimp walk you see on brothers in the 'hood? That's a man's protection walk. You don't know how to walk the walk, might as well be wearing a bull's-eye on your back. Johnny sho' was trying, but he ain't had it right. Held his shoulders hunched too high, his head way too low. He wasn't dipping enough at the knee. Blue-balling like a broke-dick dog.

Every so often the boy would take a little skip. Now, what kind of fool go skipping through the ghetto like Little Red Riding Hood? The boy was wearing them talking gym shoes, sole flapping open at the toe.

Come to find out, he was skipping to keep from tripping on them flapping soles. Trying not to get his feet wet. Po' baby. First thing I did when I got with Hot Johnny is bought him a brand-new pair of high-top Keds.

Back in those days I was freelancing. Ain't had no pimp, just worked the stroll on Madison Avenue from Keeler to Kostner. Enough to keep me in clothes and cigarettes, drinks and rent money. I'd seen Johnny going in and out the library, ain't never had no books. I guess he had sense enough to know better. You don't walk the valley of the shadow of death with no book in your hand. That be like calling every vulture out here.

I remember standing in a doorway to light my cigarette one night, Johnny come skipping by, whispering to himself.

"Phasers, men. Attack!"

The little nigga lived in a comic-book world. He could memorize and say them word for word. Captain J.C. and Count Caitiff, shit like that. Heroes and bad boys. One be running around trying to blow up the world, the other one be trying to save it. All he did in that library was read comics. Don't know how he passed a class in school. I never known him to do a page of homework. But hell, I ain't nobody to talk. I can't remember last time I even went by somebody's schoolhouse. Can't read too good, but I do know how to count my money. Lady Peaches done got a Ph.D. from the University of the Streets.

See, I been living the sporting life practically since I was born. Hard as it is out here, it was worse at home when I was coming up. Got the hell up out of there quick as I could. A kid supposed to be protected, but ain't nobody protected me. My mother and that trick she called a stepdaddy? They was too busy looking for their next high to look after me. But shit, you ain't paying twenty-five an hour to hear my sad story.

What you want to know about Hot Johnny the Gent? He was what, fifteen years old when I met him? You think that's young? Shit, I wasn't much older than that myself.

Johnny ain't had no easy life, either. Oh, no. Hardly enough food, be living on peanut butter sandwiches and Kool-Aid for days at a time. He was with his old drunk daddy then. It ain't nothing lower than a back-slid preacher. The higher they climb, the lower they fall.

When Joe's disability check came, Johnny know he got to stay outta school that day and follow the nigga down to the currency exchange. He have to tussle away a little money for his self before his daddy drank or whored it all away. I felt so sorry for that boy. Half the time the lights was cut off, Johnny had to go to the library just to have some-place warm to read his comics.

But see, a black man in the ghetto, you can't be living up in no li-brary. Book learning is one thing, street smarts is another. Hot Johnny was so sweet and innocent, these streets would have squashed him like a bug. I hadn't come along when I did, some freak or sissy might have got ahold to that tight young ass.

He wasn't no weak-looking broke-at-the-wrist dude, but he sure was tall and good-looking. Pretty eyes, baby hair, brown-complected. Would have been a damn fine bitch. Could have made a-plenty money on the stroll.

But Johnny wasn't nobody's bitch. He wasn't no sissy kind of boy, just green as grass without a lick of street sense. Wet as snot behind the ear, between the toes, under the dick. He wouldn't have made it on these streets without somebody to school him. Lucky damn thing I came along.

One winter right around sunset I stumbled up on Jimmy "Bosco Bear" Johnson. The dude was just trouble, the worst kind of lowlife. Gang-banging, jailbird, punk-ass bully. Bosco Bear ain't liked nothing better than beat somebody's butt, then turn around and fuck them in it. Remind me of my evil-ass stepdaddy. None of us working girls wanted a thing to do with Bosco. Half the time he take the ass and won't pay, then turn right around and kick it for you. Oh, you know Bosco Bear? Then you know I'm telling the truth.

I swear to God, I was going home. I was renting a room over on Ridgeland Avenue. It was late at night and it was snowing. I was walk-ing 'cross Madison Avenue with my coat buttoned up, my hands in my pocket. Now if I'd a-been working, I would open up my coat so the tricks can see what they buying. I may not look like much now, but I was a fine bitch back then. Long hair, big legs, high-rise booty. Shit, some tricks would pay a dollar just to look at me with my clothes off.

I was on my way home, and here Bosco come stumbling out this same Blues Room we sitting in, stanking drunk.

"Hey, Peaches. Come over, let me feel on that big black ass."

I played like I ain't hear him, just keep on walking.

"You heard me, ho. Come on over here."

Next thing I know, Bosco run up on me, come snatching off my coat. He slammed me up against a building and went to grinding. Right out there on West Madison Avenue, with cars passing and people looking. Let me tell you something about a punk-ass raper man, because that's what the nigga was. They don't want to fuck you as much as hurt you. Bosco wasn't even hard inside his pants. Am I sho'? Hell yes, I'm sho'. Got to see it up close before too long.

I just stand there and take it, because I know how Bosco is. He like it when you try to fight back. The harder you fight, the harder you fall. But playing along ain't helped me none. Bosco Bear knocked me down to that slushy sidewalk, unzipped his pants, and pulled out his worm.

"Suck my dick, bitch."

"Naw, Bosco," I plead with him. "Not out here in front of everybody. Come on, let's go somewhere."

I struggled to my feet, Bosco Bear knock me back down again. He went to punching, beating, kicking on me. His thang dangling loose out his zipper. His fist in my face, his knee in my chest, his hand yanking back my hair. Trying to stuff his worm down my mouth, soft and flabby like a wad of chewing gum. I'm hollering, trying to get away.

From the corner of my eyes, I could see a group of winos around a lit garbage drum. They stood and watched, warming their hands. Passing cars slowed down, some of them beeping horns and laughing out loud. Not a one of them stepped up to help me. Not until Johnny passed by, skipping like a dick-dog.

"Help me, boy!"

Johnny stopped, frowning for a second.

"What's going on?"

He had one of those voices in the middle of changing. Be starting out deep and ending up squeaky.

"Call the cops, this man 'bout to kill me!"

I ain't meant for that skinny little boy to get in no fight with big old crazy Bosco Bear. You heard what I said. I told him to call the police. I don't know what got into his head. Maybe he was still in his comic-book high, thinking he was Captain J.C. of the Space Command.

"Hey, man. Why don't you leave that lady alone?"

Bosco Bear stopped hitting and kicking, but still held on to my hair. He didn't even seem mad at first. He talked real slow, like a old man giving a young one advice.

"This ain't no lady. This is a ho." Bosco yanked my head back, giving the boy a good look at my face. "See. That ain't nothing but Poontang Peaches. Now get the hell out of my business, boy."

Johnny stepped back on the ball of his left foot, sole flapping. Shoes doing his talking for him. Crammed his hands in his pocket.

"Don't they call you Jimmy the Bosco Bear?"

"Yeah." Bosco let go of my hair, took a step toward him. "Yeah, what about it?"

"That's what I thought. Saw your momma down on Roosevelt Road."

"My momma?"

"Yeah. Your old girl tried to sell me some pussy. Broad so ugly she promised me a dollar, ain't had nothing but seventy-five cents. Told me to come find you, you'd be good for the quarter."

That was it. The boy was dead, he just sealed his own casket. Unless you ready to fight to the death, you can't be calling somebody's momma a ho. Even if she was a cheap stank ho like Bosco Bear momma musta been.

"Been missing your momma, Bosco Bear? So do every other nigga on West Madison Avenue."

Bosco was already riled up from beating on me. He balled up his fists, came after the boy. I got to my feet, ready to run. Johnny should have done the same.

Seen Bosco's ugly momma
Sitting on the graveyard fence
She was trying to make a dollar
Out of seventy-five cents.

"Little yella nigga," Bosco told him, "you getting your ass whupped good tonight."

Bosco Bear bum rushed him. The boy was quick on his feet; he stepped away.

You miss, you miss,
You miss like this . . .

He kept singing, dodging blows, dancing. Had him a little Ali action going on—"float like a butterfly, sting like a bee, you too big and clumsy to catch up with me."

Yo' momma don't wear no drawers
I saw her when she took them off.

That wasn't no real signifying, that was a training rhyme. It was just a silly little tune kids tossed at each other when they were practicing to play the dozens. Maybe that wasn't even what made Bosco Bear so mad. Maybe it was the other folks snapping, the winos on the corner slapping five.

"Damn, man. He talking 'bout your old lady. Wouldn't take that shit if I was you."

She hung them on the wall
and the roaches refused to crawl.

"Ooh, do. Sigged all over you."

This time Bosco's blow landed, busting Johnny upside the jaw. The boy slid across the snow, but he didn't fall. Not that time.

She put them on the line
and the sun refused to shine.

"Scared the sun right out the sky! Them musta been some funky-ass drawers."

The winos was steady instigating, like announcers at a boxing match. Bosco busted Johnny again, knocking him in the chest. It must have winded him, because he stopped singing. But one of the winos had picked up the song.

> *She put them on the fence*
> *and I haven't seen the mailman since.*

Bosco looked around, his fists in the air.

"Who said that? Come on, nigga. Jump to my chest. I'll whip your ass like I did this punk."

He turned around to point him out, but the punk was on his feet and flying toward him. Johnny's punch wasn't that hard, but it caught Bosco off guard. He went down on his knees. The winos on the corner were do-wopping now, making it up as they went along.

> *(A ding-dong)*
> *She put them in my sink*
> *and my sink turned yellow-pink.*

"Fool, that ain't no lyrics. 'My sink turned yellow-pink.' Can't you do no better than that?"

"Let's see what you got, you so big and bad."

Bosco struggled up, slow and drunk. By then Johnny had raised up them holey gym shoes and was running like greased lightning.

> *(A ding-dong)*
> *She put them on the railroad track*
> *and the train shot ten miles back.*

"Man, look at that dude's johnson flapping in the breeze. Hey, Bosco! Less'n you got some bullets in it, you better put that pistol back in your pocket. A-heh-heh."

Johnny ran for the corner. He crashed into the crowd that was standing there, singing for blood. Hands went to grabbing on him, pushing him back to the fight. They held him there until the Bear caught up with him.

> *(A ding-dong)*
> *Bosco momma don't wear no drawers*
> *I saw her when she took them off.*

Bosco ran at the trapped boy, ramming him like Gayle Sayers or something. The crowd broke open. The boy fell, holding on to his middle.

"Y'all boys stop it now," some woman whined. "Somebody gonna get hurt."

"Go on ahead and let them fight," one of the winos told her. "Toughen 'em up, baby. Toughen 'em up."

> *(A ding-dong)*
> *She put them on the ground*
> *and the green grass turned to brown.*

Bosco went to stomp the boy laying on the ground. Missed. Johnny done a quick roll, snow went to flying.

> *(A ding-dong)*
> *She dropped them on the bedroom floor*
> *and the floor walked out the door.*

Different people tell different stories. Some said Johnny bounced a brick off Bosco's head. Others say he pulled a knife. But I was there, I saw it all. Johnny ain't done nothing to Bosco but roll out of the way.

That was it. Johnny rolled out from under Bosco's boot, like the stone rolling away from Jesus' tomb. Sunset shot a glare across the snow. And Bosco tripped over his own two feet. I remember it just like it was yesterday.

You know how in the movies when the bad boy falls, seems like he falls forever? Daddy, that's just the way Bosco Bear fell, arms spread across that garbage drum, like a stocky Jesus on a flaming cross. Sprung on fire like he was soaked in gasoline. Must have been all that alcohol. Bosco screamed and hollered, rolling in the snow, trying to put his self out. The boy scrambled to his feet, looking down at Bosco like he wasn't sure what he was seeing.

". . . Six, seven, eight, nine, ten!" some drunk went to counting. "It's a knockout, folks. And the crowd went wild."

Winos came slapping Johnny's back, shaking his hand.

"Y'all know who this is? This is Joe's boy, Johnny. Joe should have been down here, man. His son did him proud tonight."

"Shit, Johnny a cold muthafucka. Kill you quick as look at you."

"Yep, we don't need no fire. Johnny done heated up the corner tonight."

The crowd broke up when we heard the sirens. Nobody waited to see if it was the cops, the ambulance, or the fire department. I grabbed Johnny's hand and ran, pulling him into the Blues Room. I grabbed a handful of ice from the cooler and wrapped it in a cocktail napkin to hold against his black eye.

"What you doing with that boy?" Big Fat Jessie hollered from behind the bar. "He way too young to be up in here."

"This boy is hot," I told her. "Ain't that right, daddy? Hot Johnny like a dick-dog."

Johnny only nodded, taking the ice pack off his face and putting it on mine. He rubbed his hand against my cheek, singing to me in some kind of foreign language. You see there? That ain't no boy. That's a gentleman. I had forgot all about my own bruises. Hell, I had it worse than Johnny.

"You're a lady, Peaches." He laid his hand alongside my face. First time anybody every called me a lady. "You don't deserve to be treated like that."

"Hot Johnny, hot damn," Jessie came back. "I don't give a shit what his name is. Just get that boy out of here, do I have cops crawling out of my ass. Look like y'all both been fighting, too. You know better than to bring that humbugging in the Blues Room."

"Johnny done already hummed Bosco's bug. This boy just saved me a ass whupping, Miss Jessie. Somebody ask who you met tonight, you tell them you met a gentleman."

I took the gentleman on over to my room, sat him on my bed, and cleaned him up. Opened a can of Vienna sausage, heated it on a hot plate, served him that with some crackers and a sip of Wild Irish. Gave him a minute to let it settle. Pulled off his shirt, his pants and drawers. Seen a scar running along his right thigh. Kissed it all up and down like my lips could heal it. Leaned him back in that bed and went to work. When I got through he was hollering my name.

"Lady Peaches! Lord, do have mercy, baby!"

That's how I leave all my tricks, crying my name and begging for more. Ask any of these dudes out here, they'll tell you Lady Peaches got some of the best pussy this side of Western Avenue.

Honey, I turned that man every which way but loose. Took him from punk to pimp and back again. You hear what I'm saying? Got that worm when it was fresh and young, wasn't even sure it could make no spunk. That boy was ripe, ready for some woman to make a man out of him. How you gonna call yourself a gang-banger when you ain't never had no trim?

"I ain't no gang-banger, Lady Peaches," he come telling me. This after he had done it two, three more times. Once the boy got the hang of it, he didn't know how to stop. "What makes you think I'm in a gang?"

"You ain't in one, you better be. Bosco Bear way up high in the war council of the Deadwood Dicks. You going to need some protection once he gets out the hospital."

I tell you, daddy. I made that boy. Bought him some new gym shoes and a black leather jacket. Took him over to Lawndale and introduced him to Antonio, captain of the K-Town Killers. Told him and the boys how Hot Johnny the Gent broke Bosco's sorry ass all the way down. You talk about respect. Man, Johnny made those Killers sit up and take notice. But he almost punked out when he had to pledge in.

Back in those days, the Killers' initiation was "find a girl, fuck a girl." It had to be somebody fresh, a bitch you ain't never met before. Somebody who wasn't ready to give it up that easy. Hot Johnny hadn't even been fucking that long, he ain't had it in him to do no rape.

So, I knew this girl named Juanita, right? She wasn't in the life yet, but she was a sho' 'nough ho at heart. Me and Johnny dragged her up in the den, playing like we had just pulled her off the street.

Juanita put on such a show, she should have been in the movies. Wiggling like a worm and throwing herself around. Screaming and hollering, "No, don't!" when you and me both know she meant "No, don't *stop*." When it was finished I paid her off, like the ho she was. This wasn't no favor, it was a service. I didn't wanted Juanita thinking we owed her nothing. Unless she was ready to do some business, wouldn't be no more for her where that came from.

After that, Johnny was in. The boys had his back, I was in his corner. He had money, clothes, a place to stay, all the pussy he wanted. Man, he was living the life. K-Town Killers and them had a little chop shop operation going. He learned to jack cars, kick a little ass. Smoke a little weed, pop a few pills. Holding up his signs, tagging his turf. He ain't even had to fight that much, because he already had a rep. Plus he could ball.

I even had to teach him that. Took him over to the court at Dummies High, had him practice free throws and one-on-one. Shit, I wasn't that nigga's woman, I was his natural daddy. Can you believe it? Black man in the city of Chicago don't even know the hoops? Hell, I was a bitch and even I had played my B-ball coming up.

All that height on him, going to waste. Shit, if I had that height and I was a dude, you better know I'd be in somebody's NBA. But I took care of my daddy. Hot Johnny took to the court like a fish to water. I turned that boy into one basketball-playing muthafucka, you hear me? Shit, that's what a man's supposed to do.

Juanita came creeping around just like I figured. Always did like them pretty brown-skin dudes.

It was the first time we went out in public. Our coming out, so to speak. Lady Peaches and Hot Johnny the Gent. I dressed up my daddy real nice that night. A white-on-white leisure suit, Big Apple hat, white patent leathers with a platform heel. Shit, that man was looking good! Almost as pretty as me. I had on a gold lamé halter top and white leather hot pants, so tight you could see the crack of my ass. You know how brothers is, they all into that ass.

We went strolling on up in the Player's Ball, every eye in the place on us. I seen Juanita and her friend Hollywood sitting over at the bar, eyeballing Johnny. Next thing I know, that skanky Hollywood had pulled me out on the dance floor, asking me to show her how to Bus Stop. Out the corner of my eye, I seen Juanita slide over to Johnny and stick her tongue in his ear. Who she think I was, Boo-Boo the Fool?

You know what? I took care of her real good. Call herself trying to play Lady Peaches. Well, the player got played. I put her right on the stroll. That's right, I turned her black ass all the way out. You want to come licking and lapping on my man, you better be ready to pay some money.

You know the funny thing? I ain't sure Johnny even knew he was macking. See, I was the one who put the shit together. He be laying up reading comic books, drinking, hanging out with his boys. Me and Juanita, we went out and worked, came home with the cash. Anybody even try to mess with us, I got them told real quick.

"You know Hot Johnny the Gent? That crazy nigga, burn somebody quick as look at him? That's my man. You want some of what he gave Bosco Bear?"

It wasn't just his face that got messed up. The same dick that old trick tried to stuff in my mouth got fried like a hot dog when Bosco fell against that garbage drum. Word on the street was Bosco Bear couldn't even get it up no more. Good on his ugly ass. Every ho on Madison Avenue was happy. If not for nothing else, Hot Johnny deserved to be paid for that piece of work.

First time we brought home our money, Johnny was like a kid at Christmas.

"A hundred dollars, for me? Wow, thanks a lot."

First time in life I had my respect. I wasn't Poontang Peaches no more. I was Lady Peaches. People look at you different when they know you got a man watching your back. Somebody who's going to the wall for you, no matter what. Long as I had Hot Johnny the Gent, I wasn't just some bitch you could do any old kinda way. I was somebody's lady. Plus, prostitution pays a whole lot better when you got representation. Daddy, that man was my rainbow and my pot of gold, both.

Johnny was the front, I was the brains of the operation. I made sure he looked good, always had some money in his pocket. I had to watch his cash for him. Juanita got to where she was holding out. I knew the ho could pull a good fifty dollars on an average night. But sometimes she would roll in there with a twenty-dollar bill, claiming business was slow or some john had jacked her.

"She's holding out," I kept telling Hot Johnny. "Stealing from you. You got her back, she supposed to watch yours. Kick her ass. That's what a man's supposed to do."

He never could bring himself to beat Juanita, but I did it for him. Near about beat the black off her ass. She ain't never held out on Johnny after that, you better believe it. See, I was building Johnny up, trying to make him into something.

He had the looks, he had the game. He learned to walk that walk and talk that talk. But he never had the killer edge a man needs to make it big on the streets. That's what I was there for. Next time you see his ass, tell him what Lady Peaches said. He had the game, but I had the balls.

I still remember the day Juanita come running up, telling me the cops had Hot Johnny outside the Honeybee Hair Palace. I ran over there and they were still working him over, beating his ass like a sorry bitch. Two nigga cops, jealous and evil. Pushing him all up against the concrete wall, slamming him with their nigga beaters.

"Do you feel good, pretty boy?" Like two raper men with nightsticks. "A half-white thug. Wait until the jailbirds get ahold of that ass. You be the prettiest bitch at the ball."

You think I don't know who did it? Those niggas in the K-Town Killers set him up. Antonio, Antman, Lucifer, and them. Sent him off by his self to rob that beauty shop, had the cops waiting outside when he came out. That was wrong. They was just jealous of Johnny, wishing they had his women, his money, his winning game. Wishing they could go to the hoops like he could.

Johnny had to do his time, true enough. Not in the joint, because he wasn't old enough yet. He went to Juvenile Court, got sent up to the Audy Home for almost a year. But you know what? Vengeance is a sho' 'nough muthafucka.

Those K-Town Killers, they ain't even around no more. While Johnny was away, Bosco and the Dicks shot up every last one of them. Lucky thing Johnny was put away for a while. There but for the grace of God go he.

Hot Johnny the Gent was better than all of those niggas put together. Anybody with balls enough to go up against Bosco like he did, he could have been a star. Ain't no telling how large he would be now. Fine as he was, with a little hard work, he could have had a string of hos from here to Halsted. He be up there with the great pimps of all time: Wookie Hughes, Loverboy Lucius, Hambone Benitez.

But when that little yella nigga come out the Audy, he act like he don't know me no more. Swinging some sanctified chick by the end of his dick. Hot Johnny done got all holy on me. All of a sudden he some big-time basketball star at Dummies High, don't want no more parts of pimping.

He run into me on the corner and look right through me, like I'm made of glass. Like he done forgot my name. Me, the one who taught his little maroni ass all he know. Busy rubbing elbows with educated womens and church girls and college recruiters and shit, ain't got no more time for Lady Peaches.

Now, don't you be looking through me like I'm made of glass. Don't be down on me because I'm a common streetwalker. You picked me up, didn't you? Ain't nothing wrong with selling it, not if somebody want to buy some. If the truth be told, everybody out here got a little ho in them. That's right. If the price is right, all y'all be down on your knees sucking somebody's dick.

Who you is, anyway? Jimmy? Jimmy the Bosco Bear? I thought you looked familiar. You just got out of the joint, didn't you? Old gangsters never die, they just get hard and ugly. What you want with me, man? Naw, you can't buy none of this. I heard you can't even get hard no more. That's all you know how to do these days, is talk?

Naw, you ain't got to prove nothing to me. Don't nobody want to see your burnt hot dog. Deadwood Dick like a muthafucka, ain't you? Juanita say she sold you some the other night. Only way you got your rocks off, she had to dig all up in your ass, mashing on your love muscle. Ain't that a bitch? Same Bosco used to beat a ho down and fuck her in the butt. Only way he can bust a nut now is getting it up his own ass. Life sho' is a muthafucka. What goes around comes right on back around.

That's all right, Bosco Bear. You keep your little money. I don't want nothing you got to give. I do sell pussy, but I never go up nobody's ass. This a lady you looking at here. They say ho's make money on our back, but that ain't strictly true. Do this ass look wore out to you? Naw, it's the feet. You do more walking than you do screwing, and I got the bunions to prove it. You do your time on your knees, and it sho' ain't praying.

Be damned if I know where Hot Johnny is. I wish to hell I did. I'm not gonna lie to you now. Hell yes, I'm tired of ho'ing. This life is hard. You got to dodge the man, cop your tricks, do your thang, get your money, and struggle just to stay alive. Don't be no Social Security waiting when you get out the game.

If I had played my cards right, I could be retired by now. The Gent's Lady Peaches, sitting pretty. Could have been off the stroll, running the business and counting the cash. Aw, man. I had big plans for Hot Johnny. My pot of gold and rainbow too. That man could have sat me down.

Shit, that's what a man supposed to do.

Merilee

Wasn't nobody to help me be a mother

MENDEZ: This deposition taken on the twelfth day of August, 1979, the law offices of Rohm, Lipsholtz, and Barnes, of Mary Lee Wright—

BAPTISTE: I go by my maiden name, Merilee Baptiste. That's M-e-r-i-l-e-e.

MENDEZ: Correction, Merilee Baptiste, testate case two-one-one-two-dash-six. Now. Are you comfortable, Mrs. Baptiste? Just relax and I'll be asking you a few questions.

BAPTISTE: Is she going to be copying down everything I say? All on that machine there?

MENDEZ: Yes, Mrs. Baptiste.

BAPTISTE: Well, I hope I don't talk too fast for her. People always tell me I talk real fast. I'll try to slow down a little bit.

MENDEZ: That won't be necessary. Just speak at your normal speed.

BAPTISTE: Well, the way I feel about it is this. I gave Mr. Gooden the best years of my life, and I gave him the best years of his life. I made that man's last days the happiest ones he ever had on this earth, he used to tell me, say, "Miss Mella, you sure do know how to make an old man happy."

MENDEZ: Hold on, hold on. We seem to be getting ahead of ourselves. Now, I'll be the one asking the questions, and you will answer them to the best of your ability. Do you understand?

BAPTISTE: Well, hey. Ask me anything you want to know. I ain't got no secrets.

MENDEZ: We'll start with your name. Can you tell me your full legal name and your date of birth?

BAPTISTE: Merilee Reina Baptiste. I was born January fifteenth, same day as Martin Luther King. January fifteenth, 1943.

MENDEZ: Now what is this name you say Joseph Gooden called you? "Mella"?

BAPTISTE: Well, that is just a name people give me. Years back they use to call me "Mellow Yellow," me being so light and all. It's just something folks call me.

MENDEZ: Like a nickname?

BAPTISTE: A nickname. But like I was saying, Mr. Gooden meant me to have that house. I don't care what Gina, Coretta, and them have to say about it. That was always Mr. Gooden's wishes. He told me time and time again, "Miss Mells, when I'm gone I want you to have this place and everything in it. It's not much, but it's yours." Was saying that up until his dying day. Gina and them will tell you about it.

MENDEZ: Mrs. Baptiste, will you let me ask the questions?

BAPTISTE: Well, excuse me.

MENDEZ: Can you tell me how long you knew Joseph Gooden?

BAPTISTE: Let's see, this September will make seven years me and Mr. Gooden been living together. But really, we hooked up almost a year before that. So I guess it's going on eight years.

MENDEZ: I notice you refer to him as Mr. Gooden. Why didn't you call him by his first name?

BAPTISTE: Well, it's a funny kind of thing. See, he had the same name as my ex-husband, Joseph. When I met him, I told him, "I sure can't call you that name if we going to get along. My husband just ruined that name for me." So he say, "But you got to call me something." I say, "Why don't I just call you Mr. Gooden and let it be like that?" He say, "That suits me. Just as long as you call me." And that's the way it went.

MENDEZ: How did you meet Joseph Gooden?

BAPTISTE: *(Laughter)* Oh, Lord. Honey, that was something else. See, I was at Sears. You know the one out on Seventy-ninth Street? I was in the washroom, just coming out the toilet, when this man comes up in there. I mean running, like he got some important business to take care of. I said to myself, "Lord, what's this man doing in the ladies' room?" So honey, he ran up in the toilet, just a-talking away. Didn't even bother to close the door. "Oh, miss, I sure hate to barge in on you like this. But this here is an emergency. When you got to go, you got to go." Mr. Gooden always did have trouble holding his water.

But I didn't know it at the time. I got pissed off. Excuse me, miss. I got mad. Man standing in the ladies' room doing his business, chitchatting. I liked to curse him out. "You sure got your nerve, mister. I could have been in here naked or anything. Come running up in here on me. I got a mind to call security on you."

He coming out the stall looking all nervous and shame-faceded, zipping his self up. "Now, miss. Ain't no cause for that. You know I'm sorry. How can I make it up to you?" Then he asked me what I come to Sears to buy, and I told him an ironing board. So he say, "My treat." Do you know the man went and bought me an ironing board?

We laughed about that for years. Anytime Mr. Gooden want to get on my good side, he offer to buy me an ironing board.

MENDEZ: You say that you and Mr. Gooden lived together for seven years. Yet you never married.

BAPTISTE: Well, it wasn't because he didn't ask. Mr. Gooden was always on me to marry him. Wouldn't leave me alone about it. He must have asked me a hundred times.

MENDEZ: Why didn't you?

BAPTISTE: Now, I ain't come up in here to answer no stupid questions. You know good and damn well why I never married to him.

MENDEZ: Just answer the question, please.

BAPTISTE: Me and Mr. Gooden never married because I was already married and never got no divorce. Okay? It's just something I always meant to do and never did do. And then it was too late.

MENDEZ: So legally you are still married to your first husband. How long have you been estranged?

BAPTISTE: Say what?

MENDEZ: How long have you been living apart?

BAPTISTE: We wasn't hardly together to begin with. I was just married for a minute, then it was over. This is what, 1979? Shoot, I haven't seen the man in fifteen years.

MENDEZ: Where did you meet?

BAPTISTE: Who, Joe? Right in front of my house. My grandmother's house, really. That's where I lived most of my life, over in the Ida B. Wells Homes. You know, the projects over on Pershing Road?

MENDEZ: Your grandmother reared you? What about your mother?

BAPTISTE: Oh, she was around now and then. Honoré was totally out there. She did her own thing.

MENDEZ: What do you mean by that?

BAPTISTE: Little Gracita, that's my grandmother, she was church. Honoré, that's my mother, she was street. You know. Always running some kind of game, whether it was policies or hot property or the con. That was Honoré. But like I said, little Gracita raised me up.

MENDEZ: How long did you live with her?

BAPTISTE: Up until I got married. I was about seventeen at the time. Oh, you want to know how it happened. Okay. I was sitting on my front step sucking on a strawberry snow cone. I always did like me something sweet. That's why my teeth ain't no good now. It was just hot that day and I was sitting outside trying to catch me a little breeze. Here come this little man riding on a bicycle. He shout at me, "Evening, sister." So I say, "Evening yourself." Next thing I know he turn around and ride back again. He stop and ask me, "Do you know the Lord?" I say, "No, but maybe you can introduce me."

I didn't really mean nothing by it. Just young and full of sass. This man, Joe Wright. He a short, skinny dude. Hair cut real short, and men was into wearing them high-top dos back then. He was old-fashioned, just the kind of man my grandmama liked. He got in good with her. He used to come ask her to let me go to Bible study, or revival, or whatnot. Would ask her, not me. Just like she the one he trying to court. Little Gracita just kind of pushed him at me. She wouldn't have been so particular if she knew the boy was pushing forty. He didn't look it, though. Always did have a young look about him, riding around on that little raggedy bicycle.

MENDEZ: So your husband would have been at least twenty years older than you when you married him.

BAPTISTE: Was then and still is, I guess.

MENDEZ: What led to your breakup?

BAPTISTE: You getting mighty personal here, ain't you, miss?

MENDEZ: Mrs. Baptiste, these are questions that I have to ask. Now, your attorney promised us your full cooperation.

BAPTISTE: I came here to say my piece. I didn't come here to sit up and answer a bunch of nosy-ass questions. I don't give a damn, Mr. Grenshaw. You may be my lawyer, but this don't make no sense.

GRENSHAW: Toni, may I please have a word with my client?

(Break in testimony. Transcription resumed.)

MENDEZ: Please bear with me, Mrs. Baptiste. The sooner we get this over with, the sooner we can all go home. Please answer the question. What caused you and your estranged husband to separate?

BAPTISTE: We was just two different people. Joe was what folks called a jack-leg preacher. When he had a job, he worked security for a living. He sang gospel sometimes with a little quartet. And he preached on Sunday, didn't have a regular church. He just went all over, church to church. He come from sanctified folks, real strict. You wasn't supposed to drink, you wasn't supposed to dance. You couldn't wear no makeup and you had to keep yourself all covered up, nothing showing. I was seventeen years old and looking like an old lady, sitting up there in those mammy-made dresses. I couldn't have no fun.

MENDEZ: So you left him because of religious differences?

BAPTISTE: Well, yes and no. Really, Joe had me put out. He was always accusing me of stepping out on him.

MENDEZ: Your husband thought you were seeing other men. Were there other men?

BAPTISTE: I had acquaintances, yes. I mean, I was seventeen years old and married to a dude who wouldn't even take me out for a hot dog. What was I supposed to do? Sit up and rot?

MENDEZ: What about children?

BAPTISTE: What about them?

MENDEZ: You and your husband had children.

BAPTISTE: One little boy, name of Johnny.

MENDEZ: Can you tell me about that?

BAPTISTE: Ain't nothing to tell. Joe named the boy John the Baptist Wright. Can you believe that? Said it was going to make him righteous. Johnny was supposed to had been born two months premature. At least that's the story Joe put out. Tell you the truth, I was pregnant when we got married but Joe didn't want the church folks to know we had been screwing. Anyway, I had the baby seven months after we got married. When I left, his daddy kept him.

MENDEZ: Why?

BAPTISTE: I just couldn't handle no baby. All that crying, those dirty diapers. Not a minute to myself. I didn't want to have the baby to begin with, okay? You know how birth control was back then. It wasn't shit.

And those rubbers, I wouldn't be surprised if Joe sat up and poked holes in them. He was always on the case about how he wanted a son and how his first wife couldn't make nothing but girls. He was sure enough glad when little Johnny was born.

MENDEZ: Mrs. Baptiste, do you love your son?

BAPTISTE: Of course I love him. What kind of mother wouldn't love her own child?

MENDEZ: Then why did you leave him at such a tender age?

BAPTISTE: I just couldn't keep him. I was nineteen years old. I was in the streets. I just couldn't give him a home life.

MENDEZ: What did you do for a living at that time?

BAPTISTE: What did I do? I was on aid sometime. Worked in a liquor store. Was a crossing guard. A bar waitress. Shake dancer. That kind of thing.

MENDEZ: Were you receiving money from men at this time?

BAPTISTE: Look, why don't you just come out and say it? I know what Gina and them been telling you. And it's a goddamn, chicken-shit lie.

MENDEZ: Please don't use profanity.

BAPTISTE: I never been a whore in my life. Any bitch that tell you different is a liar and the truth ain't in her.

MENDEZ: But is it true that you were accepting money from men?

BAPTISTE: I had men spend money on me. Haven't you? That jewelry and them clothes you got on, I know they cost you a pretty penny. You or somebody else.

MENDEZ: Who pays for my clothing is not the issue here, Mrs. Baptiste.

BAPTISTE: I was just trying to make a point. You a good-looking chick, just like I was. Men liked me. I was young and had all my teeth and a good grade of hair. This ain't no Jheri curl here, honey. This is the real thing. So what if men wanted to spend some cash on me, show me a good time. What's wrong with that?

MENDEZ: How many?

BAPTISTE: What the hell? Excuse me, but this is some bullshit. How I'm supposed to know how many men? You think I sat up and counted them?

MENDEZ: More than ten? More than twenty?

BAPTISTE: I already told you, I don't know. I couldn't even guess. Maybe more than ten. Maybe more than fifty. But I will tell you this: Since I been with Mr. Gooden there hasn't been no one else but him. And that's the truth. As far as I'm concerned, I was his wife and he was my husband.

MENDEZ: Is that so? Then tell me this, Mrs. Baptiste. Are you acquainted with a Mr. Wookie Hughes?

BAPTISTE: Honey, hush. You know that man name his self after that old thing in the movie. You know. Big, shaggy, ugly-ass thing. Looks just like him, too. Yes, I've known Wookie since grade school, when folks called him Wishes.

MENDEZ: Wishes?

BAPTISTE: Yep. In high school they used to call him Alley. Aloysius was his real name. It's funny how a name can mess you up. That's probably how he turned out like he did. His mama stuck him with that sissy-ass name and he was always fighting somebody about it. I know how it is to have an odd name. Kids was always following up behind me, singing, "Merrily we roll along."

MENDEZ: Are you aware what kind of work he did?

BAPTISTE: Wookie Hughes ain't never done a lick of work in his life. He was a hustler, a gambler, a dope man.

MENDEZ: A pimp?

BAPTISTE: I wouldn't be surprised.

MENDEZ: And he was one of your acquaintances.

BAPTISTE: Look, girl, I know all kinds of people. Doctors, lawyers, Indian chiefs. If I go with a baker, do that make me a biscuit? Besides, Wookie Hughes as dead as a doorknob. Been dead. So what's the deal?

MENDEZ: Mrs. Baptiste, when was the last time you saw your son?

BAPTISTE: Look, I don't get it. Why do you want to talk about the boy? The boy don't have nothing to do with it. Mr. Grenshaw, do I have to talk about the boy?

GRENSHAW: Just answer her question, Merilee.

BAPTISTE: We had him with us for a while. That was about five, six years ago. The boy was twelve, going on thirteen. Right now he's about eighteen years old.

MENDEZ: He stayed with the two of you? For how long?

BAPTISTE: It wasn't too long. Things just didn't go right. See, it happened one day I was over on the West Side. A girl I knew say, "Mella, you better go see about your son. He been done left his stepmama's place, went to stay with his daddy. Joe can't hardly take care of him no more." I come to find out that old holy roller had got the bottle near about as bad as he had religion. Same man that used to crucify me for taking a drink every now and then. He was in detox. So I went and got the boy and took him home with me. I thought, "Well, I got a man now. Maybe I can make a home for him."

MENDEZ: What went wrong?

BAPTISTE: Mr. Gooden and Johnny just did not take to each other. You see, Mr. Gooden had already raised up his family. He had girls too. Girls is easier to train than boys. He wasn't the youngest man either. It was too hard on him. Johnny's funky socks laying all over the place. Johnny's funky self all over the place. The boy didn't want to do no work, didn't want to be chastised neither. "You ain't my daddy, you ain't laying a hand on me. I don't take no beatings from nobody." He sassed Mr. Gooden one time too many, and Mr. Gooden like to broke his neck. I tried to be a mother to that boy. I really tried. But he was too mannish. I couldn't keep him.

MENDEZ: Where is he now?

BAPTISTE: With his daddy, I guess.

MENDEZ: You guess? A teenage boy with his alcoholic father? Very nice.

BAPTISTE: Look, miss, the boy is just fine. He's the head of his basketball team at school and he's just as tall and good-looking as he can be. He's doing all right. He's like his mama. He a cat, got his nine lives and then some. Johnny always do land on his feet.

MENDEZ: How do you know that? Are you in touch?

BAPTISTE: Lord, have mercy. I'm sorry I brought this up. I keep my eye on him, okay? I go to the games sometimes. I sit real far back so he can't see me. But I just watches him. He looks more like me than I look like myself. Hey, it hurts my heart that I couldn't keep my boy. Don't a day pass by when I don't wonder about him and worry about him and pray that he makes out all right. But you don't know how it is. You got kids?

MENDEZ: No, I don't.

BAPTISTE: I didn't think so. You try and see it my way. I gave up my freedom before I even knew what it was. First when I wasn't but seventeen years old to an old freak hiding behind a Bible. Then I had a baby. Johnny shouldn't never have been born. I'm like my mama that way. I just wasn't made for no kids.

I loved him well enough. I still do. But I swear, miss, I used to walk around that piss-stank kitchenette we lived in, that boy would just be hanging on my leg while I walked. You know how some kids speak that baby talk? Not Johnny. He would be jabbering at me in that old foreign talk my grandmama taught him. I speak to him in plain English, he answer me back in Spanish. Can you believe that?

MENDEZ: It upset you to hear your son speaking Spanish?

BAPTISTE: I used to talk like that myself until Curtina set me straight. Everytime my mama caught me jabbering that *señoree, señorina,* she would take me to the kitchen and wash my mouth out with soap. I soon got shed of that habit. We living in America, in case you ain't noticed.

But it wasn't just about that Spanish. Johnny wasn't no easy child to raise. I tried to nurse him, but I couldn't have nobody hanging on me, sucking the life out of me. I had to put him on the bottle, then he start getting sick. My grandmama, Little Gracita, used to keep him for me. All of a sudden she got tired one day, told me Johnny couldn't come there no more. Joe was long gone by then. Wasn't nobody to help me be a mother.

I ain't had no job, no money. Pretty soon the sheriff came and put us outdoors. How I'm going to raise a baby, both of us outdoors? Hard enough for me to look after my ownself. Felt like I was trying to keep my head above water and this boy was a weight steady dragging me down.

Anyway, he loved his old daddy. He look like me, but he was his daddy's child. Joe would be practicing his sermons around the house, preaching up and down the floors—"sinners going to burn in Satan's barbecue pit," that kind of mess. Little Johnny could hardly walk, less more talk. But he'd be following up behind Joe, just a-preaching as he go. I was just something to hang on to when Joe wasn't around.

MENDEZ: Do you have any idea why Joseph Gooden didn't leave a will?

BAPTISTE: I don't know, miss. Lord knows I don't. But Mr. Gooden meant for me to have that house, I can guarantee you that. When I come to live with Mr. Gooden he had the place jammed with dusty old tore-up furniture and whatnot. Didn't have but one or two dishes and looked like it hadn't seen a good cleaning since Gina and Coretta left there. I made that place a home for Mr. Gooden. And I made me a home.

I ain't even forty. Johnny's eighteen now, older than I was when I went out on my own. But what if he need someplace to come home one of these days? Since I been grown, I've lived in every back alley, every little piss hole, in every corner of this city. That place been my home for the past seven years. Mr. Gooden in the ground now. That's all I got left of him. You a woman, miss. You ought to understand that.

MENDEZ: Regina Mathers and Coretta Gooden are women too. You might consider how they feel about giving up their inheritance to a woman their father never even married. That home is also the only thing they have left of their father.

BAPTISTE: Those womens is young womens. They got they educations, got good jobs and good money. Gina is married into that family, them Mathers Funeral Home folks. You know that's some money. All I got is that house and Mr. Gooden's memory.

MENDEZ: That will be all, Mrs. Baptiste. Thank you for your time.

BAPTISTE: Hey, this is my story. I'm going to tell it, now.

I gave him eight good years when neither one of those girls was nowhere to be seen. And I'll tell you this. When Mr. Gooden got sick and wasn't his self no more, I cleaned his natural ass. That's right. Cleaned his ass just like he was a baby. Where was they at? Neither Gina nor Coretta gave diddly-squat about they father or his house. Didn't bring him so much as a get-well card. And when he died, they wouldn't let me sit in my rightful place as the widow. Said I wasn't none of his wife.

But I was his family and he was mine. As God is my witness, I gave up my son for that man. Mr. Gooden meant for me to have that place. You tell Gina and Coretta this one thing: If my boy Johnny ever need to, he going to know he got a place to come home to. That there is my house. I ain't about to be moved.

Gracita Reina

I am the foreigner in your blood

Sana, sana
colita de rana
Si no sanas hoy,
sanarás mañana.

Why the hell am I singing that old shit? Demon babble, that's what Sister Baby used to call it. "Monkey brother, quit talking that demon babble!"

You are trying to find the language of angels, Johnny. If only you would listen to me and not to the voice of your grief.

What is all this wetness running down my face? Am I in a dream? Could I really be stumbling toward some half-frozen lagoon with a pint in my hand, drinking like a fish and crying like a sap?

It is only me, the thing you feel brushing against your cheek.

This ain't tears, it ain't nothing but some melting snow. Crying would be too much like right tonight. I don't even deserve the comfort of tears.

Can you hear me? Do you even know that you have called me here?

Who's that staring at me from the bottom of the water? Hey, you down there! I hate to drink alone. Want some of this libation? Here, let me pour you a taste.

Yes, you have had enough for one night. Not a bad idea to empty away your bottled spirits. To open yourself up to receive others.

Damn, I'm drunk. I must be seeing things. Ain't nothing looking back at me but my own reflection. Hot Johnny, you are one pitiful waste of a human being, you know that? A muthafucking muthafucka. No, you're even worse than that; a man who pollutes his own bloodline. Not even worthy of the word "father."

Ay, nieto. Wallowing on the banks of despair. Why are you drawn to these troubled waters?

Look at that yella nigga staring at me with those guilty green eyes. You ain't shit, you know that? You ain't shit, you ain't never been shit, you ain't never gonna be shit. Acting like some kind of comic book superhero, gonna save your baby's life by sheer force of will. Thought you could take on death in a game of run-and-gun alley-ball. Well, you fumbled, fool. You dropped the ball. Just a big shit-ass is what you are. An everlasting failure, a giant fuck-up.

No, Juanito mio. Do not do this to yourself.

I want me some more liquor, that's what I want. Bartender! More fire water for the brother.

No, nieto. That is not what you want. They have already taken your reason, those spirits; and I do not mean the saints.

Where the hell is that bottle? Empty. Damn, I poured it down this muddy lagoon, throwing good liquor after bad. Hey, didn't the Lord turn water into wine? Look at it out there, shimmering in the moonlight. Look at that pretty mermaid, offering me a bottle of her finest blues. "Hold on Elizabeth, I'm coming to join you!" Hot Johnny's gonna trouble the waters.

No, you will not. Do not go down into that water. Resist the suck of mud, the lick of water against your legs. That is no woman waiting to tuck you into bed. She is *La Sirena*, wanting to pull you down. She is *la patrona de los dolores*, the patron saint of sadness. Do not let the siren's song seep into your soul.

What loss would it be? I've done nothing but rage through life like a wildfire, leaving a blaze of destruction wherever I passed. A little cold water ought to put it out.

Ay, nieto. Can't you hear me? Here, take my hand. Surely you recognize the sound of my voice, the touch of my embrace. I throb in the cadence of unforgotten pain, the thunderbolt scars on each of your thighs.

I know your lusts and frailties, great-grandson. In this moment of sorrow you are weak for the charms of women. You are flirting with the harlot of no tomorrow. Left alone, you might pull lagoon waters over your head and sleep forever.

I will not leave you alone, Johnny. Step through this curtain of darkness. Turn away from the water and into the little forest. People in this city call it Independence Park. No harm will find you when there is someone guiding your footsteps.

This is no hungry beggar tugging your sleeve. It is I, your great-grandmother, *'Lita Gracita.* Do not think me a selfish old woman, incapable of sacrifice. I could be in the sunshine right now, *nieto.* Might have found my way to the outskirts of a certain city in Veracruz. I could be wandering rain forests instead of snowy parks. I could be breathing the fragrance of growing things, smells that lingers in the air as you reach Córdoba. The brazen green of coffee trees, the scent of vanilla orchids in bloom.

I would have no worry now. I am in the sanctuary of *los viejos.* It is only the young who are taken tender, then soured into curdled milk. No one bothers with women whose breasts are fallen and hair whitened. No *patrón cafételero* would want me now. I could be happy as a virgin again.

" *'Lita Gracita, why you always liked to sit by the stove?"*

Ay, Juanito, that stove was my sun, the place I warmed myself with memory. I never imagined growing old in this country. In eighty years here, I have always been cold. The ends of my fingers, the tips of my toes, always chilly to the touch. Even in summer I would sit by the lighted stove with you on my lap. Remembering Yanga, the African slave who seized his own freedom. Singing to you *los sones* and *corridos*, the songs strummed by firelight on Papí's four-stringed guitar.

> *Para bailar la bamba*
> *Para bailar la bamba*

Se necesita
Una poca de gracia

Ay, sí. I see you still remember. Please know how sorry I was not being there to see you grow. How powerless I was to protect you all these years. Yes, you were born a boy. But the world has changed, my great-grandson. Once we had only two types of *patrónes*: the Catholic saints, which we revered, and the labor bosses, which we feared. But *los patrónes* of this world, they will piss in any chamber pot. It is not only the girls who must be guarded.

You tower over me in your manhood, but I still remember you small. Racing through the house like a rabbit. Reaching toward the stovetop fire, not knowing yet that fire burns.

It pained me to have to slap your hands. I know you only wanted to hold the sun, not hot enough to burn, only to warm. An African ancestor who lives in your blood. A Mexican sun you never saw but still long for. Do you realize the people you are from? Do you know what we have come through?

Yo soy jarocha, a woman of Veracruz. *Yo soy mestiza,* a mixed-race Mexican. *Y yo soy negra,* a black woman. I had to leave my homeland to learn this third truth. Through the years we learned to revere the Spanish and endure the Indian in our blood. We did not acknowledge the third race, *nuestro africanismo,* the African within ourselves.

We knew *la bamba* as an African rhythm. "In order to dance *la bamba*, it is necessary to have a little grace." The ancestors called from the beat of *la tarima*, the drum one dances upon with the feet. We heard the rhythm and we danced with grace. But in the last moment we turned away. Maybe that is why they were silent when the coffee boss came to our cabin. I never knew him by any other name than *el patrón cafételero*.

When it is over, the blood trickles down my legs. I am asked to bring the chamber pot. He pisses in it, almost filling it to overflowing. He orders me to empty it and I carry it away, liquid sloshing over the sides. When he is gone I take the straw broom and brush away wetness on the dirt floor. I do not know which spots are made by his piss and which are my blood.

You think that you have suffered? And so what if you have? Does that give you the right to end your life? I might have killed myself then, Juanito. You would not be here contemplating suicide, because you would not have been born.

I was once beautiful. My beauty survived my ruin, as milk will look fresh for a time when it has soured. Even after I was touched by *el patrón*, my hair still drifted about my face like a rain cloud. My skin was still brown as fresh cinnamon.

When women become as old as I, some believe it is only by *brujería*. If I could gather the powers of this witchcraft, reach back across miles and years to rescue the child you were, I wonder if I would do so. If you had not suffered, would you be the man you have become? If I had not suffered, would I be the woman that I am?

I could have been no more than thirteen years old, leaving the hacienda in darkness, burlap sacks slung across the back of my burro. I would walk into a darkness so deep it seemed a living thing. No protection for me against spirits who roamed the night.

Away from my village for days at a time, I would carry food that was never enough to last. Hunger became my cross. I would trudge through rain forests and villages, one night and one day. I walked a main road frequented by robbers and bad men. This had not always been my lot in life, but it seemed suitable enough now for a girl of ruined virtue.

To leave the sleepy hacienda for the bustling, bullying city. *El puerto villa rica de la veracruz.* The rich port city of the one true cross. The first landfall of Hernán Cortés. The conquistador master, *el primer patrón*. To sleep by night in the shadows of San Juan de Ulúa fortress, wrapped up in my poncho like a package.

To squat by day at the waterfront. To spread open my burlap sacks, green beans drying in the sun. To grind them with my mortar and pestle. To put them on the fire, roasting them with brown sugar, adding water. To strain out the fragrant brown liquid. To catch it piping hot in earthenware mugs. To serve it to the same gringos who months before had fired upon the city from their foreign warships.

"Café Córdoba," I call into the crowd. *"Muy bueno."*

When the gringo sailors came ashore to stroll amongst us, laughing the laugh of the *conquistadores*, a solitary dark one stopped before me. I didn't know his language then. He was *negron*, a black giant, an African pureblood. He was Yanga from Papí's song stories. A runaway slave who had founded a *palenque* of rebels and mulattos, thieves and renegade Indians. The place against which Córdoba was built in defense.

The gringo who looked like Yanga did not want to buy my Córdoba coffee. Squatting on his heels, reaching out his hand, he grasps mine. He holds them up to the sunlight, black and bronze entwined.

"See. Look at your color, my color. Yours is like mine."

"Ay, señor, no entiendo. ¿Quiere café?"

I could not hear his language, but I did understand. I didn't say so, but still I knew. No, I am not like you. *No soy prieta. No soy negra. Soy jarocha. Soy mulata.* But still I smiled into my bitter brew. Still I sold him beans to take back to his warship, ground and roasted, wrapped in a patch of burlap.

He came to me many times over the months, each time with a little more Spanish in his mouth. Each time asking a little more to go with his *café negro. Tiene café de olla* with brown sugar, cinnamon, and cloves? *¿Café leche, con azúcar, con un besito?* With sweetened milk, with sugar, with a little kiss? It was no small sacrifice. I already was *la puta del patrón.*

El patrón cafételero *had already come to our cabin. This was back in 1914, but it may still be happening in Córdoba today.*

El patrón orders us out. *Papí,* mostly Totonac Indian. Tired from a day of coffee picking, mending his huaraches by firelight. He picks them up and puts them on his feet. Mamí, mostly African from an unremembered tribe. Exhausted from sorting and washing coffee beans, preparing dinner. She snatches tortillas from the fire, puts away the pot of pintos. No questions are asked.

They gather us together. My younger brother, Jacinto, my twin sisters, Jimena and Josefa, my unmarried aunt Gracia, whom I am named for. And me. We file through the front door, the only door in the cabin.

Before I step out into the night, el patrón grabs my arm and pulls me back inside. No one tries to stop him. It is only Mamí who glances back with knowing eyes as the door shuts in her face.

There is no bed in our wooden cabin, only crude pallets piled in the corner, coffee sacks sewn together and filled with moss. He frowns and prods with the toe of one boot, as if expecting to see something crawling out.

He does not trust them after all. That night el patrón has me on the bare floor, before the warmth of Mamí's cooking fire. I catch splinters in my bare back, but he is protected by the shield of my body. He eventually brings a bed for our purposes. A big bed that dwarfs all the furniture in the room, all polished wood and feather mattresses. On nights when I am not visited by el patrón, my mother and father sleep there.

Some nights I hear Papí crying from the big wooden bed. The harsh, impotent sobs of a dark man who cannot protect his daughter. Mamí tries to console him. Even in the dark I can hear the shrug in her voice.

"Ay bueno, hombre. Para mejorar a la familia."

Ah well, man. A daughter may be ruined. But at least the blood of el patrón would improve the family, producing a lighter shade of offspring. My dark mother, covered in sheets of embroidered cotton much finer than anything we had ever worn. Perhaps when I left Córdoba, Mamí made them into dresses for herself and Tia Gracia, Josefa and Jimena.

Until that night I had been a child, making maracas from dried gourds, singing sones and playing games on moonlit nights. Now I was soured milk. No good for anything but the goats. I had a new name. *"La puta del patrón,"* the boss's bitch. I would soon receive another: *Malinche,* the whore traitor.

"Yo te quiero."—In Spanish this can mean "I love you" or "I want you." I chose to believe the former. I bundled my few belongings, took the large black hand of a *gringo negro* named Jean Baptiste, and went onboard with him. When his ship left port, I was stowed away beneath his bunk. Moving toward a place where I would find a new home and begin to build a new name. Gracita Reina Baptiste, "baptized queen of little graces."

I did not leave my home at fourteen, cross the Gulf of Mexico into another world, did not live my life and die my death only to see you drowned here tonight.

Jean Baptiste was no *conquistador*. This Yanga in a Yankee uniform spent his duty shut away in the galley, cooking meals for the white sailors aboard. He was not a real gringo either, I would soon learn. This is not just because he was a black man.

He was a foreigner once removed, the son of *Haitianos*, poor Haitian farmers who burned candles to their saints and spoke a sort of French that still frustrates my tongue. I would learn to speak it myself, before I had even mastered English.

Jean took me to his parents in New Iberia and left me there, pregnant with *el patrón*'s son, although we didn't know it at the time. You never met your great-uncle Romel, who one day went to New Orleans to live as a white man.

I became wet nurse for one *patróna americana*, leaving Romel with his Haitian grandmother and her saints, her candles and asafetida bags. When two years were over and the child was weaned, *la patróna* had given birth to another one who needed my milk.

Your great-grandfather Jean was away at war, making meals to fill the white sailors' stomachs. He came home on leave after four years, took a hard look at the pale child who had been born in his absence, and led me at once to bed.

I didn't go to *la patróna* at all during that month. When Jean left again for war, I was pregnant with Honoré and Gloria, your grandmother and great-aunt. Remember Josefa and Jimena? Twins seem to run in our family, *nieto*. Jean went into a world war and came home unharmed, only to die at the hand of a white American. They sent his body back in military uniform, the knife holes in the back stiff with dried blood.

I might have killed myself back then, but I had children to care for.

My widow's benefits were denied because I was not the wife of my daughters' father. Romel was left behind to aid the aged Baptistes, to replace the son they had lost in battle. They loved him, though he was not the son of their son. I suspect they continued to love him even after the blood of *el patrón* moved him to New Orleans.

In 1920 I took my twins and worked my way north along the Mississippi River, all the way up to Illinois. I didn't know it then, but I followed the same route marked by another Haitian named Jean Baptiste some centuries before.

I was not the only Mexican in Chicago. There were people from Michoacán and Mexico City, Chihuahua and Guadalajara. Every now and then I would see someone who looked *jarocho*, whose Spanish hair was softened with African curl, a Yanga nose in an Indian face.

But to most Mexicanos in Chicago I was *el otro*, "the other." Another *negra* to be ignored. I rode the bus to South Chicago for my *adobo*, corn flour, and *mole*. Spanish would be spoken before me boldly, unafraid of being answered. *Mira la prieta, la fea india María.* Look at the black woman, the ugly Indian. I suppose by then I was no longer beautiful.

Those who hate *el otro* come in all colors. None of us is innocent. Sometimes we even hate *el otro* within ourselves. We turn up our noses at cinnamon-flavored coffee, crease our foreheads at accented English.

"If you don't want to speak American," we say with a glare, pretending not to understand, "then go back to where you came from."

Even as insults fly from their mouths, they cannot say the place where I come from. Puerto Rico? South America? Africa? They would never guess this old black woman was a "wetback," their favorite foreigner to despise. They would never know I was here before their parents came up from Mississippi, their grandparents arrived from Ireland. I was not the first outsider to come to this city. That man's name was Jean Baptiste and he did not speak English at all. If anyone can say I do not belong, it is only *los indios*, whose place this was before. We are all foreigners here.

I lived among factory and stockyard workers. Women fresh from Mississippi and Arkansas ran their fingers through my crinkly curls.

"Girl, you got some pretty hair. You talk right funny, though."

Dark-skinned domestics taught me to ride the North Shore line to where the wealthy *patrónas* lived. One or two North Shore matrons would recognize in my language something different from their other "girls." They would stand above me frowning as I scrubbed floors of ceramic tile and hardwood on my hands and knees.

"Gracita, what an unusual accent. I can't quite put my finger on it. Where are you from, dear?"

"Louisiana," I would always answer.

"Ah, Creole." They would nod knowingly. "I thought so."

I never betrayed Veracruz, never admitted to Córdoba. It was a strange kind of comfort to keep my origins locked inside me.

So it was Bronzeville where I stayed, even when the friends I made had died off or moved on. Even when the beauty shops and restaurants and jazz clubs closed, when the bulldozers cut a path through the bronze village to build the Dan Ryan Expressway. Even when mini-mansions along South Park Boulevard were cut into kitchenettes, and cold-water flats torn down to build housing projects like the Robert Taylor Homes and Ida B. Wells Homes. I stayed on, tired of moving. A middle-aged colored woman from Veracruz, forgetting more Spanish than I remembered.

I was here when World War II washed the second wave of migrants up from the South, when the Puerto Ricans and Cubans came. I rode the El to the North Side, bought candles and spells at their *botánicas*. I listened to their music, their island-accented Spanish. They are not my people, *los boricua, los cubanos*. But they are not so very different. African is spoken here.

There was safety in numbers, in shades of cream and tan, black and brown. *Café negro, lechero, de olla.* The housing projects were beautiful in those days, clean and new. A place with separate bedrooms for me and my girls. No one had lived there before us. No cooking smells had seeped into the walls and floors, no bathtubs rusted by dripping water. I made a home for my daughters, far from the reaches of coffee bosses. Or so I thought.

It was not so simple, like in Veracruz. Here *los patrónes* flickered like tricksters in different shapes and colors. They lived at the bottom of whiskey bottles, in powders and syringes. Here they prowled the streets in Cadillacs, wearing shiny suits, with names like Honey Boy Brown. They floated in through windows on marijuana fumes.

I soon learned the lesson of my parents: Poor people are powerless to protect their daughters. I lost both of the twins born to bring glory and honor to their father's name. Your great-aunt Gloria stabbed a man in the back, killing him the same way her father died. Your grandmother Honoré sold herself body and soul and came home pregnant by a gringo who would not give her his name. She gave birth, before dying of alcohol and shame, to a green-eyed daughter she would name Merilee. Your mother, Merilee.

I might have killed myself back then too. But there was you.

I was happy to know my seventeen-year-old granddaughter had a son, though like me she gave birth too young. I could not save my daughters, but I thought a son would be safer. He could capture his freedom, like Yanga, or redirect his future, like Romel. A son could be more easily protected.

Your father was so proud of you. "My boy, Johnny, he heard his call at an early age. You know he been preaching since he could talk."

It was not preaching, I told him. Yours were the words of a parrot, repeating whatever you had heard before. You could speak Reverend Joe's sermons word for word. But you also repeated his drunken ravings and Merilee's curses. You could even tell me what the cartoon rabbit on TV said, or the words of the Mexican song I sang to you whenever you were sick or hurt.

Sana, sana
colita de rana
Si no sanas hoy,
sanarás mañana.

You always had your pockets bulging with stones. To you they were like jewels. Smooth brown pebbles, shiny black quartz, chunks of concrete and brick from bulldozed buildings. You never even kept them for yourself. You would save them to give away; to me, your mother, to perfect strangers.

You had many words to say, many places to wander. You had hardly learned how to walk before you were running. Whenever you were free, you took off toward the concrete stairs. Where were you headed besides death, Juanito? If this old woman hadn't been able to move so fast, you would have fallen down them a dozen times. You wouldn't been the first dead baby in the Ida B. Wells housing projects. You wouldn't have been the last.

I did not save you then only to lose you now.

"Digame, 'Lita Gracita, how you see me when your back is turned?"

"Where you are concerned, Juanito, I have extra eyes. I see around all sides of a situation."

"It's 'X-ray eyes,' Little Gracita." Your mother stayed missing most of the day, but always came back in time to correct my English. "Not 'extra eyes.' "

"And I am your *abuelita*. *'Lita* Gracita, not *Little*."

Though she is more right than she has ways of knowing. *In order to dance* la bamba, *it is necessary to have a little grace.* My brother Jacinto always called me "queen of little grace."

My granddaughter soon learned to serve *el patrón* of the streets, just like her mother before her. I had been caring for you nearly every day since your birth. Merilee said she had gone back to school. I should have known better. What high school has classes until seven, eight, sometimes nine o'clock at night? Saturdays, also. I finally opened my eyes and spoke my mind.

"This is your child, Merilee. I am not the mother of Johnny, you are. Take your son and take him home."

She brought you back not a week later, with the story that she had some business waiting.

"What is this business, Merilee?"

She said she was looking for a job.

"When you get this job, who will be caring for Johnny?"

She kissed her teeth and rolled her eyes.

"Why you want to do me like that, Little Gracita? You ain't got nothing else taking up your time."

"I told you this so many times, *nieta*. I raised my children and I raised you. I have been raising babies since I was fourteen. I am old and tired now. You had that little monkey, you raise him now."

I didn't intend to sacrifice the son. I was only trying to save the mother. I never turned my back on my blood—not my son of *el patrón cafételero*, not my twins, not my grandchild, not my great-grandchild. I just wanted Merilee to be the mother she was. We all have *nuestras cruces verdaderas*, our own true crosses, to carry. But do you know how it is to drag someone else's?

Yes, that day I called you a monkey. I also called you a *colita de rana*, "little tail of a frog." I also called you a *negrito lindo*, pretty little black one. You didn't mind it, did you, Johnny? These are soft words, not insults. Your father sometimes called you monkey himself. Merilee had heard me say this many times before. Why at that certain moment did she suddenly find it unhearable? She exploded into a volley of insults, cursing me like a whore on Forty-third Street. I should have known the Thunderbird was talking with her tongue that day.

"You calling my son a monkey, with your monkey ass? Speaking to him in foreign, when I already told you I don't want him talking that Spanish. You don't want to speak American, you shouldn't have come here."

"And where would you be?" I remind her. "Would you be there with me, speaking the Spanish you hate to hear? Or maybe you would not be born, you or your son. You would have no child to raise, no need to be dropping your duty in the arms of others."

"You're just selfish, Little Gracita, ain't nothing else to it. You don't do nothing all day but sit and watch white folks on TV. If you don't want to watch my baby, then you ain't got to look neither one of us in the face again. Come on, Johnny."

At that moment I could have stopped her. I should not have let that anger come between us. But yes, Johnny, I was angry at this child who thought she knew the world.

The love of a grandmother cannot make up for a missing mother. Merilee should have known this herself. I did not want to see my granddaughter lose her son, as her own mother had lost her daughter. As I had lost mine.

So I watched *los patrónes* from the safe distance of the TV set, where I could see them but they couldn't see me. I studied them, the way they are, the things they do now. Not for myself; I was beyond their harm by then. It was for the last of my blood, for your mother and for you.

Mira, nieto. One gringa on TV with many of her own children. It was not enough to love those children, she had to love monkeys. Real monkeys, *verdad*! Circus monkeys, laboratory monkeys, runaway monkey pets. To see her house and yard, you would not believe it. *Ay, Dios mío!* It was not a nice thing. Monkeys running everywhere, screaming, shitting, crawling, climbing.

She had a baby monkey whose mother wouldn't feed it. I have seen this myself, at the hacienda outside Cordóba, on the farm at New Iberia. There are sometimes *las malas madres*, the bad mothers. A mother cat will eat her litter, a mother pig will trample her young. La Llorona, who killed her babies and was doomed to wail and wander the world, preying on other people's children.

Do you know what that *gringa loca* did? She wet-nursed that baby monkey like it was a child. I saw it right there on the TV screen. If a crazy gringa can do so for a hairy little monkey child, what would I not do for my own blood? You think I would not come back even from death? To save you from the sinking sadness inside of your own soul? I remember your deepest hunger, your thirst for the mother's milk taken from you too soon.

That powdered milk never agreed with you. Merilee never knew, she would not understand this kind of love. Maybe it was from all those years of wet-nursing in Louisiana, but even as an old woman I had milk to give you. I would sit by the stove side and nurse you, remembering "La Bamba." Singing the songs of Veracruz with very little grace. But still, they were my songs. Still, they were my memories.

You were weaned long before you were ready. Merilee took you away to where I could not find you. I looked for you, please know this. I found your father serving *el patrón* of the bottle and your mother following *el patrón* of the streets. But where were you, Juanito? I could not see you anywhere.

I might have killed myself even then. But I did not. I did not go looking for death, but I was ready when it found me.

I am more than a woman now. With no body to weight me, I have gained power. There are many of us here, Johnny. The ancestor saints, the spirit protectors. We have been there with you in the gang den and the prison, in the homes of unloved or unloving women, among blood and strangers, among *los patrónes* of your world in all their powers. My own heart has beaten in your scars, throbbing out a warning when danger threatened. When you felt yourself ready to fall, I have held you up, pushed you back upon your feet. In my death I have helped you to live your life.

After your mother took you away I stayed inside with the TV turned up loud. I was in my mortal weakness still, growing weaker in body but stronger in spirit. I would watch *los patrónes* and their horrors, fearing all the while for my missing great-grandson.

When the grandmother will not baby-sit for a party one night, a young girl drops the child down the project garbage chute.

Eres tu, Juanito?

On the Spanish-language TV, a bottle blonde smiles up at a singing black man whose name is also Johnny: "You are every white woman's dream, a big black man."

Eres tu, Juanito?

I know it is not you, Johnny. *Los patrónes* will not have you. You are a son of Yanga, of Jean Baptiste. Of your great-grandmother Lita Gracita, who gave you your name, gave you her milk, sang *sones jarochos* by a lit stove.

People think it is your preacher father who chose to call you John the Baptist. But that name was from your mother's side. I remember the day you were born, when I held you in my arms and told your father you would be Jean Baptiste. He thought it sounded Catholic, and to his mind Catholics were not true Christians.

"Now, Miss Gracita." He ruffled himself up to preach. "I don't hold with the mixing of religions. God commands me to give this child a good biblical name, so that he may walk in the way of the Lord."

"How much holier," I answered him, "than the man who washed Jesus?"

So John the Baptist you became. My lost son, my slain husband, my Jean Baptiste returned to me.

Lo africano dentro de nosotros. The African within us. One day I smelled it brewing on an unlit stove—the scent of black coffee laced with cinnamon and cloves, just the way my mother made it. It was then that I knew it. My parents had not sent me into darkness because I was beyond salvation. I was spirited away to a place of protection.

It was my time to enter the darkness, to learn to embrace it. I was destined to be a female Yanga, finding my own village in the wilderness of the world.

Do you know how you left here as a very young man? It is so that I sent you from this place, away from those who would do you harm. I whispered love into the ear of a broken-hearted sister, and you were spirited south. Along the way the Mississippi flows, the same route another Jean Baptiste traveled when he left behind the city he settled.

Your ancestors are not ready for your life to be over. We have gone too far to bring you here. I come to you now, strong as *café negro. Soy una bruja vieja,* an old black witch, powerful with love.

Your fear that you will always fail. *Why is my life so fucked up? I might as well just end it now.*

You are contemplating your Destiny. Your mind twists in anguish over the unthinkable, the unnameable. *How could I actually make love to my daughter? Could my sin be the source of our own daughter's illness?*

You are mourning your Beauty. *Is her death punishment for what I've done? Of course it is, fool. God would never let such an abomination loose upon the world.*

I feel the despair rising in your blood, pulling you toward the place of self-destruction. You will not go there. Your heart holds the answer to all these questions, *nieto*. Look into the darkness, the thing inside yourself that you have not claimed.

Now is the time to forget everything you have learned. There is no such thing as too much love. Those who love you are not all *sirenas*, lurking in the depths to draw you down. There is a path in all your journeying from woman to woman, bed to bed.

You have been everywhere with me, from Córdoba to New Iberia to Chicago. Before and between and beyond. You are everything I am and more. *Delante, durante, siguiente.* Do not turn from the path of life because you stumble upon potholes of pain. You will live to learn certain truths. Love can endure even death, great-grandson. You must bury the loss and bear the pain. *Sana, sana, colita de rana.* If you do not heal today, you will heal tomorrow.

You are no sacrifice for the patron saint of suicide. No prey for the jaws of a wounded bear. I am with you here. The voice in your ear. I am the foreigner in your blood, the scent of *café de olla* brewing.

As you part the veil of night and reenter your own life, look down at the ground below you. Do you see the stone, sharp and shiny black? Pick it up. Keep it in your pocket and remember where you've been.

I am 'Lita Gracita, your guardian spirit who sings by the stove. And you are not alone. In your life a miracle is waiting to be born.

Sanctuary

I will gather all thy lovers with whom thou has taken pleasure,
and all them that thou hast loved

EZEKIEL 16:37

Processional

> Look at the pretty flowers, the people all dressed up.
> *Because it's a party, all for you.*
> Really? For me?
> *See how many people love you.*
> They love me? But I don't even know most of them.
> Ay, *but they know you. Come, little one. Let us sit right in front.*
> *We wouldn't want to miss a thing.*

Call to Worship

"The Celebatarian Saints Social Club welcomes you, one and all. Everybody take your seats now. It's filling up pretty quick, yet we still got people coming in. Soon it'll be standing room only, just like it was before Bishop Pleasant died.

"Oh, yes, mallanee salla jeema! Surely God is good. Touched a father's heart and brought him back to his old church home. After twenty-something years, he found his sanctuary from worldly corruption. Ain't that right, Brother John?"

> Brother John, that's my daddy. Where my daddy at?
> *You see him, standing right over there?*
> Oh yes. He's talking to that tall lady. Look. She got a baby.

Daddy's holding the baby, Now he's kissing the baby. Who's that lady? Who's the baby?

"Let us open our hearts to these words of solace and encouragement from our own dear pastor, the Right Reverend Lucius Sandifer."

Eulogy

"Welcome unto you all. Members, visitors, family, and friends. I'm not going to lie to you, now. The Pentecostal Sanctuary Church of God in Christ is not a perfect place."

(Watch yo'self, now.)

"No church is perfect, don't fool yourselves. Everything bad outside these doors will happen within them too, so long as people are lovers of themselves, lovers of money, boastful, proud, abusive, disobedient to their parents, ungrateful, and unholy."

(Preach, Reverend Sandifer. Sinners in the house of God.)

> What is that man saying?
> *Listen hard. You'll understand.*
> Why are the people answering him back?
> *Because they agree with what he is saying.*
> Well. What is he saying?
> Ay, *child. Too many questions. Not enough listening.*
> Sorry.

"Going to church don't mean a thing. What? I said, *going* to church don't mean a thing. Not getting all bathed and squeaky clean, powdered up and smelling nice. Not putting on your Sunday clothes, them too-tight shoes you can't hardly walk in. Y'all ladies know what I'm talking about."

(Well. Fancy clothes won't save your mortal soul.)

"Not sloshing through the snow to get on the bus, calling up a cab, nor driving your car. Not walking through these doors or sitting in those chairs. For God said, 'My sanctuary shall be in the midst of them.' "

(In the midst of them, Lord.)

"In the midst of them. Not in the brink and mortar. Not in plaster and lathe. It is not your mere presence within these walls that makes a church. It's about opening up your soul and letting the Holy Ghost come inside. Saying, 'Lawd, make me a vessel for your divine love! Abide with me for just a while. Take your shoes off, Savior. Make yourself at home.' "

(Take your time, Reverend.)

"So today we do not *go to church*, the physical act. We are *having church* in the spiritual sense. Can I get an amen?"

(Amen, amen.)

"I'll tell you something else you might not know. Today is a joyful occasion. Y'all don't hear me, now. I said that *today* is an occasion of *joy*. For didn't the Good Book say that 'ye shall be sorrowful, but your sorrow shall be turned to joy'?"

(Oh, my soul.)

"God told me, 'Reverend Sandifer, something bad in the physical world might just mean good in the spiritual realm.' We need not weep for the home-going journey of this child. We come together not to mourn her death but to celebrate her life. And though it was short, Beauty Lynn Wright's space on this earth held a special measure of joy."

(Yes, it did. Sho'ly it did.)

    He's talking about me, 'Lita Gracita.
    I know, bonita, *I know.*

"Now when her father, John the Baptist Wright, first approached me about a memorial service here, it gave me pause for concern. You see, John hadn't been in regular attendance for over two decades. Y'all can look at me and see that I'm a young man. So this would have been before my tenure as pastor. Way back during Bishop Pleasant's day."

(Old Bishop Pleasant. God rest his sainted soul.)

"John's journey on the good ship Sanctuary wasn't all smooth sailing, so I've been told. A troubled teen by his own account, sinning up a storm but searching for a source of salvation. Praise God! Here's a living witness, church. It's never too late to be saved, hallelujah!"

(Hallelujah!)

"I don't put much stock in empty rituals. Y'all know that I have never preached a funeral or sanctified a marriage, baptized a member nor blessed a baby, but that I knew it was someone who knew the Lawd."

(That's right, Reverend Sandifer. Got to know the Lawd.)

"John's beloved daughter, Beauty—not many of us knew her well, or indeed knew her at all. She lived her brief years down yonder in the mountains of Carolina. Who knew whether she was churched? Was raised up in the ways of God? 'Reverend Sandifer,' I said to myself, 'can you in good conscience preach a memorial for this child?' Oh, when the mind is troubled and the soul unrested, I take it to the Lawd!"

(Take your troubles to the Lawd!)

"God told me, 'look into this man's heart and tell me what you see.' Brother John was like someone who had been on a long journey, the kind of trial that tests a man's faith. And who among us wasn't touched by Beauty? Who didn't pray for her recovery? We read the newspaper, listened to the radio, watched stories on TV of that brave little girl child struggling for her life. When the Lord saw fit to call her home, the pain of that loss was felt by us all. While few of us actually have met her, we felt we truly knew her."

So that's how they knew me!
Yes, they did.

(Yes, we did.)

"Even as she journeys on to her maker, that child's good works go on in her name. Her illness allowed Brother John to reunite with scattered friends and family all across Chicagoland. To even discover kinfolk he never knew he had. To bring him back to his old church home. Something bad in the physical world created something good in the spiritual."

(Praise the Lord.)

"I think y'all just about ready to have me stop talking and let somebody make a joyful noise."

(Preach on, Reverend.)

"Now, this sister has called the Pentecostal Sanctuary her church home since the day she was born. In fact, I'm told by some of the church mothers that Pearlene Pleasant was actually born right here in this very building. Can I get another amen?"

(Amen, bless her heart. Poor Pearlene, you know she ain't quite right.)

"That's what sanctuary is all about, church; a place for the weary to be rested, for the sick to be healed, for the sinner to be redeemed. Our sister Pearlene has been a selfless and dedicated saint. For so many years she's put church welfare before her own well-being. As long as I'm alive and in my right mind, this will always be her home. We are proud to say the Pentecostal Sanctuary takes care of its own."

(Sho' you right, Reverend Sandifer.)

"A choir selection has been specially chosen for this occasion, with a solo performance by Sister Pearlene. Aw, I feel the presence of angels in here!"

(Tell it, Reverend. Speak the truth.)

Look at those people coming up. Even the men got dresses on. *Choir robes,* bonita. *I think they will be singing soon.*

"So let the angels sing, and let the church say amen."
(Amen, amen.)

Musical Selection

All night, all day
Angels watching over me, my Lord.
All night, all day
Angels watching over me.

Do you like the music, bonita?

It don't sound too good, but I still like it. I don't think she likes it, though. Who's that lady?

That is your father's half-sister, the one who raised him. Sister Baby Ruth.

Look at Pearlene cutting up. She need to sit her butt right on down. Who told that girl she could sing? All those years in the choir, she still can't carry a tune. Her voice ain't no better than her mother's, and I ain't talking about Mother Pleasant.

> *Oh, ramallee samanee*
> *Angels, Lord, angels*
> *In the Pentecostal Sanctuary*
> *Church of God in Christ!*

Whoever heard of singing in tongues? She acts just like her Aunt Samaritan, with all that false holiness. Was always one to show holy, pull up them long skirts, let some man get a look-see. Serve her right somebody noticed.

God, please forgive me. Bless my sister Samaritan, wherever she may be. Lift from me the burden of bitterness she left behind for me to bear. What happened to me and my sister wasn't no more our fault than whatever killed Johnny's baby.

I left my child in a house of prayer, knowing in my heart it was a house of sin. Just like I inherited Samaritan's cross, my little Pearlene wound up carrying mine. I didn't hold my daughter, and she wouldn't keep hers.

Lord, it has been a long time. My last time in the Sanctuary was for another service, back when Momma Niece passed on. I was on my drug then, the demon monkey riding my back. I was stoned like a fallen woman, flying high and living low. Bishop Pleasant had me read out the church and I ain't been back since.

Well, I ain't high no more, praise God and thank Johnny. The night he left for Memphis was the last night of my addiction. I woke up from my DTs with clean eyes, the craving gone from my gut. I thought I done him a favor, but he was really blessing me. My brother made a miracle in my life. Johnny was my Good Samaritan and didn't even know it.

He ain't never asked much of me. Yet I wasted so much of my life in blame of my half-brother. Begrudging him his little needs, Momma Niece's love, his place in my life when he ain't had nobody to lean on.

Given up by his parents, then cast off by me too. Oh, yes. You can forsake somebody sitting right there with you. I gave him too much chastisement and not enough praise. So bitter over my burden, I couldn't see my blessings. I had a little brother who thought his butt-ugly big sister was the prettiest woman in the world.

When he came to know Pearlene, I faulted him for laying with a girl he couldn't have known was my child, his own half-niece. I was jealous of him holding her when I couldn't hold her myself.

Like everybody else here, I put it on Johnny when Pearlene turned up pregnant, after she came back talking all out of her head. I thought it was for the best she left that abomination down south. I remember the night Johnny set off on that wild-goose chase. I let him leave, thinking he'd find Pearlene in Memphis, when she was back here in Pleasant's house of sin. Yet somewhere along the way he met his Destiny. The one I know is my grandchild.

> Do you think my daddy's sister knows the truth?
> *I think so,* nieta. *I think so.*

If he don't know already, Johnny need to know. Soon as I get my chance, I'm going over and tell him. We been keeping secrets in this family way too long. Look at that girl. How could people even think that Destiny was his child?

Look at my granddaughter sitting so silent at Johnny's side. I can tell something ain't right. Something's broken between them. You can see that marriage is weighted down with so much sorrow. It's real hard to lose your only child.

Yes, I can see it in him. Ain't had much pattern to make himself from. Yet I truly believe Johnny was a good father. That little monkey grew to be a man, in spite of everything he never got from me. Or maybe just because of it.

> Sun is a-setting in the west
> Angels watching over me, my Lord.
> Sleep my child, take your rest
> Angels watching over me.

Reading of Obituary and Acknowledgments

Look at her eyes, Little Gracita. I know those eyes.

Of course you do, angelita. *You are looking at your father's eyes, repeated in his oldest daughter.*

That's my big sister? She looks so sad. It is because of me?

Something else is eating her. Gnawing at her from the inside.

What is eating my sister?

A hungry mouse called guilt.

Obituary

Beauty Lynn Wright came into this world on January 15, 1999. She was born to Destiny and John the Baptist Wright in Asheville, North Carolina, where she lived most of her life. A bright and happy child, despite longstanding health problems, Beauty was a delight to her parents and all who knew her. Her brave struggle to overcome a debilitating genetic disease drew attention and support from people all over the country. Her journey ended just shy of her second birthday. She died at Children's Hospital at Duke University in Durham, North Carolina, January 10, 2001. She is survived by her mother, her father, two sisters, and many relatives and friends.

"Hello, everyone. Thank you all for coming out. You might not know who I am. My name is Jonavis Ransom. I happen to be the half-sister of the deceased. We weren't raised together, so I didn't really know her.

"I just wanted to tell everyone here, my mother, my stepfather, the new family members I'm just getting to know, and especially . . . my father . . . Ah, excuse me, I don't usually get emotional like this. . . . I want my father, John the Baptist Wright, to know how very sorry I am that I couldn't give what was asked of me during this difficult time. I'm young and I'm selfish and I know that's no excuse.

"When Johnny sensed my fear and confusion, he gave me a graceful way out. He said we had new options now, that we could hold out for something a little less invasive. But Beauty died before it came to pass. That's the question that I'll be living with for the rest of my life. If I had given her my bone marrow instead of making her wait, would my sister be alive today?

"No, it's all right, Mom, Gunther, Johnny. I really did need to say this. Confession is good for the soul and so is forgiveness. Johnny, I have forgiven you for so many things you couldn't know I held against you. I hope you can find it in your heart to forgive me, too.

"I also want to thank those who, in lieu of flowers, made donations to the Sickle Cell Association in the name of Beauty Lynn Wright. Sickle cell disease affects seventy thousand Americans, most of them of African descent. Chances are most of you in this room know and love a person struggling with this disease.

"My sister was on the waiting list for stem cell therapy, which is a transplant of blood cells from the umbilical cord of a newborn. She died just before the baby was born who might have been her donor. If Beauty had lived and the operation had succeeded, the new blood cells would have migrated to the bone marrow and started producing healthy ones.

"The risks of such an operation are high, but the potential results are more effective than a traditional bone marrow transplant. The odds for survival would have been seventy percent. It is your donation to the Sickle Cell Association that makes this kind of treatment possible, as well as new breakthroughs in sickle cell research. It's an important and worthy cause, and one I hope you will continue to give your full support.

"Now is the time for testimony. Let all who loved Beauty and support this family come forth and testify. Let each one witness before the congregation, or reflect in the silence or his or her own soul."

Testimony

"Whew, my feets! Took me a while to make it up here, 'cause my dogs sho' is barking in these tight-ass boots. How y'all doing this afternoon? I'm here for Hot Johnny baby funeral.

"Hell naw, I ain't drunk, just a little toasted. Shit, it's cold outside. Just a little Wild Irish to knock the chill off. I'm here to pay my respects, just like the rest of y'all. I ain't just somebody off the street. I'm a friend of the family. You go ask Hot Johnny, he tell you who I am. Let him know Lady Peaches in the house.

"Look at all these peoples! I can't hardly make out a face in all this crowd. I sho' hope I get to see Hot Johnny, 'cause that's what I came here for. My respects to the deceased, but I ain't really knew her.

"I thought this was suppose to be a funeral . . . Oh, a memorial service. Tell me something, then. I don't know squat from no memorial service. Where the casket at? That baby musta died hard. Still they coulda had a closed-casket funeral. This a gyp here, calling people out to pay respect, ain't even got no body up in the muthafucka. Oh, 'scuse my filthy mouth. Been so long since I was in church, I be forgetting myself.

"Beauty, that's the baby's name? That's a pretty name. Pretty little ol' girl too. This a real nice picture of her. She look just like Johnny, don't she? Too bad she had to die so young. That's got to be a hurting thing. Where Hot Johnny at?

"Oh, there you is. Well hey, daddy. You look good, you know that? You got so many people around, I had a devil of a time making you out. You don't remember me? Lady Peaches McCoy, they used to call me Poontang Peaches.

"Wait a minute, now. Why these fools grabbing hold to me? You don't know me, nigga. I'm a lady, don't nobody be grabbing on me like that. Johnny, tell these peoples I'm a lady.

"All right, I see my business ain't wanted here. Take your hands off me, I'm fixing to go back to my seat. But first I'm going to say this one last thing. You, girl. That tall, tree-looking something sitting in the back row. Don't you be shamed just because these church folk act like they ain't never seen a naked titty. You go ahead on and do your thang, baby. Bunch of Bible-thumping holy rollers, trying to tell me I can't say hello to my ex-pimp."

What? Am I the one they're staring at, then averting their eyes? Yes, it must be me. A woman who dares breastfeed in public. I guess I should have gone to the ladies' room, sat on the toilet seat or something. I can't worry about that now. There are too many other worries on my mind.

I worry about this milk. It looks so thin, so watery. Almost blue. Can something so weak and insubstantial keep a baby alive? Can I find enough in me to mother this newborn being? Johnny loves her already, loves her with a passion so fierce and urgent it breaks my heart.

It's a terrible thing, a terrible thing. A terrible thing to be jealous of your own child.

Johnny, what have you done to me? I look down at her face and I see you. Your mouth, your skin, your eyes. I've tried to be strong, I swear I have. But something is broken in me, leaking out. Tears pouring down my face—where did they come from? Liquid leaking from my breasts—what is this? Who is this warm bundle of need, these greedy lips pulling at my nipple? This stranger tugging at my heart?

> Hi, little baby. Hi, hi. Look, she's smiling at me.
> *Newborns always smile when angels whisper in their ears.*
> Is she old enough to have a name?
> *She bears the one of your father's blessing.* Milagro. *Miracle.*

Benediction

"Now don't be alarmed because you see me back up here. You'll notice I'm at the podium, not the pulpit. Reverend Sandifer has said his piece. I just have a word of comfort for the grieving parents.

"Brother John, Sister Destiny. Know that you are not alone. The grace of God is upon you. 'Thy sun shall no more go down; neither shall thy moon withdraw itself: for the Lord shall be thine everlasting light, and the days of thy mourning shall be ended.'

"John the Baptist Wright will now come forward and share a few words from the Holy Scripture."

Scriptural Selection

"An old sinner like me, I feel a bit of a fraud coming up to the pulpit with a Bible in my hand. Although my sister says I used to preach a mean sermon back when I was small. Pearls of wisdom from the mouths of babes, right? Well, maybe I spent all my wisdom long before I even knew I had any. Still, the Reverend Sandifer said it best. Sanctuary is a place where even a sinner can be redeemed.

"Sometimes I marvel that I've made it this far. Like that old church song, 'my soul looks back and wonders how I got over.' I could have been a drunk or a druggie, and I was saved. I could have been a gangbanger or a career criminal, and I was saved. I could have been killed in the streets or maimed in the service. And I was saved too many times to remember.

"I'm going to tell the truth, now. I could have even ended my own life. The day had started out sunny and ended with a freak blizzard. My flight to Asheville had just been cancelled. I was stranded at the airport when news reached me of my daughter's untimely passing. She died the same day her sister Miracle was born just hours too late to save her life. I took a cab back into town, stopped for a pint to get my courage up, and walked straight over to Independence Park. I was going to say goodnight, turn out the light, and pull lagoon waters up over my head. And somehow I was saved.

"Even then I had the nerve to question my blessing. 'Lord, why take my child? Why not me?' All I can think is that God was not through with me yet. He must have a plan in his grand design for old John the Baptist Wright. I've been trying to figure out what it is. It's a powerful thing for a man to face the truth of his own life. Most of us don't do it until our deathbed.

"I've lived so many lives in my forty-odd years on this earth. I've been known by so many names. John the Baptist, Juanito, monkey, Sergeant Hershey, Hot Johnny, the Gent. And the most precious one of all, Daddy. I've been a student, an athlete, a serviceman. A brother, a husband, a father. But who am I, really? What am I here for?

"My buddies in the force had a nickname for me, one I dare not repeat in church. A word that meant I was popular with the ladies. I do confess that love has always come easily to me. At times I considered this a burden, a curse. But the only reason I'm here today is because somebody loved me. Love has been my salvation, brothers and sisters. My sanctuary in the midst of a storm.

"I look out into this congregation at faces I haven't seen in years, and I feel like Lazarus. I've traveled a long road to be with you today. I'm not just talking about South Side Chicago. I'm not just talking about North Carolina. I've floated up from the chilly waters of Independence Park Lagoon, reborn. I've risen up from the depths of despair, because somebody loved me. When I thought I had lost my reason for living, I was given a second chance: a perfect little pearl named Miracle.

"So my heart is filled with hope today. Doesn't the good book say that 'every man that hath this hope in him purifieth himself, even as he is pure'? My heart is full of joy because I know in my life that I have loved, and I have been loved. This is the lesson I want you to carry home in your hearts: 'Let us not love in word, neither in tongue; but in deed and in truth. I have no greater joy than to hear that my children walk in truth.'

"For Beauty Lynn Wright, the joy of my life. . . .

Daddy's talking to me, 'Litla Gracita.
Yes, Bonita. *I hear him.*

" 'I trust I shall shortly see thee, and we shall speak face to face. Peace be to thee. Our friends salute thee. Greet the friends by name.'

"From the Book of John, chapters one, two, and three."

Recessional

"Lord have mercy, look at you. Minute I saw you, I knew you had to be Johnny's child. Even got a name like his. Jonavis. Looks just like Johnny spit you out."

"That's what everybody's been telling me. You look kind of familiar too."

"I'm Ruth Wright, Johnny's half-sister. Your Aunt Sister Baby. Now, don't you believe none of that gossip. You know how some folks talk."

"What gossip?"

"That Destiny is Johnny's child."

"My father's wife, Destiny? His own daughter? Oh, that's absurd."

"Don't I know it, child. Come walk me a piece."

"Well, okay. I guess so."

"You see here, along these walls? We call this Pastors' Row. Everyone who done shepherded the Sanctuary got his picture hanging along here."

"Yes, I see. That's a nice one of Reverend Sandifer. A very good likeness."

"Look at this one. Bishop Pleasant was pastor just before him. Who he look like to you?"

"Oh, my God."

"Destiny look more like her old devil daddy than he did himself. What would possess Bishop Pleasant to lay with Pearlene, to breed his own daughter? Did he think he wouldn't be found out? Well, now the Lord done found him out. The vengeance is sho'ly his. People 'round here forever praising the name of Bishop Pleasant. That old sinner probably busting rocks in hell right now."

"This is all a shock to me. I don't know quite what to say."

"All you got to do is tell your daddy. Make sure he knows it. You hear me, girl?"

"Absolutely, Aunt Sister Baby. You have my word, and my word is my bond."

"Lord, you talk just as pretty and proper. Your daddy, he always had a way with words. That little monkey done us proud today. Preaching from first John, the gospel of love. 'And this commandment have we from him, that he who loveth God loves his brother also.' That boy ain't forgot his Bible. God's holy wisdom just a-flowing from his mouth. Bishop Peter Paul Pleasant was right after all, that old demon in saint's clothing. Sister Baby Ruth Wright done raised her up a prophet."

Miracle

I was born to save a life

My name is Miracle Lita Wright. I am five years old.

My aquarium has only a chameleon left. I think Chester is a little lonely. My turtle's name was Feather. He was bad. He ate up all the goldfish. Feather died when Mommy gave him plantains to eat. She didn't mean to kill him. She just thought that turtles liked plantains.

Chester likes to sleep on a stone. He turns black and shiny, just like the stone. Daddy says he found that stone the night I was born.

They're both real old. Sometimes people think they're my grand-parents. My father loves me too much and my mother loves me too little. It's true.

Mommy is like a man and Daddy's like a lady. Daddy kisses and hugs a lot, cries sometimes too. Mommy doesn't hardly kiss at all, and she never cries.

Mommy doesn't cook too much. She microwaves. Daddy is a good cook. He makes fricassee chicken and green beans, new potatoes and pearl onions. I asked Daddy what's a pearl onion.

"Peel away the layers and what do you get? The bud inside the blossom, baby."

Blossom, that's what he calls an onion. Daddy calls a lot of things by different names. He calls me "sweet stuff," "honey bun," "sugar dumpling," "baby cakes." He calls me "new potatoes" and pretends to eat me up. Sometimes he even calls me Beauty.

"But Daddy, that's not my name."

He puts his face in my hair. He cries without making a noise. He thinks I don't know he's crying, but I feel his tears in my hair. I rub his eyes to make it better. Like I always I do the scars on his two thighs. I sing to him, just like he sings to me when I have an ouchie:

> *Sana, sana*
> *colita de rana*
> *si no sanas hoy,*
> *sanarás mañana.*

Mommy says I'm lucky to have two homes. I call one the Tree House, but it's not in the trees. It's because my mommy's nickname is Tree. She looks kind of like a tree too. She's tall and very strong. She plays basketball better than most kids' daddies. Trees are nice.

Mommy says I'll be tall too, because it's in my genes. I used to think it was something in my blue jeans pocket. Like the pill Alice in Wonderland took to make her tall. Like a stone with a little piece of me inside. That was when I was four years old. Now I know better. Now I'm five.

I live in Winston-Salem at the Tree House during the week. I go to my father's house in Asheville every other weekend. I spend some holidays with him too. Sometimes I call things by different names, too. I call my daddy "Dad Gummit." That makes him laugh.

"Smile when you say that, pardner."

Daddy's real name is John the Baptist Wright, but some people call him Hot Johnny. I asked him how he got that name. He says it's his job to make the people he loves feel warm. I know who gave me my name.

"Do you know that you're my miracle, sugar dumpling?"

Yes, I do. I was a gift to everyone except myself. I was Mommy's gift to Daddy, to make him love her better. I don't think I did. I was Daddy's gift to Beauty. I was born to save a life. But Beauty died before I could save her.

My daddy misses Beauty. He makes a mistake and calls me by her name. I wonder if he's mad at me. I didn't do what I was born to do. I didn't make a miracle. I didn't save a life. I didn't make Daddy love my mommy better.

Daddy tries to answer all my questions. He doesn't believe in keeping secrets. He says secrets weigh you down like stones.

"What happened to Beauty's mother? Did she die too?"

"No, sugar pie. We had to break up."

"Did you love Beauty's mother?"

"We loved each other very much."

"Then why did you have to break up?"

"We were never meant to be together. I still care for her a great deal."

"Do you love me?"

"More than life itself."

"Do you love Mommy?"

"I'll always love her. She gave me the most wonderful gift a woman can give a man. She gave me you."

"Why aren't you and Mommy married?"

"We love each other, but we're not in love."

"Do you have a girlfriend?"

"Do you see any girlfriends around here? Let's look under the dinner plate. No? How about the silverware drawer? No? In the dishwasher. No? No girlfriends for me, I guess."

"Maybe she comes over when I'm not here."

"No, baby. I used to be a loveoholic. Now I'm anorexic."

"What's anorexic, Daddy?"

"Someone who's afraid of food."

We laugh because he's eating. He's not afraid of fricassee chicken.

"Daddy, why did you call yourself anorexic?"

"Because I'm allergic to love. I'm taking a break from relationships for now. The only woman in my life is you. I'm in a serious place, sweet cakes. Family. Fatherhood. Right now it's hard for me to be what somebody else needs. I'm too busy learning how to be myself."

"I don't want you to be anybody else except my daddy."

Daddy looks like he's going to cry, but he doesn't this time.

Daddy says I'm his last hope. He had two and a half daughters he never got to be a father to. I count them. One is me, the last to arrive. Two is my grown-up sister Jonavis. I see her when we go to Chicago. She's going to have a baby soon and then I'll be an auntie. Three, my other sister Beauty, who is an angel now. Then there's Destiny, Beauty's mother. She isn't really a daughter, but his great-half-niece. Daddy says he loves her like a daughter.

"Daddy, how can you marry your great-half-niece?"

He shakes his head. That's the one secret Daddy won't tell me.

"I couldn't even begin to explain it to you. Maybe when you're older."

That secret must be real, real bad.

Sometimes I feel like I have to be all three of my daddy's other daughters. That's too much love for me sometimes. He hugs me tight and holds me. Sometimes he cries. But he laughs a lot too. And he cooks.

Every other Saturday night we have a big dinner. Daddy always cooks my favorite meal. Fricassee chicken and green beans, new potatoes and pearl onions.

I ask him why he likes pearl onions so much. He tells me they're the sweetest kind.

"I've been peeling away the layers of my life looking for something in the center. You know what I've found? You! You're the bud in the middle of my blossom, baby."

I asked Mommy how come we call ourselves black when none of us really is. Mommy is dark brown, and I'm medium brown. Daddy looks kind of gold. Mommy says blackness isn't a complexion, it's a state of mind.

I've seen red onions and white onions and yellow onions. But I've never seen a black onion. I wonder if black onions are a state of mind.

Me and my daddy have a lot of fun. We eat our Saturday dinner. We watch wrestling. We play computer games. Sometimes we listen to the oldies station. Daddy sings along. He knows all the songs.

I know an old song too. It's called "Who Is He, and What Is He to You?" I sing it to him. That's where I got "Dad Gummit" from. It really means the g.d. word. If you say it like that, you don't really have to cuss.

I like to look at Daddy's photo album. It is a book full of faces. Most are people I don't know. A lot of them are ladies. Dad Gummit tells me who is she and what is she to him.

"That's your mother when we were in college. My stepmother, Momma Niece. That's Jonavis's mother. Oh, Lola Belle, an old friend I'd almost forgotten about. Here's my ex-wife, Destiny. That's my great-grandmother. I used to call her 'Lita Gracita."

I don't remember most of them. Every time we look at pictures I have to ask again. Sometimes Daddy makes up silly names.

"Don't you remember Chiquita Banana? This one here is Nanook of the North. Oh, look at her. Lady Greensleeves."

Daddy calls them little pieces of my past. Sometimes I wonder if my Daddy is a Play-Doh man, made up of little pieces of his past, too. Sometimes I'm scared of all those hungry faces.

It's fun to see old pictures of my daddy. He had hair and was way more handsomer. He's still medium handsome. He says he doesn't care about looks anymore. He wears Mr. Magoo glasses when he has to read. They're real ugly glasses. Sometimes he puts on mitch-mack socks. He shaves his head bald. He says he was going bald anyway and might as well finish the job.

"Most people couldn't care less how it is," Daddy says. "They only care about how it looks. It's never about you, it's always about them."

He wants people to see him on the inside.

I look in his mouth with a flashlight. His inside is pink. I love him on the inside and outside, both.

My daddy tells me bedtime stories. I can read myself now, but Daddy likes our story time. Sometimes he tells made up stories, but sometimes they're real. I like the one about stone soup. I think that one's real.

Everyone in the neighborhood is real hungry. A magic man teaches women how to make stone soup. He takes a stone from his pocket. It has a little piece of him inside, like the rock in the jeans. He throws it in the pot. He gets all the women to add something to it. Water, salt, vegetables, meat. They cook it until it's done. They all get to eat stone soup. Get it while it's hot! Yum, yum. Everybody's happy until he leaves, taking with him his magic stone. But they all know the secret now. They wouldn't have to be hungry again.

That's where the story ends. But Daddy isn't finished yet.

"You know what? I think they left something out of that recipe."

"What, Daddy?" I already know the answer. "What did they leave out?"

"The blossom, baby! Give me my pearl onion, please."

I give my daddy a good-night kiss. He makes up his own ending.

"Hmm, delicious! The man was very happy. He had been wandering the world, sharing stone soup in so many places. For the first time in his life he realized that he never got to taste any of what he made. From that day on, when the man made his special soup for special people, he always made sure that he got some too. Along with fricasse chicken and new potatoes, green beans and . . . Hey, what's that other thing? Wait a minute, don't tell me. . . ."

"Pearl onions," I tell him anyway. "Don't forget the pearl onion."

There's something I like better than bedtime stories. When the moon is full we stay up late. We go outside and catch fireflies. We get Daddy's telescope and look for constellations: Ursa Major, with the Big Dipper; Ursa Minor, with the North Star.

The crickets make a kind of music. My daddy sings to me. He dances with me under the stars. He holds me up to the moonlight. He sings about a black pearl, even though my name is Miracle. A pretty little girl he has built his world around.

He calls me the pearl in the center of his onion. I've never seen a black onion before. But Daddy says that black pearls really do exist.

ACKNOWLEDGMENTS

A number of readers provided literary critique and cultural commentary during the various stages of development of this work. They include Liz Lehrman and participants in her Critical Response workshop at Columbia College, Chicago; members of OBAC Writers Workshop, who provided feedback on very early chapters; the Summer 2000 Mixed Genre Workshop at Warren Wilson College; Giselle Mercier and Luis Rodriquez, for correcting my tortured Spanglish; Dr. Maria Stampino for helping with Italian translations; Njoki Kamau offered cultural observations and the inspiration of her resistance; M. Evelina Galang made recommendations regarding Filipino dialect and voice; Michael Thelwell gave helpful suggestions on an early draft; and long-time cohort and companion Michael West shared his insights into the black Pentecostal experience.

There were many sources of influence and inspiration, both large and small. I thank La Negra Graciana, for bringing the spirit and music of black Veracruz to Chicago; Luis "Chikome Tochtli" Rodriquez, for remembering that the black ones "are in our blood"; Diana Collins for her *carabinieri* stories; and my aunt Judy Ingram, for reflections on her first year of high school counseling.

My network of support has included the Alumni Affairs Office of the University of Massachusetts, Amherst, which generously extended a work space at a crucial point in the revision process; dance partner and "dilettante" Hamlet Theodore, who knows "a little bit about everything"; candid conversations with Bisola Marignay; my wonderful children, Adjoa and Kimathi Opoku, for their patience and understanding; my wise and gifted editor, Cheryl Woodruff, for helping me hone my vision and truly get to know Hot Johnny; and my ever-encouraging and supportive agent, Susan Bergholz.

A number of sources provided useful cultural background on Somalia. These include "Women and Words," by Amina H. Adan (*Ufahamu* 10:3, 1989); *Aman: The Story of a Somali Girl,* as told to Virginia Lee Barnes and Janice Boddy; *Desert Flower: The Extraordinary Journey of a Desert Nomad,* by Waris Dirie and Cathleen Miller; *Xiddigis Astrology,* by Mahmoud Adan Jama; the novels of Nuruddin Farah; and *Yesterday, Today: Voices from the Somali Diaspora*, also by Farah.

An earlier version of the chapter "Merilee" appeared in *Nommo: A Literary Legacy of Black Chicago*, ObaHouse Press, 1987, under the title "Mr. Gooden's House."

This work was made possible, in part, by a grant from the Illinois Arts Council, a state agency.